GLENN PATTERSON

burning your own

BLACKSTAFF
PRESS
BELFAST

First published in 1988
by Chatto & Windus Ltd

This edition published in 2008 by
Blackstaff Press
4c Heron Wharf, Sydenham Business Park
Belfast BT3 9LE
with the assistance of
The Arts Council of Northern Ireland

Glenn Patterson has asserted his right under
the Copyright, Designs and Patents Act 1988
to be identified as the author of this work.

Typeset by CJWT Solutions, St Helens, England

Printed in England by Athenaeum Press

A CIP catalogue record for this book is available
from the British Library

ISBN 978-0-85640-810-6

www.blackstaffpress.com

ONE

1

'In the beginning' – said Francy – 'was the dump.'

He stamped both feet on the mound on which his toilet squatted and fixed the boy before him with fiercely twinkling, black eyes, beguiling him with his knowledge.

Mal nodded, convinced, though it was his body, not his mind, which came closest to understanding that the world could seem a very different place from the world into which he walked that morning, hands dug so deep in his jeans pockets that the waistband chafed the knobbles of his hips, knowing Francy and the dump only by legend and hearsay.

There had been another argument at breakfast. Or, rather, the same old arguments were revived and repeated. Mal glided through the tortuous twists and turns, shifting as easily as his parents from point to unconnected point, all the time anticipating the inevitable descent into name-calling: his names. When it occurred, he slipped away to his room, hoping to sit out the too-familiar finale.

From his window, he watched the gang gather at the top of

Everest Street. He longed to run and join them, to establish, before the school holiday progressed any further, a stronger contact with them than he had yet been able to. Maybe this once, he thought, they would call for him and his parents would have to stop arguing and then ...

And then, on cue, to the accompaniment of shouts and banging doors, the argument downstairs became a fight. Mal drew back from the window as the faces outside turned towards the house. Through the gap between the curtain and the wall, he saw Mucker and Les – as Punch and Judy – pantomime a brawl.

They soon tired of the game, though. Mucker dismissed the house with a derisory flick of his wrist and the gang drifted out of sight along the street.

Mal's parents were not so easily exhausted, and the boys were long gone by the time he was allowed to go out. He descended the steep hill from the front of the estate, meandering backwards and forwards on the dusty road, kicking loose tarmac chips off the footpath, halting eventually before the sprawl of the park.

A path, running from the road to a wooden creosoted pavilion, halfway across the grass, effectively split the park in two. To the left of the path, tended by an official keeper, was the park proper: football pitches of varying size and quality – arranged in no particular order, so that, unless you knew them, the impression gained was of randomly distributed goalposts – and, beside the pavilion, a crazy-golf course, the gate to which was permanently padlocked. The grass on the right was less regularly cut; except for patches trampled flat by the smaller children to make their own playing fields, it tumbled long and weedy to the fence of a rubbish dump separating the park from the main road along the side of the estate.

Behind all of this stretched the woods, thick beyond the football pitches, extending back as far as the next town, growing sparser and ever more scraggy as they ran towards the road, before finally petering out in a confusion of overgrown hedge and a solitary, drooping willow tree at the bottom of the dump.

It was to the woods that Mal looked now, deciding whether to cross the pitches to the large group milling around the bonfire site in front of the trees. The desire not to be left out might have overcome his shyness at going alone, but the certain knowledge that the gang from his street had heard his parents' fight and would not let the fact pass unnoticed made him hesitate, his cheeks swollen red.

As he rocked his heels on the kerb, he became aware of a commotion in the cul-de-sac on his right. A bin lorry was parked at the end of the street, where the grass sloped down towards the dump; three binmen and a boy about his own age, armed with a broom handle, were gathered round the wall of a nearby house, a knot of anxious bystanders at their backs. Mal had been warned against playing anywhere near the dump, and so always avoided this street, but that was forgotten now as he was drawn into it by the frantic, raised voices.

'Kick the bastard – he's going to spring.'

Heavy workboots lashed out.

'Kick it again, don't let it out that end. Use the fucking stick, wee man.'

The broom handle was brought down with a dull crumple.

A small girl, her hand up her skirt, clutching her knickers to stop herself peeing from fear and excitement, hopped beside Mal from halfway down the street, chanting. 'It's a rat, it's a rat – from out of the dump. Our Eddie's helping the men kill it, but I seen it first. It's huge, so it is, horrible and black with a big long tail. And I seen it first.'

She danced away to a neighbour, who had ventured to the bottom of his path.

'It's a rat, Mr Taggart, it's a rat. And I seen it first …'

Mal himself had never seen a rat, but the girl's description fitted exactly with the identikit image in his mind. He bobbed from foot to foot on the fringe of the spectators, straining to peer over the shoulders of the people in front, barely able to maintain his balance in his dread and anticipation.

He managed to catch sight of the rat at last and shuddered, as he expected he would. But, after the initial revulsion, he had the peculiar feeling that he was somehow disappointed. The rat was not black, as promised, but a light greyey-brown; and it wasn't that huge either, when glimpsed among the flailing feet.

'We've g-g-g-got it n-now,' a bearded binman stuttered, reaching out a hand. 'G-g-g-give us the broom pole till I fu-fu-finish the bastard.'

Mal didn't think he could bear to watch anymore, even though, for all his disappointment, he still hated rats. He faced away and, as he did so, he was struck by the sight of a figure moving at some speed over the debris of the dump.

It straightened a moment and yelled; a boy's voice, but dredged from the belly, and hacked and coarsened along the way; urgent, grating, unnerving: 'One more fucking move and you won't live to regret it.'

The rest of the crowd turned; the stammering binman froze, broom handle poised above his head, ready to strike. The boy-figure negotiated the dump's remaining obstacles nimbly and leapt the wire fence that bordered it, landing on the grass.

His head seemed enormous, an impression accentuated by its wild burst of bright rust hair, sprouting unchecked in every direction. His feet and hands also looked to be the wrong size, as if he had yet to grow into them. Coming up the slight incline he walked awkwardly, setting his feet down with a curious, heavy plod. Even his T-shirt was too big; it hung loose on his stumpy trunk, and from beneath it a pitted wooden handle protruded down the thigh of his grubby jeans.

A murmur ran back through the crowd to the binmen: 'Francy Hagan.'

The company of Francy Hagan was, like playing on the dump, forbidden to Mal, as it was, for that matter, to every other child on the estate. His very name was a byword for unseemly behaviour: he was how you would turn out if you cheeked your elders, or refused to eat mashed turnip. But Mal's family had only been in Larkview since Easter and, just as a few minutes before he had never seen a real live rat, so, too, now was the first time he ever set eyes on the juvenile bogeyman. He pushed forward through the ranks in the hope of a better view.

Francy Hagan appeared to be about fourteen, though it was hard to be sure. Red hair, soft like down, only denser, was already beginning to spill along the line of his jaw and collect in tufts on his chin and top lip. What could be seen of his face beneath the hair was heavily freckled; dark freckles, clumped together in constellations, like a starry night in reverse, as Mal would remember it in years to come, so that the dark was light and the light dark. A short piece of cigarette was clamped so tightly between his lips at the left side of his mouth that it looked like a natural, though angry, smoking growth.

As Francy brushed past, Mal recoiled involuntarily; a stale, meaty smell came off him, as if something had crawled up him and died. Mal's instinctive reaction would have pleased his parents no end. And yet, as with the rat, he was left feeling oddly let down. This stubby body and outsized head in no way resembled the picture he had pieced together of the fabled wild man of the dump.

Francy stopped before the binmen. The little girl's brother, Eddie, who had originally wielded the broom handle, faded into the crowd and began backing cautiously away from the scene. Francy let him go, interested only in the man with the beard.

'What are you going to do with that?' he asked, nodding to the raised pole.

'I'm g-g-g-going to k-kill that rat.'

The rat lay at the foot of the wall, in a pool of blood, seemingly too weak to move. Its side heaved up and down and its black eyes bulged so that they looked as though they would burst. Francy collapsed his cheeks, hauling the smoking growth into his mouth,

7

then spat with all the force he could muster, sending the butt looping over the bearded binman's head.

'You're fu-fu-fu-fucking not, you know.'

The man's chin dropped and the stick clattered to the ground behind him. He forgot about the rat and drew back a fist as if to floor Francy.

'Why you ch-cheeky wee g-g-g ...'

He stopped, mid-swing, mid-stutter. Mal felt his stomach flip: Francy had whipped a hatchet from the belt of his jeans beneath his T-shirt.

'Go ahead, big fella,' he challenged. 'I dare you.'

Mal stepped back with everyone else, hardly conscious in the confusion of emotions tumbling inside him that his feet were moving. The other binmen retreated, circling silently behind Francy. Francy's gaze never once left the bearded man, but still he was aware of everything going on about him.

'Tell your mates, if I so much as feel their breath on me, I'll cleave your skull in two.'

The binman facing him smirked a smirk that said he thought Francy was all mouth and clenched his fists tighter. Francy responded by increasing the pressure of his grip on the hatchet shaft. His knuckles showed white, then continued to swell, until in the end they seemed to have grown out of all proportion with even his already too-big hands.

The driver of the bin lorry had been looking on from his cab since Francy appeared, bent forward, resting his heavily tattooed arms on the steering wheel.

Now he opened the door and shouted, 'The wee lad's a nutcase; it's a known fact. Come on to fuck out of that and leave him with his stupid rat. Sure the frigging thing's kicked near to death anyway.'

The bearded binman sagged and relaxed his fists. He shook his head, glowing and brushed with sweat, and walked back with his colleagues to the bin lorry. It pulled away from the bottom of the cul-de-sac, but slowed again as it drew level with Francy. The driver leaned across and stabbed a finger out the window of the cab.

'You ought to be put away, you mad Taig bastard,' he said. 'Some day you'll realise you should have been. Then you'll be sorry.'

Then you'll be sorry. The phrase had dogged Mal all year. He was going to be sorry too. Sorry that he had screamed himself hoarse one afternoon and refused point-blank to go to his piano teacher's house. Some day, his mother was forever telling him, he would wish he'd stuck at his lessons (never mind that, after Easter, he couldn't have had them even if he *had* wanted them). That was January, since when scarcely a day went by without someone trotting the words out to someone else – in the streets, in the newspapers, on the television – so that, by that July of 1969, it seemed that just about everybody in Northern Ireland was going to be sorry, one way or another. And now Francy. Mal couldn't see why anyone would ever regret not being put away. But he couldn't see either why Francy found it so hilarious.

For Francy was laughing and laughing, body jerking, hatchet waving dangerously.

The driver's finger faltered. 'Nutcase,' he spat and slammed the lorry into gear.

It careered out of the cul-de-sac and the laugh died in Francy's throat as if a switch had been thrown. He shoved the hatchet into the belt of his jeans – but outside his T-shirt this time, in case anybody should forget he had it – and crouched by the wall. Gently he lifted the rat, which looked in his hands even smaller than before, and held it close to his face, mumbling into its blood-matted fur. The rat did not strike out or bite, and Mal, whose fear of rats had been nourished by stories of their viciousness when faced with death, realised it was beyond helping itself, as it allowed Francy to stroke and probe it lightly with his thumbs.

'Bastards,' he said, feeling the broken bones.

He plodded forward with the injured animal, and the crowd

parted, making noises of disgust. Only Mal stood his ground, despite the remnants of his terror and the flip he'd felt in his stomach. Francy halted a moment and stared at him with small, hard, black eyes. Mal caught his breath. He could have sworn he heard the rat purr quietly.

Francy climbed the fence into the dump and picked his way across the rubbish with care, so that his outstretched hands remained balanced. At the far end of the dump, where it merged with the woods in a tangled thicket, he disappeared through the low-hanging branches of the solitary willow.

Mal lingered by the roadside while the crowd dispersed, then, hands in pockets, he wandered away from the dead end to the pavilion path. The gang had not moved from the edge of the woods. There was little more than a week to go to the Twelfth, and the Eleventh Night bonfire was being worked on and guarded round the clock. Mucker's dad had got a centre pole from the timberyard where he worked and this morning it was being taken into the woods to be hidden. Mal'd have missed that by now. If only his parents hadn't rowed at breakfast. Mind you, if they hadn't, he would never have seen the rat or Francy or the bust-up with the binmen.

Francy and the binmen – that was it. None of the ones at the bonfire could know what had happened yet. Just wait till he told them; he had no reason at all to feel awkward. He hurried, half-run, half-skip, across the playing fields.

Everyone lent a hand to build the bonfire and, as he drew nearer to the woods, Mal could see that the Everest Street gang were mingling with boys from all over the estate; there were even half a dozen girls standing by a few of the bigger lads. All were gathered round listening to someone talking.

'And so doesn't he go and pull a hatchet. There I am, right by the rest of them, thinking: "I'm ready for it." But then Big Bobby calls from the truck: "No need you getting involved," he says to me. "It's not your fight, but ours." And I shrugs: "It's up to you, Bobby." So I came on over here.'

It was Eddie, the boy who had helped the binmen batter the rat. He paused, noticing Mal approach.

'Ask your wee man, there,' he said. 'He seen it too.'

Mucker pointed and sneered.

'Who, that tube? I'll bet he did nothing.'

'Nah,' said Eddie. 'Just cowered by the wee dolls, watching.'

Mal flushed, angry and ashamed: angry at Eddie's twisting of the story, ashamed because some of it was true – he *had* stood by and watched. He wanted to say something, but didn't know what. It was useless anyway: nobody would believe him now. And there was no point him running away either, unless he wanted to be made fun of more.

All around, boys were punching their palms and feigning head-butts, saying they'd have to do Hagan. They could get hatchets too; the Rebel bastard wouldn't be rid of them so easy.

'You'll have to plan it carefully,' Pickles told them. 'They say he's tamed rats in the dump.'

'That's right,' Andy Hardy backed him up. 'I heard he fed them miscarriages he stole from the hospital and now they'll attack anyone he tells them to.'

The gang wagged their heads, muttering. A strange mood had stolen over them. If Mal had been older he might have had words for it. Instead he looked on, trying to account for their actions, as though they were characters in a film he had missed the start of.

Two girls whispered together in an exaggerated fashion and began to titter.

'What's the matter with youse?' Mucker asked. The girls nudged each other, disputing which should speak, until finally the taller, more daring of the two said: 'Did you know he stands perched on a barrel sometimes at the side of the dump, waving his ... you know – cock – at passing cars. And' – she dropped her voice, rubbing her chapped nose with her thumb, while her friend nudged her again – 'one night he paid a certain someone, who shall remain nameless, but isn't standing a million miles from me ...'

11

'God forgive you, Sonia Kerr.' The other girl thumped her. 'It wasn't me and you know it.'

'… to suck it for him.'

'That's nothing, sure,' Mucker said gruffly. 'I've had mine sucked loads of times. And I've had three bucks and all.'

And Les snickered. 'Yeah, but you'd buck a black eye.'

Mucker wrestled him to the ground and the others joined in, tussling and laughing.

Mal was glad of the diversion to be able to withdraw more. He didn't always understand everything when they talked like that, and he was afraid of being embarrassed if he was asked a question. He lay on his tummy, gazing off to the left where the woods tapered to a point at the bottom of the dump. He could make out the drop of the willow tree, but he could not make any sense of the feeling the sight of it aroused in him.

'Hey!'

Behind him, the wrestling had stopped. Andy Hardy was calling him.

'What?'

'We're going off on the scavenge. You're to stay here and help keep dick.'

Mal rolled on to his tummy again and focused on the distant tree.

'Can't,' he said.

'What do you mean "can't"? *Can*. Fucking will.'

'I've to be home for lunch,' Mal said quickly, getting to his feet and edging towards the playing fields. 'Got to help my mum with the shopping this afternoon.'

'Lunch? Shopping? For dear sake, wee lad, what age are you?'

'Time someone gave your ma a good stiff talking to,' Mucker told him, gyrating his hips. 'Want me to do it? God knows, your da doesn't seem able. Got the droop, he has.'

A stick cut the air, end over end, and landed at Mal's feet. Another followed, then another. He broke into a run, not caring now what they said, just so long as he wasn't there to hear it. He continued to run even after the last stick fell hopelessly short and the sound of laughter subsided. Only when he had reached the road at the bottom of the hill did he think it safe to pull up. The bulk of the boys had set out in the opposite direction, towards the streets on the far side of the fields, leaving only a token guard at the bonfire site.

Satisfied he wasn't being watched, Mal crossed his fingers and strode purposefully along the cul-de-sac. Sliding down the low bank, he clambered over the wire fence into the dump.

2

In front of the willow tree, on top of the mound on which it grew, stood a toilet with two red cushions tied to the seat. Through the curtain of branches, Mal could see sheets of tin sloping from the ground into the bushes. He shouted hello, but there was no answer, no sign that anyone was inside. He wavered, his heart pounding. All the way across the dump he had gritted his teeth and tried to blot out thoughts of trained rats. Now, his nerve was failing him. He glanced behind at the expanse of weeds and grass, strewn with ripped garbage bags, spring-burst chairs, sodden mattresses, bottles and cans. He thought of the danger he had already run, the numerous bumps and jolts he had suffered, and somehow it seemed less of a risk to go forward than back again over the junk.

Warily, he mounted the small rise and eased aside the outer branches of the willow tree ... *Whoosh!* – he was drenched by a shower of water ... *Whoosh!* – the breath was punched out of him and he was knocked to the ground by a red streak that caught him square in the chest. He thrashed on the grass, soaked and spluttering. By the time he had recovered himself, Francy Hagan was bending over him.

'What the fuck are you doing snooping around here?'

He spat a smoke spit and, dragging Mal up by his shirt front, peered at him with his small black eyes.

'Oh,' he said, somewhat softer, but at the same time releasing his grip so that Mal fell again. 'It's you.'

He walked in the shade of the tree, picking up an empty bucket and a boxing glove on a stick. He saw Mal watching him.

'Booby traps,' he said. 'Fucking nobody's going to take me by surprise.'

Mal lay still for a time, but when he realised that Francy wasn't going to do anything else he stood, mopping his face and hair with his sleeves.

'Well, what *do* you want?' Francy asked him.

'The ones at the bonfire,' he blurted. 'They're coming to get you.'

As soon as the words were out, Mal wondered why he had spoken them. He knew the gang had forgotten about Francy in all their talk. Still, he told himself, maybe another day they would come.

'So they sent you to scare me?'

'Oh no,' Mal explained, terrified of what might happen if Francy thought he was mixed up with the others. 'No one knows I'm here, I was just warning you.'

Francy almost managed a smile.

'Don't worry about me,' he said. 'I'm not afraid of anyone on this estate. I know things – the first person tries anything on me, I'll … Well, just let them try. They haven't seen the half of it yet.'

His manner had become aggressive again. Mal hurriedly changed the subject.

'And I was … I was … I wanted to ask about the rat.'

That statement surprised him too.

'Bastards,' Francy swore. 'It's dead. I'd to kill it myself.'

He stared past Mal an instant.

'D'you want to see it?' he asked, and nodded to the sloping tin.

Mal shrank inwardly at the thought and his stomach flipped

15

again as he remembered the hatchet and the jumbled stories of miscarriages and sucking cocks. He swallowed, and followed Francy towards the den.

'No you don't.' Francy held out a big hand to halt him. 'D'you think I'm some sort of headcase letting you in there? Wait outside.'

Passing out through the branches, Mal was engulfed in a torrent of sunlight, pouring from a sudden rent in the low summer cloud. He shivered, inexplicably, and crumpled to his knees, next to the toilet, rubbing his eyes with the backs of his hands. A moment later the rent passed on, leaving the sky once more a shifting waste of white. But long after sunspots had ceased to dance before his eyes, Mal was still gazing straight ahead, bewildered.

Beyond the dump, across the grass, a solid mass of red-brick walled in his vision. Roofs merged in strange teetering formations, half-houses, quarter-houses were grafted on to the sides of others, filling every gap, blinding every alley and driveway. He lived here, but he did not recognise this place, could not reconcile the jumble with the neatly hedged rows he walked through day to day.

'I thought you wanted to see this?'

Francy's voice was suspicious and challenging.

Mal turned guiltily. Francy cradled the rat in his hands; lengths of string and bootlace dangled from his belt where once the hatchet had been. He tugged on the cigarette screwed into the corner of his mouth.

'Might have known you weren't fucking interested.'

Mal had expected anger and was not prepared for the pained, almost sad squint in Francy's eyes.

'I am interested,' he assured him. 'Why'd you have to kill it?'

'Why d'you think?' Francy snapped, sitting down with a thump on the cushioned toilet seat. He laid the rat on the ground beside him and pulled the strings from his belt. 'It was suffering – they cry, you know. There was nothing else I could do, so I broke its neck.'

16

He began tying together the lengths of string, his thick fingers fashioning knots of his own invention, and Mal's attention returned to the red-bricked disorder beyond the fence.

'Do you not think the estate looks funny?'

'No,' Francy said, without raising his head.

'I'd never have believed it could look like that.'

Francy made a clucking noise at the back of his throat.

'There's a lot about this place you wouldn't believe – I could teach you a thing or two.'

He hauled so hard on his cigarette that it smouldered with the dark smell of burning filter.

'Lesson number one: when all that' – he waved a hand in the direction of the houses – 'was still no more than barren fields for cows to shit and sick grass in, the dump was here.'

Mal frowned. It was not so much that he found it difficult to imagine the houses not being there, to rub them out, to pluck the goalposts and the crazy-golf course from the park – though that was hard enough; but to imagine a time before they had ever been ... The effort made his temples ache dully.

'When the builders came, this was their yard – though even before that it was set apart, distinct. They drove their stakes into the ground, where the fenceposts are now, and behind corrugated iron sheets they erected their workmen's huts and offices.'

In one fluid movement, Francy swivelled the No 6 butt from the left of his mouth to the centre and spat it some ten yards to indicate the spot.

'There.'

Mal accepted without question that the dog-end was well aimed.

'That was the first estate, you know: a compound of diggers, bulldozers, braziers, planks and bricks. Those houses out there all started off in here, every one of them – a million fucking pieces. And there were people of course, the workmen. Each morning they'd clock in at the site and when the weather was too bad for work they'd stay in the huts, drinking tea and playing cards, waiting. Hundreds of them: navvies, asphalters, boys for the drains and the water, others to lay the electric and the gas; and then you're only just up to the house plots. On top of that lot you've your brickies, chippies, sparks and plumbers, tilers, glaziers, not forgetting every bastard type of foreman, overlooker and white-collar worker you'd care to mention.'

He spat a dry spit.

'Hundreds of them. And they'd be out sometimes in the winter before the fucking sun was right up. Day in, day out, week after week, for months on end, they dug up earth, put down foundations, put down pipes, connected mains and cables, churned cement in hand-turned mixers, laid bricks, battened floors, framed doors, wired up, roofed in and planed off, until the whole fucking lot was finished. Out of nothing from this compound they raised an estate: streets, roads, parks, avenues, drives, cul-de-sacs; houses, detached and semi-detached, on the high ground at the front, terraced row upon terraced row down here at the back. And all in the same time that it takes to make a baby, dipping to dropping.'

His beady eyes probed Mal.

'Except, of course, you can't make a baby with just men, as you well know.'

Mal blushed, looking at the ground. Francy rummaged in his butt box and struck a match.

'For a week it stood like that ...'

Francy began talking again and Mal, who had expected something else, lifted his head, relieved. Eager too. In Francy's words he had seen the estate grow, brick by brick.

'... stood complete and empty, while the workmen dismantled the yard. They loaded the huts and braziers, tar burners, mixers, planks and bricks on to trucks. The stakes surrounding the compound were uprooted and the corrugated iron sheets that had filled the gaps between them were piled high and driven to new sites. And on the last day, with the first cars and vans already nosing along the newly tarmacked streets, a workman steered the sole remaining bulldozer to one end of the now bare yard and there, at the foot of an ancient willow tree, shovelled earth, grass, broken wood and brick dust and covered in the piss trench.'

Mal's eyes opened wide in recognition. He jumped to his feet, dusting the seat of his trousers. Francy cackled and hackled a smoke spit.

'Man, dear, that was fifteen years ago. The tree hasn't suffered, has it? And the grass grows well enough here.'

He tied a final knot in the strings he had painstakingly been twisting together, attaching a long black football lace to the rope of assorted colours.

'And this rat' – he lifted it by the tail – 'didn't die of fucking piss poison. Did it?'

'No,' Mal said quietly. 'It didn't.'

'Didn't is fucking right,' Francy snarled. 'It was people killed this rat. Lesson number two: rats never kill for fun.'

He spat, absent-mindedly, the cigarette stub he had lit only moments before. It spiralled through the air, trailing smoke, like a strafed bomber, and crashed against the neck of a grass-green bottle.

'That nearly went in,' Mal told him.

'What?' Francy screwed up his face. 'Oh, yeah. I can get them in most times. When I remember.'

Mal didn't doubt it. They watched the butt's glowing tip slide down the glass and fizzle in the long tangled grass, where even at this hour the dew had not yet lifted.

'Anyway' – Francy placed the rat on his lap – 'the story. The builders slipped unnoticed through the back here, while the people, owners of the houses they'd made, entered the estate by the front. And fuck did the people ever come. Can you imagine it?'

Mal tried, couldn't, shook his head.

They came from everywhere: from Newtownards Road, Beersbridge Road and Ballymacarrett in the east; from Ardoyne, the Oldpark, Legoniel, in the north; from Ormeau, Annadale,

Sandy Row, the Village, in the south; and in the west, from Shankill, Springfield, Woodvale – aye, and even a few from the Falls and Whiterock Road.'

Francy winked, leaning forward, licking spittle from the corner of his mouth.

'And we're not yet out of the city limits, haven't begun to consider the ones who came from the towns round about: from Bangor and Lisburn, Carrick, Larne, Ballymena, Downpatrick, Portadown. Beyond that too: from Armagh, Dungannon and Omagh, Enniskillen, Newry, Strabane, Derry – and all the countryside in between; people that had scarcely ever seen a town, never mind a city.'

He paused again.

'You'd think that'd be an end to it, wouldn't you?'

Mal, his mind reeling with the vision of the hordes conjured by Francy bearing down on the empty estate, nodded dumbly.

'Not a bit of it,' he said. 'There were the lost ones as well; the ones who'd emigrated when they were young, had had their fill and now wanted to settle down.'

He shook one end of the rope.

'They felt the tug: felt it in Glasgow, Liverpool, Manchester, Birmingham, London; felt it in Toronto, Chicago, New York, Detroit, Wellington, Sydney, Perth and places whose names you've never in your life dreamed of. They felt the tug, like they all do eventually, and were drawn back to Belfast, to a space less than Belfast: an area of a quarter square mile, a collection of detached, semi-detached and terraced houses, in a network of avenues, parks, cul-de-sacs, roads and streets, raised from nothing out of the fields in the time it takes to make a baby; bounded by main roads on three sides and by a poxy wood, trailing into a dump, at its arse end.'

Francy smiled broadly for the first time. His teeth were yellow, going green at the gums.

'Now, I bet you're wondering why,' he said.

But the question wouldn't have entered Mal's head. He was

young and listened to those who were older, even those only a few – or was it more? – years older, like Francy, in the same way that he read books. He followed the words, letting them guide him. The patterns they made were the patterns of his thoughts, he was not aware of any alternatives. Indeed, listening to Francy was like reading a book, or, at least, like hearing teachers talk who had taught so long from the same book that its language had become theirs. Though, of course, teachers didn't swear, and neither did books; not the ones that Mal had read at any rate.

'Well?' asked Francy. 'Aren't you wondering why? Or even how I know all this?'

Mal was young, the words of others were his guides. And now they suggested he wonder why, how.

'Why?' he wondered aloud. 'How?'

Francy rocked back in his seat.

'As to how,' he said, tapping the side of his nose slyly. 'That's for me to know and you to find out. But, as to why …'

He closed one eye and tilted his head sideways, scrutinising Mal.

'Well, look, they grew up in the war, most of the people that bought houses on this estate. In the war or in the thirties. Not much to fucking choose between the two if you're from Northern Ireland. There were riots in the thirties, you know, things that make the stuff today look normal – house-burnings, killings, the lot. Bit like the war, only without the uniforms and on your own doorstep. The war had that going for it: by and large it happened somewhere else. And then, it wasn't as bad as the first one – no trenches, or any of that shit, not the same danger of the men coming home all packed up in their old kitbags. And there was work too in the war, unlike the thirties. So, if you could put up with the blackout, the ration books, and the odd air raid … well, things could've been worse. Still and all, they danced in the streets and sang when it was over. Because we'd won. Good old we.

'But after the celebrations, when the rationing continued and the work didn't, people started to catch themselves on. Whole

21

areas had gone' – he snapped his fingers – 'phut! And there they were having to live in prefabs or with their relatives … Suddenly just winning didn't seem to be enough. And it wasn't only the usual sort complained. D'you see what I'm getting at?'

Mal looked as serious as he knew how, but his expression of understanding was hopelessly transparent.

'People,' Francy explained carefully, 'will accept war if you can convince them the hardship's worthwhile. But they're not going to be too happy when they find out the better world they've been fighting for's just the same old world over again. Right?'

'Right,' Mal agreed.

'So, what do you do?'

Teacher trick. Lull you and lead you with their book language, then spring a question. Mal took his time, recapping all he had heard to avoid any error in his reply.

'You change it?' he offered at length.

Francy's broad purple tongue circled the outer ring of his lips, preening the thick down. He sucked a cavity in the recesses of his mouth, watching Mal.

'Aye,' he said. 'You change it.'

He continued talking, but it seemed to Mal as though he were losing interest in his own story.

'What was needed? Jobs? Jobs it was. Not so many as in the war, but more than before it. And what else? Houses. Can't have people living in the ruined shells from war and riots – pull them down. Pull them down and build modern houses, estates full of them, on the outskirts of the city, away from the old memories. That's what they did. Then, they waited to see what happened. And what happened? The people flocked to them. And they flocked here, to Larkview, to a ready-made community.'

Francy lit a heel-flattened scrap of cigar, puffing on it like it was a cigarette, raising clouds of smoke – green, blue, brown – that obscured his face. Then, with a sudden deep breath, he sucked all the smoke inside him, up his nose, down his throat, exhaling a moment later a single off-white stream.

'Finished,' he said, rising.

He held the string above his head; it bounced taut, knots tightening with the weight of the rat hanging by its tail.

'What d'you think?'

The rat had already begun to stiffen, but Mal was no longer frightened by it. Its tail, entwined in the lengths of string, was not the whiplash he had always envisaged. After killing the rat, Francy pushed as many of the broken bones as he was able back into place; it bulged awkwardly here and there, but remained intact within its smoothed grey-brown fur. Only with the mouth was Francy unable to do anything. The lips were peeled back grotesquely and two small yellow teeth protruded over a strip of pink tongue.

'This,' said Francy, 'is a charm.'

'Really?' Mal asked.

Francy cackled until the phlegm rose in his throat.

'Really and truly. See how useful rats are, even dead ones? If you tie this round you and wear it everywhere you go for a week, it'll not only bring you luck, but tell you, too, what the future holds.'

Mal looked at the rat rope doubtfully. The problem wasn't that he didn't believe what Francy told him (he did, although he wasn't quite sure he understood perfectly) but that, much as his terror of rats had diminished, he couldn't see himself trailing one behind him for a whole week. Francy, however, forestalled his objections.

'Oh, don't worry, I'm not wasting this on you. No chance. Too ashamed to wear a rat, aren't you? I'll bet you'd even be ashamed to be seen with me.'

He took the cigar from the tip of his tongue and flicked the burning end off with a red-haired, orange-stained finger, popping the remainder into his mouth. He chewed noisily, a rivulet of bitsy juice trickling down his chin.

'I wouldn't,' Mal said, his voice little more than a whisper. 'I want to be your friend.'

Francy grinned, teeth now smeared with a film of brown mucus, and spat, heavily this time, straight down. A thick, chewed splodge landed at his feet and he ground it into the grass with his baseball boot.

'The rat charm will decide,' he said.

He crossed the mound and dragged Mal to his feet. Hitching Mal's shirt, Francy passed the string twice around his waist, knotting one end to a back belt loop. He let go and the rat thudded on the grass. Mal's jeans were tugged tight against him, with a force that made him first gasp, then colour deeply. Francy swayed from side to side, mumbling incoherently, untied the rat and repeated the ritual on himself.

'Right, then,' he told Mal. 'Fuck off.'

Mal glanced at him, hurt.

'But can't I ...'

'Come back? A week from now, like I said. And not before, mind. The message of the rat will be clear by then – provided, that is, you don't mention to another living soul that you've been here and seen me. Now, beat it. I've got to find some smokes.'

He birled Mal around so that he faced the houses and placed his open hands at the sides of his head, blinkering his eyes.

'Keep going in a straight line, it's easier. And don't stop till you're at the fence.'

Reluctantly, Mal set off, endeavouring to stick to Francy's path of compacted rubbish, cutting out the worst of the brambles and nettle banks. This morning, he thought, all of this – the dump, the rats, Francy himself – had been part of another world, a world known to him through others' stories and his own imaginings. One afternoon, the like of which he had never before lived through, had changed all that. Now, he was learning its secrets. And there was the sensation in his privates, when Francy let go the rope, straining his trousers against them. He had glimpsed for an instant the vague outlines of still another world; but the faint image quickly died, and he was left once more with the half-remembered, barely understood mutterings of the older boys.

He had reached the end of the track. It occurred to him that Francy hadn't thought to ask his name. He spun on his heel, intending to go back, but the toilet was gone from before the willow and Francy was nowhere to be seen. He turned again and paused, staring at the estate. It *did* look odd from there. The angle was to blame, of course; he wasn't used to it. He climbed the fence and started up the cul-de-sac to the hill. Tomorrow would be time enough for giving the bonfire another go.

3

'One week from now, not before. And don't mention to another living soul that you've been here and seen me.'

Mal accepted as Holy Writ the conditions set upon his returning to the dump and solemnly vowed that he would observe them to the letter.

At first it was easy. He sailed through Friday, Saturday and Sunday, excited by the very idea of keeping such a secret from everyone he met and by the assurance that – whatever the outcome of it might be – at least one more rendezvous lay in store. He even took to avoiding the hill, in case he passed too close to Francy's domain and spoiled the rat charm. Instead now, when he walked each day to the bonfire site, he chose an alternative route that wound along the front of the estate and down the far side, bringing him out by Brookeborough Close, at the opposite end of the park from the dump.

With the start of the new week, however, Thursday seemed as far away as ever. The Twelfth Fortnight was only days off and everywhere factories, offices and businesses were already slowing in preparation for the break, so that it was next to impossible not to be contaminated by the lethargy. The boys at the woods, it was true, were conspicuous by their continued activity, but Mal found it increasingly difficult to share their panic at the prospect of not having the bonfire ready in time for Friday night. Monday dragged past and dribbled into Tuesday while Mal lay, sleepless, in bed, convincing himself that Francy's second condition was an unfair, additional bind. Waiting wouldn't be half so bad, if only he could tell someone what he was waiting for. But who was there to tell?

Mucker and Andy could be ruled out for a start. They were the oldest and most important gang leaders and would have been the obvious choices, if their reaction hadn't been so predictable. They hated Francy and anything connected with him. No ifs, no buts. Mal wasn't so desperate to talk that he was willing to run the risk of having that hatred turned on him.

For a while, Andy's brother, Peter, seemed a likely candidate. He had been in the year above Mal at school and, of all those at the bonfire, he was probably the person Mal knew best. But there was something sly in Peter Hardy's manner and, although he claimed to despise his older brother, there was no guarantee that he wouldn't go home and repeat to Andy everything Mal told him. His name was removed from Mal's list of possibilities, to be followed, the longer Tuesday wore on, by many others, until at dinner Mal decided that Pickles Austin would be his safest – and last – bet. Like Peter he was not much older than Mal and, more importantly, like Francy he was a Catholic (Mucker had nicknamed him Pickles because his parents' was a mixed marriage). Mal had actually opened the Austins' gate that evening before he remembered that Pickles was present last Thursday when the story of Francy pulling the hatchet was brought to the woods. Then, he had been as loud as anyone else in his threats of revenge.

Mal closed the gate and headed home, dismayed. Francy's warning was neither here nor there; no matter how much Mal might want to, there wasn't, in fact, a single living soul to whom he could mention his visit to the dump. No one liked Francy Hagan. And clearly it wasn't simply because he was a Catholic.

For as well as Pickles, there were other Catholics from the estate who ran with the gangs: Gerardy McMahon and his cousin Barry, who lived with Gerardy's family because his own parents were dead, Seth Dunne and the Kelly twins. And recently Mad Mitch Campbell had been helping at the bonfire. They were all of them Catholics, and nobody had it in for them. But then, Francy was something more than just a Catholic; he was a Rebel and a Taig.

A Rebel and a Taig. The words had no history in Mal's mind. They had been coined for Civil Rights marchers and student demonstrators; coined for rioters in Londonderry, Dungannon and Armagh, places Mal had never been; coined for John Hume and Gerry Fitt, Bernadette Devlin and Eamonn McCann, faces on TV. Why, then, for Francy Hagan? Because he sat on a toilet and not a seat, in a filthy dump infested with rats?

While he was still unsure, Mal resigned himself to saying nothing. So he waited in silence, and the silence and the waiting fed off each other, until both became almost more than he could bear and his secret seared his chest like heartburn.

He awoke early on Wednesday morning, despite his efforts to oversleep, and thought he would tidy his bedroom before allowing himself breakfast. But his mother came in every day to dust and vacuum while he was out and he could find little to do. He made and remade his bed and went downstairs.

Mrs Martin was at the kitchen sink, resting her head on the wall cabinet where the best china was kept. Mal kissed her good morning and she smiled, her face puffy and red, stooping to hug him with her elbows, while her sudsy hands dangled at his back. Her breath rasped in his ear and her hold, gentle to begin with, became tighter and tighter. Mal broke from her with a startled yelp as her chin dug into his shoulder. His mother straightened, pushing stray wisps of light brown hair inside the headscarf she was wearing. The back of her hand brushed her cheek, leaving a streak of tiny, bursting bubbles.

'Have your breakfast and get outside,' she said hoarsely. 'It's too good a morning to be stuck indoors. Dear only knows, they're rare enough.'

Mal ate alone at the dinette table, dawdling over his toast and cereal, counting each chew until he reached thirty-two before swallowing a mouthful. He listened to his mother across the kitchen divide, humming snatches of tunes as she washed up, passing the dishes through soapy water, from the right side of the draining board to the left, emptying the sink and refilling it with cold water, passing the dishes through again, from left to right.

In the centre of the table stood a heavy brass bowl. The bowl was already old when it was given to Mr and Mrs Martin as a wedding present, and its base was not properly balanced, so that the slightest bump of the table set it clattering. They had never quite made up their minds whether to leave it as an ornament, pure and simple, or put it to a more practical use. From time to time, a sediment of safety pins and elastic bands would build up at the bottom, until somewhere better could be found to keep them, and at Christmas it wore a belt of tinsel. As he drank his tea, Mal traced the intricate lines of its Eastern, hand-beaten design with his fingernail, but the bowl began rocking gently and he stopped scratching, in case his mother heard the rattle and told him off for fiddling with it. He drained his cup to the tea-leaves and carried his dishes into the kitchen.

'Thank you,' he said, though he had made his own breakfast.

His mother swivelled to face him, head pivoted on the wall cabinet.

'Take the milk bottles out when you go,' she said, and her voice drifted, trembling, into a hum.

Mal walked through the living room, rolling the milk bottles in his hand, so that they caught the sunlight with a sheen of shifting green and purple. His mother always said theirs were the cleanest milk bottles in this – or any other – street. His father told her she was being foolish taking so much trouble over them; there were machines for washing them and, clean or not, her bottles would go through with the rest when they got to the dairy. But still she washed them, and still they were left on the front step every day, gleaming.

Mal set down the bottles and sat beside them on the doormat. It was early yet, not quite nine o'clock, and the sun was struggling to clear the rooftops of the Crosiers' house opposite. It appeared to Mal so round and close and one-dimensional that it might have been cut out of dull red-orange paper and stuck on to the unmixed paint-blue of the sky. The air was warm when he breathed in. His mother was right, fine weather was too short-lived this holiday to waste it.

In the garden, kneeling on a flattened cardboard box, Mal's father was cutting the grass with a pair of shears. In the old house, gardening day was always Sunday, the day when his father did not go to work. But his father had not been to work since they moved to Larkview, and Sundays were no different from any other day (which suited him fine, he would sometimes joke to Mal, because now he could do the garden whenever it took his toe). They had brought an electric mower with them from Belmont Road, but the square of grass in front of the new house was so small that no sooner had his father started the engine than he had to stop again to turn, and before long he got rid of it for a hand mower. But that didn't satisfy him either; the wheels left ruts, he said, and now he used the shears that previously he had kept for the verges. He could take a long time over the grass, on occasion whole mornings, even when you would have thought it didn't need cutting at all. But then, there was not much else to occupy him in this garden.

A privet hedge ran along the bottom of it, next the street, and up one side, bordering their neighbour's path, to an elaborate, rusting, wrought-iron fence between the two front doors. The hedge grew at a slant, away from the garden, and when the family arrived had bulged over the footpath in an unruly mess, broken and tatty from people brushing past and from being used by the boys of the street as a goal for shooty-in.

'The first job,' Mr Martin had said, eyeing the fractured branches, 'is to train the hedge into shape. Just like hair, really, if the ends are split and unhealthy: cut back to grow strong.'

He was a great believer in education, said he'd always wished he had a proper one. At the same time, though, he claimed to have got ahead by teaching himself and that there wasn't anything he couldn't learn if he put his mind to it. He read a few books on subjects that interested him, but in most instances proceeded by a mixture of what he called common sense and comparison. The trial and error approach, as Mal's mother referred to it.

The hedge was duly taken back level with the low concrete wall which separated the garden from the street. That was three months ago and, while the privet no longer impeded the footpath, few green leaves had grown since. Shorn of the overhanging branches, the hedge looked sparse and twiggy, as peculiar, Mal's mother said one afternoon, as a newly scalped sheepdog. He had been watching with her, from the living room window, his father on his daily walk around the hedge, checking for progress.

'Look at him,' she muttered. 'He can't wait for that to grow again, so as he's something else to cut.'

On the two sides of the garden where there was no hedge, the previous owners had dug two narrow flower beds. Once, while hoeing them, Mal's father unearthed a few wizened and rootless plant stumps.

'Roses,' he said, scooping a handful of soil and crumbling it with his thumb. 'Never been properly nourished. We'll have to be careful with these beds if we're ever to have anything take here again.'

This morning his father was dressed in his usual gardening clothes: a pair of baggy trousers, green-stained and splashed with paint, and a pink nylon shirt, missing the bottom two buttons. Hearing the clink of the bottles, he stopped clipping and leaned on the shears to push himself up, yawning inside without opening his mouth.

31

Years before, half a lifetime ago, Mal sat on the edge of the bath while his father at the bathroom mirror dabbed, with a coarse white towel, his face, razored smoothly red.

He tensed his stomach and called to his son: 'Hit me, hard as you like.'

Mal came forward unsurely and jabbed at his father, hard as he dared.

'Harder than that,' he laughed.

Mal punched again, hard as a small boy could. His fist jarred and buckled against the girdle of solid muscle.

He watched as his father yawned now, stretching, shirt pulled taut across his belly. In the gap left by the missing buttons, he saw clearly the ring of dark hair plunging into the deep hole of his navel and wondered had he ever remembered punching his father at all, or remembered only his father's retelling.

'So you're up at last?' Mr Martin said, running his hand over his blackly shining hair. Drops of sweat clung to the thick, Brylcreemed strands and glistened on the reddish patch of scalp beneath them at the crown. 'Changed days, I can tell you. See when I was young, I was off at the crack of dawn, summer and winter, doing things you wee lads today never dream of doing: hiking around the countryside, blackberrying, fishing; you name it, I did it.'

He frowned, but the flesh about his mouth dimpled in a way that suggested he was only half serious.

'Better than that, I'd my first job when I was the age you are now. Just turned nine when I started – Jackie Wylie's shop in Longstone Street. All day Saturday and four days a week after school. And do you know how much I got for that?'

Mal had heard this many times before. If he had been bothered to try he could have recalled exactly how much his father earned. If he had been bothered.

'Don't know.'

'Go on,' his father pressed him. 'Guess.'

'A pound?'

'A pound?' Mr Martin laughed sharply. 'No fear. We were lucky ever to see a pound when we were young. I'll tell you – two shillings.'

He pointed the shears at his son and his frown became deeper.

'Less than you get for pocket money, mark you, and I had to work for it.'

Mal squirmed against the doorpost, flicking a flat stone over with the toe of his gutty. His weekly half-crown had used to come from his mother, out of the housekeeping, but a month ago it had been stopped. There was no warning, no apology and no one had mentioned the subject since. Did his father not know, or had he simply forgotten?

'But money was different then,' Mal said.

They were his father's own words and he said them to show that he understood already, to haul him back from the brood he saw him slipping into. They seemed, however, to have the opposite effect.

'And isn't that the truth,' his father said, more absently than ever. 'Two shillings was two shillings, and we were glad of it.'

His eyes stared straight at Mal, but his mind was focused on something much further away in time.

A small black terrier snuffled along the open gateway and turned into the drive, cocking its leg at the hedge. Before it could do anything, though, Mal scooped the flat stone from the path and shied it at it. The stone bounced back harmlessly from the gate into the garden, but the dog fled, a line of damp specks trailing in its wake on the dusty gravel.

The sudden movement broke his father's trance. He spun round to see the terrier's hind legs disappear through the gate into the street.

'Good lad,' he said. 'That's the last thing that flaming hedge needs at the minute.'

Mal spotted his chance and stood up.

'Want me to sweep the grass?' he asked, pointing to the stiff-bristled yard brush leaning by the front window.

'If you like,' his father answered brightly. He bent to resume clipping and chuckled. 'Talking of dogs – did you ever hear tell of Sammy Slipper, a cousin of Mr Turtle used to come in the shop?'

Mal didn't think so.

'His wife, Sadie,' Mr Martin began, 'had a dog, a yappy little peke, name of Bobo, and between the two of them they'd poor Sammy nagged ragged.'

He continued round the garden as the story progressed and Mal followed, sweeping as best he could with the long brush the grass his father cut.

'One day, Sadie's mother and father were coming and she wanted to have her hair permed, so Sammy had to mind Bobo for an hour or two. And, Sadie told him, he was to do something with that backyard, which was in such a state it'd make anyone ashamed to look at it. Anything for a quiet life, Sammy set to work the minute she was out the front door. But no sooner had he started than the wee dog was yelping about his heels, distracting him.

'"What do you want?" he asked, and the dog motioned with its tongue that it was after a drink. So, Sam filled its dish with water and tried to get back to work. Quick as you like, though, there was the dog under his feet again, snapping and yapping. "What now?" he asked and the dog lifted its leg, as much as to say it would like to go to the toilet. Out Sam went with the dog on a lead, till it did its business at the first lamp post they came to.'

He broke off to cast an eye along the strip of grass he had been clipping. The sun was yellowing and growing more distant. Soon it would fade in a haze and, by lunch, clouds would have bubbled up across the sky. But, for now, the atmosphere was muggy. Mal took off his T-shirt and stuffed the collar in his jeans pocket. Although his parents said they thought he had filled out this past few months, his shoulders still protruded like wire coat hangers and between the visible rack of his ribs his stomach was the round hard ball of a child much younger than his ten years. Hot or not, he would have been too embarrassed to go without a shirt at all, if the street hadn't been so sleepily deserted.

'Back at the house,' his father went on, 'it was the same drill as before: Sam wanting to work, Bobo wanting attention – looking fed, if you please. Now Sammy'd begun to wonder whether the dog wasn't doing this on purpose, to get him into trouble for not finishing the yard. For they're vindictive wee dogs, pekes, and crafty with it. He decided he'd teach the thing a lesson and mixed a whole pot of mustard in with the dog food, thinking, do you see, it'd take one taste, realise it was rumbled and leave him be.

'But here, didn't the greedy beggar scoff the lot without even pausing for breath. And when it was done, it looked at Sam kind of cockeyed, then let out the wildest howl ever you heard and set off as fast as its legs could carry it round the backyard, foaming at the mouth. Sammy tore after it with the water dish, but Bobo was convinced he was out to poison it and ran for all it was worth, a full half hour, always one step ahead. Finally though, it had a seizure, rolled over, legs in the air, and Sammy, who was near beat himself, made a last dive and grabbed it. The second he laid hands on it the eyes started out of its head and the breath left it in a whimper and a sigh. Quaking in his boots, Sammy put his ear to where he thought its heart ought to be: not a dickybird.

'Well, he was in a right panic now. Sadie'd be home any time, the yard was never cleared, and there was the pet dog she loved more than she loved him, dead at his feet. Nothing to lose, he ran into the hall and opened the door a dog's-breadth. Then, he found a binbag, dropped Bobo in, tied the top and buried it at the bottom of his wee vegetable patch. He did a lightning job on the yard and just had the place in order as Sadie stomped up the alley by the side of the house.

'First thing she wanted to know, of course, was where her precious Bobo was. Sammy played the innocent and said he presumed it was inside sleeping, for the last he saw it, it was following her to the front door to say goodbye. Sadie was straight into the house and out again in a flash, crying: What a fool she was, she must have left the door open and Bobo had slipped out and got lost. There, there, Sammy told her, all concern, she wasn't to upset herself. He'd go and look for it at once, he had a feeling it wouldn't be far away.

'At this, big Sadie sniffed and gave him a hefty hug. "Sammy Slipper, I've had you all wrong. There was me thinking this ten years you hated that dog. Can you ever forgive me?" So, boys, but if everything wasn't turning out even better than Sammy expected. Off he walked, her hero, and popped in for a private celebration at the local hostelry.'

The word was a new one on Mal, but he didn't have to ask his father what he meant. He had any number of words for it, as many, in fact, as he had stories of the long-ago. Inn and rest house, tavern and snug. Mrs Martin scowled at these stories. She had only the one word: pub. Word like a burp. A pub was a pub, whatever you called it. A pub you sneaked out to, like Sammy Slipper was sneaking out; like Mal's father sneaked out, last night and the night before, thinking Mal was asleep in bed.

'Meantime, Sadie's mother and father arrived and Sadie told them her tale of woe and told them too what a great fella her Sammy was. "Well," said her father, looking out the scullery window, "I see he's started turning the vegetable patch. Why don't I do some for him as a bit of a surprise?"

'Sammy was already on his way home, reckoning if he'd searched for that blasted dog a minute longer he'd be in no fit state to walk. Up the alley he came, shouting: "Darling, it's me. I'm sorry, but I haven't seen hide nor hair of poor Bobo." And then, just as he was in the gate, his father-in-law dug a spade into the ground, the bin bag ripped ... And what do you think? Before their very eyes, out jumped Bobo. Sammy was no better versed in dog-doctoring than the man in the moon: the thing was never dead at all, it had only passed out.'

Mal was sceptical.

'But how did it stay alive in the ground?'

Mr Martin raised a finger, as if he'd anticipated the question.

'Sammy tied the bin bag, didn't he? Made an air-pocket and that kept the dog breathing when it came round from the faint.'

He hadn't thought of that. He tried to catch his father's eye, but he was hunched over snipping a tuft of grass no one but himself would have noticed.

'Why don't I remember hearing about Sammy Slipper before, then?'

His father tutted and looked saddened.

'A fine world we're living in when a son doesn't believe his own father. You must remember Sammy – Mr Turtle's cousin. You can still see him to this day over that end of town. Walks with his head down, duncher near covering his eyeballs, a big woman nagging at his back, a wee dog snapping at his heels, tormenting the life out of him and never letting him forget what he did.'

He arched his shoulders, nursing the base of his spine as he got to his feet and walked stiffly to the front door.

'That'll have to do, I'm afraid. There's a lot more needs taking care of if I'm to have a few days' break over the Twelfth. Wait here a minute while I have a drink of water, then I'll fetch a box and a shovel for the grass.'

Mal rolled the smooth round dome of the brush handle on his cheek. A handle such as this had crashed down repeatedly on the skull and spine of the rat. So small. Battered and bloodied in Francy's too-big hands. Still. Purring. Dead. If only, like the dog, it had been dead and not dead. Sammy Slipper, Sammy Slipper. The name had begun to sound familiar.

Farther down the street, Mucker left his house, called at Les's door and went inside.

'Right, come on,' his father said returning. 'There's no time for lazing. Didn't I say there was a lot to be done?'

The friendly, easy tone had vanished from his voice and it crackled now with the edge of rising temper.

'I'll hold the shovel, you brush the grass on to it,' he snapped. 'And watch, I don't want any spilt in the flower beds.'

While he had managed the brush well enough to sweep the grass into three rough piles, Mal wasn't at all sure he was capable of such precision with it. He crouched low, grasping the handle near the bottom.

'No, no, no,' his father said irritably. 'You're holding it all wrong. You have to get over it, like the road sweeps do.'

Mal did as he was shown, pressing the palm of his right hand on the top of the brush and placing his left hand six inches below that.

'Feels better, doesn't it?'

Mal nodded. He did indeed have control of the brush, and when he pushed against the first pile it moved forward, a single, solid mass.

'Slowly you go, slowly,' his father cautioned. 'Take it a bit at a time.'

Carefully, Mal directed half the grass on to the shovel which Mr Martin held steady beneath the lawn's verge.

'That's the way,' he told his son, tipping the grass into a cardboard box. 'Now the next bit.'

Mal positioned the brush behind the remainder of the pile and pushed forward again. This time, though, he struck something hard in the garden. It was the stone he had thrown at the terrier, which had been tramped into the ground; the more he forced, the deeper it became embedded and the less he was able to budge the stiff bristles.

'I didn't mean you to go that slow,' his father said.

Mal pressed down with all his might on the top of the brush. The bristles jerked up into the pile, scattering grass over the shovel and into the dry soil of the flower bed.

His father lowered his head.

'You stupid, stupid fool,' he groaned. 'What in the name of all that's holy do you think you're playing at?'

His parents never swore and this was the closest either of them came to blasphemy. Mal stared blankly at the ground.

'The brush hit a bump and slipped,' he said.

'I'll give you slipped.'

His father took a step towards him, raising his hand. Mal ducked and hopped past him on to the driveway. His father glared a moment, then snatched the brush from the garden.

'I'll sweep,' he said. 'You obviously aren't to be trusted.' The grass was cleared from the garden and flower bed, although Mal couldn't prevent the shovel shaking occasionally, sprinkling the gravel with short showers of green blades. His father merely wagged his head at this and Mal felt even worse, since it was clear he was too disdainful to speak.

As Mal was patting down the last of the clippings, Mr Martin started towards the house, hesitated, then turned back and lifted the cardboard box.

'Go and get me the car keys from the kitchen,' he ordered.

Mal was about to ask him why, but bit his tongue, as much afraid of what the answer might be as he was of what his father would say to him questioning his command. He ran obediently round the side of the house.

The sun didn't reach the yard until early afternoon, and at this time of day, when the door to the living room was shut, the kitchen was gloomy, in a way that summer not only failed to cheer, but actually made more noticeable. Mal opened the back door and stopped dead, sniffing, listening. The smell he re-cognised at once: Duraglit. That was why his father's mood had switched so suddenly. Whenever all other chores were done, his mother polished the brasses – four, five, even six times a week – and the faintest whiff of metal polish was enough to set his father shouting: 'Would you for pity's sake leave those flaming things be and get on with something useful.'

The smell he could place, but the sound – what was that? A low rumble that grew louder and ever more erratic as he tiptoed towards the dinette.

Mrs Martin was sitting at the table, surrounded by horses' heads and horseshoes, bookends, letter racks and paperweights.

39

The tin of Duraglit stood open before her and she clutched a rag in one hand. But she wasn't polishing now. Instead, with her free hand, she was spinning the old brass bowl. It drummed and rattled and hobbled on the table's varnished surface and Mal watched, jaw slack in amazement, as her long, bony fingers flicked the intricately patterned sides, sending it still faster, faster, faster …

She clamped both hands on the bowl, bringing it to an abrupt halt, and looked up, eyes drained of expression. Seeing Mal, her tensed shoulders wilted. She seemed faded against the drab background; her face was blanched and her hair was pulled so severely inside her headscarf that the puffiness had been stretched out of the skin about her eyes.

'What?' she asked.

Mal groped for the sideboard behind him.

'Where are the car keys?'

'Why?'

'Don't know. My daddy just told me to get them.'

His mother rose distractedly.

'On the windowsill, by the cooker,' she said, passing him and opening the door to the living room.

Mal grabbed the leather key pouch and sprinted into the yard. But he was already too late. Coming out the back gate into the drive, he could hear his parents' voices raised in argument at the front of the house. He leaned against the gable-end's rough red brick, breathing deeply, watching the sharp division between light and shade, where the shadow of the house fell at an angle on the gravel. He had played here for hours one day, shuffling backwards, inch by inch, with the shrinking patch of darkness as the sun moved from the front, until eventually it was directly overhead. The shadow was eaten up and Mal stood with his back pressed to the flaking paint of the garage door, blinded by the glare.

'Mal,' his father called. 'Have you never got those keys yet?'

He stepped into the light and rounded the corner to the

garden. His mother was on the doorstep, the polish-blackened rag still clutched in her hand.

'I just don't see what right you have coming out here, quizzing me in public,' Mr Martin was telling her. 'But, if you must know, me and the boy's taking this grass to the dump, crime that it is.'

She slammed the door and Mal's heart sank. It was the answer he had feared,

'The dump?' he asked his father.

'What are you, a flipping parrot? Yes, the dump. Now get a move on, I've two months' clippings I want out of the way.'

Mal panicked. What if they saw Francy? The week wouldn't be up until tomorrow and the charm would be ruined. Or, worse, Francy might speak to him, his father would discover he'd been hanging around there and he'd be in for a hiding when he got home. Yet he knew how his parents had been lately once they got an idea in their heads (the days when his tantrums could sway them were long gone), and he wondered, as he caught up with his father in the garage, if he could bring himself to say anything. He had no time to find out, for at that moment a box was shoved against his bare chest.

'You take that. One at a time'll do for you.'

His father walked off, confidently balancing a precarious stack of cartons. Mal looked down at his box. The grass on top was parched yellow and brown, but when his fingers searched the bottom for a firmer grip they sank into damp cardboard and the smell of rotting grass stung his nostrils. He *couldn't* go with his father. He would have to tell him.

Mr Martin was bending over the boot of the car, loading the boxes.

'Daddy?'

Beneath his shirt, the muscles of his father's back flinched, as though in pain, but he didn't answer.

'Daddy,' Mal persisted. 'D'you think it'd be all right if I didn't come to the dump? Only …'

His father faced him slowly. His eyes were heavy and his top

41

lip curled at the corner. Words failed Mal. Then, suddenly, the eyes lightened and the curl creased into a smile.

'Ach, Philip, son. How's it going?'

With perfect, cavalry timing, Mucker and Les were making towards Mal and his father.

'Not so bad thanks, not so bad,' Mucker replied.

He was fifteen and all the grown-ups spoke to him. Even to most of them – Mr Martin was one of the few exceptions – he was 'Mucker', because that was what he usually called everyone else. This time next year he would be left school and would have outgrown the street gangs. Already he was spending evenings at the park with the older teenagers, drinking cider and playing pitch-and-toss behind the pavilion. The girls loved him and he knew it; his brown, wavy hair was longer than any of the other boys' on the estate and his face put people in mind of somebody famous, though they could never quite think who. He was tall and sturdily built and, it was agreed, labouring would make him stronger still. As once, long ago, it had Mal's father.

'And how's Leslie?'

Les's large, round head joggled up and down. He had no father of his own and was a bit simple, but he was also Mucker's sidekick, so nobody dared tease him. Except Mucker himself, when he was bored or had run out of people to pick on. If Les minded, he never complained, and when Mucker got outnumbered in a fight he was always the first to help. He had a smooth skin that was always slightly yellow and a thick helmet of dark hair, cut short at the back and sides. He, too, would leave school in a year, but unlike Mucker, it was hard to see him breaking away from the kids in the street.

'Where are you off to, then?' Mr Martin asked.

'Here and there,' Mucker answered coolly. 'The bonfire eventually.'

'You call that a bonfire?' Mr Martin sounded incredulous. 'I was down that way the other day and I had a look across the fields at it. And I'll tell you, I've seen bigger campfires.'

The car creaked as he hoisted a buttock on to the rim of the boot.

'I remember a bonfire we had in Lisburn ... Let me see, that must have been the first July after the war – for, I don't suppose you know this, but we weren't allowed to have them while the blackout was on – and no word of a lie, that bonfire was so big that people in the centre of Belfast said they could see it. Imagine – ten miles away.'

He sighed at the recollection.

'But our wood's all spread out, so's nobody can burn it on us,' Mucker told him. 'Plus, we've a whole stack of tyres hid from the cops. You'll see the smoke from them, all right, in Lisburn and beyond.'

Mr Martin jabbed his temple with a no-nailed finger.

'It's the height you need. That's the secret – the height. Now, that one after the war ...'

'We're not stupid,' Mucker cut him short. 'We've a huge centre pole my dad got us from the timber yard. You know, where he works.'

Mr Martin stood up, his tongue fluttering drily over his lips, and hitched his trousers, making his belly bounce. Mal saw again the black, hairy hole and wished his shirt would close properly. He laid a rough hand on his son's shoulder.

'Is our wee Biafran going with you?'

Mal remembered his own exposed tummy, hard, white and round, with a belly button like a knot in a balloon. He fumbled for his T-shirt.

'We need all the help we can get,' Mucker said.

Mr Martin laughed an empty laugh.

'Help?' he said, and laughed again.

Mucker nodded to Les and without another word the two of them carried on their way. Mr Martin stared after them. Red blotches had appeared on his neck and cheeks. His hand sought his son's shoulder once more and he squeezed it. Hard.

'On you go,' he said. His voice was strained but gentle. 'I can manage this on my own.'

Mal was so relieved at having got out of going to the dump that he forgot even to say thank you. He ran up the street after Mucker and Les.

'Hey, wait youse ones. I'm coming too.'

They broke off a whispered conversation as he drew level. Mucker's expression was hovering uncomfortably between a smile and a snarl.

'No,' he told Les, as though he had doubted him. 'I wouldn't wish it on a dog.'

The snarl seemed to be winning, but then the smile got the better of it and he cuffed the back of Mal's head.

'Your old man's wrong,' he said. 'Biafrans are fat compared with you.'

4

They turned left into Larkview Avenue and headed for the front of the estate. There was a fierce racket coming from the last house, opposite the roundabout; but, then, there was nothing unusual in that. This was where Mad Mitch Campbell lived. Mal's mother hated the place – an eyesore, she called it – and especially *that* car. 'That car' was an Austin 1100 which sat in the driveway, covered with a mouldy tarpaulin. It had no wheels and the body rested on four piles of paving stones. Every time she saw it, Mrs Martin repeated her secret wish: some day she was going to phone the AA pretending to be Mitch's mother and have them tow it away.

Mitch was perched on the windowsill outside the box room. A transistor blared on the other side of the window and he was making windmill motions with his arm, letting on to play a non-existent guitar. Even in Mal's limited experience of the breed, he was an unlikely looking guitarist. He was thin as a rake and one tooth protruded to rest on his bottom lip like permanent spittle. He wore glasses too, more often than not with one or other leg missing. Once, Mal had been told, he managed to break both legs at the same time and for a week walked around with the frames stuck to his nose by a plaster.

His sister's voice could be heard from downstairs.

'Mu-um, he won't answer me. You ask him.'

'Brian!' Mrs Campbell shrieked. 'Tell Anne-Marie where it is.'

Mucker whistled to him and he switched off the transistor.

'Right there, mucker.'

'Hello-o-o,' Mitch howled his werewolf's greeting. 'Hello-o-o, hello-o-o.'

'Giving us a hand the day?'

They never found out, for before Mitch could reply his mother yanked him in the window.

'For the last time, Brian, what have you done with the cat? And when I say get the jam out of the toaster, I mean get the jam out of the toaster.'

She pulled the window to and made a fist at the boys outside. Mitch saluted them, like a man about to face a firing squad.

'He's gone,' Mucker said. 'Definitely gone.' And you could tell he admired him.

They crossed the road, running from the entrance of the estate, to the Larkview shopping precinct: five shops in all, each a division of a single, square, one-storey building, each with the same blank, glassy front, surrounded by breeze blocks and smooth, purplish brick. They marched, three abreast – Mal trotting to keep his place in the line – past the supermarket, the chemist, the fruit shop, and wheeled round the corner towards the newsagent's and the chippy. A dozen or so boys were waiting, clustered about the three-brick-high wall separating the pavement outside the shops from a shallow lay-by, where the young people of the estate gathered when there was nothing better to do. They were all from the Crawford Drive gang, known as the Hook, after their street, which began deep in the estate and curved in a slow loop, past the shops, to the entrance.

Andy Hardy leaned against the padlocked gate to the precinct's service bay, as far apart from the others as he could possibly get. He nodded a barely perceptible welcome, tugging at the back of his hair, which was hacked in a wedge across the nape of his neck. Being a grammar school boy he wasn't allowed to grow it any longer and his habit of tugging, bad at the best of times, was even more pronounced if Mucker was about. When he talked to him he held his head tilted back slightly, so that his hair wisped over his collar. Not that they talked much normally. While the two of them had never fought one to one – and there was a lot of argument as to who would win if they ever got round to it – there was no love lost between Andy and Mucker; and this feeling had spilt over into their respective gangs, who had become fiercely competitive in everything from football to fashion. But the bonfire was the bonfire. It was their estate against others in the area, and in the weeks leading up to the Eleventh and Twelfth all rivalries were laid aside.

'What are you looking so happy about?' Mucker asked Andy.

Andy took a quick drag on the cigarette pinched between his forefinger and thumb and shielded from view by the back of his hand.

'My ma said I'd to bring the fucking kid with me, didn't she?'

He pointed to the chippy wall. Peter Hardy, dressed as always as though for a Sunday-school outing, right down to his freshly polished shoes, flapped his hand in a deliberately prissy wave. Andy retched.

'Look at him,' he said. 'Make a buzzard boke.'

His stare switched to Mal and for a horrible moment he seemed to be about to start in on him. Mucker too was eyeing him narrowly, but then, improbably, he put his hand on Andy's arm and turned away talking, as if Mal didn't exist. Mal had never been more grateful for a snub. He went and sat on the steps down to the lay-by where he was soon joined by Les.

'What's going on?' he asked.

Les looked dead ahead, sullen. Mal wasn't the only one being ignored.

'Your guess is as good as mine. We were meant to be collecting off people that promised us wood, but you know what those two are like when they're together.'

Mal knew all right. No matter what was being done or what the plans were, Andy and Mucker could set off, without warning, into mad fits of daring, goading, bullying. It was as though one was the plug and the other the socket and between them they made work some vast tyrannical machine. Worse than that, either plug or socket – or both – was faulty and there was no telling where the machine would stop once it was in motion. All you could do was keep your head down and pray.

'Hey,' Mucker called.

Down went the heads, up went the prayers.

'Mongol!'

Everywhere there was relief; except to Mal's right. Les's body remained rigid. He closed his eyes and got to his feet reluctantly, his face turning a darker shade of yellow, as it always did if he was angry or embarrassed.

'Go and buy us a blue Creme Egg,' Mucker told him.

Les held out his hand for the money, but Mucker ducked to light a cigarette from Andy's match. The others, thankful to have escaped themselves, snickered and gabbled excitedly while Les was in the newsagent's. He returned at length and handed over the chocolate.

'What's this?' Mucker wanted to know.

'A Creme Egg.'

'And what did I ask you for?'

Les shrugged, mumbling. A savage grin slashed Andy's face.

'A blue one,' Mucker said. 'Didn't I? This one's fucking green. I hate green Creme Eggs.'

'But they're near sold out,' Les complained. 'And sure, there's no difference ...'

'Shite,' Mucker interrupted. 'Take it back.'

Les's skin had grown so dark as to be almost brown. Mucker dropped the egg, smashing it, and went back to talking to Andy, who was rubbing his sides from laughing.

'Mucker doesn't mean it,' Les said sadly, sinking down on the steps beside Mal. 'That bastard Hardy puts him up to it.'

Mal wasn't so sure. Mucker had been cruel, very cruel, but he had been many times before, without Andy's coaxing. Then, in fact, Les had been a party to the bullying, and other people – Mal in particular – had suffered. He looked at the back of Les's head, hung between his knees. Another day, he thought, and Les would be there again, next to Mucker, and someone who was watching this morning would find themselves on the receiving end. Maybe he was worrying too much in the past when he was the butt; it was all part of being accepted in the gang. He felt less sorry for Les, but more understanding.

'Andy's probably jealous because you don't have spots,' he whispered.

If Andy'd heard Mal say that, he'd likely have killed him. No one, but no one ever mentioned Andy's skin within earshot of him. He had a beard and moustache of spots and boils at the back of his neck where he longed only to have hair.

'All that yellow, red and green – it's like looking at a set of traffic lights.'

They were both laughing, chins pulled tight against their chests, when Peter Hardy stopped before them.

'What's the joke?'

His eyes flitted constantly from face to face when he spoke. With Peter it wasn't so much conversation as interrogation.

'Nothing,' Les said, scrabbling backwards to the top step.

A look of loathing came over Peter's face.

'God save us,' he said. 'I only asked you a question. How much older than me are you supposed to be?'

He crouched on the ground, sidling up to Mal.

'D'you not hate all this? My mum only makes me come out with our Andy because she thinks I'm bored on my own. I'm not, you know. Rather be on my own than waste my time with this bunch of no-hopers. Fancy you and me going round to my house to play with the Scalextric?'

Mal was sorely tempted. Peter Hardy's Scalextric track was renowned; it wasn't everyone got asked to play with it. But no,

Peter had already done his Qualifying and next year he would be at the grammar school with his brother. Mal wouldn't see much of him once term started. The gang from his street, however, he would have to see every day. It was better he stayed with them.

'No thanks,' he said. 'We're going collecting wood.'

'Suit yourself,' Peter said, not even deigning to look at Les as he dandered on to Crawford Drive.

All that afternoon, Mal helped Les push a handcart from house to house round the streets at the front of the estate, while from the yards was carried whatever could be spared for the bonfire: planks, boards, crates and boxes, bits of hedge and dead branches, even the odd kitchen chair without a seat, broken stepladders and old bedsteads. Everything was piled on to the cart and pushed to the bonfire site; load after load, trip after trip, until, finally, at five o'clock Mucker called a halt. They could do the rest of the collecting tomorrow, he said, and the day after – the Eleventh itself – they'd build the bonfire.

As guards were being selected for over dinner time, Mal surveyed the scene around him. It looked like a bomb had hit it. He couldn't believe that in a short time these bits and pieces could be transformed into the giant, blazing bonfire that the rest of the boys were envisaging.

Les spoke from behind him. 'Me and Mucker's going to check on the centre pole. Want to come?'

Mal looked doubtfully to where Mucker waited by the entrance to the woods. He hadn't apologised to Les yet and, indeed, until Andy left just a minute before he had hardly spoken to him at all.

'Don't worry about Mucker,' Les jollied him. 'He was only messing earlier. I told you he didn't mean it.'

Everyone went through it and still they came back for more. Mal had gone through it and still he wanted to be friends and have them call at his door like they did for the other boys.

'Honest,' Les assured him. 'He said it was okay.'

'All right, then,' Mal said.

He had been in the woods several times since work started on the bonfire, but always he kept to where he could see the entrance and had never gone further than the electricity pylon a hundred yards in. Here the path forked in two directions. To the left, it turned sharply and ran parallel to the front of the woods until it reached a large barley field, where it bent right again and sloped down to a farmhouse at the far end of the field. This farmhouse marked the beginning of Derrybeg, the first town to the south of Belfast. Years before, when Mal's father was young, it had been an insignificant place, with a Tuesday market and a few rows of cottages clumped about a linen mill by the old Dublin road; but as Belfast swelled in size, so Derrybeg spread along the road to meet it. Until Larkview had been built, however, it still seemed cut off. Now, said Mr Martin, the only things between it and the rest of the city were the woods and the memories of people like him.

But it was the other fork down which Mal followed Mucker and Les. The path here swerved around the pylon and then continued in roughly the same direction as the original track. The air was moist and cool and when the paint-smooth edge of a sign, poking from the bushes, stroked Mal's arm, he shivered, making his skin break out in goose pimples. The sign was inclined to one side and much of the writing was obscured by leaves and branches. At the top, though, Mal was able to read the words 'Northern Ireland Housing Trust' and, further down, 'commencing July 1969'.

'Les,' he said and tugged his shirt. 'D'you see this?'

Mucker and Les both turned and regarded the sign without curiosity.

'That? That was there last year, only then it said 1968,' Mucker told him.

'And the year before that,' Les added, 'it said 196–nothing.'

Mal looked more closely and saw that, while the first three numbers were painted, the final '9' was stuck on.

'There's been houses meant for here this donkey's,' Mucker said. 'But they never can get the money.'

They were approaching a break in the trees; Mucker put a finger to his lips and they slowed down, listening. Cars could be heard faintly in the distance, but the trees made little noise and in the stillness of the early evening all else was silent.

Mucker beckoned to them and they darted forward into a clearing, streaked with wood-dusty light. An unpaved road cut across their path from between the trees on the right, passed a low wooden building with a pointed roof, and disappeared off to the left in the direction of the farmhouse. The simple building was a chapel, used for the most part by the people of Derrybeg, and beside it stood an old pebble-dashed cottage where Father Riordan, the priest, lived. A bicycle was drawn up by the front porch, but otherwise there was no sign of life. They slipped up the blind side of the chapel.

At the back, the trees closed in once again and the atmosphere now was cold rather than cool, so that even Mucker and Les were shivering. Large grey stones lay scattered on the ground and, as they progressed, the stones appeared more and more frequently, until, at last, a broken, moss-covered wall could be made out. It started low then staggered to a height of about six feet, where it met another, similar wall, at a right angle to it. A topless, square hole, where once a window must have been, broke the flow of the second wall and after ten yards it too gave out and the stones became random again.

These two walls were all that remained of the first chapel built in the woods. Mal recognised the ruins, though he had never seen them before. He had read once (or had someone told him? – he couldn't remember) that the old chapel had been destroyed during a skirmish outside Derrybeg, when King Billy was passing through from Carrick on his way to the Boyne, hundreds of years ago.

Behind the second wall, the bushes were so dense and confused that, as Mucker said, nobody in their right mind would ever think to go poking about in them. This was where the centre pole was hidden. They swung down from the window like commandos. Mal was pricked and jagged through his jeans and T-shirt, but so infected was he by the mood of subterfuge that he was loath to cry out. Mucker and Les parted the bushes with sticks, revealing a length of bark-stripped wood.

'Took fifteen of us to get that up here,' Les whispered. 'It's twenty foot long, easy.'

Mal could not see much beyond the base, but this was so thick that he saw no reason to doubt him. Mucker patted the pale creamy wood.

'You are going to make one fuck of a fire,' he told it.

Mal was able now to imagine the pole, ringed with tyres, surrounded by layer upon layer of branches, bushes, headboards, tables and chairs.

'One fuck of a fire,' Mucker repeated.

Mal nodded, agreeing.

And so he returned home, finding himself, for the second time in under a week, sworn to secrecy. But if anything this was more exciting – this was closer to conspiracy. All the gangs in the know; a nod, a wink, but not a word about the centre pole. And then, too, it wasn't just for their own benefit, it was in everyone's interests that the hiding place be kept secret until the eleventh of July. That length of wood guaranteed, after all, that the Larkview bonfire would be the best anywhere on this side of the city.

The sun was in the backyard now; weak sun, like September or April sun, strained through a fine mesh of cloud. But the door was wide open, bent back on its hinges and hooked to the wall by the drainpipe. Summer was summer, whatever the weather. The deckchair-striped curtain flapping in the doorway looked out of place in this house, but Mal liked it none the less. He stood with his face to it, feeling the material suck around him as the breeze died down. Slowly he began to walk through; the curtain rode up over his body and the kitchen took shape before him, bit by bit.

At his knees, the yellowed glass of the oven appeared, followed, at his stomach, by its surround, a scoured, bathtub white. Same

53

height, to his left, buried beneath the counter, the vegetable basket, dwarfed by the washing machine, parked for the night, hoses grey and ridged like elephants' trunks coiled on the twin-tub lids. Above it, chest height, the work surface came into view and next it the divide between the kitchen and dinette, a crisscross of wooden slats, like a garden wall-frame, on which hung a solitary Star of Bethlehem, whose flowers, sunned only in the afternoon, never opened beyond narrow, arrow-headed points. Curtain to his face now, combing back his hair; on his right the sink, basin standing on its end on one side of the draining board, on the other side, bottles drying. Two bottles, tall and brown. Mal let the curtain fall limp behind him.

In the old days, the only time alcohol was brought into the house was Christmas: a bottle of whiskey and one of sherry, for guests. Whatever was left after the holiday would be brought out on special occasions in the months that followed until the bottles were done. And that would be it for another year. Then, the year before Mal and his parents had to leave Belmont, Aunt Pat and Uncle Simon moved from their house further along the road to a new one – designed and built by Uncle Simon's own firm of contractors – in the north of the city. They began visiting every other fortnight, instead of dropping in any time they happened to be passing, and Mr and Mrs Martin made sure there was always something to offer them.

But Aunt Pat and Uncle Simon hardly ever called at this house and these weren't whiskey or sherry bottles. Mal turned them around looking for the labels. Red Heart: Guinness. The very name reminded him of the sound of bottles belching open, of the smell of the dark, bitter liquid foaming out the tops, down the brown sides to gather in thick pools on fusty trestle tables. Last year, his father's cousin's wedding. Lisburn Blues' Supporters' Club. Same bottles. That was where his father was spending the evenings now.

He opened the living room door. His mother and father were standing in the middle of the floor, their arms around each other's waists. They started at his entrance and his father jumped back in pretend embarrassment.

'Oh dear, oh dear,' he said. 'The master has come home and caught the servants canoodling. Please, sir, thank you, sir, we weren't idling. We've all our work done, sir.'

His wife scatted him with a tea towel.

'Fool,' she said. 'Away and get out of these old clothes till I get your dinner on the table.'

'The table? What's the matter – no plates left?'

He winked, unsuccessfully, with both eyes and went out into the hall, laughing to himself.

'Beer on an empty stomach, he's not used to it,' Mrs Martin excused him as he walked heavily up the stairs. 'Goes straight to his head.'

Mal had never heard her being so understanding about drinking. She dusted the spotless mantelpiece with a corner of the tea towel, talking on, as though to the Hummel figures and not him.

'Of course, he wouldn't have it normally, but it's thirsty work out there.'

Mal lay in bed, listening. Nine o'clock came and went, then ten, and still there was no sound of his father leaving. As he was dropping off to sleep, they were switching out the lights and creaking quietly upstairs together.

5

'I said, Leslie's at the door for you.'

Mal rolled on to his back. His mother stood by the foot of the bed.

'Didn't you hear me, sleepy head? I've been calling for ages.'

'What time is it?'

'Half nine. I let you lie on, I knew you were tired.'

Mal waited until his mother left the room before scrambling out of bed. Even in summer, she made him wear pyjamas – for cleanliness – and he didn't want her to see he kept the bottoms under the pillow.

He struggled into his pants and jeans. Of all the days to sleep in. Why hadn't he been woken earlier? In the kitchen the washing machine sloshed and churned dully. No wonder he couldn't hear his mother shout.

'Sorry, Les,' he called, charging downstairs. 'I didn't realise the time.'

Les was staring at the doorstep.

'How d'youse get your milk bottles so clean?' he asked.

'Just washing.' Mal was trying to pull on his gutties without undoing the laces. 'Have they started putting up the bonfire yet?'

'Huh?' Les tilted his yellow face to one side. 'Sure that's not till tomorrow.'

'But is today not ... Is this only Thursday?'

Les grinned shyly.

'Were you thinking this was the Eleventh?'

Mal was too annoyed with himself to reply. All the agonies he had gone through waiting for Thursday to come round again and in the end it had slipped his mind totally. For the life of him, he couldn't think why.

'Well, are you comin' out or aren't you?'

'What? Oh, no. No, I can't. At least, not till later.'

Les glanced glumly over his shoulder. Mucker was in the street, plucking what leaves he could find from the twiggy hedge.

'Didn't I tell you?' he asked Les. 'See what happens when you have ideas?'

Mal spoke past Les.

'I'll be along in a while, honest I will. I've just a few things to do before I can go out.'

'You mean they want you to act as referee?' Mucker sneered. 'Come on ahead, mucker, you're only wasting your time here.'

'I'll see youse both this afternoon, then, will I?' Mal called, but they walked off without looking back.

Mal could have kicked himself. The first time anyone in the street had bothered to call for him and he'd said no, he wasn't coming out. But the Eleventh was so close that he knew once he was at the bonfire it would be very difficult to make an excuse to get away. And he had to go to the dump. It had been around lunchtime when he got there last Thursday and he was determined not to arrive before then today.

In the kitchen the washing machine still sloshed and churned. Mal hated the sound – like running on the spot with a bellyful of liquid – especially when it was accompanied, as it was now, by the dentist-drill whine of the spin dryer. His mother was hanging dripping clothes on the line at the bottom of the garden. Mal wondered where he ever got the idea that he had to see the week out to the minute. He wouldn't have thought of it himself, so it must have been Francy's suggestion. He concentrated to remember his exact words, but somehow, after days of reciting them and committing them to memory like the catechism, they now escaped him.

He became peeved at the thought of spending the morning in the house when there was so much else he could be doing. He lifted a pepper grinder from the counter and unscrewed the top to see what was inside. There was nothing. Mrs Martin entered by the back door, carrying an empty clothes basket.

'Aren't you away with Leslie?' she asked.

Mal had dropped the screw that fastened the handle to the grinder and couldn't fit it back together again.

'Yeah, I left ten minutes ago,' he grumped, searching on the floor for the screw. He found it by his foot. He shouldn't have fired up like that, he'd get a clout if he wasn't careful.

'I'm not leaving for a while yet,' he said more politely, his mother's son now, not his father's. 'After lunch probably.'

'Hm?'

His mother raised the lid of the spin dryer and it whirred to a creaking halt. He needn't have worried, she obviously hadn't heard him cheek her.

'I'm staying in until after lunch, I said.' He was choosing his words carefully. 'They're going to be at the bonfire this afternoon.'

Mrs Martin was filling the basket with more badly wrung clothes. She turned to him, her hair falling loose about her face. Although she claimed she hated it being straggly and untidy, Mr Martin said he preferred it not tied up and Mal did too. Her face was red, but only from standing over the steam from the washing machine, and the puffiness about her eyes, if not gone completely, was much less noticeable than it had been of late. Mal thought she looked very pretty, in an old sort of way. She smiled at him, vaguely, but pleasantly.

'That'll be fun,' she said, going out into the yard again.

Mal ate his cereal sitting on the back step, watching his mother hang the washing. It was what she called a good drying day, fresher than the previous morning with a stiff sea breeze blowing in off the lough. She was humming as usual, but, even though odd notes were lost in the flutter of shirts, sheets and towels, for once Mal was able to recognise a single, consistent tune.

Far away, far away. The wedding in Lisburn? No, another wedding, the summer before. Aunt Pat's sister, with Cathy and Alex as bridesmaids. His mother's heels click and his father's soles squeak on mirror-shiny tiles as they twirl effortlessly, face-to-face, around the deserted dance floor. Far away, far away. That same summer they went to Jersey. Some day, his father said, when the shop made him rich, they would move there. Far away, far away.

> Love me now, for now is all the time there may be,
> Oh, if you love me, Mary, Mary, marry me.

His father had come from the side door of the garage, singing the words to the tune his mother hummed. She poked her head between two sheets.

'Wrong girl, buster. Who's this Mary?'

Mal's father shook his head and continued towards her, arms apart, still singing:

'I hear the sound of distant drums, far away, far away.'

He hugged his wife, winding her in the sheets that billowed around her. The clothes pegs couldn't support their weight and gave way, tipping them on to the grass, giggling. Mal slinked into the house to finish his breakfast.

At midday he helped his mother prepare lunch – soup and open sandwiches, just like the ones they had had on holiday in Jersey, Mal said. The only difference, his mother pointed out, was that in the Channel Islands they didn't make them with wheaten bread.

'Ah, well,' his father said, rubbing his hands together as his plate was set before him. 'Their loss is our gain,'

'Did you tell your daddy who called for you this morning?' his mother asked, pouring the tea.

Mal had just taken a bite of bread.

'Young Leslie,' she answered for him.

'That a fact?' His father's tone was even and unsurprised, but his delight was evident in his smile.

'He's meeting them at the bonfire this afternoon, aren't you?'

That wasn't quite the way Mal had said it; he'd been careful not to be so definite. But his father was looking him straight in the eye. He couldn't deny it now, yet at the same time he couldn't bring himself to tell a deliberate lie. He pointed to his mouth and gulped some tea to help him swallow. No speaking with your mouth full.

'See now?' Mr Martin leaned back in his chair; he was older and had learnt how to speak and eat all at once without choking. 'What did I say? Only takes a bit of time. Isn't that what I said?'

Mal thought rapidly as he cleared his mouth of food.

'It's a quer laugh at the bonfire. Everyone's dead friendly to me now.'

That was true enough. They had been yesterday.

'Of course they are,' his father said. 'You just have to give people a chance to get to know you.'

He winked to his wife and grasped her hand across the table. Mal finished his lunch at a gallop and stole a glance at the clock above the cooker: twenty to one. He was sure he had waited long enough.

'Please may I leave the table?'

'Well, you certainly can't take it with you,' his father told him. 'Not to the bonfire, at any rate.'

'Don't listen to him,' his mother smiled. 'Enjoy yourself.'

Mal began to trot as soon as he was outside the house and at the top of the hill he broke into a run, not stopping until he arrived, panting, at the edge of the dump. He rested on the fence to catch his breath and looked across to see the toilet in place before the willow tree. Francy was about somewhere.

It suddenly struck him, now that he was finally so close, that he had been so impatient all week just to get back to the dump, he had barely taken time to think what he might do if Francy said they couldn't be friends. As if all he had to do was see out the seven days, turn up, and everything would be fine. In fact, he couldn't recall either having given any thought to whether or not *he* actually wanted to be Francy's mate. He could be sure that even if Mucker and the rest weren't after him when they found out they certainly wouldn't call for him again. But, then, today was the first time they had and he'd messed that up, so he'd no way of knowing they'd be back for him anyway.

At least with Francy there'd always be somewhere to go and he wouldn't be left to play by himself. And, come to think of it, he'd already managed to hold his silence for a week, so if he did have to keep his friendship with Francy a secret for good and all, so much the better. He imagined the Everest Street boys asking him was he coming round the shops, and him saying: 'Nah, thanks all the same, but I've something better to do.' Ha! The look on their faces when he went off down the hill by himself. They'd be curious about him then, all right.

He placed one hand on a wooden post and swung himself over the wire fence, twisting his body at the last moment to avoid landing in a deep pothole on the other side. At this end of the dump, the refuse was mainly the overflow from household bins, plastic bags and cartons filled too early or too late for collection by the council trucks. The boxes had been upset and holes chewed in the sides of the bags, so that the ground was cluttered with eggshells, potato peelings and blackened cabbage stalks. There were magazines, corrugated by damp and now dried brittle, stained with tea leaves, and a smell like dirty nappies drifted back and forth on the breeze.

Mal tiptoed carefully past the severed legs of an ironing board and around a ripped tractor tyre, encrusted with snails. With every step he took, scores of blue-green flies rose from the rubbish, landing a couple of feet further on, rubbing their wings with their back legs until he approached again. Just when he was convinced he had found the path he had followed last week, Mal stopped short, in front of a dead-end tangle of brambles and cans.

He couldn't understand it. He had definitely come over the wire at the same point as before; so why was the way now so difficult? He was thinking he would have to double back and skirt along the fence, when he noticed a teetering tower of boxes to his right. He pushed them over on to the brambles, making them sag in the middle. As the boxes fell, grass spilt in all directions, and Mal recognised them as the ones his father had taken from behind the garage the previous afternoon.

He wavered, gripped by guilt. He thought of his parents, last night and this morning, and he knew that part of the reason they were happy was because they believed he was settling down. It didn't matter what way you looked at it, he'd been lying when he talked about the bonfire at lunch. And he would have to go on lying to them for as long as he continued to come to the dump. They would hate Francy. He was dirty and stank; he smoked practically non-stop and he swore like a trooper. They'd be shocked enough at the knowledge that their son even knew someone like that, let alone that he was his best friend.

But he wasn't Francy's friend yet. There was no harm in going along to find out what his decision was. He didn't have to be friends with Francy just because Francy said it was okay – and then there was the chance he would say no, so it'd be no skin off anybody's nose anyway.

Mal tested the first box to make sure it would hold him, then, using the rest as stepping stones, he crossed the bramble patch and carried on towards the next rise, Francy's mound. He contemplated walking up and knocking on the tin, but he remembered the soaking he got the last time and decided to call from where he was.

'Francy,' he shouted. 'It's me, M –'

He left off, glimpsing the outline of Francy's short body through the branches; the detail, though, was obscured by a dark tracery of shadow, cast from the foliage by the sun. A butt glowed fiercely orange from the blackness of Francy's mouth as he drew in breath.

'Hello,' Mal said, his voice strangely weak.

Francy stepped into the light and placed his feet solidly apart. He was wearing the same clothes as last Thursday: muddied black baseball boots, with the white rubber toes peeling from them, blue jeans, shapeless with filth and wear, and a white T-shirt, run pink, from beneath the arms of which semicircular sweat stains, of varying degrees of dampness, spread out, like ink on blotting paper.

'What?' Francy asked.

Mal was aware he had been staring and raised his eyes to Francy's face. Even out of the shadow his features were dark, though now from frowning. The scowl clotted his freckles, and the reasoning conversations Mal had been having with himself as he approached crumbled.

'It's a week since I was here,' he said.

His mouth was dry and his tongue felt thick and useless.

'So it is,' said Francy tiredly. 'Ten out of ten. Take two giant steps and go to the top of the class.'

Mal's feet twitched. There was no string around Francy's waist and as far as he could see nothing was hanging down behind him. Surely he hadn't forgotten? Francy's jaw was set hard and he glowered from beneath darkened brows, narrowing his unblinking eyes until only the cold black of his pupils showed. Mal couldn't hold his stare and his head slumped forward, defeated. No, he couldn't have forgotten. Could he? Mal's eyes smarted with the salty sting of tears and he squeezed them together to prevent any escaping.

'Where were you this morning?' Francy asked savagely.

That was it, he should have been there earlier. But how was he supposed to know that?

'I didn't think I was meant to come till this afternoon.'

'What the fuck are you on about, bollock bake?' Francy shouted. 'Watch my lips this time: where – were – you – this - morning?'

But Mal didn't look up, because he didn't dare open his eyes.

'I was at home,' he said, suppressing a sob. Francy *had* for-gotten. 'I was at home waiting to come down and see you.'

There was a brief silence. A cigarette zinged past Mal's ear and a tear found its way out of the corner of his eye and trickled down his nose. He couldn't hold back much longer.

'Nah,' Francy said. 'I don't suppose you would have had anything to do with it.'

Mal was scarcely listening to him. The willow branches rustled and, sensing he was alone, he gave up the struggle and his whole body jerked absurdly as he began to cry. He stumbled back across the dump. How could Francy forget? It wouldn't have been so bad if his answer had been no, just so long as he'd remembered he was to give an answer in the first place. Mal couldn't believe that he had found this all so important. Francy hadn't meant a single word he said last week.

'Where are you going?' Francy's voice reached him from the mound.

'Leave me alone.'

Mal started to run and he heard Francy lumbering after him.

'Come back a minute.'

Mal was sprinting now, his vision blurred by tears.

'Fuck away off,' he shouted, then pain seared his ankle as he blundered into a pothole and fell flat on his face.

Francy's big hands were on him, trying to roll him over. Mal resisted, but Francy was too strong and he soon managed to turn him on to his back. Mal covered his face with his forearms. He hurt everywhere: his ankle was in agony where he'd wrenched it; his pride was pricked by the shame of being seen crying; his conscience racked by the torment of his first swear word; and more than ever his heart ached at Francy's rebuff.

'You all right?' Francy asked.

Mal refused to remove his arms from his face.

'You said you'd let me know today and you forgot.'

'No, I didn't,' said Francy. 'I'm sorry I was like that back there. I was pissed off about something, that's all.'

Brackish liquid was dripping from both Mal's nostrils, but the crying had stopped. He sniffed.

'Are you able to get up?' Francy asked.

Mal rubbed his nose with his bare wrist, making the light, fair hairs dark and sticky. He balanced on his right leg, setting his left foot down gingerly and shifting his weight on to it. The pain jabbed again and he grimaced, falling backwards. Francy caught him.

'Here,' he said, passing his arm about Mal's middle. 'Your ankle's likely staved. Let's get you to the den, I'm sure I've a bandage somewhere.'

They retraced their steps slowly, Mal hobbling, eyes screwed tight in pain, and Francy plodding alongside, supporting him.

'Sit here a minute,' Francy said, easing Mal down at the top of the rise and hurrying into the hut.

Mal clutched his ankle, bending his leg to his chest, and rocked backwards and forwards. It was some moments before he realised where he was sitting; Francy had given him his toilet. He squirmed on the red rayon cushion, trying to get comfortable in the depression left by Francy's bottom. He scanned the dump and the peculiar view of the estate – that wasn't so peculiar really, the more he saw it – and attempted a spit towards the row of bottles. The saliva was weak and only just missed his shirt front, landing white and foamy at the base of the toilet. Mal looked down at the bursting bubbles mournfully, and then his heart quickened as, immediately to the right, he saw the rat.

The rat's fur was ruffled and littered with tiny stones and bits of twig. It looked longer and thinner than Mal had remembered. He prodded it with the toe of his good foot.

'A couple of teeth got broken off.'

Mal twisted in his seat to find Francy standing behind him.

'Otherwise,' he went on, 'it's not too bad. D'you not think?'

'It's a bit flat,' Mal observed.

'The dragging around does that – stretches it.'

'But doesn't it ...' Mal trod warily; he didn't want to get on the wrong side of Francy again by upsetting him. 'Don't they, you know, come apart?'

'Sure, isn't that the whole idea of the charm?' Francy said with an air of finality. He sat on his haunches by the toilet, puffing on his cigarette, each puff in time with an intake of breath.

'What is?'

'Look,' said Francy, not impatiently. 'If the rat was torn to pieces it wouldn't exactly be a good omen. Right? But since it wasn't ...' He grinned. 'Well, what's two teeth between friends?'

While Mal held his left leg outstretched, Francy strapped his ankle with a strip of elasticated bandage that was stained purple and stank of dried meths.

'Right, then; try walking on that,' Francy said, pinning the bandage with a George Best badge.

Mal limped around the mound. The ankle still twinged but the pain was only slight now.

'What was it was bothering you earlier?' he asked when he came back to face Francy.

'Don't stop.' Francy sat on the toilet and fished in his box for a butt. The walking's the best thing for it.'

Mal started off again, forgetting his question in his haste to obey the command. Round and round he walked, slowly at first, wobbling off balance, then faster, as he felt his ankle become stronger beneath the strapping. Round and round, faster and faster; woods, fields, houses, road; woods, fields, houses, road. Round and round, faster and faster; round and round, faster ...

'Whoa! Whoa! For God's sake, whoa!' Francy yelled. 'You'll wear the fucking place out and I can't afford a new one.'

Mal sank to the ground. His head was spinning and a kaleidoscope of shapes throbbed at the back of his eyes. But he was laughing and he could hear Francy laugh too, his hoarse, smoky cackle tearing at his throat and lungs, until a fit of coughing wrenched him from his seat and threw him on to the grass.

They lay on their backs, trying to regulate their breathing. Mal rolled on to his side to speak, but his gaze fell on one of the rat's beady, black eyes; he spluttered and was away again, laughing. Francy turned to see what was up and met with the other eye, and he joined in once more, his body jumping like frying bacon as the cough cut in and out of his cackle.

'Oh, no, no,' Francy said at last. 'Stop this before I die.'

He pressed one hand on his chest and shielded his eyes with the other.

'Bastarding sun's too strong,' he said. 'I'm getting out of it.' Mal stopped sniggering.

'Aye, all right,' he said gloomily. He was hoping that Francy wouldn't go in yet a while. 'Can I meet you later?'

Francy gobbed straight in the air and opened his mouth, throwing his head back in an effort to catch the phlegm again. But it whipped back on the breeze and landed on his forehead.

'Shite.' He jumped up, mopping his brow with his T-shirt, then looked at Mal. 'I'm only going into the hut. You can come as well, if you like.'

He drew back the curtain of willow branches and bowed elaborately. Mal was still having difficulty focusing on the opening.

'Sure this isn't a trick?'

'Sure,' Francy said and the two of them entered the shadow.

They had to duck low behind the corrugated iron sheets; Mal was surprised how small and narrow it was inside – dark too. So dark, in fact, that he couldn't even see Francy ahead of him. He groped along the tin until he reached a hedge, blocking the opposite end. He discovered now the reason he couldn't see Francy was because Francy was simply no longer there. His body went momentarily rigid and panic welled within him. He turned about three times, completely disoriented, and began scrabbling away from the hedge, all the time wondering what had become of the light in front. He stumbled against something bulky and opened his mouth to scream; but nothing came out.

'Where the fuck were you?'

It was Francy.

'Me?' Mal asked, fighting hysteria and still fighting to get to where he supposed the exit must be. 'Where were *you*, more like. I've been all up and down this hut and you weren't here.'

'Calm yourself, will you. I thought you could see me better. This is only a passage, the hut's up this way.'

He took Mal's hand. Mal drew back, not because he didn't trust Francy, but because he knew it wasn't right boys holding each other's hands.

'Don't be a dick,' Francy said, clutching him more firmly and dragging him into a gap in the hedge the iron sheets rested against.

This led into a second passage, along which they had practically to crawl to avoid the mesh of branches above them. After a short time, however, they emerged into ... well, Mal couldn't be altogether certain at first what it was exactly they had emerged into.

It appeared to be a clearing, roughly square in shape, each side being some ten feet in length. Indeed, it was not much smaller than the living room at home, and the more he thought about it, the more Mal was forced to admit that the space was more like a room than a clearing in a thicket. He got to his feet, dusting himself down, amazed. Above his head, a couple of yards from the ground, a plastic sheet was spread – a ceiling through which he could make out the dark shapes of stalks and branches, but little daylight. The walls (because he had to call them walls) were made up of odd pieces of chipboard, planks, sides of crates and more corrugated iron. The back one even had a section which seemed to consist entirely of books.

'I found an old bookcase once,' Francy said, seeing the direction of his stare. 'I patched the back and stuck it in there against the hedge. The books didn't come with it, of course.'

'How did you ever manage to get it in?'

'How else? Took it apart and put it back together again,' Francy said. The only way there is to get anything in here. Or out. Bit by fucking bit.'

He was perched on a card table in the centre of the floor. An oil-fuelled roadworks lamp beside him supplied the room with a peculiar orange light which stopped at their knees. Below, all was murky.

'Have a seat,' Francy said and indicated three around the table.

Mal chose an armchair, upholstered in vinyl, but with a rayon-covered cushion, like the one on the toilet, in preference to a deckchair and a kitchen stool.

'Well?' Francy spread his arms wide. 'What d'you think?'

Mal hunched his shoulders.

'But whereabouts are we?' he asked.

'You know rightly where we are,' said Francy. 'At the end of the dump, behind a hedge, among the trees.'

He turned his head to the side and spat. There was a sharp plink sound. Mal squinted into the murk at the foot of the right-hand wall. His eyes roved over obscure lumps that gradually took on the form of bundles of newspapers, tied with string, more books, stacked in piles, and a row of files, like the ledgers his father had brooded over for hours every night in the last house. Finally, they came to rest on a squat object which refused to assume a more clearly definable identity. Mal left the armchair and edged forward, curious. The object was fat-bellied and sat on a square base. As he drew closer, he noticed that the surface was of a marbled effect, grey-white, and that there was – lettering? – yes, gold lettering on the side. He stopped before it and spelt the letters in his head. P-A-R-K-E-R. R-I-P.

He peered at the top; curved wire mesh dripped spit into a shallow pool at the bottom.

'D'you know what this is?' he asked Francy, unable to disguise his shock.

'A spittoon.'

'It's a flower urn off a grave, is what it is.'

Francy laughed sarcastically.

'Here it's a *spit*urn. Lesson number … whatever: their rules' – he jerked a thumb vaguely over his shoulder – 'stop at the fence.

When they dumped that, it ceased to mean anything but what I wanted it to mean.'

He rose from the table and walked to the far corner by the wall of books. Mal wished now that he hadn't appeared so scandalised; he didn't suppose spitting into the urn was any worse than throwing it on a dump. And Francy's voice had such a hard cutting edge to it.

'I thought you might have understood that by now,' he went on, facing Mal. 'But maybe I've been over-estimating you.'

'I'm sorry, I do see. Really I do,' Mal said. 'I was just a bit surprised.'

Francy pointed a menacing finger.

'I hope for your sake you're not lying. Make sure you know before we go any further. And make sure you believe; if you have any doubts whatsoever, you can get out right now. This is no game; my secrets are dangerous.'

'I've said I'm sorry,' Mal pleaded. 'What more do you want me to do?'

The words seemed to echo about the hut, but in reality they reverberated only within Mal's temples. There was complete silence as Francy sized him up.

'Shift the lantern to the edge of the table,' he commanded.

As Mal moved toward the card table something scurried from behind the spiturn, making for the passage. But Francy took no notice and Mal quelled a shudder. He placed the oil lamp so that its orange light fell in an arc on the book wall and the corner where Francy was crouching before a tall, narrow structure, draped in a patterned bedspread.

He straightened and beckoned Mal.

'Kneel there,' he said, stepping aside.

Mal faced the bedspread and his shadow darkened it. He was undecided, but he felt Francy's hand on his shoulder and he was forced to his knees.

'Now, bow your head,' Francy ordered. 'And don't look up again until I tell you.'

Mal complied without objection, nestling his chin on his chest. At first he closed his eyes, convinced, for the moment, that he was meant to be praying. Then he opened them and looked out as best he could through his fringe. The bedspread drew away from the ground, revealing a solid base of large, grey stones. Out of sight, Francy was shambling along the wall, lifting books from the shelves and replacing them. Mal peered up past the bridge of his nose at the stones; so cold looking, so grey and old.

Suddenly he recalled where he had seen such stones before.

'The chapel,' he said, about to turn to Francy. 'You got those up at the old chapel, didn't you?'

'Keep your fucking head down,' Francy snapped. 'And did you hear me saying you could talk?'

Mal shook his bowed head.

'Well, then,' Francy's voice tailed off, and when he spoke again was much less strident. 'You're right,' he said. 'They've just been lying up there for years, no use to no one. So, I thought, what the fuck, I'll have some of that.'

He paused again. The back of Mal's neck was beginning to ache and he wished Francy would get on with whatever it was he was going to do. But Francy was still interested in the chapel.

'So you know the ruins, do you?'

'Yeah,' said Mal. 'I was up there the other day with a couple of the lads from my street to see if the ...'

He hesitated, remembering what Mucker had said about not letting on to anyone where the centre pole was hidden.

'To see if ...'

He looked behind him, powerless to invent. Francy was watching him, the bedspread around his shoulders like a cape.

'What did I tell you about lifting your head?' he asked, and he smiled and frowned both at the same time.

He resumed picking through the books and Mal hoped the subject of the chapel had been dropped, relieved that he had got away without letting anything slip.

Finally, Francy's black baseball boots – tight at the toes –

moved within range of his downcast eyes. Mal was instructed to raise his head and, as he did so, he saw Francy strike a match and light two candles, one in an ornate brass candlestick, the other in a cracked Union Jack egg cup. He shuffled away from the shrine, and Mal found himself staring into a shaving mirror, set in an embossed gilt frame, his reflection distorted by the glass and by the molten air above the flames.

'Now, repeat after me,' Francy said, opening a thick book, without spine or boards. 'I, Mal – '

Mal glanced at him quickly. How did he know his Christian name? Francy merely nodded, smiling beatifically.

'I, Mal – ,' he coaxed again; and when Mal responded added: ' – achy.'

Mal flinched, but Francy's recitation went on relentlessly and he had to devote all his powers of concentration to keeping up his mumbled repetition.

'Malarkey, Malakos, Malcontent … Malentendu, Malevolent, Malfeasance, Malformation, Malfunction … Malice, Malign, Malignant … Malingering, Malison, Malleable, Mallemaroking Martin – hereinafter, Mal du Siècle, Malkin the Ill, The Great Malacophilous …'

Mal stumbled through the words, bewildered. Francy set the thick book on the floor and began reading from a second, smaller one in a buff dust jacket.

'In the presence of' – Francy surveyed the hut – 'in the presence of Fuckallatall, do solemnly swear allegiance to the dump, now verbally established; and that I will do my utmost, at every risk, while life lasts, to defend its dilapidation and perversity; and finally, that I will yield implicit obedience in all things not contrary to the laws of morality …'

'… to defend its dilapidation and perversity,' Mal recited. 'And, finally, that I will yield implicit obedience in all things not contrary to the laws of morality …'

He waited for Francy to continue, but for a long time he said nothing more; his brow was wrinkled in thought.

'Nah,' he said, tearing a page from the smaller book. He screwed it up and threw book and page across the room. 'Scrap all that yielding obedience stuff.'

He dropped the bedspread to the ground and, taking hold of Mal by the fleshy part of the upper arms, helped him to his feet. Mal thought then and ever afterwards that he had never seen kinder eyes than Francy's at that moment.

'Do you agree to be my friend?' he asked. 'And do you swear, no matter what, to stick by me and the dump?'

'I do,' Mal replied.

Francy pulled him towards him and kissed him on both cheeks; his breath smelt of old nappies.

'It is done,' he said.

Hot, transparent wax dripped from the fissure in the egg cup and trickled down the front, cooling and congealing in primitive formation around its base.

6

With the weather being so fine, Mrs Martin decided they would have ice cream instead of whipped cream on their dessert that evening. She gave Mal four shillings and asked him to run to the shops to buy some. Mal had taken Francy's bandage off before going into the house and his ankle was giving him no trouble. He did run, literally: out of Everest Street, along Larkview Avenue, past the supermarket, the chemist, the fruit shop, and round the corner to the newsagent's. He bought a family block of raspberry ripple and began running home again: round the corner, past the fruit shop, the chemist, the supermarket ... and straight into Andy Hardy, who was running in the opposite direction.

He shoved Mal roughly, making him drop his brick of ice cream. The white paper bag in which the shop assistant had wrapped it was ripped and one corner of the carton had buckled. But the ice cream itself was, thank goodness, undamaged.

'Sorry, Andy,' Mal apologised. 'I didn't see you.'

'You weren't watching where you were fucking going. You've broke my fag.'

He showed him his cigarette. The glowing tip hung by threads of tobacco, but smoked on independently, and there was a second break just above the filter. Andy attempted to keep the whole lot together, using three fingers, and puffed on it a few times. Then he tore the filter off completely; but the end of the stump was so ragged that he stopped after one draw, spitting out flakes of tobacco and paper, and rubbing his tongue with his fingertips.

'I can't bloody smoke that.'

Francy could have, Mal thought.

'I really didn't mean it,' he said, although he wasn't entirely sure that the collision had been his fault alone.

'Fuck all use that is to me,' Andy said. 'That was my last one too.'

He toyed with his cigarette sulkily. Mal was back-pedalling towards the road, but Andy stopped him.

'Not so fast. D'you think you're getting away that easy?' he said. 'Show us your odds.'

'Aw, come on, Andy,' Mal said. 'I've to get home. I haven't any odds, I'm skint. I'll buy you your fag tomorrow.'

But Andy wouldn't let him go.

'I suppose there was no change from that?' He pointed to the block of ice cream.

The ice cream only cost three and six and Mal was holding the other sixpence in his hand. But the price was on the packet and his mother would know if he took it off. He didn't even have any money in the house to replace the change with. Since his pocket money was stopped, he had to ask when he wanted money and say what it was for.

'It's my mum's.'

He tightened his fist round the sixpenny bit and Andy made a grab for his wrist.

'Tough,' he said, squeezing Mal's fingernails until he cried out and dropped the money. Andy killed it with his foot. 'Dead on. Now, go and get me a single and a couple of bubblies.'

'Look, Andy,' Mal begged. 'Why do you not just take the money and let me go home?'

'Principle, short arse, that's why. A Protestant virtue – time you learnt the meaning of the word.'

He twisted Mal's arm behind his back, frogmarched him to the door of the newsagent's, and flung him inside.

'Here,' he said when Mal came out. 'Have a bubbly.'

Mal thanked him – more grateful that he could now leave than he was for the gum.

'What time've we to be at the bonfire tomorrow?'

'Early as you can. Me and Mucker and a few others are camping out there tonight. And talking of that, what happened to you today?'

'Oh, I'd to go into town with my mum and dad. Did I miss much?'

'I'll say. Remember last week that bastard Hagan pulled a hatchet on Big Bobby Parker's bin squad?'

Mal started at the mention of Francy's name, but straight away checked himself and frowned, nodding sternly.

'As you know, I was all for going after him there and then. But, no, the rest said, he might still be having a fit over his frigging rat and hack out at anybody. Fucked if I'd have been bothered, like. Anyway, we got him back for it today.'

He lit the cigarette. Mal turned his package around and around in his hands. They must have done it after he left the dump, for Francy had been all right when he last saw him.

'Why, what did youse do?' he asked.

'D'you know his house?'

Mal was thrown on the defensive.

'No,' he said. 'How could I? I've only ever seen him the once in my life.'

'Aye, well, this morning, when we were down the back of the estate collecting wood, we met the bin lorry at Brookeborough Close and we're talking away to the whole crew, and I says did they realise this was the street the Hagans lived in, and Mucker says, right enough, so it is …'

'Brookeborough Close?' Mal asked. He knew the street: it was in front of the park at the end of the circuitous route he'd been taking to the woods. 'But I thought he was meant to live on the …'

'Dump?' said Andy with a sneer. 'Balls. That's just a fairy tale. I know, I've been down there and looked. All's there is a poxy bit of tin shoved against a hedge. He no more lives there than I do. Anyhow, Bobby says: "I've been wanting to teach that wee git a lesson." So here, they decide that when they're carrying the bin, they'll accidently-on-purpose spill it over the path. And fuck me, when they do, your man's ma comes running out the house, squawking: "You'll pick every last bit of that up," and there's all sorts of crap on the ground. And Bobby says: "It's not our fault, missus; there's a hole in your bin. We're not even supposed to lift them when they're in this state." And she says, "There's never a hole," and Bobby sticks his boot through it and says, "See, there is too."

'I swear, I thought I was going to bust myself laughing. Your woman's ripping it, yelling she's going to get the police, she's reporting them. "Wise up, love," Bobby tells her. "You know you wouldn't, for the first person they'd fucking lift would be that mad bastard son of yours." Then they got back on to the truck and drove off, and the grey-haired old hag was crying like a wee doll.'

Mal could hardly believe what he was hearing. He had never thought of asking Francy if he lived anywhere other than the dump. He tried to imagine the house, but could see in his mind's eye only a more outlandish version of Mitch Campbell's, a topsy-turvy eyesore. And as for a mother and father; well, his imagination failed him utterly. And then there was the business with the bin. He realised now what had been pissing Francy off earlier.

'Hey,' Andy said. 'You've come all over your hand.'

The ice cream was melting and oozed out of its carton, soaking the grubby bag and coursing over Mal's fingers, spattering on the tarmac.

'Flipping heck,' he said and he was away like the billy-o.

'Thanks for the fag,' Andy called after him, laughing.

'There you are,' his mother said. 'We were just about to organise a search party. I tell you, I'd hate to send you for sorrow.'

She was opening a tin of pear halves and doling them out in their thick syrup into glass bowls.

'What did you get us, son?' his father asked from the dinette. 'Vanilla or raspberry ripple?'

Mal didn't say anything. He lingered by the door, hands at his back.

'Where's the ice cream, then?' his mother asked when she was finished dishing up the pears.

Mal could feel his ears burn.

'Mal? What's the matter?'

He drew the package from behind him: a gooey mass of cardboard, paper and red-streaked white liquid.

'I'm sorry,' he said. 'I fell over.'

'Ach, Mal,' Mrs Martin groaned.

'What is it?' Mr Martin came into the kitchen.

'Nothing, nothing,' Mrs Martin said quickly, snatching a damp cloth from the sink and wiping her son's hands. 'He fell, that's all. We can save some of the ice cream.'

'Fell?' Mr Martin said, irritated. 'I'll bet he was running. Were you? Were you running?'

'He probably just wanted to get home with it before it melted. You can't blame the wee fella, I told him to be quick.'

'We can't eat this.' Mr Martin prodded the soggy bag on the draining board. 'There's stones in it and everything.'

'That's all right.' His wife dropped the ice cream in the pedal bin. 'There's whipping cream in the fridge will do just as well.'

Mal felt ashamed eating his dessert. His mother chatted away like nothing had happened, but his father didn't speak, except to say pears weren't the same without ice cream.

He was clearing the table when his mother asked him where her change was. Mal blushed furiously once more.

'Well?' she said. 'There should be sixpence. Am I right?'

'I ... ah ... I lost it when I fell.'

It wasn't too much of a lie.

Mr Martin tutted, smiling wryly. But his wife wasn't so amused.

'Lost it? Spent it, more like. Do you think your daddy and I have money to throw around? If I'd been going to let you keep the change I'd've said so.'

'For dear sake,' Mr Martin said. 'It's a sixpence we're talking about. Surely to goodness things haven't come to the point where we're arguing over half a bob.'

'Oh no,' Mrs Martin said. 'I don't expect you would understand, the way you go gallivanting to the blasted Blues' Club. But you're not the one has to pay the groceries every week, more's the pity. Maybe if you'd had any idea at all of money, we'd never be in this mess.'

'What's that supposed to mean?'

'You're asking me? You who thought he could run a shop giving credit to every sad sack that spun you a yarn? Is it a bit of wonder our Malachy ...'

'Mal,' Mr Martin said through gritted teeth. 'It's just Mal. How many times do you have to be told?'

'*Malachy!*' Mrs Martin's voice rose. 'I gave my son a name and neither you nor anyone else on the face of this earth will stop me using it when I want to.'

'Read the birth certificate,' her husband said. 'You'll find no Malachy there.'

'Because you cheated me,' she shouted. 'Cheated me when I was too sick from having him to fight you.'

'Look!' Mr Martin thumped the table. 'We compromised, remember? Mal we would christen him and Mal we would always call him. Right?'

Mal shrank lower and lower in his chair. Every day, it seemed, since they'd come to the estate, the same argument.

'Ignoramus!' Mrs Martin burst out. Her laughter was feverish. 'Terrified people will think he's Catholic when if you'd an ounce of education you'd know the name's Hebrew.'

'I don't care if it's flaming Zulu, it *sounds* Catholic.'

Mal jumped from his chair, on the verge of tears.

'Stop it,' he yelled. 'Why can't youse stop it? I'm sorry I dropped the ice cream, I'm sorry I didn't bring home the change, just don't fight anymore.'

Both his parents stared at him. Then slowly, deliberately, his father crossed the room and slapped him, jerking his head back against the dinette wall.

'Bed. Now,' he told him, then pointed at his wife. 'And don't you open your mouth if you don't want the same.'

The front door slammed as Mal lay in the premature darkness of his bedroom. He craned his neck over the side of the bed, trying to work out from the noises downstairs which of his parents was still in. For a long while he could hear nothing distinct, but gradually he became aware of movement in the kitchen: cupboards opening and closing. And then it started. Low and rumbling at first, growing louder and louder: clatter, clatter, clatter. The brass bowl was spinning, drumming on the dinette table.

7

They gathered after breakfast at the entrance to the woods; most had no intention of going home until the early hours the following day. They came by the street or by the gang. Andy Hardy, who had gone for something to eat after camping out the previous night on guard, led the Hook across the playing fields and when they saw the boys already assembled they broke into a spontaneous goosestep, laying two fingers on their top lips, signifying moustaches.

'Nazi bastards,' Mucker shouted and dived to the ground, his hands closed in loose fists, one before the other, as though they held a machine gun. 'Eh-eh-eh-eh-eh-eh-eh.'

Les and Mal joined in his staccato stuttering, pitching forward on to their stomachs. Most of the Hook died instantly and elaborately, but Andy and Peter began to run, crouching low, shooting back. Andy fired from the hip, making a swooshing sound that rose and fell with his hands as he advanced. At the long reedy grass where the ground sloped up to the woods, he yelled and charged, swooshing covering fire for his brother. He rushed first at Mucker, then (seeing him jump up), at the last minute flung himself on to Les, giving him no time to get to his feet. Peter was left facing Mucker.

'Dow-dow-de-dow,' he said hopefully, though he ought to have known that when it came to hand-to-hand combat, onomatopoeia alone was ineffective. Mucker knew.

'Biff, you cunt,' he said and punched Peter square in the face.

'Fuck sake, Mucker, take it easy.' Andy scrambled up off Les. 'There's no need for that.'

'You know what they say,' Mucker told him, dusting his hands. 'All's fair ...'

'Anyway,' Les scowled. 'Youse'd both have been done for ages ago. Those were tommy guns we had, weren't they, Mucker?'

'Dead right.'

Andy screwed up his face into a sneer and pinched Les's cheek.

'Well, a tommy gun's no fucking use against a flame-thrower. Is it, bumface? Make a mess of your Mongol skin that would.'

Les pushed his hand out of the way. Andy made as if to slap him, but in the end only ruffled his hair and went over to his younger brother who was still lying on the ground, snuffling. He pulled him up by the belt of his trousers.

'Grow up and quit your girning, or else away home,' he said.

Andy joined Mucker in conference and Peter stood alone.

'You hurt?' Mal asked him.

'Yesh.'

His lip was cut and swollen and when he spoke it ballooned forward, spraying blood down his chin. Peter didn't exactly invite sympathy; he made no bones of the fact that he didn't rate any of the other boys on the estate and never missed an opportunity to let you know he had nothing whatsoever in common with them. Even so, Mal felt for him now. Since yesterday, he was secure in the knowledge that he himself had, in Francy, at least one real friend he could turn to and he didn't like to see anyone else excluded, whether *they* claimed to like it or not.

'Don't mind Mucker, he's not really that bad,' Mal said. 'Half the time he doesn't mean it seriously.'

'Yesh he doesh,' Peter lisped, touching his lip. 'Yesh he doesh.'

Since they'd likely be carrying on through lunch and dinner

many people had brought sandwiches and lemonade to keep them going. Mucker told all those with food to give it in to Sonia Kerr, who had a large cardboard box which was to be placed in the ditch before the trees, covered with grass and branches, to keep the food from going rancid.

'Haven't you anything?' Peter asked Mal.

'Nah.'

'Nor me. Going to the chippy?'

'No money.'

Mal started to walk away.

'What'sh the matter? Mummy not love you anymore?'

Mal now thought that Mucker hadn't hit Peter half hard enough. What business was it of his what Mal ate or didn't eat? Anyway, he *would* have asked his mother for sandwiches that morning, he just didn't want to bother her, that was all.

She was sitting at the table when he came downstairs, her head resting on her hands. The brasses were spread out around her, but they were only half finished. The Duraglit tin lay empty on its side and the once-moist pads of polish were heaped in a pile, blackened and dry. Mal told her he was going out, and she said, 'Fine.' He said he'd probably not be home for lunch, and again she said, 'Fine.' And maybe, he ventured, not even tea either.

'Fine, fine, *fine!*' She shooed his words away with her long, bony fingers, ridged and stained from polishing.

Mal looked to see was there any bread he could make a sandwich out of, but there was nothing in the breadbin save an empty waxed wrapper. He knew it wasn't like his mother not to be worried about him not getting anything to eat, but guessed she was still annoyed with him over the change from the ice cream, and that was why she didn't offer him money. He looked at her sitting there, elbows raw and nobbly, reflected on the smooth, polished surface of the table.

'Bye,' he said.

'Bye.'

Outside, the garage door was wide open, but the car wasn't

there. Nor was it parked in the driveway. Mal's heart beat fast and he glanced over his shoulder at the house. But it was all right: his father must have come home, for the curtains were drawn, and his mother would never have left them closed this late if he wasn't still in bed. He was no longer worried, but he was puzzled, as he turned out of Everest Street and started down the hill, head bowed, fists dug deep in his pockets ...

'*A*.'

A hand patted Mal's head, making him jump. He blinked rapidly, trying to separate this jolt from the shock of bumping into his father's car, parked half on, half off the pavement on the hill. He saw Andy pass on to Peter.

'*B*,' Andy said scornfully. 'For "baby brother bastard".'

The uncertainties of the morning receded for the time being as Mal caught up with what was going on around him.

'Okay, listen,' Andy said. 'Youse should each have a letter. Now don't worry about what one you've got, they're given out at random just to make things a bit easier and speed them up.'

'God Almighty,' Mucker interrupted. 'Would you speed it up, then. Look, it's simple. *A*s, come with us for the pole. *B*s, youse are on tyres; *C*s, stay here and start gathering the wood into piles – furniture in one pile, logs in another, and so on. Right?'

Everyone nodded. Right. The *A*s walked into the woods, with Mal at the tail end. At the pylon where the paths diverged, Les dropped out to tie his shoelace. All morning he had been behaving oddly towards Mal, staring at him until he spoke or smiled, and then turning away, cutting him dead. Seeing him now, he ran to the front of the line, pointing back along the path.

'Why's he with us?' he asked.

'It was either him or my kid brother,' Andy said. 'And there was no way I was having *him* along with me.'

'Couldn't you have got Sonia or one of the other girls?' Mucker wanted to know.

'Heh-eh-eh-eh-eh-eh-eh.' Les's put-on laugh sounded like a machine gun.

Mal trudged behind them, almost wishing he'd never come. He thought of the afternoon before when he was leaving the dump and Francy said he supposed he'd be at the bonfire all the next day and Mal said yes, he supposed he would. He felt bad at once, and after a second told Francy he would come down to the dump instead and play with him if he wanted.

'Don't bother your head,' Francy said. 'I've too much to do. Just you have a good time with your mates.'

He felt the sting of Francy's sarcasm even more now than he had then. And yet, at the same time, he had to admit that he wouldn't have missed this for the world. There was something about helping at the bonfire that made him ready to put up with almost anything; a satisfaction at being a part of a team – no matter how insignificant that part was – all pitching in together, knowing that the end they'd been working towards was now in sight. Francy couldn't begin to understand that, and it was clear, too, that Mal couldn't make him understand by bringing him along. Not because he was a Catholic, but simply because he seemed to have absolutely no interest in joining in with what other people were doing. But then again, maybe you couldn't expect him to, since just about every one of those other people hated his guts.

They had reached the clearing in front of the chapel. But whereas the last time Mal was there, Mucker had ordered him and Les to keep silent, now he was actually orchestrating the boys' singing and shouting. There were more of them this time, of course, but that wasn't the whole reason. It was bonfire day and they were picking up their centre pole from its hiding place. The need for secrecy was past, and they didn't care who knew they were there now.

An elderly woman in an apron, the priest's housekeeper, appeared at an upstairs window of the cottage, peering round the curtain. The lads spotted her and waved; some of them made faces or pulled up their shirts and stuck their bellies out.

'See enough, missus?' they shouted.

Andy held up one hand, making a circle with his thumb and

forefinger, and darted the index finger of his other hand in and out of it.

'Are you getting plenty? Is he giving you it?' he yelled and the woman let go the curtain, stepping back from the window.

They continued up the side of the chapel, whooping and leaping around, scuffling with each other, singing:

We are – We are – We are the Billy Boys,
We are – We are – We are the Billy Boys.
We're up to our necks in *Fenian* blood, surrender or you'll die,
For we are the Billy, Billy Boys.

They trampled through the dense, dark undergrowth at the back of the chapel until they came to the old ruins.

'Let's get organised,' Mucker told them, and they all fell silent. 'Now, we want the big fellas over the wall to lift the pole out and then we'll hoist it through the window and feed it down to the rest of youse.'

The boys gave him the okay. All except Mal. He was preoccupied by the large grey stones scattered on the ground. So cold, so grey and old.

'Wait a second,' Andy said. 'Sure, aren't we going to need some of the big ones over here to take the pole as it's fed through? You can't expect the wee lads to manage it on their own.'

Everyone looked to Mucker, including Mal this time: it wasn't every day you heard him contradicted. He dropped his head and gripped his right bicep with his left hand. A long, silvery string of spit descended from his mouth and swung as he made small circles with his head. The string grew longer and the middle became thinner and thinner, until eventually the weight at the bottom caused it to break entirely and Mucker sucked the remains into his mouth with a loud smack of his lips.

'The man's right,' he said with a crooked smile.

Everyone else agreed with Andy now, although they'd known all along he was talking sense. It was decided that Mucker and Les would lead a squad of eight down the other side of the ruin and

Andy would take charge of the rest. Mal was in Andy's group and he lined up in the middle of the rank that formed in readiness for the pole, thinking that, there, he wouldn't have to take so much of the weight.

Mucker and Les hauled themselves into the headless window frame and dropped down behind the wall. Eddie was in the gap when a scream from Mucker shattered the silence of the earnest preparations: '*Bastards! Bastards! Bastards!*'

Eddie nearly toppled over, his mouth gaping.

'What's the matter?' Andy asked him.

'*Bastards! Bastards! Bastards!*'

Andy couldn't wait any longer and trailed Eddie backwards from the window, climbing up in his place.

'Holy fuck,' he whispered.

The other boys, taking this cue, surged forward, fighting for position on the walls, or shoving in around Andy. Mal squeezed to the front, so that he stood looking through Andy's legs. The first thing he saw was Mucker, with his head thrown back and his eyes closed; his face was a deep red, almost purple in places, and the veins in his neck protruded like thin blue canes supporting his keening jaw.

'*Bastards! Bastards! Bastards!*'

Mal leaned further over the edge and saw Les thrashing the undergrowth with a branch, and finally his eyes focused on what everyone else's had already seen. Directly below the back wall of the ruin, a black scorch mark extended twenty to thirty feet into the scrub. The grass on either side was singed and bent black. It looked like a flame-thrower had been taken to it. A raised line ran, straight as a backbone, the length of the scorch mark. In places it was no more than a stretch of grey-white ashes, in others a charred black shell of brittle wood still smouldered. The centre pole had been burnt.

Mal's heart sank. He threaded his way through the crush and sat down on a stone. So cold, so grey and old. He saw himself kneeling, his bewildered face contorted in the haze of guttering candles, and at once he knew; and the knowledge made him sick to his stomach.

Mucker was eventually prevailed upon to come back through the ruined window, but even then they had difficulty talking him out of going out the far side of the woods to Derrybeg and giving the first Catholic he saw a hiding. Nobody else could have done it, he was convinced; it had to be those Micks hanging around after Mass. He quietened down, but as they passed by the chapel the housekeeper ventured a look out the window once more and Mucker suddenly broke away, hurtling towards the house.

'Fenian whore, I'll kill you for this.'

He shovelled stones from the shingle roadway and hurled them wildly at the cottage and the front of the chapel. A small pane of glass in the porch of the cottage broke with a hollow pock and immediately the door opened and the priest himself came out in his vest.

Father Riordan was a familiar enough figure in Larkview, visiting parishioners, and sometimes he would stand, always smiling, on the sidelines of the football pitches, watching the boys play football. It was said he played football himself in his day – for Finn Harps in the League of Ireland. But no, other people said, it wasn't soccer he played, but Gaelic, for Roscommon in the All Ireland Final. Whatever, there was no doubting that he ran a boxing team at the local Catholic boys' school and, although he was short and balding, you could see he was no mug. You could see too that he wasn't smiling now.

Andy and Les dashed forward and grabbed Mucker by the arms, whispering low and urgent in his ears. He fought to free himself, his feet flailing in the direction of the father.

'Let go, you bastards,' he ranted. 'Priest or no priest, I'll ...'

Father Riordan stopped before him and with practised ease undid the buckle of his belt and slid it from his trouser loops so that it dangled like a scourge in his hand. A piece of soft-boiled egg wobbled on his lower lip with each heavy breath from his nostrils.

'He didn't mean it, Father,' Les said.

'I did, I fucking did,' Mucker yelled, lashing out again with his feet. 'Take your hands off me and I'll show youse how much I did.'

Father Riordan eyed him carefully, as though the question in his mind wasn't so much *if* he should hit him as *where* he should. He wound the belt tightly around his hand.

'He's ... He's ... He's epileptic,' Andy stalled. 'He takes these fits now and then, doesn't know what he's doing.'

The priest smirked and moistened his lips with a coated tongue, dislodging the translucent egg white.

'I suppose you've no idea what they used to do to epileptics in the old days?' he asked. His accent was refined, like that of a newsreader, and only occasionally did it betray traces of his native brogue. 'Still do in some heathen parts of the world. Well, I'll tell you, it's a lot worse than taking a belt to them.'

'Look,' Andy said. 'We'll have a whip round; we'll pay you back for the window – today; as soon as we can.'

Father Riordan brushed the palm of his hand with the rolled-up belt. He stared hard, first at Andy, then at Mucker. A glazed look had come over Mucker so that you might well have thought that not only was he an epileptic, but that epilepsy was indeed a form of possession, as Father Riordan seemed to be hinting. The priest lowered his eyes and smiled a quick, nervous smile.

'See that you do that,' he said and turned back towards the cottage.

'We'll do no such thing,' Mucker shouted as the cottage door was shut. 'Anybody gives money and I'll want to know the reason why.'

But behind him the boys were already making dejectedly for the entrance. They had to step aside to avoid the Housing Trust sign which had been completely uprooted and dumped on the path. Two workmen were hammering a new notice in its place. 'Commencing 26 July 1969', the bottom line read. But no one was in much of a mood to pay it any mind.

'*Bastards! Bastards! Bastards!*'

Back at the bonfire, they tried glumly to decide what to do next. From time to time, the name of someone who might have torched the centre pole would be suggested. Francy's wasn't one of them, but Mal was worried none the less. He was raging with Francy, yet he knew, too, that it had been his slip that had tipped him off. There was no way he could tell on Francy without giving everything away. And, then, there was the oath he had taken the day before; God alone knew what might happen if he broke that. He could understand Francy being angry at what the binmen had done to his house, but he couldn't see how this was getting even with them.

His T-shirt felt tight and uncomfortable; he tugged at the sides to move it from his underarms, which had become hot, and his fingers touched a sticky dampness. He inclined his head, sniffing, and an acrid smell like rotting grass and sodden cardboard made him flinch. He glanced round, suddenly self-conscious. Peter Hardy was watching him fixedly. Mal averted his eyes, taking an exaggerated interest in the proceedings.

Mucker was stalking the circle of boys and girls, as if looking for someone to hit. But there was no one to hit: only the oldest and biggest lads had camped out the previous night, and that included Mucker himself; they were all adamant they'd seen no one approach the woods. That was the one problem in Mal's mind: for all that he was in no doubt that Francy was the culprit, he could not work out how he had got into the woods unnoticed. Mucker was sticking to his original theory of Rebels from Derrybeg being responsible, but he was in a minority of one. Finally, Andy rose and spoke above the rest.

'It's already after ten, and every minute we sit moaning and complaining is a minute lost,' he said. 'Maybe we were putting too much hope in the centre pole, maybe we should have made plans in case something like this happened. But we did and we didn't, and that's that. But there's still going to be a bonfire here tonight. Now until we know for sure who did this, I see no point in going looking to get even. So, I say, find something else to stick up the middle and make the best of what we've got.'

He faced Mucker, who was sitting with Sonia on a pile of tyres, chewing a stem of grass.

'What d'you think, Mucker? Carry on as planned?'

'Suit yourselves,' he replied, without removing the grass.

All eyes watched him a moment and he looked up, irritated.

'I said yes, didn't I?'

'Right,' Andy said quickly; 'let's get cracking.'

They started at once and worked on through the morning and into the afternoon, those with sandwiches not even sitting down to have them, but eating as they laboured. Andy went back into the woods, taking Les and three other helpers, armed with hatchets. Before he left, while Mucker and Sonia were fooling about elsewhere, he did the rounds of all the boys, asking them to put their hands in their pockets and give what they could towards the cottage window. Mal had nothing in his pockets but Kleenex and feared the worst when it came his turn. But Andy shrugged it off magnanimously.

'Remember that fag last night?' he said, showing Mal sixpence of his own and adding it to the pool. 'Well, this is us quits.'

In the end, they managed to collect just under two pounds. They had no idea if that was too much or too little, but, as Andy pointed out, the important thing was to get the money to the priest before he thought of calling the cops.

Andy and Les brought back with them a young tree, which they immediately set about stripping of branches. It was nothing like as big as the pole Mucker's dad had got them from the timberyard, but it was something. The tree was replanted in the centre of a wide circle of dry earth, the site of every bonfire since the estate was built.

'It'll never fucking work,' Mucker mumbled, to no one in particular, it seemed.

Tyres were hoopla-ed over the tree and more were packed around its base to keep it sturdy. Next to these were placed the heaviest articles: the chairs, the mattresses, planks and pallets, the sideboards and thick, short logs. Lastly came the thinner branches, which sloped from the ground and converged in a point at the top, so that the bonfire looked like a tepee. The gaps between the branches were stuffed with all available odds and ends: newspapers, rags, collapsed cardboard boxes and broken lemonade crates. When it was eventually finished in the late afternoon, the bonfire stood no more than twelve feet high, less than half the height originally intended. It certainly wouldn't be the tallest bonfire in Belfast that year; but there was no denying it was fat, and, they all agreed, it would burn like a bastard.

Mal had already skipped breakfast and lunch and the sight of the sandwich box being fetched again from the ditch persuaded him he really ought to go home for dinner after all. He had only got as far as the playing fields, however, when Peter Hardy called on him to wait.

'Heading up the road?' he said. 'I'm coming too.'

Mal smiled, but he was angry inside. For Peter's arrival forced him to own up to what, in reality, he had known from the outset, that hunger was the least of his reasons for going home. The uneasiness of that morning had returned to niggle him: the memory of his mother at the table – elbows raw and nobbly, reflected on the polished surface – and of his father's car, parked on the hill, more on the kerb than off. How was he going to explain it away to Peter if the car was still there?

They walked for a while in silence before Peter said, almost casually: 'You knew about the centre pole, didn't you?'

Mal stopped short and faced him, his jaw working, but no words coming out.

'Oh, don't worry,' Peter said. He no longer lisped when he spoke, but there was still a hard, swollen lump where his lip had been split. 'There's no danger me telling anyone. Can't see why they're so het up about a mingy bonfire anyway. My brother's the worst, really – he ought to have more sense.'

'How did you know?' Mal said with difficulty.

'I'm not stupid. I *passed* my eleven-plus, don't forget, not like most of those dunces back there. I've seen how you've been acting. And I saw how *he* was looking at you.'

'Who?'

'Don't come that. You know rightly who. The big soft lad, Les; all dopy and guilty, heartscared of you squealing on him. I knew he did it straight off.'

Mal didn't say anything. For a minute he thought Peter might even be right, that Les *did* burn the centre pole.

'I don't blame him at all, the way they treat him,' Peter continued. 'Mucker and our Andy especially. The names they call him and the things they say about him whenever there are girls around. Anyway, it's obvious it was someone who was there yesterday evening, nobody saw anyone else near the woods the whole night. I bet they just raked him once too often and he sneaked away while they were playing cards or snogging with their girlfriends and *whumph*! – Bye-bye centre pole.'

Mal began to realise that for all that Peter was clever and had passed his eleven-plus, he didn't know everything; and he certainly knew nothing whatsoever about Les. No matter how far Les was pushed, he would never do a thing like that. If he was watching Mal strangely, it was probably because he felt bad for having taken the hand out of him earlier. But Peter wasn't finished yet.

'Then I thought to myself, someone like Les would never be able to keep it a secret – first important thing he's done in his life off his own bat. The question was: who was there for him to tell? And the answer, of course, was that it had to be you. Like a couple of days ago round at the shops – you were the only person bothered with him after he got picked on. Then, too, he's bigger than you, and can threaten you, and also … Well, like I say, he's bigger than you.'

Peter smirked and, even with the lump on his lip, he reminded Mal of Andy. Despite the fact that he had said he would keep quiet about what he thought he knew – which, after all, was half right – Mal still didn't trust Peter, or like him much. They were at the top of the hill.

'D'you think anyone else caught on?' Mal asked.

'Not a chance,' Peter told him. 'My brother was too busy playing generals and Mucker was too busy moping to notice anything. And the rest are just too thick.'

Mal thought that, even if he were to tell the truth now, Peter wouldn't believe him. He had everything so well worked out for himself.

'See you,' Peter said.

'See you tonight.'

'I doubt it,' said Peter. 'I've had enough of their useless bonfire.'

And with that, he walked on up Larkview Avenue towards the Hook. Only when Peter was out of sight did Mal remember about the car. He glanced back down the hill, but the car was gone. The driveway and garage were again empty and Mal quickened his step, round the side of the house and in the back door. His father's absence was no great surprise, but Mal's disquiet increased when it became clear that his mother was not at home either. He could not recall a single occasion, ever, when she had been out of the house at dinner time. On the mantelpiece he found a note in her handwriting:

Mal, tea in the fridge just in case.

And that was all. Just in case what? In case he *did* come home, or in case they ...

Mal scrunched the note in his hand and tore upstairs, fear tightening his throat. He pushed open the door of his parents' bedroom. The bed was made and the floor and furniture were spotlessly tidy, like they always were. Despite the thumping of his heart that made the blood pound in his ears, he tiptoed carefully across the carpet – vacuumed so that the pile leaned first one way, then the other, in broad swathes, showing up any heavy footprint that disturbed the pattern. He reached out a hand for the wardrobe doors, withdrew it, then reached out again and flung them apart.

Tension broke from him in a noise that was somewhere between a laugh and a cry. He buried his face in the fur collar of his mother's camel-hair coat and ran his hands along her dresses and his father's suits and shirts, hung, neatly pressed, beside them.

Downstairs again, feeling calmer, Mal lifted the food from the fridge. It was a salad, but it looked all wrong. The eggs were grey-white where they should have been just white and the yolks were tinged a blackish green. His mother had covered the plate with a second, smaller plate, but this had slipped to one side and broken the tomato segments, the juice from which had soaked into the lettuce, so that it was soggy and stuck to the plate. Only the slivers of ham were at all appetising.

Mal took his tea in the living room, in front of the TV, since he was forbidden to watch it while he ate when his parents were at home. But there was nothing on except the news. The glum faces and wagging heads of the politicians amused him at first and he thought of the kids from the estate sitting in a circle that morning, wondering what to do about the burnt centre pole. But all the talk quickly bored him and he grew restless. His plate kept shifting and he had difficulty balancing it on his knee. In the end, he went back to the dinette, telling himself that was all right too, since he was eating there from choice.

There was something about the dinette that struck him as peculiar, but he couldn't quite put his finger on it. He turned his attention once more to his plate and gamely attempted another few mouthfuls. It was no use, though; the sight of the eggs and lettuce put him off and, in the sun that came through the window, even the ham had begun to look odd, with a sheen that reminded him of washed-up milk bottles and the blue-green bottoms of the fat flies that buzzed around the dump.

The dump. He pushed his chair back and got up from the table. He was wasting time when he had the perfect opportunity to see Francy and put it to him about the attack on the bonfire. He wrapped the remnants of his tea in Kleenex, ran his plate under the hot tap, and left it on the draining board on his way out to the yard. He lifted the bin lid and made a hole in the rubbish with the coal shovel, kept next to the yard brush by the drain. The shovel hit against something, making a dull metallic clang. Mal peered into the bin and at once realised what had been different about the dinette; for there, halfway down, buried in dust from a vacuum bag and surrounded by dried polish pads, was the brass bowl from the table.

Mechanically, he dropped his Kleenex-wrapped package into the cavity, covered it and the bowl with refuse, and replaced the bin lid. His head was reeling: his mother's note, the bowl in the bin, the burnt centre pole, Les, Peter – everything today seemed beyond his grasp. He didn't feel like arguing with Francy any more; he just needed to talk to him.

But Francy wasn't there. Mal knew the second the dump came into view and the toilet was nowhere to be seen. He picked a path across to the willow tree all the same, too pre-occupied to notice how easily he followed the route and avoided potholes.

He called out to Francy, never really expecting him to reply, and then, after a moment's hesitation, he stepped forward decisively and parted the branches of the willow. Nothing happened. It seemed Francy only set traps whenever he was actually in the hut. But why was he not afraid of it being found when he was not there? Andy didn't mention any booby traps when he talked of being at the dump; in fact, he claimed that all there was to the hut was a couple of sheets of tin, leaned against a hedge. But Mal knew there was more than that. He'd seen for himself. Hadn't he? He ducked behind the corrugated iron.

He began at the top and worked his way along methodically, feeling with both hands for the gap in the hedge through which he had followed Francy the previous day, and when he reached the bottom, he turned and worked back again, searching.

Mal couldn't say he was really surprised when he emerged, not having found the breach. A hut that was only there when Francy was. His mind, so tired and confused such a short time before, felt, for an instant, supremely relaxed.

'Lesson number ... whatever,' he repeated to himself. 'Their rules stop at the fence.'

But the further he walked from the dump and the nearer he drew to the woods, the less he was able to remember what it was he had found comforting in what had passed. It had not needed articulation at the time and, now that he strove to hold on to the vision, he felt the lack of the words to make it concrete. He saw the boys and girls milling around the bonfire and he frowned deeply.

Les watched him approach, his staring eyes round and guilty. But when he got to the slope up from the playing fields, Les turned his back and went to the bonfire, laying a line of boards and planks from the wide base to the apex where the branches of the outer shell converged. Nearby, Andy was directing Pickles and another boy who were binding with lengths of string the legs of a man-sized doll, made up of old clothes, stuffed with newspaper and dried grass: the Pope for the top of the bonfire.

The young men of the estate, with whom Mucker already played pitch-and-toss sometimes and who this time next year, it was assumed, he would have joined for good and all, were starting to gather now. They drank openly from bottles of cider and cans of beer, hooting at the contingent of girls who passed before them, linked in couples, and trying to catch their skirts with the toes of their shoes. The girls broke formation, arching their backs out of the way, then regrouped further on and passed in front of the boys again, arm in arm.

There were other clumps of people drinking, but they were under-age and sat back from the bonfire in the shade of the first trees, swallowing in quick gulps and setting the bottles on the ground behind them between mouthfuls. Half a dozen teenagers with flutes ran through their repertoire of party tunes, rehearsing for both the night's celebrations and the following day's parades. They stamped their feet in time to their playing and around them jigged a circle of very young children (some no more than toddlers) who wouldn't be allowed to stay up for the fire itself but were making the most of their Eleventh Night anyway.

Mucker was walking between the various groups, swigging from whatever was offered to him. Sonia Kerr hung on to him and took her turn at the bottles and cans when he had finished with them. Drunk, she looked a more awkward mishmash of girl and woman than normal. Her nose, which seemed to be permanently chapped from a head cold, showed up still redder with the alcohol and a thin snail trail of liquid glistened on her top lip. But, at the same time, there was a coarse, almost muscular, maturity about her, and when she stretched to kiss Mucker's cheek, Mal glimpsed a deep, blue-purple blotch on her neck. He willed the sight away, thinking he had unwittingly discovered a dark secret, and his stomach churned with a curious mixture of repulsion and attraction. He tensed the muscles at the top of his thighs, feeling the weight on his privates of a rat hanging taut on a string.

He was suddenly distressed, lost among so many people. He almost wished Peter had been there, or that Les would make up his mind whether he was sorry or annoyed.

'Yo!'

Andy was beckoning him and he trotted over to the bonfire.

'I want you to shin up there and stick this at the top. Anyone heavier might go through.'

He held the dummy out to Mal. It wasn't a Pope now, but instead, as a piece of cardboard around its neck bore witness, *Gerry Fitt. Agent of Rome.* Mal looked dubiously at the flimsy walkway.

'Go on,' Andy urged him. 'It'll take you, no problem.'

'He's scared,' Les said.

'No, I'm not,' Mal told them, though he was.

'Well then.' Andy offered the Gerry Fitt doll. 'Take it.'

Mal started to climb, on all fours, with the dummy slung across his back like a wounded comrade. At the junction of the first and second planks, he felt his wooden footboard shift slightly. The branches below him rustled and sighed. He froze, glancing behind him through his rigid arms. Andy and Les waved him on. He breathed deep, steeling himself, then slowly and carefully continued to the top of the bonfire.

He could be seen now by everyone around the entrance to the woods. Bobby Parker, the bin-lorry driver, was arriving at that moment, lugging his massive Lambeg drum. He set it down and cheered as Mal kneaded the dummy's middle to make it sit straight. The cheer was taken up by the young men drinkers, who raised their bottles and cans. Those who had built the bonfire whoop-whoop-whooped and the tiniest boys and girls jumped up and down, clapping. Mal bowed to them, milking the applause. He felt important and central. Then, all too quickly, the cheering stuttered and died. Mal turned to descend the blind side of the bonfire. But there were no planks, only a stretch of branches, like the blank face of a tall hedge. Les was leaning on one of the boards, while Andy stood looking on, snickering.

'Aw, come on,' Mal pleaded. 'Put them back. How'm I meant to get down?'

'Try jumping,' Les said and laughed his machine-gun laugh.

Mal tried to lower himself, but Andy put a foot on a branch and began to roll it on his instep so that it moved under him. Les joined in, using both feet and his hands until all the branches shifted and swayed. Mal scrabbled to the top again and clung to the effigy. Fear made him dizzy; fear of falling, of crashing down; down through the branches, past the chairs, the mattresses, planks and pallets, the sideboards and thick short logs, the hoopla-ed tyres; and still falling ...

He heard a muffled thump and a groan and the branches stopped moving. He opened his eyes cautiously. Les was stretched out on the ground, clutching his groin, and Mucker was squaring up to Andy.

'What the fuck are youse at?' he asked.

'It's only a frigging joke,' Andy replied.

'Some joke. Did youse want to pull the whole bonfire down too?'

The flute players interrupted their tune and people drifted round to see what was happening.

'Now wait a minute here,' Andy said. 'Glad you're interested in the welfare of the bonfire again all of a sudden. You weren't so bothered this morning at the chapel. If that priest had called the cops on us they'd have taken our tyres for sure. And then what would we have been left with? You don't know because you never thought about it – and don't forget who it was who organised the building of all this when you were too sulky to be arsed doing anything today.'

'Today?' Mucker shouted. 'What about this past month? How d'you think you were able to do what you did this afternoon? Because I fucking arranged everything weeks ago, that's how.'

Mal watched, fascinated, forgetting his precarious position. It looked like this was it at last: Mucker and Andy were going to have it out. And then Big Bobby stepped between them.

'Okay, okay,' he said, pacifying them. 'Cut it out, the both of youse. For Christ's sake, it's the Eleventh Night, let's have no fighting among ourselves. The bonfire's as much due to the one as it is to the other. How's that? Now stop your arguing and have a drink.'

He passed a can of beer to Andy, who reluctantly took a pull before holding it out in front of him. Mucker didn't move, so Bobby took the can and offered it more insistently. Mucker ignored him too.

'Put the fucking planks back and let the wee lad down,' he said to Andy.

Andy shrugged.

'I never touched them.'

Les picked himself up sheepishly, one hand still on his groin and, without a word, began to replace the planks on the side of the bonfire. Bobby jerked the beer can towards Mucker a third time. He paused for a long moment, then accepted it and, wiping the mouthpiece with his sleeve, drank from it. The spectators dispersed and Mal descended to the ground, embarrassed now at having been the cause of so much trouble; especially since, once he was down, nobody paid any further attention to him.

He flitted alone through the crowd for the rest of the evening. Darkness rolled off the mountains, seeped through the trees and swallowed the estate. The night air grew chillier and small fires were lit on the slope up from the playing fields. Lights shone in the open doorways of the houses facing the woods as street parties began, and the numbers around the bonfire increased steadily with more and more grown-ups coming out to mingle with the young people. There was pressure to light the bonfire early for the benefit of the smaller children, but the boys held out, saying midnight it had always been, and midnight it would be this year.

Mal was becoming drowsy; he had eaten next to nothing all day and felt weak. Only the cold kept him from dropping off, and he was looking for somewhere warm to lie and wait when his father lurched into view with his hand on Bobby Parker's sleeve. It was the first Mal had seen of him since dinner time the night before, and he drew back into the shadows, frightened, for his father was obviously drunk. Mal had known him to be tipsy, but never like this, and never in public. He waved his free hand in the air as he talked loudly.

'These Civil Rights yahoos make me laugh,' he was saying. 'Too lazy to get off their behinds and do things for themselves. Instead they expect to be lifted and laid, have everything done for them. Wait'll I tell you ... Bobby, is it? Wait'll I tell you, Bobby. I had nothing, and there was nobody took to the streets demonstrating for me. Ha! If that's what I'd been looking for, I'd still be looking to this day.'

He was going to continue, but Bobby extricated himself, moving out of his reach.

'Oh, you're right there,' he said. 'You're right there, okay. But, here, I must get on: time I was ready with the Lambeg.'

Mr Martin stood alone, pitching forward every now and then and shooting a leg out to steady himself. He was by far and away the neatest person in sight and wore his best navy suit – saved from being unfashionable by a pinkly patterned tie. But his black, slip-on shoes had been scuffed at the toes and, worse, one side of his face was raw and grazed. Mal came out of the shadows to speak.

'Ach, if it isn't me own wee True Blue himself,' his father said thickly. He seemed to want either to hug his son or give him an affectionate pat, but his hands were fumbling and he succeeded only in jiggling him awkwardly.

'What have you done to your face?' Mal asked.

His father pushed him away.

'Oh aye, oh aye,' he said. 'That's your mother's game, is it? I seen her by the pavilion, watching me like a hawk. Spends the afternoon at that brother of hers complaining about me, and now she's sent you snooping. Is that it, hm?'

'I was just worried something had happened to you,' Mal said, hoping he would quieten down.

'Worried?' Mr Martin lowered his face until he was staring directly into Mal's eyes. 'Listen, son, the day I need you to worry for me is the day I'll really start to worry for myself.'

He hauled himself up by his suit trousers and turned away from Mal.

'Did youse hear that?' he appealed to everyone within earshot. 'Worried.'

He tried to buttonhole passers-by and eventually put himself in the path of Sonia and Mucker so that they were obliged to stop and listen to him. Mal sprinted across the playing fields to the pavilion, where he found his mother talking to Mrs Clark. Immediately she saw him, his mother dropped to her knees and hugged him tightly. Looking over her shoulder, Mal noticed Mrs Clark was as uncomfortable as he was.

'Mum,' he said in a low voice.

'Are you not cold?' she interrupted, plucking at his T-shirt.

'I'm all right,' he said. 'Mum, listen.'

'You can't tell them anything,' his mother said.

Mrs Clark smiled awkwardly. 'I know, I know. Our Leslie's the same.'

'Mummy, please,' Mal insisted. 'It's my daddy. He's …'

He stopped; he felt exhausted and thought he would fall down at any moment. His mother stared at him, then glanced at Mrs Clark.

'Will you excuse me, Sadie?' she said, strainedly polite, and drew the collar of her coat close to her throat.

Mal led her to the bonfire, where Mr Martin was still holding forth to Sonia and Mucker.

'See, you youngsters, you don't know the meaning of the word. There's only one way to be a success in this world, and that's to *work* for it yourself.'

He swung round abruptly, aware that Mucker was looking at someone behind him. Mrs Martin touched his grazed cheek with the back of her hand. His head recoiled.

'Now don't start,' he threatened her. 'I slipped – fell off a kerb. Anyone could have done it; the state of the footpaths in this place is a disgrace, they're crumbling to bits.'

But it seemed as though Mrs Martin was indeed about to start. Her concern rejected, she was shaping up for a tirade. Somewhat unstably, her husband stood his ground.

'What's that over there?' someone shouted from the edge of the woods.

Beyond the houses at the top of the estate the sky was tinged a light orange.

'And there,' Mucker said.

On the horizon, to the left, the black smoke of burning tyres, denser than darkness, rose in a vertical pall.

103

Bonfires. It was not quite half eleven, but it did not matter any more. The boys had managed to wait longer than at least some of the neighbouring areas; they had not been the first to give, and now they listened to the calls to for God's sake get on with it and light theirs.

As sticks with petrol-soaked rags wrapped around them were driven in at points around the base of the bonfire, people converged on it from all sides: the Bells, the McMinns, the McMahons and the Crosiers, Tommy Duncan and his family, the Smyllie twins with their wives, the Garritys, the Presses, the Kerrs and the Boyles, the Sinclairs, the Hugheses, the Jamisons and Stinsons, Mrs Clark and old Mrs Parker, the Hemmings, the Taggarts, the Greys, the Whites, all of the Campbells except for the father, the Tookeys, the Clearys, the Kellys and Craigs, McClures, Milligans, Hawthorns and O'Days, the Wheatcrofts, the McDevitts, the Viles, wee Ernie Buchanan with his Bible-tract sandwich boards. More faces in the end than Mal could identify. And when everything was in place, Andy lit a final torch and touched off all the others. The bonfire had begun.

Mal stood between his parents, watching with them, painfully intent. A reverent hush descended as the flames took hold. The dry leaves and twigs of the outer branches crackled and burned yellow, but they were only the accompaniment to the real fire. The heart of the bonfire began to glow a deep, powerful orange. For what felt like an age, flames hued with fantastical reds, purples, blues and greens from blistering varnish and paintwork burned in circles, rolling round and round as if fuelling them-selves, spreading neither upwards nor outwards, while the glow grew ever more bright, ever more intense. Then, on an instant, the flames burst with a whoosh, erupting through the top of the bonfire, engulfing the Gerry Fitt doll.

The silence broke and cheers and whistles pierced the crackling air; the flutes began to trill again, joined now by the monotonous, penetrating rumble of Big Bobby's Lambeg drum: *rat-tat-a-rat-ta-ta-tat, rat-tat-a-rat-ta-ta-tat*. People danced, linking arms and laughing, and Mal felt his parents move closer together behind him. The flames stretched higher and thick smoke belched and billowed up into the night sky above the trees.

Suddenly there was an almighty crash; whiplash flames exploded sideways from the fire and showers of sparks and splinters of burning timber poured down on the scattering, screaming onlookers. The weight of the sides, the devouring intensity of the inner ball of flame, had proved too much for the improvised centre pole and the bonfire had caved in. It blazed on, but it was no longer the bonfire which had been so many weeks in the planning. When the debris settled and the smoke cleared, Mal saw Andy and Les running around the increased circumference of the fire, using long bundles of sticks in a desperate attempt to sweep it back together again. But no sooner did they succeed in shoring up one spot than another was undermined and subsided; the brushes themselves ignited and were dropped, increasing still further the extent of the fire.

'I knew it,' Mucker grumbled. 'I fucking knew it.'

He was only yards from Mal and his parents.

'Hey, Philip,' Mr Martin shouted, eyes twinkling, reflecting the fire. 'I thought you told me they'd see this one in Lisburn. Have you given them all binoculars?'

Mal could never quite get straight in his mind what exactly happened next. From the flickering, broken images that tumbled before and behind his eyes then, he was able later to piece together only an impression of the rapid movement of silhouettes, jagged flashes of arms and legs and a random scuffling. When it was over, a matter of seconds, no more, his father was on the ground, propelling himself backwards with his elbows, and his mother was stooped over him, crying, trying to protect him.

Mucker seemed to pulsate with rage and his mouth, a fire-lit gash, worked frantically:

'Don't talk to me about failure, mister, for you're the biggest failure ever drew breath as sure as I'm standing here.'

And then a wall of bodies blotted Mucker from view and Mal helped his mother lift his father to his feet.

As the family limped across the playing fields, Mal noticed a squat figure emerge from the darkness of the now deserted pavilion. It plodded along at a distance, shadowing them, and then veered away at the bottom of the hill towards the dump.

'Who do you think that is?' Mrs Martin asked, scared in case anyone should try to renew the attack on her husband.

'Nobody I know,' Mal told her, without hesitation.

They started up the hill, followed by the trill of the flutes and the dull beat of the Lambeg drum: *rat-tat-a-rat-ta-ta-tat.*

TWO

1

Dawn was not at all how Mal always imagined it would be. The day did not burst triumphantly red into the living room, but instead leaked, gradually and unannounced, through the open blinds, so that when the first rays of strong sunlight did spill on to the carpet before him, he felt cheated, as though sneaked up on from behind.

Nobody had bothered to send him to bed, but, although awake the whole time, he seemed to have drifted far from his body, which ached now as he sat forward, becoming conscious of it once more. He rubbed his eyes, remembering his tiredness of the night before, and, in his mind, the Mal of then and now and the boy who had sat through the darkness appeared as two entirely separate people. To the left of the patch of sunlight, at the foot of the settee, his father lay, curled in on himself, exhaling in a strange, whistling snore. He had his back to Mal and his hands were driven between his thighs, with only the tips of the fingers protruding, swollen purple and meeting as if in prayer. Mal stood unsteadily; his head whirled with nausea and he thought he must have got up too quickly. He pressed the heels of his hands on his eyebrows until the feeling subsided, then blinked his eyes open again, trying to root himself more firmly in his surroundings.

The carpet was strewn with teacups, which, as the night wore on, even his mother could not bring herself to clear away: the small delft cups of everyday use, their mud-brown backgrounds thickly splodged with orange paint (a crude floral design that always suggested to Mal blinding, desert suns); the mugs-for-men, sloganed or stout and glazed blue; and even the special-occasion china cups, to the white sides of which clung frail purple wildflowers. Every cup in the house, it seemed, had been used and in all of them a film of milk was formed, pale and separated like an oil slick. They were arranged in a pattern Mal could not understand, and he weaved in and out them to the hall door, where he faltered, listening.

In the hallway, his mother was speaking into the telephone. She was not deliberately lowering her voice, but it was so weak and tired that only a wordless murmur reached Mal's ears. He leaned against the door's cool paint, lulled by the murmur and the rhythmic wheeze of his father's snores. He had rolled on to his other side now, facing Mal. His shirt front was spattered with blood; and there was more blood, dried black, partially blocking one nostril. It was this that caused him to whistle whenever he breathed. Mal stared across the room, seeing his father, but seeing, too, the jagged images of the bonfire-lit night and, behind all, Francy's figure watching from the shadows of the pavilion. Saliva frothed hotly in his mouth and he wanted to spit.

The telephone bell dinged as the receiver was replaced. Mal crossed quickly into the kitchen, easing the door shut after him, and busied himself preparing his breakfast. But his mother did not come into the kitchen, or even into the living room. Her footsteps sighed furtively on the stairs and Mal followed the muffled tread down the landing and into his room. Then all was silent.

He poured milk straight from the bottle on to his dish of cereal, but despite the hollow gurgling of his stomach he had no appetite, and poked and prodded the cornflakes with his spoon. He had no idea how long he continued in that trance-like state, but when the door at last opened, the kitchen clock read a quarter past seven and the orange of the flakes had discoloured the milk.

Uncle Simon smiled a narrow-lipped greeting. Mrs Martin came into the dinette behind her brother and touched his sleeve lightly. Although the sun had been up for some time now, she wore her camel-hair coat with the fur collar tucked around her chin like a neck brace. A crammed sports grip dangled by its strap from her wrist.

'Eat up quick,' she told Mal.

Mal began spooning his cereal unquestioningly. He knew without asking that he was going to stay with Uncle Simon and Aunt Pat, just like the last time, when his father first lost the shop. He ate as fast as he could, trying his best to oblige; but, if anything, it seemed to take him longer than usual getting to the bottom of the bowl. The milk from each spoonful slipped straight down his throat until if felt like it was congested in a long column, reaching to his stomach. The cereal was left stranded on his tongue, bulging his cheeks and pressing on the milk column. He gagged, spluttering half-chewed flakes back into the bowl.

'*Mal!*'

'He's okay; he's okay,' said Uncle Simon, shushing his sister. 'Plenty of time, son, there's no rush.'

Mrs Martin left the room and Uncle Simon smiled more broadly, making his lips disappear altogether, raising his eyebrows in a way that was meant to suggest that he was on his nephew's side. Mal looked at him quizzically, bemused by his inane expression and by the boyish flick of his wispy, sandy hair that contrasted more markedly every time he saw him with its greying sides. Uncle Simon scratched the outside of his thigh with the car keys.

'So ... Ah ... How've you been getting on at school?' he asked, then slapped his head in a pantomime of forgetfulness. 'Oh, but of course, it's the holiday now, isn't it. No time to be thinking about school, eh?'

Mal, his mouth still full, moved his head vaguely in reply, unsure whether he should be shaking it or nodding it.

'The man only looks like a simpleton,' his father once confided in him. 'Stands to reason: nobody gets to where he has without a bit of the sly in him.'

Uncle Simon pulled at a short hair on the flesh of his ear lobe and sidled over to the sink for a glass of water. Mal swallowed in short, painful gulps until his cheeks had lost their pouchiness and he was able to force the word 'Finished' through what remained in his mouth. His uncle smiled briefly.

'Right then. I'll just get your mum, shall I?'

Mal slid down from the seat and tailed his uncle into the living room, taking care to negotiate the scattered cups. They paused awkwardly to contemplate his father (since it was harder to ignore him) still asleep at the foot of the settee. The clotted blood breezed like snot from his nostril and his belly bulged, exposed, between his elbows, the black hole plunging bottomless in the shade. Mal turned to offer some excuse. Uncle Simon's face was stretched, his mouth and doubling chin downwards, his nose and brow upwards, as if he'd smelt something foul. He caught his nephew's eye and attempted to scale his face down to its earlier look of complicity, but he failed hopelessly and gave instead an apologetic grimace.

'Are we ready?' Mrs Martin asked from the hallway.

She had tied her hair with a paisley headscarf, fastened at the nape of her neck in a tight knot. Uncle Simon's lips flickered with relief and he skipped quickly to open the front door for her.

The street hadn't woken well from the party. Bottles and cans had been swept roughly into piles against the low walls in a half-hearted effort at clearing up, and the bunting strung between the houses sagged limp in the windless, soot-flecked air. Everywhere there was a smell of wood smoke mingled with stale beer. No one spoke as Uncle Simon steered the car away from the kerb and on out of Larkview.

Alone in the back seat, Mal finally swallowed the last of his cereal. The car was stifling and he rested against the window to take the heat out of his face. So quietly did the Rover engine hum that he let himself believe it wasn't the car which was moving through the streets, but the streets themselves that were running, in the opposite direction, past the car, away from the city. An estate like his own sped by, closely followed by another of uniform stucco (Housing Trust grey) dragging in its wake a chain of flat-roofed shops and a panic-stricken ramshackle of prefab bungalows. A long, straight road of suburban houses, with their hedges hitched to their middles, outstripped the car, dumping it smack in the midst of row upon row of dingy terraces, which promptly took to their heels and fled as fast as their twists and turns would allow them. Only in the centre was there calm. The grand shops and offices of Donegall Square stood unperturbed, flanking the City Hall, the heart of Belfast, its domed top exposed as a bared belly.

Uncle Simon stopped at a green light to let a solitary lodge file past. The car purred impatiently behind them for a time through the main shopping streets, then made its break at the bottom of North Street, skirted the Shankill, and raced along Clifton Street, bypassing the Orangemen and beating them to Carlisle Circus, where many other lodges and bands had already converged in preparation for the march through the city. Mal flopped in his seat, dismayed that this was the closest he would get to the parades this year. His uncle glanced at him in the driving mirror.

'What do you say we catch them tonight on their way back from the field?'

Mal shrugged, squinting at a banner that was being carefully unfurled: Derry, Aughrim, Enniskillen and the Boyne in the four corners; in the centre King Billy on a white horse, sword pointing. A silken signpost.

'Not fussed,' he said.

The Rover turned in an easy swerve into the driveway of the double-fronted house, its tyres sliding over the deep gravel like sled runners on snow. Uncle Simon had obviously had someone in since last Mal stayed there at the turn of the year, for the pebble-dash of the walls was now glossed stickily white where formerly it had been beige, and the window frames, drainpipes and doors had been coated a shade of pale lemon. Aunt Pat was waiting in the glass porch and, as the car braked confidently close to a large rhododendron, she came down the three front steps to greet Mal and his mother. She shook a deliberately stray ringlet aside and bent to kiss Mal with sticky lips, painted a pale, pale pink on the outside, but puckering to show their natural meaty colour of bluish red on the inside near her gums.

'How've you been getting on then, hm?' She held a white filtered cigarette behind her shoulder, out of the way of Mal's face. 'New school fun?'

Mal didn't think there was a single thing he could say to her. Uncle Simon checked her with a faint movement of his head and Aunt Pat's smile creased the flesh around her nose, furrowing the finely powdered skin, making of her face a cracked mask. She stroked Mal's face with the backs of her fingers, the large marbled stone of one of her rings coolly sliding over his flushed cheek, and passed on to speak to his mother.

His aunt and uncle seemed to think it necessary to drop their voices when they talked in his presence. He was disgusted with them for treating him like a child who knew nothing. He wondered where their concern had been last night and was too bored even to strain to hear what they were saying. He crunched deliberately across the driveway to the edge of the neatly shorn lawn, which sloped into a rockery of soft ferns and mosses and delicate china-teacup flowers, overhanging the pavement.

It was still not quite eight o'clock, but already the air shimmered and Belfast stretched out before him like a mirage, so that even the rundown terraces away to the right, which he had been driven through only minutes previously, were fused into a warm red mass. On his left was Bellevue Zoo and behind him towered the Cave Hill and the jutting black rock of Napoleon's Nose.

114

The house seemed to be cut into the very hillside and Mal now grasped something of his father's desire to move here, the passion that spurred him to work past closing time in the shop for as many years as Mal could remember, spending what free time was left him devising plans for improvement and expansion. He understood now his hurt when last year it had all stopped and the Belmont Road house went up for sale and Mal was sent here to his aunt and uncle. When his parents came for him again it was to drive him not east, but south, past the town houses to the estate on the edge of the city, closer by almost a mile to the tired, grey market town where his father was born than to the centre of Belfast.

The sun caught the lough and it glistened and winked like tinsel.

'Don't you want some breakfast?'

Aunt Pat was on the doorstep, shielding her eyes from the sun's reflected rays.

'I've had mine,' Mal said, turning only briefly.

He gazed down into the valley again. Dazzled, he saw the city dance before his eyes in a thousand broken shapes and he shuddered, so that the backs of his thighs were set trembling, and he took a step back lest he topple headlong from his perch. He seized upon the giant staple of Goliath, the shipyard crane, and gradually stared the city into focus, harmonious between the hills.

He shouldn't go making things so difficult for Aunt Pat when she only wanted to make him feel welcome. He faced her once more.

'D'you think I could just have some orange, please?'

She crinkled her face in pleasure, exhaling a brown gush of cigarette smoke from between her pale pink lips, and extended a hand for him to clasp as he crossed the driveway to the open door.

Mal's cousins, Alex, who was sixteen, and Cathy, who was a year younger, were away that weekend on holiday in England with a girl who boarded at their school. Mal was glad; he was sure they didn't like him at all and were bored having to entertain him whenever he came to the house. The last time he stayed, he had taken to sitting in the same room as his aunt and uncle after tea, while the girls went to Cathy's room and listened to records, singing along and stamping their feet if ever Mal happened past the door (which their father insisted should always be left slightly ajar). Mal didn't mind a bit staying downstairs with the grown-ups. They appeared to worry so much about what they ought to say to him that, more often than not, they ended up saying nothing whatsoever and usually he could watch TV undisturbed until they packed him off to bed, much later than he was sent at home.

One night, though, Uncle Simon had to attend a builders' conference and the girls spent the evening in the lounge with their mother and Mal. Aunt Pat seemed totally transformed. She flipped off her Scholls and tucked her legs beneath her, kidding her daughters about boyfriends, while they teased her back audaciously over boys *she* had known before she met their father. Mal was enthralled by her easy talk about the old days. The names of dance halls and picture houses, long gone, conjured up a Belfast remote from the one he knew. It wasn't difficult to imagine Aunt Pat dancing till two in the morning and getting up for work at seven, as she sat on the sofa wearing a short, belted dress, boldly patterned, that might well have belonged to one or other of her daughters, and twisted a loose ringlet round her index finger. But his own mother ... That was different. Whenever her name cropped up in reminiscence, it jarred, and spoiled the picture in Mal's mind. Even an old photograph which his aunt found for him in a shoebox in the bureau was no help. His mother looked at the camera in wide-eyed surprise; clutching a small white bag, the size of a dishcloth, to her stomach, she stood awkwardly on open-toed stilettos, so that it seemed only her ballooning taffeta skirt kept her balanced.

'I remember the night that was taken,' Aunt Pat said. 'It was a May Ball – the first dance your mum ever went to. Uncle

Simon chaperoned her and had to dance with her all night because she was petrified of anyone else asking her.'

She looked fondly at the picture and Mal wondered if she saw anything different from what he saw: a slight, serious girl with his mother's face, whose sleeveless top hung like a vest.

'Oh, but she was very pretty,' Aunt Pat went on hurriedly, noticing Mal's despondent eyes. 'And not in the least shy after that first dance. We had some times, your mother and I – your Uncle Simon used to ask me who I was going out with: him or his sister.'

Alex snickered and her mother shot out a foot and prodded her with a stockinged toe.

'Things were different in our day,' she said. 'We didn't know what one of them was.'

She made a limp sign with her wrist that set Alex off again.

'Is that where she met my daddy?'

Aunt Pat breathed audibly through her nose, but was smiling when Mal looked up at her.

'No, no. She didn't meet your father for nearly two years after that. Old Year's Night, 1954, at Morelli's in Newtownards.' She paused. 'Your grandparents were living on the Woodvale then, right up the top of the Shankill – though, of course, the Woodvale was a far different place in those days – and your father would visit every night and stay until your grandpa threw him out, which was usually after the last bus. And so he'd have to walk back to Lisburn – ten miles, if it's a yard.'

'Too keen,' Cathy said, and Alex gave a low impressed whistle.

'Oh, he wasn't the only one would have,' their mother told them. 'God knows, there was many a one would gladly have swapped places with him.'

Mal looked again at the narrow-waisted girl with hair twisted and pinned into a flat, round hat. It was still hard to think of her as being young.

It was even harder that morning as they sat at the breakfast bar, watching yet more tea grow cold. Her face was unprettily puffy, but, at the same time, grey and drawn. From the way she dabbed periodically at her red-rimmed eyes and avoided her brother's gaze, Mal thought that something must have been said to upset her. Although he had to struggle to keep his own eyes open, he sat by her all morning, politely refusing when his aunt said he could go upstairs to rest. At length, Uncle Simon said it was mild enough for them to have lunch on the patio and Mrs Martin was persuaded to sit outside while Aunt Pat got everything ready. Uncle Simon emerged from the garage, carrying folded canvas picnic chairs under one arm and an old, leather football tucked under the other.

'Fancy a game?' he asked Mal.

Mal hovered by the patio table, uncertain. He loved football, although he preferred not to play with the lads on the estate because they were mostly bigger than him; he was easily knocked off the ball and, boy, did they ever get angry if he gave it away too often. His mother had at last taken off her coat and signalled to him impatiently that she was all right and he wasn't to make such a fuss.

He stepped on to the grass, so tidily swathed in a criss-cross of alternating light and dark that it appeared to have been vacuumed, not mown, and Uncle Simon bowled the ball towards him. The ball wasn't quite round, it swelled from age, an age-old soaking and from being dried too close to a fire, but Mal did not even have to stretch to reach it. He trapped it inexpertly, took aim and launched it back up the garden with the front of his foot. The lacing was raised and hardened and stubbed Mal's toes with such an acute pain that he felt the jolt course through his whole body. He staggered dizzily.

'You're not going to tell me you're still toe-poking at your age,' his uncle said. 'See what happens if you don't kick properly? Look here till I show you.'

He tapped the ball from instep to instep and then stroked it easily, side-footed, skimming it across the short grass to his nephew.

'Right?' he said.

Mal had a go at steadying himself for the kick, though his head still throbbed sickeningly and his calves twitched a tired tic. He caught the ball too far up his foot and it span abysmally askew, so that his uncle had to sprint to prevent it bouncing into the herbaceous border. They tried again and again; a dozen times all told. But even when Mal managed a firm, clean strike, he was unable to compensate for the bias in the ball and it still bobbled in practically every direction save the one he intended.

Aunt Pat called from the kitchen asking for help with the plates. Mrs Martin made to rise, but Uncle Simon raced across the lawn and eased her back into her seat, telling her not to bother herself, he could do it.

Mal didn't eat any lunch, despite his aunt's goading and saying surely he must be hungry now. He was, but he knew if he ate he would sleep and he didn't want to let his mother out of his sight for that long. If she herself had nagged him for not sitting down with them, he would have had no option, but her only reaction was to smile absently when Aunt Pat suggested, pouting, that maybe Mal didn't like anyone's cooking but his mummy's.

Lunch was dragged out until it blended with afternoon tea. The fine weather of the morning showed signs of breaking, and swift grey-white clouds alternately obscured and revealed the sun, causing the temperature to rise and fall with such rapidity that Mal began to feel as though he were sweating and shivering at one and the same time. Thoughts swam in his head as in a waking dream; incidents, faces, sounds, smells of the previous hectic days lurched in and out of his consciousness in a procession of fast-increasing pandemonium. He strove desperately to pin everything down, to remember which happenings went with which days, to put the right words in the right person's mouth, but every effort only brought more confusion. And still he felt the need to keep moving, stumbling up and down the garden time after time behind the miscued caser, until finally he lost sight of it altogether.

He scanned the garden with great difficulty, adjusting his eyes to cloud-diffused light one moment and squinting into the glare the next. The ground seemed to shift beneath him; there was so little friction between his shoes and the too-close-cropped grass that he was slipping and sliding at random, running, running, running, without ever catching sight of the ball or coming any nearer to tracking it down. He tried to concentrate on the sounds around him, the better to weight himself in the present: the scrape and chatter of teacups on saucers, the rumble of grown-up conversation, a distant lawnmower's droning whirr. But they escaped his grasping brain, filtering into his wake-dream, fuelling it, so that now he ran from unseen blades, whirring ever closer to his heels, dodging a china-strewn carpet of grass, towards a constantly receding figure, beckoning, bloody snatters tripping him ... 'I hate to say we told you so, from that very first night in Morelli's, but you do know what he's becoming at this rate ...' And the barbed, low-whispered word ricocheted in his head, suddenly full of lapping beer, black beer, in blue-glazed mugs-for-men; lap, lap, lick, lick, until it was all around him and he was drowning in the black shifting sea, with the snapping at his heels, and he clung to a dummy, crying: Stop, stop, how am I supposed to get off? He fought a swoon at the thought of falling, crashing down, down, through the writhing scrimmage of faces; down, down, and still falling; teacups tinkled, the dummy cackled and hackled a smoke spit, telling him: 'An alcoholic, that's what.' And the stench from the sign around its neck, a rat from which the insides were spilling, made him recoil, floundering, and Francy waved a lifeline and he reached, then recognised, and refused. His knees buckled and he was sucked back; refusing he fell, fell, fell ...

His uncle had seen him start to topple and caught him before he hit the ground. He carried him to the patio where he came to briefly to feel the dry, ragged lips of his mother on his cheek. Her breath was old and tired, but its familiarity comforted him and he clung to her neck, feeling her breast against him; his mother's body. Her eyes were moist and she crouched over him, steadying his head for him to sip a cup of hot, sweet tea that his aunt brought through from the kitchen. His throat was keen, but his mind rebelled and only his mother's coaxing helped him manage the half cup that he did before his eyelids went together again and he was borne into the regulated warmth of the house.

2

When next Mal awoke he knew by the pink-shaded light and the depth of the quilt under which he lay that he was not in his own room. The bed smelled of small flowers and Germolene – Cathy. He was in Cathy's room where he had used to stay. He poked his head above the quilt, sleepy, but no longer tired. A man with lank hair, curtained to reveal a thin face, dominated by a large-boned nose on which were perched gold, round-framed glasses, stared at him sourly from the wall. He had not been there when last Mal visited and for a moment in waking, before he identified the Beatle, Mal entertained the possibility that he had been roused by this steady gaze. Blinking the picture from his mind he turned his head aside quickly to see another face looming, although the spectacles of this one had heavy, black frames and lenses so thick that the eyeballs in them were trapped, as in paperweights.

'Hello, Mal,' the face said, smelling, too, of Germolene. 'Feeling any better?'

Mal nodded. A chair sighed out of sight and Mal guessed his mother was somewhere in the room. He allowed himself to be examined, rolling whichever way the light touch of the man's hands suggested without complaint. He opened his mouth and eyes wide in turn, breathed deeply, held a thermometer under his tongue and counted fingers before his face as bidden. He knew he had fainted, but he did not feel unwell, only a little hot when a clammy palm moulded itself to his forehead.

'Tough as old boots,' the doctor said, patting the quilt under Mal's chin. He straightened up, using the bedside table for support, and winked, slipping his glasses into a worn leather pouch. Mrs Martin rose from the sighing chair and accompanied him to the bedroom door.

'Just plain exhausted,' the doctor told her. 'Fought it so long he went down like a ton of bricks when it finally got the better of him.'

'And?' Mrs Martin asked.

'And,' the doctor held her hand, 'I'll give him a wee pick-me-up, and if you're not ringing back in a couple of days from now asking for something to calm him down again, I'll trade in my stethoscope.'

He winked once more at Mal and the bedroom light winked out as the door was eased shut. Mal lay on his side in the draped blackness and endeavoured to decipher the time from the luminous dial of an alarm clock on the dressing table over by the window. But the ring of dots and glowing strips of hands meant nothing to him and he gave up puzzling, rolling restlessly on to his stomach. The chair sighed again, unexpectedly, and his mother sniffed. Mal hadn't realised she was still in the room and he wondered now what she could be doing. She drew in breath sharply at irregular intervals, as though someone else were there in the darkness, nipping her flesh. Mal thought to make some sign that he was awake, and when the gasps of breath were joined by a muffled bleat he was on the point of swinging out of bed to go to her. But as he pushed back the quilt, the sounds combined and modulated into a steady sobbing, and Mal froze, hearing for the first time in his life his mother cry.

'Mummy,' he whispered.

The crying stopped at once and his mother coughed self-consciously. She came to kneel by the bed and Mal stretched a hand into the murk to touch her face.

'Watch mummy's scarf,' she said, and at that began crying again. 'Oh, Mal,' she said. 'I'm sorry.' And she repeated the last word over and over: 'Sorry, sorry, sorry.'

Eventually she raised herself from her knees.

'I have to go now, son. Uncle Simon's running me over home. I waited till I knew you were all right, but your daddy and I have things need to be done.'

'I know,' Mal said simply. He did not feel ten years old.

His mother brushed his hairline roughly with her lips.

'Goodnight,' Mal said, and then, as his mother's bare feet padded across the carpet, he called: 'Could I have the light back on?'

The room snapped into rose light in time for Mal to see his mother's hand withdraw behind the closing door. He could read the clock clearly now and was disheartened to find that it was only just after twenty past eight. His mind was free of its wearying jumble and the prospect of staying in bed until this time the following morning made his skin prickle in anticipated discomfort. He thrashed his head on the yielding pillows, suddenly annoyed by their depth and their folds about his face. He tried to palm them flatter, then sat up on his haunches and kneaded them, like he had the Gerry Fitt effigy only twenty-four hours before. He grew more and more aggravated and aggressive until he was pummelling the pillows, grinding his teeth in an inexplicable rage.

'Bastards! Bastards! *Bastards!*' he hissed.

The stairs outside the bedroom door creaked and Mal dived back under the quilt. His aunt must have been checking on him. But when there was no further noise it occurred to him that what he had heard might simply have been the wooden stairs contracting and that his aunt might have gone in the car to keep his uncle company on the journey back home. Still listening, he raised himself on his elbow and came face to face with the picture on the wall. The small black eyes held his stare for a terrifying instant, then broke it.

Mal jumped out of bed, his stomach a fizzling pit of gall. He looked about the room frantically for his clothes and when he couldn't see them anywhere he dragged open the drawers of Cathy's dressing table, rummaging for something to cover himself with. He pulled on a pair of patchwork denims, hitching them to the bottom of his ribcage and twisting the waistband in his fist to hold them closed. The wide bottoms caught up his feet as he fled the room and thumped down the stairs, hoping against hope now that his aunt was in the house.

The television was on in the sitting room, but the volume had been turned down to a whisper and the room was empty; so too were the dining room, the kitchen and the reception room. He hurtled back upstairs, calling his aunt, searching all the bedrooms.

'Auntie Pat! Auntie Pat!' he yelled, then, dissolving into tears, he sat on the top step. 'Oh, Auntie Pat!'

'Mal?' Her voice came from behind the door at his back. He'd forgotten the bathroom.

'Auntie Pat?'

'What's all the banging? Why are you out of bed?'

'I can't sleep any more.' He paused. 'What are you doing, Auntie Pat?'

'What do you think I'm doing?' his aunt answered shrilly. 'Now have some manners and shoo away downstairs. I hope you know your mother'll have a fit if she hears you've been up.'

Mal was only too glad to shoo away. In his confusion, he genuinely hadn't thought that she might be on the toilet; although, in truth, he admitted, turning up the television, it probably wouldn't have entered his mind at the best of times. Of course everyone had to do it, women as well as men, but that didn't mean it wasn't difficult to accept. He sat on the sofa, remembering Mucker's impersonation of the Queen shitting. But, if anything, the Queen was easier to imagine than Aunt Pat.

He pictured her with her flowery gold-belted dress hoisted decorously – or maybe, he thought, she took her dress off altogether. He squirmed in his bagging, borrowed jeans, seeing his aunt naked on the toilet. The details were hazy, but the general impression was clear enough as her elegant fingers drew a cigarette from between her pale, pink lips.

'Oh, God,' he said aloud, and clutched his groin in amazement.

Canned laughter filled the lounge and Mal's body was torn this way and that by successive waves of mortification and pleasure. The first he knew of the door opening was a sudden rush of cool air on his bare back. He turned awkwardly in his seat, trying to move his legs into some position that compensated for and disguised his tentative erection.

'I'm sorry, Auntie Pat,' he began, feeling he ought to explain about the jeans. But he stopped short, seeing his uncle enter the room – his eyes darkly angry – followed by his mother, who looked only slightly less peeved and a good deal more agitated.

'I'm sorry,' Mal began again, thinking now he should offer some reason for being out of bed in the first place. But once more he got no further with his apology, for at the that moment his aunt appeared, cigarette held limply over her shoulder, her face the perfect image of bewildered surprise.

'My goodness,' she said, looking at the three of them in turn. 'Is there anything the matter?'

Mrs Martin jerked her head and shoulders. Uncle Simon stood, sombre, on the hearthrug with his back to the fireplace. The bars of the electric fire had not been lit, but the glass-fibre coals were illuminated by an unseen bulb and beneath them a fan whirred almost inaudibly.

'The parade was petrol-bombed at Unity Flats,' he spluttered. 'I didn't want to chance the city, there's rioting at the bottom of the Shankill.'

Aunt Pat moaned and lowered herself on to the cushion next

to Mal, but so quickly and completely had he forgotten his embarrassment that he scarcely noticed her.

A long ash shell toppled from his aunt's cigarette. The glowing red tip at the filter seared her fingers and she dropped the butt on to the intricately scrolled carpet. Before she was able to scoop it into an ashtray it scorched a narrow black mark.

'*Pa-tricia!*' Uncle Simon scolded.

3

There were windows broken in the new Orange Hall at Dungiven. Fingers of flame, grey-white, clawed at the wheels of the police tenders ranged outside in protection and it seemed only the exertions of the local priests prevented the seething crowd from turning the building into an extempore Twelfth Night bonfire.

The sinister import of the reversal was not lost on Uncle Simon.

'What more do you bloody want, Bernadette?'

On the TV screen a straggle-haired girl spoke rapidly, teeth flashing, spaced like seed markers, pounding her palm for emphasis.

'You've got everything you moaned about, now what more do you bloody want?'

Mal reclined on the sofa, a cushion at his back, legs lost in a blue blanket, watching the pictures and hearing the words for the third time that day. He could have answered his uncle before Bernadette did: the immediate banning of all parades until the end of August.

Sunday was a day of news, and Mal rested before the television through the morning, afternoon and into evening, the programmes between bulletins appearing as nothing more than long intermissions in the main feature. He paraphrased statements and scrutinised faces, placing each person in one of the two makeshift categories he had constructed that day: Decent People and Troublemakers. He had paid scant heed to the news till now. The black and white scenes of rioting that had recurred with increasing frequency in previous months had seemed a world away from the living room in Larkview and made little impression on him. But the trouble on the Shankill had changed all that. The Shankill was less than a mile and a half from here; the Shankill was practically the middle of Belfast.

There were no petrol bombs that he could see at Unity Flats, but he had no time to dwell on that as he absorbed, second-hand, the violence of the day before; a camera-woven tapestry of trouble spread over the whole of Northern Ireland. A fire in Dungiven was more to him now than just a fire in Dungiven.

'It galls me to have to say it,' Uncle Simon told the TV, 'but your man Paisley was right: the Civil Rights is nothing but a bunch of IRA men and Communists.'

The last word chilled Mal's brain. The year before, in his old school, they had said special prayers one morning after assembly for Czechoslovakia. Something had happened there with the Communists. The headmaster showed a photograph on the overhead projector. Of what? A building in ruins; a church. That was it. Communists didn't believe in God; they wanted to take from people all they had earned, to destroy everything.

A thought came to him with the force of revelation. The Civil Rights were wrecking things because they said they were left out, but they didn't want to be a part of them in the first instance. Like Francy. Mal had got it all wrong before; Francy was hated *because* he wouldn't join in, not the other way round.

There was hymn singing on the TV now. Aunt Pat changed channels. Another church, another hymn. She switched the set off with a petulant flick of the wrist.

'Sundays!' she exclaimed, and Mal half expected her to stamp her foot.

His aunt noticed him watching her. Her mouth began to mould itself into a serene smile, but a sudden shudder wiped it clean away and she chafed the sides of her arms, where goose pimples bubbled and the fine hair bristled. Mal lowered his eyes and Aunt Pat took a cigarette from the box on the mantelpiece. She lit it, swallowing smoke hungrily.

'Tea anyone?' she asked in a bright voice that wavered as she rocked her heels on the hearth.

Mrs Martin had finally left for home that Sunday morning, saying she would be back soon. Mal knew what that meant. Last time, 'soon' turned out to be a fortnight. Not that he cared now, though. He didn't want to go home to the fighting again, didn't want to face the people who had seen his father punched to the ground by someone less than half his age, a boy not yet out of school.

But early the following day, as he sat on the doorstep scouring the *News Letter* before taking it in to Uncle Simon, his mother came round the final bend of the driveway, laden with a small suitcase and a shopping basket, from the top of which a slipper heel showed.

'Why the surprised look?' she asked, setting the bags down on the driveway.

Mal was crushing the front page of the newspaper absent-mindedly in his fist.

'I ... I ...'

'Wheesht!' His mother flapped a hand towards him. 'Uncle Simon'll skin you if you ruin that.'

Mal dropped the paper on to his knees. An already blurred photograph of the disturbances at Unity Flats was mangled out of all recognition and the print of the accompanying story had smudged the white spacings between the lines, leaving the whole illegible. Mrs Martin snatched the paper from him.

'Didn't I tell you yesterday I'd be back soon?' she said, smoothing the crumpled page with the flat of her hand.

'Aunt Pat didn't say anything at breakfast.'

'Oh, I didn't want to bother them.'

She indicated with the newspaper that he was to pick up her shopping basket. Mal stole a glance down the drive.

'I took the bus over,' his mother told him. 'He's not there.'

Mal's head dropped guiltily. That was what he had been hoping.

'I didn't think he was.'

His mother walked past him into the glass porch, then turned. In her smile was a hint of a person Mal had never known.

'You're not to worry about anything. It'll all work out fine.' She held up the folded newspaper. 'We'll say I trod on this in the porch. Okay?'

The doctor told Mal to be sure and take his tonic and not to overdo things for a week or so. After his rest on Sunday, though, Mal maintained that there was nothing at all the matter with him and he ran about the back garden, practising with the misshapen caser, whenever the grown-ups were on the patio, to prove the point. Even so, at some stage in the day he would find time to sit on the edge of the front lawn by himself, looking down on the city.

Each time he was there, it seemed, he was able to see more. His eyes could still distinguish only the outlines of areas and the vague shapes of buildings, but his imagination now supplemented this with detail gleaned from the fragments he saw night by night on the television screen. He constructed actual streets and peopled them with real individuals, whose lives and actions had bearing on his own. What they did – and didn't do – was of importance to him, of importance to everyone. If they could only see the city from where he saw it, could see how it was linked, built up, each part depending on the others, they wouldn't cause trouble anywhere, knowing that if they did they put everything at risk.

He continued to watch the news, at lunchtime, at teatime and in the evening before bed; but, while there were daily reports of violence it was on nothing like the scale it had been at the weekend. The deluge was reduced to a trickle and Belfast, in particular, appeared to be returning to normal. On the subject of his father, meanwhile, his mother offered nothing more, and Mal, for his part, asked nothing further of her.

Then, on Wednesday, everything at the house changed. First thing that morning, Uncle Simon drove to Larne to meet Cathy and Alex off the Stranraer ferry. They must have been warned in advance that Mal and his mother were staying, for they showed no surprise at seeing them when they came into the kitchen. They sat on high stools amid a rubble of bags and, while their mother made coffee, related all that had happened on holiday, Alex languidly undercutting Cathy's stories, Cathy fighting Alex for the punchlines to hers. They talked easily to their aunt, but took little more than polite notice of Mal, who kept in the background, overawed, as always, by their confident, outgoing manner. When they had eventually exhausted everything that was of prime importance to tell, they stumbled upstairs to unpack and show off the clothes they had picked up on Carnaby Street, coming through London.

Aunt Pat followed them into the hall.

'Ally?' she shouted. 'You're in with Cathy, love, for the time being. All right?'

There was a bump of a rucksack being dropped. Uncle Simon had evidently neglected to warn them of *that*.

'Oh, mu-um,' Alex groaned over the banister.

'It's only for a day or two,' Aunt Pat said, in a whisper that nevertheless sounded plainly in the kitchen. 'We'd to put Mal in your room.'

Mrs Martin smiled weakly at her brother, who fidgeted with his car keys by the back door. Mal closed his eyes, humiliated, thinking of the fear which had led him to ask to be moved from Cathy's room on Saturday night and which now kept him from even setting foot in it. He knew he was being irrational, that it was only a picture, but try as he might, he could not shake off the feeling that it was somehow accusing him.

'But why my room?' Alex insisted.

Aunt Pat looked swiftly over her shoulder into the kitchen and stepped on to the stairs. Her whisper was too low now to be understood, but the knowledge of what she must be saying only made Mal feel worse, and the silence in the kitchen seemed all the more glaring. Uncle Simon strode into the hall.

'Pat, get in that kitchen!' He watched her go, then spoke firmly to his daughters. 'Right, you two, you heard what your mother said. You're both to sleep in Cathy's room until told otherwise. Understand?'

Bags were dragged across Cathy's bedroom carpet.

'Do you understand?' Uncle Simon repeated.

His persistence was rewarded with a ready 'Yes, daddy,' from Cathy. His elder daughter's response was slower in coming.

'Understood,' she said curtly.

'Girls!' Aunt Pat laughed. 'They're so jealous of their space.'

'Oh, you've no need to tell me,' Mrs Martin placated her. 'I well remember what I was like. I screamed blue murder if I thought Simon so much as opened my door while I was out.'

She giggled behind her hand as her brother came through from the hall.

'I was just saying,' she told him. 'Nothing really changes, does it?'

He brushed past her without replying and snapped at his wife in a voice whose unexpected sharpness reminded Mal, momentarily, of his father's: 'Don't ever let me hear you make excuses to those wee girls again. They might think they're grown up, but they still have to answer to someone.'

He banged the back door on his way to the garage.

'Nothing really changes,' Mrs Martin said again and tittered.

Aunt Pat's bottom lip quivered, alternatively pale pink and a meaty bluish red.

'What are you watching?'

Cathy stood behind Mal, one hand resting on the back of the sofa.

'The Apollo launch,' Mal said. 'They're putting a man on the moon this time.'

'Cos-mic!' Alex said sarcastically, entering the room and flopping into an armchair so that her legs dangled over the side.

It had come on to rain during lunch and the afternoon had been blurred by drizzle. Mal's mother and aunt had gone shopping and Uncle Simon was in his garage workshop. He felt uncomfortably trapped with his cousins.

'Oh, shut up, you. Why d'you have to be so bored by everything?' Cathy said.

She sat down and Mal noted with a quickening of his pulse that she was wearing the patched denims he had borrowed on Saturday night when her mother had sat where she sat now.

'God,' she said, staring at the TV. 'Wouldn't get me in one of those.'

Alex balanced a loose sandal on the end of her foot and tutted, unimpressed. 'It's just a giant cock.'

'Alex!' Cathy croaked, pleasantly outraged by her sister's offhand comment.

Alex feigned surprise.

'What?'

Cathy twitched her head at Mal, as if to say Alex should watch her mouth in front of him.

'If Simon was to hear that coming from you he'd have your life.'

Alex lay back over the arm of the chair and spread her arms apart. Her long hair trailed the hearth and she jiggled her head, chanting nonchalantly: 'Cock, cock, cock, cock, cock, cock, cock.'

Cathy squeezed against the back cushion of the sofa, her fist pressed to her mouth, and Mal was so astonished he forgot to be embarrassed.

'Cock, cock, cock ...'

The back door's rubber draft excluder squeaked across the kitchen floor. Alex swung her legs off the arm of the chair on to the ground before her, sitting bolt upright, and Cathy gulped a lungful of air. Uncle Simon came in, looking from face to face, puzzled by the unnatural silence.

'What are you all up to?' he asked, adopting his most vacuous expression.

'We're thrilling to the rocket launch,' Alex drawled. Her cheeks were still flushed from hanging upside down.

'Of course,' Uncle Simon said, with an almost boyish excitement. 'It's the moon shot, isn't it?'

As he crossed the room to the armchair by the television, Alex leaned over to the settee and mouthed the word 'cock' at her sister, flicking her tongue savagely in and out her lips for punctuation. Cathy's face coloured and swelled with pent-up laughter; she gripped Mal's arm in an effort to contain herself, her varnish-hardened nails piercing his nylon pullover.

Pain made him flinch and another time he might not have been able to stop himself crying out. But this was the first he could remember having been close to either of the girls, ceasing to be simply their younger cousin. He bit his lip till Cathy finally pulled herself together and the pressure of her nails eased.

That evening, after the dishes had been done, Cathy was waiting for him halfway up the stairs and motioned him to follow her to the top.

'Thanks a lot for this afternoon,' she said when they reached the landing. 'I didn't hurt you too much, did I?'

Mal shook his head, but Cathy sensed he wasn't telling the truth and caught hold of his left arm, pushing back his sleeve. Three blue-purple crescents indented the flesh below his elbow.

'Oh, I'm terrible,' she said, bashful. Then, brightening again she asked: 'Want to listen to records with us?'

She turned and went into her room, assuming he was right behind her; but Mal hung back. Still that picture haunted him, reminding him of the giddy instants before he collapsed in the garden. Reminding him ultimately of Francy. He knew then what the eyes were accusing him of: he had denied Francy, and broken the promise he made on the dump.

'Aren't you coming?' Cathy poked her head around the door frame.

He might have to stay here for days yet, for all he knew; he couldn't waste such a chance to start getting on better with his cousins by being foolish and childish. And then, too, he thought, he could not have known when he swore his oath what Francy had planned for the centre pole. Yet he had let slip its where-abouts *before* the ceremony had properly begun. He was sure now that Francy had tricked him and that the conditions of his pledge no longer applied.

He walked boldly into the room, although it felt for a moment like there was an eyelash in his right eye and he was that busy rubbing it he didn't get to look at the wall. He crouched on the floor with his back to the bed.

Alex's stare was far from welcoming. She pulled the door behind him, pointedly inserting her foot lengthways against the jamb and stopping it with her toe.

'Always leave the bedroom door at least a foot ajar,' she said gruffly, doubling her chin and raising her brows in an expression of wide-eyed innocence. 'Otherwise the bad air will make you sluggish and irritable.' She fell back on the bed and went on wearily in her own voice: 'Worse still, you might actually have some fun.'

Cathy ignored her and continued sorting through a rack of records.

'Uncle Simon's not that bad, is he?' Mal asked.

Alex rolled to the edge of the bed so that her hair fell across his shoulder and he could feel her breath warm on his neck when she spoke.

'You'd better believe it, small boy.'

Mal recoiled. She never called him by his proper name, but it had been some time since she referred to him as 'the small boy'. It was an unkind reminder of how things stood between himself and the girls before this afternoon.

'D'you think we like playing records here night after night?' she asked him. 'We do it because it's about the only thing we're allowed to do. No going out unless daddy drives us there and back and no driving anywhere at all if he considers it unsuitable. Which leaves us with the church and not much else.' She stared at the ceiling. 'Hypocrite.'

Cathy turned, holding the arm of the record player poised over an LP.

'I wouldn't say that ...'

'No?' Alex got up from the bed and walked in long, lazy strides to the window. 'Well, what would you say, then? What would you say about someone who gets all high and mighty churchy where his daughters are concerned, but can never be arsed to set foot in one himself? Hm? What would you say?'

Cathy thought about it, pursing her lips.

'I don't know, but not hypocrite,' she said weakly, lowering the needle on to the record.

'Well, that, sister of mine,' Alex waved a hand airily, 'is where you and I differ.' Then as the chop chords of an acoustic guitar and Ringo Starr's flat, nasal voice drifted from the speaker, she pointed to the record player with exaggerated disdain. 'As is *that*.'

'Give my head peace,' Cathy said, stretching out on her back and studying the record sleeve close to her nose.

'The Beatles are all very well, Ca-ther-ine,' Alex pouted, flicking her hair back melodramatically and draping a hand over her shoulder as though she held a cigarette. 'But your father and

I don't want them for breakfast, dinner and tea, thank you very much. Besides,' her voice became whining and antagonistic, 'it's kiddies' music.'

She stomped about the room, legs rigid, arms straight before her.

'Dum. Dum. Dum.'

She sang the simple tune, twisting her face to look like Frankenstein's monster; then she skipped from side to side, pretending to hold the hem of a short dress between thumb and forefinger as she joined in the chorus, a cutesie five-year-old.

> We all live in a yellow submarine,
> Yellow submarine, yellow submarine.

She had reached the bed again and sat down heavily on it.

'Don't you agree?' she asked Mal.

Mal had watched her performance, fascinated, and was as surprised to hear himself addressed as he would have been had the television suddenly called him by name. He didn't quite know what to say. He remembered having sung the song at a Sunday-school party and thought that backed up what Alex said, but Cathy was looking at him expectantly and he couldn't bring himself to disappoint her.

Alex cackled, a laugh of such pitch and endurance that only sheer force of will could have sustained it.

'The small boy's afraid to speak in case he offends Cathy. He fancies her. Imagine! Fancies his own cousin.'

'Wise up,' Cathy said, but Alex kept on laughing.

'He does. He does.'

An accusing finger hung limp over the side of the bed. Cathy scurried over on all fours and bit it, briefly but sharply. Alex yelped in pain.

'You fucking cow,' she shouted and leapt at Cathy, landing on the floor with a thud and trailing her to the carpet.

There was a scuffle too at that moment at the foot of the stairs.

'Right,' Uncle Simon shouted. 'What's going on up there?'

'Leave it to me, leave it to me,' Aunt Pat pleaded.

Her footsteps sounded on the stairs and Cathy and Alex rolled apart, punching each other in the small of the back. Mal was already at the door, clawing it open. The telephone rang and Aunt Pat halted.

'Quieten down and stop all the rough-housing,' she cautioned, then tumbled down the stairs in her haste to reach the telephone. 'It's okay, Simon. I've got it.'

Mal backed out of the room, unnoticed by the girls, who continued to eye each other warily. He was shocked into complete silence by Alex's suggestion. But then he thought of Cathy's legs against the denim of her patchwork jeans, of his own legs in them on Saturday night, of the image of his aunt, naked on the toilet. He slumped in the semi-darkness at the top of the stairs, nursing his head in pained confusion.

In the hallway below, he made out the furious whispers of his mother and aunt. Aunt Pat had covered the mouthpiece of the telephone with her hand and was offering the receiver to his mother. But she was having none of it.

'Tell him I'm not here.'

'I can't. I've already said he could speak to you.'

'Well, then, tell him I'm ... having a bath.'

'Come off it, he'll know that's a lie.'

'No he won't. Anyway, so what if he does?'

Mr Martin's telephone-distorted voice called Pat's name and she put the receiver to her ear again.

'Yes, yes, I'm still here,' she assured him. 'Ah, listen, do you think you could ring back later? Only she's in the bath right now.'

Mrs Martin knelt by the banister, gnawing the flesh of her upper arm, crooked about her neck. There was a long pause, during which Aunt Pat held the phone out once more for her to hear.

'Okay then, Pat.'

Mal heard the words, weak, thin and acquiescent. There was

a click and the dialling tone burred. His aunt and mother looked at each other an instant, then spluttered with laughter.

Feeling too awkward now to reveal himself, Mal decided to go to Alex's room. But, as he passed again by Cathy's open door, she called him inside. Alex was kneeling behind her sister, braiding her hair. She appeared to have altered her opinion of the Beatles, for she was singing along now, unsarcastically, to the record.

> One, two, three, four, can I have a little more?
> Five, six, seveneightnine, ten, I love you.

'Say sorry, Alex,' Cathy ordered her, through her fringe.

'Sorry,' Alex said and grinned, 'Small boy.'

The name didn't sound anything like as bad as it had earlier, Mal smiled back.

'Thanks for having me up.'

'Whenever you want,' Cathy said and waved clumsily so as not to lose her balance.

Alex wagged her head from side to side and it was hard to tell if she was saying goodbye or keeping time to the music. Mal made to leave the room, forgetting until it was too late to avert his eyes from the wall above the bed. He realised immediately, however, that the picture there now was not the one that had troubled him so much at the weekend. The eyes of this one were not rat-like and reproachful, but deep, shining, even inviting.

'That picture,' he murmured.

Alex glanced up.

'Mm. You like it?'

'Yes, yes. But the other one …'

'Lennon?' Cathy said, hair-blinded. 'I told Ally to hide it somewhere out of my sight. I hate him. He'd have broken them up by now if it hadn't been for Paul.'

'And,' Alex mimed absently, swaying with the rhythm.

'And,' Cathy continued, 'he married that witch.'

Mal gazed longingly at the picture. He'd found a new hero.

'See you,' he said.

'All together now,' the record exhorted.

'All together now,' Cathy and Alex returned.

'All together now ... All together now ... All together now ...'

The next time Mr Martin called, Aunt Pat told him his wife wasn't at home, even though she was in the lounge watching television. But when the phone rang the following evening at dinner, Mrs Martin herself sprang out to the hall to answer it.

She was away, though, for what seemed only seconds. Uncle Simon showed no interest in her coming and going and made a point of talking loudly over both about tennis, a pet subject. Aunt Pat watched eagerly as her sister-in-law smoothed her skirt and got into her seat before asking her a question with her eyebrows. But Mrs Martin's only response was a fond glance at her son, which caused him to concentrate on his plate in a vain attempt to press peas on to his fork. Patience was not one of Aunt Pat's strong points. She tried one more facial question, then could wait no longer.

'Well?' she enquired aloud.

Uncle Simon's monologue had petered out and the girls' attention strayed to their mother and aunt. Unabashed, Mrs Martin spread more butter on her bread than was her custom. Aunt Pat was becoming exasperated.

'Are you going to tell me or not?'

Uncle Simon looked at the two women, his features betraying his conviction that they and the rest of their sex were beyond understanding.

'Of course, Newcombe really ought to have won Wimbledon.' He spoke in a sudden desperate burst, tapping Cathy's wrist with the flat of his knife. 'I mean, he is far and away the most accomplished player on the circuit.'

Below the resurrected tennis conversation, Mrs Martin spoke at last, calm and unhurried.

'He wanted to know why I hadn't come to the phone before and when I said I would have if I'd been in he called me a liar and lost his temper.'

Aunt Pat looked indignant on her behalf, but when nothing more was forthcoming, her frustration returned and she gave a little vexed squeak, which even Uncle Simon's vigorous denouncement of Rod Laver failed to drown totally. Mrs Martin seemed almost to be enjoying herself.

'So, I told him he would never have got away with that in the old days and that he'd no right to think he could now. Then I hung up.'

Aunt Pat smiled her amusement and admiration, but her husband appeared cross, and a vein wormed across the chafed red skin at his hairline.

'Will you girls clear the table please?' he asked, rising from the table and walking through the archway to the lounge.

Cathy stacked the used plates, cups and saucers and Aunt Pat fumbled in the pocket of her cardigan for her cigarettes. Mal's mother squeezed his arm affectionately, but she caught the still tender prints of Cathy's nails and Mal eased his arm out of her grasp.

'Never mind all that,' she said quietly, misinterpreting his movement. 'It's just a bit of fun. Your daddy's getting everything sorted out at home. We'll all be back together before long, you'll see.'

Mal was far from comforted by her assurances, although he did his best to conceal it. He thought of the last time he had seen his father, bloodied and dishevelled on the living room floor. He thought of him at the bonfire, swaying drunkenly from side to side, hanging on to anyone within reach. He thought of the fight and the violence the next day. Down there in the city was where the trouble was. It was different here. He had seen a change come over his mother, so that she barely resembled the woman who had haunted the kitchen of the Everest Street house all these months. Even in the happiest times there she never came close to the mood of this week, which she and Aunt Pat passed like school friends; seldom apart, talking, laughing, shopping, even trying on make-up together at the mirror on Aunt Pat's dressing table.

The table was cleared and Aunt Pat rested her elbows on it, lighting a cigarette.

'Pat, do you mind if I have one of those?'

Mal saw his mother take the cigarette precariously in the tips of her fingers and draw back her head in quick jerks as every puff enveloped her head in dense, pale smoke. He didn't find it anything like as unusual as he would have a week ago.

His father's phone calls became more and more frequent, and each time he rang his mother spoke a little longer. Mal was forced to admit that much of her change of mood had to be attributed to the fact that, although apart, she and his father were hitting it off in a way they had not done for some considerable time. He himself felt as fit and well as he had ever done, if not slightly stronger; in a matter of days, his bottle of tonic was pushed to the back of the bathroom cabinet and forgotten. There was a steady improvement in the news from around the Province – Mal watched now only in the evening and then more in the cursory manner he had used to – until, by the end of the week, the troubles of the Twelfth were as distant and unreal to his mind as the delusions brought on by his exhaustion.

He began to take it for granted that he would be included in all that his cousins did. Not that they did much. They divided their time between Cathy's room and the lounge, when there was no one else there. Together they charted the progress of the Apollo moon shot, although Mal struggled with the idea of a rocket travelling through the no-atmosphere of space and had to check regularly on the neat, grey paisley-patterned planet in the corner of the screen to convince himself of what he was watching.

On Sunday, after dinner, the three of them played in the garden with the football, Mal kicking it and the girls catching and throwing it back. After a short time, however, Uncle Simon shouted at them to mind the roses and Alex walked away, saying that football gave her a sore ear, to spend the rest of the afternoon in the shade of the garage, painting with poster paints on a sheet of pink card. When she had finished she hung the card with clothes pegs on the washing line. Mal looked at it, perplexed and disappointed. The painting was dreadful: bright random swirls of unmixed yellows, reds and blues, and in the centre a tiny square of black, under which were written the words: *You Are Here*.

'It's a street map,' Cathy told him, by way of explanation.

'A world map,' Alex corrected her, and wagged her head to a song running through her mind.

4

A hand touched Mal's cheek.

'It's time.'

He crawled from under the quilt, eyes sealed green with sleep, and shuffled on to the landing.

'It's a sin to wake him.'

'He asked.'

By the lounge door his mother, dressed in a towelling house-coat, waited for him in the almost daylight.

'All right?'

He tried to speak, but the words were lost in a face-stretching yawn which moistened his caked eyes. He nodded tiredly. His mother guided him to the sofa, where Aunt Pat, in movements that whispered of silk beneath her dressing gown, draped his shoulders with a blue blanket. His cousins sat on the floor before the sofa, Alex zipped into a sleeping bag, Cathy's long T-shirt making a tent for her legs which she hugged to her chest. Mal forced his eyes open and shut to rid them of blear, focusing on the television.

A squat capsule bulged into view on the left of the screen, pressing down on Meccano-spindly legs that you would have sworn could not have supported its bulk on earth. Steps descended from its blank side to a wilderness of white rock beneath. Mal had expected the surface to be curved, but, instead, all was flat and uniform; a near perfect straight line, two-thirds the way up the picture, separated the rocky waste from the blackness of space. Voices, distorted like long-distance telephone calls, jabbered incoherently, and Uncle Simon leaned forward in his armchair.

'Here he comes,' he said. His hair stood on end, as though his face alone could no longer adequately express his amazement. Turn it up.'

Alex caterpillared to the television and switched the volume up full. A cacophony of hisses and crackles, punctuated by long, piercing beeps, swamped the lounge's silence as the cabin door was opened.

An arm, distinguishable by the minute grey markings of the flag on the shoulder flash, appeared against the white, and grew into an astronaut. He moved down the steps in a fuzzy, weightless bob, jumping from the last one like a deep-sea diver off a boat.

'That's one small step for a man, one giant leap for mankind.'

'Russians take a rotten tomato,' Alex said under her breath, and Cathy laughed noiselessly, so that only the tremor of her shoulders gave her away.

There was no earth now in the corner of the screen and Mal's eyebrows puckered as he tried desperately to believe in what he was hearing: words carrying from behind a blank helmet visor, over the moon's surface waste, through thousands of miles of no-coloured void, to a planet, a ball suspended – how? where? – in space.

I am here, he told himself, in this room, in this house, on this street, in this country, on this island … But already he could feel himself losing control and the enormity of the distances swirled inside his head, making a nonsense of his efforts. He concentrated on the smooth leather of the cushion beneath his bottom and thighs, willing himself to become, with it, an unquestionable part of all that surrounded him: mother, uncle, aunt, cousins, in the almost daylight of the lounge, watching television. He banished from his mind any thoughts of the vastness of space. The astronaut waved. In his visor was reflected the capsule, the capsule whose camera filmed him. Waving reflecting. Encapsulated within the television set, which Mal's mother, uncle, aunt, cousins watched. Which Mal watched, forcing his weight upon the cushion. Merging.

Mal sat up in bed, shielding his eyes from the artificial glare of the electric light. On the covers of Alex's bed, sunlight bubbled and flowed in time to the blinds gently blowing in the morning breeze. He shook himself fully awake, banishing dream images from his mind; identifying them, neutralising them. For a time, though, as he dressed, one lodged there unexplained. A helmeted pilot, waving. Only when he switched off the light and left the room did he succeed in placing him. In those first moments of waking, the sight of a man walking on the moon seemed to belong more to the world of dreams than the real world.

His mother and aunt, still in their housecoats, were in the kitchen, hunched over a catalogue spread on the countertop.

'Where is everyone?' Mal asked.

'Hm?' Aunt Pat looked up, a broken halo of smoke writhing above her head.

Mrs Martin snaked out a hand and stroked his arm.

'No kisses this morning? Still tired?'

'I'm okay.' He walked to the kitchen window. 'Are they outside?'

'Your Uncle Simon was called out to a meeting.'

It wasn't his uncle he had in mind.

'I should hope it's important, whatever it is,' Mrs Martin said. 'Ringing him like that in the middle of the holidays.'

'Holidays make no difference to Simon,' Aunt Pat griped. This is him all the time with that damned business.'

Mal let them finish.

'What about Cathy and Alex?'

'I'm the last person to ask. They tell me nothing,' said Aunt Pat. Town, I expect. They were away first thing. I'm only surprised we've seen so much of them this past few days.' She leaned across the breakfast bar to her sister-in-law. Their father, you know, doesn't like them out on their own. But what can you do?'

Mrs Martin tutted, understanding. 'Nothing, can you?'

'Nights, now, well that's different, of course …'

'Of course,' Mrs Martin echoed. 'Of course.'

'But you can't keep them in the house all the time.'

Mal was already out the back door, crossing the patio. His brain was so full it felt empty, and, stooping to collect the caser from where he'd left it the previous day, he noted without curiosity the square of shadow fluttering on the grass close to his nose. He straightened and bounced the ball on it, once, twice, then swayed a little as the shadow wavered to the left and the right; bouncing the ball, once, twice. Gradually the shadow folded over upon itself, growing smaller as it approached him and he retreated, still bouncing the ball. He took a final step backwards and the only shadow cast now was his own. A knife-edged sharpness trailed the back of his neck and he spun on his heel. Alex's painting flapped stiffly in his face.

His mind suddenly focused, Mal kicked the ball ferociously against the garage wall, trapping it as it bobbled back and kicking it again. Again and again he thumped the ball in a rage of disappointment and frustration. They had appeared to be getting on so well and then the minute Uncle Simon was out the house …

Thump, thump, thump, the ball struck the garage wall, until, by degrees, the game itself came to preoccupy him and he thought only of volleys and half-volleys, side-foots and headers. His playing had improved beyond all recognition since he had been at his aunt and uncle's, although he still had to have his wits about him to compensate for the ball's swelling. He commentated on fictitious games, in which he played for Northern Ireland, inventing players to line up beside the few stars whose names he actually knew.

'Mal!'

His mother's voice broke in as he drew his foot to score yet another goal from his long career. He had gone too far to stop, but when he followed through, he caught the bump with his instep, making a complete hash of it. He must get a proper ball.

His mother was dressed now, in a pair of flared slacks and a halter-neck top which hung like a vest on her narrow body. Mal saw then what he had not seen in the photo his aunt showed him all those months ago: his mother had been young once, was, even now, not yet old.

'Do you like it?' she asked shyly, plucking a ruffled shoulder strap. 'It's Cathy's. Aunt Pat says she doesn't wear it anymore ...'

Mal nodded, equally shy, uncomfortable in the stare of this woman, his mother, in whose face his own was sketched, who was so much a part of him and so much beyond his knowledge.

'I was speaking to your daddy on the phone just now.'

Mal nodded again, knowing what was coming. His mother was excited and happy. A part and apart. He supposed he was happy too.

'Aunt Pat's asked him for dinner tonight.'

'Good,' Mal said, wishing for his mother's sake that he could have sounded more enthusiastic.

But that single word was all she needed. She smiled broadly and passed an arm around his shoulders that were her shoulders too.

'Didn't I say it wouldn't be too long before we were back together again?'

'You did,' Mal agreed and his mother's bony fingers twitched convulsively as she led him towards the house.

Mal was in the kitchen helping his mother and aunt peel and chop vegetables for dinner when Uncle Simon came in from his meeting, much earlier than expected. He skipped down the hall and messed Mal's hair in a jovial, pally way, then grabbed Aunt Pat by the waist and swung her around. She squealed and dropped the knife she had been using to dice carrots.

'Simon!' she yelled, but he took no notice and swung her again. 'Simon!'

He set her on the tiled floor and she rested one hand on the countertop to steady herself, fending him off with the other.

'I could have had your eye out with that knife, if I hadn't thought to let go,' she admonished in as stern a voice as she could muster.

'Well, you may be thankful you didn't,' Uncle Simon said indignantly, drawing himself up to his full height, level with his sister. 'Because' – he pointed to his brow with a dramatic flourish – 'these eyes foresee *big money!*'

Mal looked at his uncle's eyes, pale and watery, dry skin flaking at the corners of the lids.

Aunt Pat's own eyes widened and he gripped her arms to her sides, bracing her for what he was about to say.

'That conman McCandless has been rumbled at last – the firm's gone bankrupt. He was all set to roll on a Housing Trust contract and now they've had to award it to somebody else. And who do you think that somebody else is?'

'Oh, Simon!'

Aunt Pat hugged him, but he pulled away excitedly.

'They want us on site straight after the Twelfth Fortnight. Only four streets of twenty to start, but there'll be more. So put all this food in the fridge – the bin, even – we're eating out tonight.'

Aunt Pat made a discreet gesture towards Mal and his mother.

'Actually, Simon, we've company this evening.'

Uncle Simon threw back his head and laughed.

'Excellent,' he said. The more the merrier. We're in with the Housing Trust, now. We're made.'

'That's marvellous, love.' Mrs Martin kissed her brother.

'Marvellous is bloody right,' he told her and swung her once for good measure. 'And you'll never guess where it is? Right up by you in that bit of a wood.'

'The woods?' Mal was stunned into speech.

'Yep,' his uncle said. 'Know it?'

'That's where we have our bonfire.'

('Bonfires? Orange parades?' Uncle Simon would often scoff. 'I've better things to do than be bothered with that carry on.')

'Oh, yes,' he said. 'How *could* I forget?'

But nothing was going to spoil this mood, if he could help it.

'What do you say – maybe there'll be a job in it for you. Someone who could show us around might come in useful.'

'Up by us?' Mrs Martin said haltingly. 'A job?'

Uncle Simon's banter dried up. A pained expression came over his face; the joke was going badly wrong. He jerked a thumb unconvincingly at Mal.

'Aw, now, look, I was only having the wee fella on. It's not that simple. I can't just go giving out jobs to … There's the other partners … Pat?' he appealed to his wife, 'isn't that the case, Pat?'

Aunt Pat narrowed her eyes and returned to the vegetables. Uncle Simon kneaded his temples with his knuckles.

'Come on,' he complained. 'This was supposed to be a big day. I didn't want to start any of this.'

The telephone rang and Mrs Martin dashed from the kitchen, relieved. Uncle Simon stared at his wife's back and at her elbow, rising and falling as she chopped the carrots. He turned to Mal and shrugged, Stan Laurel.

'The woods?' Mal asked him, and in his mind's eye he saw once more Francy's conjured hordes descending on the empty houses.

Mrs Martin tiptoed in from the hall.

'That's for you, Simon.'

She waited till he had left the room, then whispered to Aunt Pat. 'I'm sorry, I just thought …'

'Michael, hello.' It was a more cheerful Uncle Simon who spoke into the telephone. 'What can I do for you, my man?'

151

'Don't apologise,' Aunt Pat hissed. 'What's family for, for heaven's sake?'

'Only it would mean so much to him, you can't imagine.'

'He's *what*?' Uncle Simon's groan silenced their whispers. 'Oh, my good God!'

Mal's mother motioned him to shut the hall door, but Aunt Pat shook her head and edged towards it, listening.

'I don't believe it. I just don't believe it. Fine payment that is for taking heed of all that bunk and hiring him ... Catch yourself on, Michael, people don't get arrested for no reason. What's a working man doing hanging around with a bunch of students in the first instance? He's asking for trouble.'

Uncle Simon paced the hall carpet, his face glowing redder as his voice became ever more shrill.

'Court, nothing. I'm not waiting that long. How's it going to look with the Housing Trust if our name gets dragged through the courts over this?'

He mulled over something, straining saliva through his teeth.

'Send him his cards.'

The voice on the other end of the line began to remonstrate. Uncle Simon listened first impassively, then impatiently, and finally cut it short.

'I don't care what *they* say. I'm the senior bloody partner and that's an end to it. All right? Now, I don't want to hear another word ... Michael, I said not another word.'

He slammed down the receiver, looking at it a while longer, as though it might at any moment jump up and answer him back. From the kitchen doorway the faces of his wife and sister stared at him. He held up both hands to prevent them speaking.

'I know what you're thinking and you can forget it at once,' he said. 'It's not the same thing. Not the same thing at all.'

The faces in the doorway remained blank. Uncle Simon sagged against the stairs, demoralised.

'Okay, okay,' he muttered into the underfelt. 'I'll see what I can do. That's all I'm saying: I'll see.'

152

He stiffened, fighting to regain some semblance of dignity.

'Will that do?' he asked his sister. 'Satisfied?' he asked his wife.

He marched through the kitchen and pulled open the back door, bumping into Cathy and Alex.

'Hello, daddy.' Cathy was breathless with surprise. 'You're home early.'

'Yes, I am, amn't I? And where have you two been?'

'Out,' Alex replied, plucking a fat purple grape from the half-eaten bunch on the sideboard.

'What do you mean "out"?'

'As opposed to in,' she said, without turning.

Uncle Simon gawped, then bounded across the kitchen, laying his hand on her shoulder and birling her about. He slapped her hard with his left hand and immediately jumped back, as if in shock. Alex dropped the grape. Her eyes brimmed with tears, but she refused to cry. Uncle Simon retreated towards the door, one forefinger pointing at Alex, the rest of his body trembling with the effort of keeping it steady.

'Hear me good,' he warned. 'There's been too much has been let get away with in this house lately. Well, there's to be no more of it. Understand? I've told your mother, we're going out for dinner tonight as a family, so I want you two girls cleaned and dressed *properly* by the time I come back in. You're celebrating with us, like it or not.'

The back door jarred and banged shut at the second attempt. Aunt Pat lit a cigarette, reducing a third of it to ash with three deep draws.

'You shouldn't goad your father like that. You know you're only asking for it.'

Alex ground her teeth together, willing the tears from her eyes, so that the heat of her anger seemed to dry them. Uncle Simon's handprint rose on her cheek, an angry red welt.

'I'm the way I am because he's the way he is.' She bent to pick up the bruised grape. 'It's not me that's asking for it.'

5

Mal sat stiffly on the sofa. His neck was already raw where his mother had scrubbed it and now the rigid collar of his new nylon shirt was bringing him out in a rash. Alex sauntered into the lounge, pulled Mal's red tie to his waist, then let it snap back on its elastic against his throat.

'You look so stupid,' she said, and switched on the television.

She wore a bright yellow, sleeveless dress, and Mal, who had seen neither of his cousins in anything other than jeans since they were bridesmaids two summers before, thought to get back at her by teasing her about it. But, in fact, the dress suited Alex. The colour set off her auburn hair, which she had tied in a ponytail, and the simple, straight cut made her body seem somehow less girlish. Mal had always thought Cathy was the looker in the family – everyone else said so – but now he wasn't so sure. The dress ended two inches short of her knees, just past the line above which she did not shave, and Mal stared at her pale, unsunned calves.

'Didn't know you had legs,' he said feebly.

Alex stopped fiddling with the tuning dial and minced across the floor.

'These legs,' she drawled, in her mother's voice, 'used to drive all the boys *wild* with excitement … in 1922.'

She sprawled in an armchair and sucked the end of her pony-tail. Her mood was brittle, and Mal, who was nervous enough as it was, hoped that Cathy would appear to lighten the atmosphere. But it was a forlorn hope.

'Where is it we're going?' he asked at length, reckoning that Alex talking was less worrying than Alex silently brooding.

'The Wayfarers. Over your end of town. Don't you know it?'

'Nah, it's ages since we ate out.'

'But, of course,' Alex gibed. 'You're our poor relations now, aren't you?'

'We're not poor,' Mal protested. 'Just because my dad's been out of work, don't think we have to depend on youse.'

Alex clapped her hands and cackled deep in her throat to see her cousin riled.

'I'm joking. I'm joking.'

'Well, you don't hear me laughing,' Mal shouted.

Alex swallowed her snigger, realising she had hurt him. 'I'm sorry,' she said, genuinely vexed. 'I'm a dopy bitch sometimes. I just don't think.'

Mal still seethed, his annoyance fuelled by the knowledge that Alex was right. He knew his mother hadn't had to fork out for a single thing since they came to stay; he knew where the very shirt came from that irritated his neck; and he knew where his father's best chance of a job now lay.

'It doesn't matter,' he said, though his jaw remained set hard.

'Who wants to be rich anyway?' Alex asked, 'when you see what having money does?'

She didn't have to explain herself, the bitterness in her voice said it all. Mal looked at her face. A faint swelling beside her eye, the imprint of a wedding ring, was the only hint now of the blow from Uncle Simon's hand.

'D'you think your dad's sorry?' Mal asked, his own pain paling.

'Sure he is,' Alex answered. 'Till the next time.'

155

'Why does there have to be a next time?'

'There just does. Nothing's ever settled, just let drop for a while. But it always comes back. Always, always, always.'

She tucked her ponytail under her chin.

'Ever wonder what you might be like if you had other parents, if you were born somewhere like ... oh, I don't know – Africa?'

'I'd be a Negro.'

'Yes.' Alex sat forward. 'Have you ever thought about that?'

'No.'

Mal was lying. He had thought it many times when his mother and father's fighting was at its worst. Indeed, he had asked much the same question of Francy on the afternoon spent in his hut on the dump. Francy dismissed the subject scornfully: you were what you were, and it was pointless to speculate. Mal rehashed Francy's argument and presented it as his own.

'If I had different parents I wouldn't be me at all. I'd be somebody else altogether, so how could I know?'

Alex heaved a sigh and slid out of the chair on to the carpet.

'But still ...,' she said. 'Everything's so haphazard. I mean, why did we have to get born here? Here of all places ...'

But before she could go any further, the door handle clicked and Alex scrambled off the floor.

'Hi,' she said with a convincing smile.

Mal glanced over the back of the sofa. Aunt Pat, a towel turbaned about her head, was showing his father into the lounge.

'I've a feeling Simon wants a word with you,' she was saying.

'Oh, aye? And what might that be about?'

Aunt Pat locked her hands together and giggled a borrowed giggle.

'Now, you should know better than to ask me about Simon's business. Some new contract he's landed. I'm not sure, but it sounds like good news. Can't think why he didn't mention it when he phoned to change the arrangements.'

Her voice trailed off into silence. Mal's eyes had met his

father's. Mr Martin passed a hand across his neatly Brylcreemed hair. His face was washed ruddy and his suit had been dry-cleaned.

'Hello,' he said, but Mal was already looking away.

'Right then, Mal,' Aunt Pat resumed briskly. 'I'll leave you in charge. Get your dad anything he wants, your mummy'll be down in a minute. She's just finishing getting ready.'

'Never watch a woman while she dresses,' Mal's father told everyone and no one. 'Like buying buns from the shop: you don't enjoy eating them half so much when you've seen what goes into the making of them.'

He hurtled through the latter part of the sentence, as though he regretted ever having started it. Aunt Pat twiddled the stitching of the towel where her hair normally hung down.

'Well, I'd better get this dried if we're to be off soon.'

She ushered Alex out of the door and drew it softly behind them, leaving Mal and his father alone in the lounge.

Mr Martin dug his hands in his trouser pockets, jingling the loose change. He whistled in his own peculiar way – not a blow, but a thin hiss squeezed between his teeth – and wandered to the hearth, where he pulled his hands from his pockets, smoothing the legs of his trousers and straightening his tie before the large mirror over the mantelpiece. He patted the knot satisfactorily, inspected his chin for shaving nicks, then spoke to his son's reflection: 'Mind if I sit down?'

In all his years, Mal had never heard a more stupid question. His father could do whatever he liked without asking his permission. He didn't bother to answer. Mr Martin pursed his lips and crossed the room to the bay window. He rested his forehead on the leaded pane.

'Some view, right enough,' he mused.

Stepping back, he wiped with a thumb the greasy mark left by his hair cream.

'All the same, gets quer and cold up here in the winter. Wouldn't fancy that, would you?'

157

At that moment, Mal despised his father. He hated him for the falseness of his chatter, for the pretence that nothing whatsoever had happened these past few weeks, and for taking him to be an idiot. Alex's gloomy prophecy resounded in his mind: nothing was ever settled, just let drop for a while; but it always came back – always, always, always.

'So you weren't well for a while?' Mr Martin was casting about in desperation. 'You seem to be over it all right now.'

He smiled and for an instant you would have believed that Uncle Simon was his, and not his wife's, brother.

'You're looking a fair bit better yourself.' Mal spoke at last, and if he could have said the words any more viciously he would have.

His father slumped against the windowsill.

'Ah, son,' he whispered, wounded. He took three shaky steps to the armchair by the TV. 'Mind if I ...? No, no, of course you don't.'

But he remained standing. His knuckles blanched as he gripped the back of the chair and looked squarely at his son. 'You've every right to say that.'

Mal had had enough, he didn't want to hear this. He was about to get up off the sofa, but his father made a sudden dart in front of him, pinning him against the back cushion.

'No you don't. You can sit here and listen to me a minute.'

Mal had no option. His father loomed over him and he wilted beneath his bulk and the overpowering smells of Brylcreem, Fairy toilet soap and a chemically cleaned suit.

'Let's not kid ourselves. I was becoming a drunk. I was making a laughing stock not just of myself, but of you and your mother as well. But that's history now. I've changed since the two of you left and I'll never revert back so long as I live. I swear.'

Not once while he spoke did his stare relent.

'I can't expect you to believe me straight away – I wish you would, but I can't expect it. That's the hardest thing for me to have to say. But your mother's told me she's prepared to come home, and I'm going to do all I can to show her she's made the right decision. So, if you'll only give me the chance, give us all the chance, well ...'

He had run out of words and his grip on his son relaxed. He sank on to the sofa beside him, limp.

Mal's gaze fell on his father's rough, clean hand, twisting the middle button of his jacket. The button's stitched core was a lighter blue than the rest of the suit. Mal recognised the thread from home and knew his mother would never have used it to strengthen a button on a suit that colour. He knew then, too, that Alex was wrong – there didn't always have to be a next time. What was true for Uncle Simon wasn't true for his father. He had admitted his mistakes and even acknowledged that Mal must still have his doubts. He wasn't trying to fool anybody. But the past was the past was the past.

Mal threw his arms about his father's neck, kissing his cheek. Mr Martin was startled rigid, but Mal clung to him all the harder and gradually he yielded, tension leaking from him in a prolonged sigh.

'Oh, son.'

He hugged his boy, fingers squeezing tentatively, stopping, shifting a little and trying again, like someone picking up an accordion after an interval of many years. Bit by bit, his touch came back to him and he collapsed Mal against his body, as though wanting to mould the two of them together. When they broke apart, Mal noticed that his father's eyes gleamed wetly.

'Oh, here,' he started, bluffly self-conscious. 'Nearly went clean out of my head.'

He fetched a plastic bag from the hallway and proffered it to Mal.

'This is for you.'

Inside the bag was a brown-papered parcel. Its shape was a dead giveaway, but Mal resisted the temptation to tear the paper to shreds and instead picked carefully at the Sellotape, his baffled expression kept in place by the strength of his resolve not to disappoint his father. The paper peel came away in a single, intact sheet and Mal held in his hands a brand-new, bright orange, leather football.

'What do you think?'

'It's brilliant,' he said, and the surprise on his face now was only half dissembled. For, aside from being completely and perfectly round, this was an actual professional caser, regulation size and weight for the Football League. 'But how did you know I wanted one?'

Mal knew well enough how his father had known, and his father knew he knew; but they both played along.

His father shrugged. 'What else do boys ever want?'

No one on the estate had a ball like this. It must have cost a packet. Mal sniffed the taut leather, imagining himself on a never-ending dribble through a maze of impressed faces.

'Hey, not now,' his father called, and Mal realised he had strayed to the door. 'We'll be going in a minute. Anyway, you've got your good clothes on.'

They laughed together at Mal's forgetfulness. Father and son.

'What's this? A new football? Suppose you won't be wanting my old one anymore.'

Uncle Simon had entered through the archway from the dining room. Mal damned him for turning up at that moment and felt for the first time the desire to be away from this house and back on Everest Street with his parents.

'Simon.' Mr Martin pumped his hand and clasped his arm familiarly. 'How's it going?'

'Bearing up. Yourself?'

'Well as can be expected,' Mr Martin said. 'Keeping myself busy and hoping. Nothing else for it, is there?'

Uncle Simon nodded unenthusiastically and sat down. Pictures of the Apollo moon landing were being replayed on the television news.

'Did you watch that this morning?' he asked Mr Martin.

'Can't say I did. Bit early for me. Old habits die hard: bed by eleven, up at seven, that's me.'

He peered at his son out of the corner of his eye, but Mal stared straight ahead at the television.

Uncle Simon sucked his cheek a second before speaking. 'Wonderful achievement, though, there's no denying it. I mean for the youngster there to have a lifetime of this ahead of him. Wonderful.'

In fact, Mal was losing interest in the moonwalk already. It had been difficult to come to terms with at first, but had been repeated throughout the day and would, no doubt, be shown again and again, each time meaning a little less to him.

'The wonder to me,' his father humphed, 'is how they can justify spending all that money up there with all the problems they have down here.'

Uncle Simon chewed his lip in a half-hearted attempt at hiding his annoyance.

Mr Martin changed gear abruptly. 'Mind you, I dare say in the long run it's money well spent. Whole new world really. Must be phenomenal scope for industries. Never know, eh, Simon – your next contract could be semis for the moon.'

His laugh was mirthless and all Uncle Simon could muster in response was a tight, no-lipped smile.

'That reminds me, Pat was saying you wanted a word.'

Uncle Simon feigned ignorance. 'Was she?'

Mal wanted to take hold of his uncle's cravat and throttle the living daylights out of him. He had it in his power to help his father and instead he was putting him through this, humiliating him. But his father persevered.

'Something to do with a new order?'

Still he said nothing. The bastard. The fucking bastard.

'Is that the one you were talking about this afternoon?' Mal asked, and his uncle found himself face to face with an image of his own wide-eyed innocence. 'In the woods up by us?'

Uncle Simon ran his tongue along his small white teeth.

'Oh, yes, that.' He turned to his brother-in-law, hand on forehead, masking the vein that pulsed on his temple. 'You'll have to excuse me, I've been miles away. Had to sack some fool today nearly landed the firm's name in court.'

'That a fact?'

'Mixed up in that damned People's Democracy crowd. I only took him on in April when there was all that flipping outcry about discrimination.'

'Don't tell me,' Mr Martin chimed in. 'Everybody knows what's best for us except ourselves. Or so they'd have you believe.'

'You're right there,' Uncle Simon conceded.

Mr Martin pointed at the TV screen. 'And there's the biggest culprit of the lot.'

American marines crouched in undergrowth, holding on to their helmets. A helicopter hovered low above a clearing some yards ahead. They darted forward in pairs, each man gripping one strap of a long, zipped bag. They hoisted the bags through the open cabin door and the helicopter lolled to the side as it received the load in its belly.

'There's another few for home. Can't sort out their own wars – can't even control their flaming Negroes, for that matter – but never mind all that, they've got a solution for Northern Ireland off pat.'

'Spot on.'

Uncle Simon stressed both words and for the first time looked him in the eye.

'Ready?' Aunt Pat called from the hall, and when they didn't appear immediately Mrs Martin came to the door to gee them up.

She wore a pair of Aunt Pat's slacks and a sunflowered blouse with a fake gold rope dangling at the waist. At the back of her head, a large, white bow hid the scaffold of hairpins that held her bun in place. Mr Martin hiss-whistled his approval.

'Well, I never,' he said, drawing her further into the room.

Uncle Simon cleared his throat of non-existent phlegm.

'Tell you what,' he said to his sister. 'You, Pat and the kids take our car.' He laid a hand on Mr Martin's shoulder. 'The two of us will follow in yours. Time we found out if the hard hat fits.'

He laughed sharply and Mal's mother and father joined in as they walked out the hall to the cars.

The young waitress seemed almost wholly unaware of the party she waited on in the lounge bar, padding wordlessly, eyes averted, from one to the other, handing each a menu. She was not much older than Alex, but, judging from her smooth, unthinking movements, she had already worked there some time.

'No expense spared,' Uncle Simon reminded them. 'Follow your stomachs, not your pockets.'

'No expense spared is right,' Mr Martin echoed. 'What will you all have to drink?'

He laid three fingers on the waitress's wrist as she turned to go.

'A sherry for me,' Aunt Pat said.

'Do you think I could have a glass of sweet white wine?' Mrs Martin asked.

'You can have anything you like,' her husband told her and tapped his fingers on the waitress's arm. 'You getting this?'

'Yes.'

Hunched over her pad, she jotted down the order, then waited, pencil poised.

'Simon ? Bush isn't it ? Bring us two Bush, love, and – you'll take a Guinness too, won't you, Simon? – two bottles of Red Heart.'

Uncle Simon touched the girl's other arm.

'Honestly,' he said. 'Just make that one Guinness.'

'Just one,' she repeated, scribbling.

Mr Martin smiled ruefully. 'Maybe you're right, the whiskey'll do us fine for the moment.'

The waitress changed the order again, uncomplaining.

'Anything else?' she asked, glancing at Cathy and Alex.

'What have you?' Mr Martin wanted to know. 'Coke? Orange? Which do you want, kids?'

'Coke,' Cathy said.

'Me too,' said Mal.

Alex scowled and scoured the menu.

'I don't want anything to drink.'

Mr Martin pressed money into the waitress's hand, parrying Uncle Simon's attempt to pay.

'Now, that's the last.' Uncle Simon wagged a cautioning finger. 'This was to be my treat.'

Mr Martin raised his hands in reluctant acceptance.

'Whatever you say. But I'm celebrating too, don't forget. The least you can let me do is buy a round of drinks.'

When they had finished ordering, a balding waiter, in a bow tie and red jacket, manoeuvred them through the busy restaurant, creaking in his shiny, slip-on shoes, and sat them at their tables. The tables were not quite pushed together and there was just room for a person to squeeze between them. Uncle Simon and Aunt Pat sat opposite Mal's mother and father at one table and Alex, Cathy and Mal sat at the other, Alex opting for the side by herself and the seat furthest away from the grown-ups.

Mal started with soup, hot and clear with pieces of vegetable floating in it that were still crunchy and satisfying to chew. He ate the soup with roll after doughy roll from a basket in the middle of the table, which he spread with butter, served in individual portions, that was beginning to melt and tasted oddly-pleasantly of silver paper.

'How's the broth?' his father asked him through a mouthful of grapefruit.

Mal told him it was fine and wiped his bowl clean with half a roll for proof.

'Bet it's not as good as your mother's, eh?'

Mrs Martin furrowed her brow to tell him not to go on so.

'Ah, you can't beat the home-made,' Uncle Simon said wistfully. 'I remember *my* mother's. With all due respect to Pat,' – he stroked her hand in appeasement, 'I never tasted the like, before or since.'

'It was great, right enough,' Mrs Martin said, her frown ironing itself out.

But her husband disagreed.

'Next to hunger, nostalgia's the greatest sauce I know,' he said. 'I'm telling you for a fact, your broth would put anyone to shame. I swear, I could eat it till the cows come home and go back out again.'

(The table in the dinette is set for three. Mal and his mother sit, home-movie silent, spooning going-cold soup. His father's seat is empty. On the place mat before it, boiled potato halves rise, blackening from a full bowl, a tidemark of overcooked vegetable scum forming around them. The tableau flickers twice and white holes appear in it, raggedly expanding, until they have devoured all detail, leaving Mal's memory clean as a wiped slate.)

The young waitress was clearing the soup plates and grapefruit dishes.

'Everything satisfactory?' The waiter came forward, smiled to the ladies and handed Mr Martin a wine list. 'Wine with your meal, sir?'

Mr Martin inclined to his wife.

'Another glass of sweet white?'

She lowered her head, colouring. At mealtimes in her brother's house, wine was always served by the bottle.

'Medium?'

'Ah, I wonder what the house red's like.' Uncle Simon attracted the waiter's attention. 'A bottle of red okay for everyone? Only, if we're having steaks ...'

'Yes, yes,' Mr Martin said good-humouredly. 'Red'll be just the ticket.'

The wine was brought while the waitress served the main courses. After the soup and the rolls, Mal wondered where he'd find room for the breast of chicken and boiled ham that the girl heaped on to his plate. Uncle Simon was offered the wine to taste and registered his satisfaction with the merest twitch of his head. As the waiter filled each of the grown-ups' glasses, Mr Martin called down to the other table.

'More Coke, kids?'

'If he calls me kid once more, I'll scream,' Alex muttered.

'Oh, give over,' Cathy told her. 'You'd scream at anything.'

Alex snatched up her fork, gripping it like a dagger. Cathy pulled her hands beneath the tablecloth.

'You wouldn't dare,' she said.

'D'you want to bet?' Alex asked her, and jabbed the prongs against her own palm.

The waitress had stopped at Alex's shoulder, a fillet of plaice held between two spoons, ready to serve. She coughed lightly and Alex rounded on her.

'See enough?' she snapped, so loud now she could be overheard by the rest of the company.

'Alex!'

'Bernadette!'

Uncle Simon and the waiter spoke simultaneously.

'What did I say earlier?' Uncle Simon's voice was stern and confident.

'It's her,' said Alex. 'She's staring at me.'

'No, I'm not,' the girl said, so bemused she was smiling.

'Fibber!' Alex was practically out of her seat. 'Look at her grinning.'

The girl's smile contracted as the waiter closed in on her.

'Bernadette, will you get into the kitchens, please.'

'I wasn't doing anything,' she said. But she had no chance. In a few deft movements, the waiter had relieved her of her tray and was now screening her from the table with his body. He fussed about Alex as he finished serving her meal, and in no time at all the adults were talking away as though nothing untoward had happened.

Mal pared the greasy skin off the chicken with his knife and fork, cutting moist chunks of white meat from the arc of breastbone, no longer hungry, but still greedy for the tastes of bought food: for carrots dished up whole in butter, not diced, for peas, swollen and tender, not burst in tinned green juice, for mashed potato in perfect scoops, and stuffing that tasted stodgily of bread; for ham served hot, not cold, and sliced thick as steak, for chicken on the bone, not carved and dry.

Alex's fish lay on her plate, untouched. Every now and then she touched her cheeks with her thumbs and licked the hollow beneath her nose. Drying tears. Only Mal noticed them, and even he pretended that he hadn't.

The waiter creaked to a halt by Uncle Simon and presented him with a bottle.

'More wine, sir?' he stage-whispered. 'Compliments of the management.'

The young waitress, meantime, had been standing, head bowed, some feet away in the aisle. Now, the waiter beckoned her forward, pointing to the spot where she must stop.

'Sorry,' she mumbled and dropped a curtsey from which it seemed at one point she would never recover.

'Slatternly wee girl that,' Aunt Pat gave off, when the waiter and waitress had withdrawn.

'Are you surprised?' Uncle Simon said. 'Name like Bernadette?'

Mr Martin papered over the momentary gaping rent.

'Now, a name's a name and nothing more.'

'Oh, don't misunderstand me,' Uncle Simon defended himself, swirling his wine redly around the bulbous glass. 'You know me, take a person as I find him.'

'That's right,' Mrs Martin agreed. 'We were always brought up to believe that you should treat people not for what they are, but for how they are.'

Mal filled his mouth with as many different tastes and sensations as he could cram in, chomping them together so that they mingled and became almost indistinguishable.

'Exactly.' Uncle Simon karate-chopped the table. That's what I'm talking about: attitude. I tell you, where authority is concerned, there's a difference in attitude between them and us.'

'They're not all bad,' Mr Martin insisted.

'I'm not saying they are.'

'Simon!' Aunt Pat admonished, rolling her eyes as though trying to see over the top of her head. 'Voice.'

He continued more quietly. 'But it's the exceptions I'm talking about. Take that business I was telling you about today. Now, God knows, they're a lot of rough diamonds in the building trade. But, trouble? Once in a while, maybe – too much drink on a payday, say: workmates in high spirits, have a disagreement, a few fists fly and there's bloody noses all round.' He speeded up, thrown for an instant. 'But, even then, a night's sleep cools them down and come eight thirty the next morning there they are, working together, side by side.'

'I don't follow,' his sister interjected.

Aunt Pat threw up her hands and laughed lightly.

'No more do I,' she assured her. 'I always say the best thing a woman can do with politics is leave it well alone and get on with her life.'

But Uncle Simon was back in his stride and, for his part, showed no intention of leaving anything alone.

'What I'm getting at is that they have respect for their work and the working day. But your man I got rid of today ...? Put it like this: there's agitation for equal opportunities – which,' he interrupted himself, 'I'm all for, as you well know; although, I don't mind saying, there's more to that than meets the eye. But that's another story ... Anyway, you go along with it, doing your bit, like anyone would. And what happens? This fella gets a job and, quick as you like, he's out there on the street, rabble-rousing. No thought for his job then. See?'

'Well, you might have something there,' Mr Martin said.

'I'll say.' Uncle Simon drained off his wine. 'And here's the best of it: while they know they can get the bru, they've no fear of being out of work – doesn't mean the same to them as it does to us. But all the time they're marching to bring down the government that pays them. For what? A United Ireland? I'd like to know how much social security they'd be getting down south.'

He banged his empty glass on the table, triumphant.

The bald head waiter returned, supervising two teenage boys, bow-tied but jacketless. The conversations at the top table fragmented as one of the boys removed the dishes from the main course and the other trailed the sweet trolley from seat to seat.

'So tell me,' Mr Martin asked his wife. 'Where did you come by all these with-it clothes?'

He grinned behind Cathy at his son, but Mal was too busy deciding what to have for dessert to pay him much attention.

Mrs Martin smiled, exasperated and pleased. 'I picked the top up in town the other day – very reasonable. The slacks are Pat's, but I've sent off for a pair the same from her catalogue.'

'Glad to see you haven't been idle,' he teased. 'Good thing I got this job, isn't it?'

'They're only forty-nine and six,' she said.

'*Only?*' he shrieked in pretend horror. 'Fifty shillings for a pair of slacks?'

'Forty-nine and six,' she corrected him.

'Fifty shillings in all but name,' he said.

'Have it your way.' She waved a hand. 'I'm not going to squabble over sixpence.'

Her coy half-wink silenced whatever it was he was starting to say. A smile of recognition creased his face and he wove his fingers in hers as they moved closer together, their voices muffled to low murmurings. Uncle Simon refilled the four wine glasses and Cathy leaned across the table, comparing the length of her fingernails with her mother's.

Mal stared disconsolately at the daunting slab of gateau on his side plate. He had thought he could manage it when he saw it on the trolley, but now he was aware of his dinner lying in his stomach, a solid, heavy mass, and he wished he had ordered coffee like everyone else. He scooped a forkful of chocolate sponge and clotting cream and balanced it before his mouth, summoning what was left of his appetite. Facing him, Alex scored shapes on the tablecloth with the handle of her teaspoon.

'That another world map?' Mal asked her.

'No,' she said, 'it's Ireland.'

Ireland; the world: Alex's maps were pretty much of a piece to Mal's eyes: none of them bore the slightest resemblance to what they claimed to be. He watched as she continued her moody scratchings.

'Looks more like a pig, if you ask me.'

'Slow, slow, quick-quick, slow,' Alex loured. That's what it's meant to be: "the old sow that eats her farrow".'

Mal scraped the gateau off the fork with his teeth. She'd lost him totally.

'What's a farrow when it's at home, then?'

'Baby pigs,' Alex lashed at him, letting fall her spoon. 'Fat, slimy, baby pigs.'

The sponge disintegrated in Mal's mouth. His tongue melted through the air-dried outer coating of cream to the sugary soft centre. He pushed the side plate into the middle of the table and in an instant all eyes were on him.

'What's the matter? Bite off more than you could chew?'

Uncle Simon was almost gleefully vindictive, but Aunt Pat's tone was one of polite concern.

'Don't force it. What you can't finish we'll get the waiter to put in a doggybag to take home.'

'Here.' Mr Martin slapped Uncle Simon's leg under the table. 'Did you ever hear tell of Sammy Slipper? Well, Sammy's wife Sadie had a dog, do you see, and ...'

'That's enough,' his wife interrupted. 'We can do without that sort of story when there's people trying to digest.'

And Mal was still trying to swallow. Liquid cream oozed to the back of his throat.

'Begging your pardon,' Mr Martin said, all contriteness, touching his greased-back forelock. 'Another time, maybe.'

Uncle Simon chuckled and sighed.

'Boy, but I've had a time and a half tonight.'

He reached for the stem of his glass and his eyebrows scaled new heights.

'A toast,' he said. 'To all the things we have to be happy for and celebrate this evening.'

'And luck in the days to come,' Aunt Pat added by rote.

Mr Martin lifted his wine, changed his mind and raised a glass of water in its stead.

'The future.' He toasted the company, but looked only to his wife. 'To jobs and contracts and – why not? – to men on the moon.'

The last of the gateau slipped down Mal's gullet, grave cold, and met a hot stinging burp halfway. He leapt from the table and ran for the toilet. His mother rose to follow him, but his father stopped her.

'He's all right,' he said. 'Just too much rich food on top of everything else. I'll go and see to him.'

THREE

1

The press of people on the pavement before the amusement arcade forced Mal back against a circus-postered pillar. They spilled off the kerb, across the road to the sea wall, and stretched, in a seemingly unbroken stream of bobbing heads and balloons, right around the front to Pickie. Even there, the rocks about the swimming pool were alive with bodies. Never had Mal seen so many people in one place at one time. He dug his hands deep into his trouser pockets and his wonder changed to contentment as one fist closed tightly around his hoard of coins. Coppers in the main, but there were a few sixpenny bits there, and a shilling or two besides; and in the safe keeping of the zip pocket at the back of his jeans there were even two, brand spanking new, ten pence pieces.

On Tuesday morning, with the same lack of explanation with which it had been stopped in the first instance, his pocket money had been reinstated. His father had called at Uncle Simon's to collect his mother and had given him half a crown – to tide him over till Saturday, he said, when Mal was to join them in Bangor. He smiled as he pressed the coin into Mal's hand: 'No getting yourself all excited again, now. Hear?'

Excited. That was the word he had used the night before,

when he walked into the toilets at the Wayfarers and found Mal hunched over the sink, puking carrots and peas, chocolate cake and chicken, into a whirlpool of hot and cold water. Without a second thought, he plunged his hand into the brimming sink and wiggled his finger to clear the plughole.

'Never mind, never mind. It's not your fault. A lot's happened all at once. You're just excited.'

Mal's chest heaved again, but this time he brought up only bile.

'That's a fella,' his father's voice sounded soothingly, from the other end of the room now. 'Get it all out of your system.'

Mal caught sight of him in the mirror that ran the length of the wall above the sinks; standing easily before a urinal, shielding himself with a loose hand, while his yellowed stream sprayed lazily out of the enamel bowl and splashed about his feet. Weak from retching, Mal rinsed his mouth with cold water, ridding it of the bitter aftertaste of regurgitated food. He pulled down a dry yard of roll towel and held it to his face: white and warm, as though freshly laundered. Perhaps his father was right; perhaps none of this would have happened if he hadn't been so keyed up.

An elderly couple had come to lean against the pillar of the amusement arcade beside Mal. Although the day was hotter than any there'd been that whole summer, they were both dressed as if for a winter's outing. The woman wore a black woollen coat, reaching almost to her ankles, and a felt hat, fastened by a tarnished silver pin at the back of her head. She carried a handbag and a shopping bag, at the top of which Mal could see a thermos flask and a set of false teeth, made from seaside rock. The man wore a dark grey suit, thinly striped. The jacket was unbuttoned and his fingers fiddled with the links of a watch chain, looped across the front of his waistcoat. There was sweat on the old woman's face and a smell off her like the boiled sweets they sold in chemists' shops.

'Have you your hanky?' she asked her husband.

The old man rooted in the breast pocket of his jacket. Mal noticed he was holding a pair of shoes and glanced furtively at the ground. The trousers of the man's suit were rolled, revealing pale, hairless shins, speckled with drying sand. His wrinkled toes curled in against each other, as if shying away from the sea air. Apart from the two big ones – which had growths like shrivelled raisins balanced on the ends – none of the toes had any nails whatsoever.

The old woman took his checked handkerchief and dabbed at her forehead and the furze of her face.

'I'm roasted,' she said.

Her husband fell to fingering his watch-chain. She turned her head to Mal.

'Know that, son? Roasted.'

Mal slipped out of sight round the other side of the pillar and jiggled his hand in his pocket, listening for the comforting clink of coins. Half a crown from his father and then, that very morning, when he himself was preparing to leave for Bangor, ten shillings from Uncle Simon.

'Not a word to anyone,' Uncle Simon whispered, slipping Mal the note. 'You say nothing, I'll say nothing.'

He didn't have to suggest it twice. Now that he was going, Mal no longer had any qualms about taking money from his uncle. After all, he'd plenty of it, and a lot more coming to him too, by the sound of things. Mal's one slight feeling of regret was that he might have been too hard on him previously: Uncle Simon wasn't so bad. Indeed, during the past week he'd been much better company than Mal had ever dreamt possible – from the moment he at last got it into his head that to treat his nephew as an equal he didn't have to act like a child himself.

'I'm awfully sorry,' he'd said, sitting down on Mal's bed the night of the celebration dinner, 'laughing at you running out to the toilets back there. I didn't realise you were that sick.'

He extended his hand.

'What do you say? No hard feelings?'

Mal accepted the hand and gave as good as he got squeezing it. 'No hard feelings.'

Uncle Simon slapped the bedclothes and stifled a yawn. 'Good man,' he said. 'Good man.'

The days that had followed seemed like a holiday in themselves, Mal spending most of them on a deckchair on the patio. Too hot in the heatwave that was washing over the tail end of July to be annoyed with his football, he sat for hours each afternoon, cautiously eyeing the prone figures of his Aunt Pat and Cathy, in their matching towelling shorts and bikini tops. His shame at imagining his aunt on the toilet was long gone and he followed the lines of their limbs, allowing himself to get as aroused as he could possibly bear, before going into the shade of the house, curious as to what the next stage might be, but satisfied that in time he would find out.

By the Saturday morning, however, Bangor was the only thing on Mal's mind. His father was waiting for him in the driveway and he was almost finished packing; only the football remained to be fitted into his holdall. But, no matter what way he tried it, it disturbed some or other of the clothes that Aunt Pat had stood the evening before ironing. Outside, the car engine revved and Mal, his patience all but exhausted, was nearing the stage where he could gladly have left the ball under the bed, when he eventually managed to squeeze it down the side of the bag and force across the zip. He drew back the curtains, for what he hoped would be the last time, opened the door, and found himself staring into Alex's face. Alex held the stare for a longer time than was comfortable and Mal searched for a way out of it. He seized on the pillowcase and sheets folded small over her arm.

'Sorry for putting you out,' he said.

Alex's expression didn't change, but she stepped aside patiently to clear the doorway. She had on again the short, yellow dress she had worn on Monday night, but Mal couldn't understand why he had thought her pretty then. The dress was plain and frumpy; his mother wouldn't have been seen dead in it. Mal edged past her to the top of the stairs. From the kitchen, Aunt Pat was calling one more piece of news he just *mustn't* forget to tell his mother, and in the driveway his father and Uncle Simon laughed beefy laughs. Three steps down the stairs, Mal put his face to the landing banister.

'Bye, Alex,' he said. 'See you soon.'

With her back still to him, Alex bobbed quickly to the floor and up again, as though she had dropped something; but from his oblique angle Mal couldn't tell what it was. Only later, as the car turned off Oxford Street on to the Queen's Bridge, towards Bangor, did it occur to him that what she had actually dropped was a curtsey.

A steady bleeping penetrated Mal's thoughts and focused them once more on the present. Somewhere in the tide of pedestrians before him a car was embedded. He could just about make out the slightly curved roof of a Mini, beneath which the driver, unseen, sounded his horn repeatedly; a thin and pitiful noise. The people nearest the car tried to steer clear and give it breathing space, but the surge of the crowd on all sides was too strong and their movement was constrained by the people next to them and theirs, in turn, by the people next to them. The ripple died without a trace and the car stayed where it was, trapped, braying.

Mal shook his head to rid his ears of the sound and struck out into the amusement arcade, with its shrieks of mechanical laughter and screeching dodgems. His father was playing two one-armed bandits at once and didn't notice him pass, but his mother soon spotted him from beneath the sign of the Kentucky Derby machine and called him enthusiastically.

'Come here till you see. I just won a shilling on this.'

A group of very young children were packed about the machine, clambering on to the panel to see into the dome. Their dirty faces watched Mal approach. The boys wore wellingtons and the girls plastic sandals with no socks under them. Gipsy children. One of the girls, who couldn't have been more than four or five herself, cradled a fat baby against her hip. She had to hold on to it with both hands, locking her fingers around its grubby rubber pants, and the weight of it had bent her fully forty-five degrees to the left.

Lights flashed to signal the start of betting and Mal turned his attention to the race. Mrs Martin dropped a penny in the slot beneath the white light.

'You're not betting on that, are you?' Mal asked her.

She looked round, her face young with excitement.

'What do you think won me my shilling? See, it's up in front again.'

So it was, but not by much. In a very close race it was pipped on the line by the red horse.

'D'you not see it only comes in once in a while to keep you putting in money?'

Mrs Martin nodded, as though taking in every word, but the lights were flashing again and she pushed her penny into the white slot with her thumb. Mal scrabbled in his pocket and just managed to get a penny on blue before the lights went out and the race began. The gipsy children peered through the dome, as interested in Mal and his mother as they were in the race.

The white horse streaked down the course, while the others juttered forward in its wake, in fits and starts. Mrs Martin clicked her fingers and nudged her son with her elbow.

'What do you say now?' she teased him.

But as she spoke the white horse stopped dead. The rest of the field came up behind it; red and blue forged ahead, with green following at their tails. Blue took it and green came through in second place. Red was third and white and yellow finished joint last.

'I tried to tell you,' Mal said, bending to collect his tuppence winnings. 'They can't afford to let white win too often. Yellow's not much better.'

The flashing lights called them again. Mal stuck to blue and his mother, despite what he'd told her, stayed with white. Blue won, white was nowhere. Next race, Mal switched to red and his mother, at the last moment, gave her penny to yellow. It was neck and neck for a time, but Mal knew red was never in any danger. He collected another tuppence. Mrs Martin's winnings were dwindling rapidly and her face was less animated than it had been a few minutes before. She looked about for her husband.

'Last one?' Mal suggested. 'I'm going on green, will I put one on for you as well?'

'Oh, go ahead,' she conceded, amiably enough, though she couldn't resist adding, as soon as the bet had been placed: 'But I know what'll happen, the white will win now I've changed.'

It didn't come anywhere near it, though. Green won by a mile. Mal scooped the winnings and offered his mother her fourpence share.

'No,' she said. 'That's yours.'

She looked at the little stock of coins in her left hand.

'In fact, you may take these too. They're more use to you than they are to me. I should listen to your Auntie Pat. Gambling's like politics, women would do better to leave well enough alone.'

The gipsy children funnelled into their places at the machine, hopefully pressing all the reject buttons. The girl holding the baby bounced it on her hip and tightened the grip of her locked hands. The veins on her wrists were as prominent as an old woman's.

Mrs Martin tickled her husband from behind as he pulled simultaneously on the levers of the two one-armed bandits.

'Hey, Rockefeller,' she said. 'What about those chips you promised us? I'm ravenous.'

The wheels of the fruit machine whirred to a halt. Mr Martin scoured the characters in search of a winning sequence, but there was no payout. He ran his hand along the collection trays before leaving.

'How did you do?' Mal asked him.

He closed one eye and made a face, waving a hand vaguely from side to side.

'Broke about even,' he said. 'Maybe a bit ahead.'

They stepped out on to the pavement and were at once swept along by the wash of holidaymakers.

'Boysadear,' Mr Martin said. 'It's a good job we're parked down this way.'

Mrs Martin gasped, nearly losing a shoe, and she grabbed on to her husband's arm to keep up.

'I've never in all my days seen the like of this in Bangor,' she laughed.

Mal remembered having thought much the same thing himself.

'Making the most of their last day off,' his father said.

A car – it might have been the same car – brayed hopelessly in the unrelenting throng.

Later, Mal awoke in the back seat of his own family's car. He was alone and one of the two car rugs had been placed loosely about his legs and midriff. He rubbed his eyes, trying to gather his thoughts. The car was parked at a picnic site, overlooking Ballyholme Yachtclub. There were lights on in the moorings and lights shining behind at the entrance to the lay-by; but the rocks that sloped between the two were in utter darkness. Mal heaved himself over into the front seats. The rug was gone from the passenger's side. He sat in the driver's seat, alone and unafraid, jingling his savings in his jeans pockets. Strings of coloured bulbs swayed in the evening breeze on the far side of the bay.

(

2

Mr Martin adjusted his short, square-bottomed tie for the umpteenth time that morning and tugged anxiously at his moleskin trousers.

'I'm not sure. I'm not sure,' he muttered.

He quizzed his reflection in the mirror and called into the kitchen.

'Tell me seriously, what do you think of these trousers?'

Mrs Martin appeared at the kitchen door, carrying a Tupperware lunchbox, yellowed with age and washing.

'I mean, assistant could mean anything: assistant manager, assistant brickie – assistant tea boy! Did Simon not say anything else to you?'

Mrs Martin shook her head and her bun shifted lightly. She was not able to get it as high as she had been with Aunt Pat's assistance and, without the white bow at the back, the framework of pins supporting it was plainly visible. She walked to the mirror and slipped her arm around her husband's waist.

'All I know is what you've told me yourself,' she said. 'But quit your worrying. If you're sitting down all day, those'll be the most comfortable things, and if you *are* working outside they'll not look out of place.'

Mr Martin's reflection smiled reassuringly and he kissed her forehead.

'You're right, of course. I know you are,' he said. 'I just wish I hadn't polished these blasted boots so much.'

Mal joined his parents in silent contemplation of the new workboots, bought that weekend in Bangor. The reinforced toecaps shone like cut coal and Mal found himself thinking of his first day at school after moving to the estate.

'You'd better watch your time,' he told his father, as his father had told him then.

Mr Martin took his old suit jacket from the back of an armchair and flattened his hair with the palm of his hand. He kissed his wife again, full on the lips this time.

'We right?' he asked Mal.

Pausing on the doorstep, Mr Martin filled his lungs full of the morning air, holding it a moment, then letting it go in a slow, contented breath. He didn't say anything, but Mal knew how he felt. *This* was the summer. It was as if everything that had gone before didn't actually count. There were still three days left of July and the whole of August yet to come before school went back. The holidays hadn't been wasted at all.

The street was already busy with men and women on their way to work; some hurrying, some sauntering or waiting for neighbours, some in cars, most on foot. Mal hugged his new orange caser to his chest. He hoped they were all taking good note of his father with his lunchbox and workboots.

Near the top of the hill a car stuttered past them, changing down the gears, making to turn into Larkview Avenue. The driver made a brief, awkward movement with his hand and jabbed his horn. It was Mucker's father, late for the timberyard. Mr Martin held up an open hand to the back of the car as it drove out of the street: not so much a wave as a sign that enough was enough.

'Hey, wait on there.'

Mr Crosier from the house opposite was panting along the road behind them.

'Danny,' Mr Martin said in greeting.

Mr Crosier placed a hand on his sleeve, completely out of puff. He was, on his own laughing admission, a wee fat pudding of a man, though he claimed that he was not especially heavy, but, rather, unusually short. That was true enough: he was smaller than Mucker, Les and a good few of the other teenagers on the street. There were folds of flesh about the collar of his shirt and the top of his head was flat with a smoothed bald patch, so that it was possible to imagine he had once been much taller and had been worn down to his present size by persistent hammering. He was generally regarded as an easy-going sort, although, until that morning, Mal had never known him to have much to do with either of his parents.

'Rumour has it you've got a start?' he half asked, half stated when he had swallowed sufficient air to speak.

'Rumour's right,' Mr Martin said.

'Done a bit of building work myself in my time.' Mr Crosier inclined his shiny head to Mal and spoke behind his hand. 'I was a steamroller, don't you know.' Then, addressing his father again: 'So, ah, what exactly are you doing?'

Mr Martin, cheerful up till now, looked for a moment deadly serious; but the shadow of a smile lingered about his lips.

'Handy man,' he said.

The deadpan look spread to Mr Crosier, as though contagious. 'Handy man?'

'Sure, I only live just across the park,' Mr Martin snapped gratefully at the feed.

Even Mal had seen that coming, but Mr Crosier still raised a chuckle.

'Very good,' he said. 'Handy. I like that. Very good.'

He patted his neighbour on the small of the back.

'Well, it's handy for me too. I go down that way each morning for a lift. I'll walk a step with you, if you don't mind.'

'Course not,' Mr Martin said.

He turned to his son. Like Mal, he was prone to irritation from stray eyelashes at inconvenient times and now he was working his little finger into his right eye to dislodge one.

'Coming then?' he asked.

'Nah,' Mal said, turning the football in his hands. 'I'm going to see if there's anyone around for a kickabout.'

'Okey-doke.' His father smiled, and Mal could tell he had said the right thing. 'See you after work.'

The two men continued down the hill and Mal watched them go, listening to their conversation as long as it was audible.

'Saw Charlie Press give you a toot.'

'How is he?'

'Ah, still taking it bad.'

Mr Martin moved his head to say there was nothing to feel bad about.

'It's history now,' he said. 'Best forgotten all round.'

'You can be forgiving all you like,' Mr Crosier said. 'But the wee lad's got to learn there's some things just aren't done: principles. No respect for anyone or anything – he's his father's head turned completely. I suppose you know they expelled him from the Lodge?'

Their voices trailed away and became indistinct, leaving Mal to deal with the overheard words on his own. He wasn't quite sure what was going on, but it certainly didn't sound too good for Mucker; and, while he was glad that people were siding with his father over the fight, he was, at the same time, scared in case Mucker would take it out on him. He thought about what he'd told his father just now, how he was going to see who was around to play with, and he had the feeling that maybe it wouldn't be as easy to do as it was to say.

Still, he had to start somewhere. He was walking away from Everest Street towards the entrance of the estate, reckoning if there was one person likely to be up and about this early it was Mad Mitch. Tommy Duncan, the milkman, swore blind he had found him in the garden one morning playing solo Scrabble, and that was at six o'clock. Drawing closer to the roundabout, however, Mal noticed that the Campbells' curtains were still closed. He wondered idly what sort of drug Mitch's parents had used on him to keep him quiet and let them get a lie-in. From drugs and pills, his thoughts moved easily to sweets. He jingled the heavy change in his pocket. At least the newsagent's was open at this hour.

He squatted by the side wall of the supermarket with his packet of Lovehearts, tucking the caser up the front of his T-shirt. He didn't care how long he had to wait for someone to happen by, there was no way he was going down to the park alone. He wouldn't allow himself to contemplate the real reason (refusing even to speak Francy's name in his mind), and pretended to think it was simply no fun kicking a ball around a football pitch by yourself. He ate the sweets one after the other, not bothering to read their messages, sucking them until the writing was worn off, then crunching the smooth discs with his back teeth. He was on the last one, his tongue swollen fuzzy with saturated sherbet, staring absently at the Campbells' house, when he realised their driveway was empty. His mother's dream come true: the tarpaulin-covered 1100 was gone, as were the four piles of paving stones on which it had rested.

'Well, well, look who's back.'

Mal twisted about, swallowing his half-sucked Loveheart whole and nearly choking in the process. Mind you, even without the sweet the sight which confronted him would have been enough to make him splutter. For both Peter Hardy, who was grinning at him, and Andy, who stood a little off to the right, were sporting crew cuts, and Andy's in particular was so severe that his head appeared at first to be completely shaved.

'Pretty good, eh?' Peter asked, showing Mal each side of his head in turn. 'Everyone's getting them done.'

Mal was really choked by that. Only the day before, his parents had decided he was old enough now to grow his hair long if he wanted. For a moment he could do nothing but gape. With his hair cropped back from it, Andy's face had taken a strong suntan and the worst of the spots about his mouth and nose had withered, leaving only faint purple scars in their place. Lighting a cigarette one-handed and breaking the match between his thumb and forefinger to extinguish it, he looked as handsome as he'd always believed he was. He appeared totally oblivious to Mal's presence and Mal began to fear that his trepidation earlier had been justified.

'Good holiday?' Peter asked him.

Mal shrugged his shoulders. In the circumstances, Peter's unsarcastic question was almost as disconcerting as his brother's continued silence.

'All right, I suppose.'

Peter nodded, frowning, as if Mal's answer was the most reasonable anyone had ever given him. He burrowed in a pocket of his new denim jacket and produced a crumpled cigarette and Mal watched in amazement while he lit it from the tip of Andy's. He never quite knew what to make of Peter Hardy at the best of times. Now, however, after more than two weeks away, it was like looking at another person altogether.

'See you put on a bit of weight while you were gone,' Peter said, and Andy smirked.

Mal remembered the football.

'Oh, this,' he said. 'I was just on my way to the park to try it out.'

He eased the ball from beneath his T-shirt. The second he saw it, Andy's whole demeanour changed. He blinked his eyes and snatched the caser.

'Fuck me,' he said. 'Where'd you nick this?'

'I didn't,' Mal told him, bracing himself. 'My dad bought me it.'

Andy wolf-whistled, caressing the orange leather.

'Want to swap das?' he said.

Not a word about the fight at the bonfire, not a single sneer at the mention of his father.

'What are we waiting for?' Peter whooped. 'Let's call for every-one and get a game going.'

Mal wasn't prepared for this at all. The best he had hoped for coming back to Larkview was that sooner or later the boys would get fed up teasing him and he would be able to ride out the meantime. He wasn't complaining, though. He even began to relax a little. He took the ball from Andy, squeezing it in his hands like his father had shown him to do to test the pressure.

'Might as well,' he said, casualness itself. 'Will we knock Mitch up?'

'You can knock there till your arms drop off,' Andy said. 'He'll not hear you.'

'Why not?'

'You mean you didn't know?' Peter chipped in. 'They're away.'

Mal looked again at the house and saw that what he had taken to be the backs of drawn curtains were, in fact, white dustsheets tacked closely about the inside window frames.

'On the head, on the head,' Andy called, back-pedalling down the street, jutting his neck forward.

'What, and have the ball ruined bouncing on the tarmac?' Mal asked him. 'No fear.'

Andy stopped calling without protest.

'You're probably right,' he said and spun on his heel. 'I'll see youse down there, I'm going for Les.'

Mal and Peter walked on together. Peter seemed happy enough not to talk, but Mal was still dogged by questions about the Campbells' empty house.

'How long are they gone?' he asked.

'Who?'

'Mitch's family.'

Peter blew smoke out the corner of his mouth.

'Couple of days.'

Even allowing for the fact that he'd been away a while, Mal couldn't help thinking their leaving was a bit rushed.

'I didn't know they were thinking of moving.'

Peter was inspecting the unlit end of his cigarette.

'No? Seems they didn't like the bands practising at the roundabout every night,' he said, as though that explained everything. 'Here, have a look at this.' He pointed to the cigarette's stained filter. 'See the shape the nicotine's made? What d'you think that is?'

'Where did they go?'

Peter glanced at him, apparently unable to believe anyone being more interested in the whereabouts of the Campbells than in the configuration of his nicotine stain.

'No idea,' he said. 'They've people over Derrybeg way. They're probably there. Best place for them too.'

He assessed the filter from another angle, then put the cigarette back in his mouth.

'A dog,' he told Mal. 'The shape – it looked like a dog.'

Mal was irked by Peter's evasiveness and was sure he was taking the hand out of him. Peter had fallen silent again and puffed comfortably on his cigarette; but halfway down the hill, he sniggered and slapped Mal between the shoulder blades.

'What's the fuss?' he said. 'Listen, it's simple: things change. If you accept them, well and good; but if you don't it's nobody's lookout but your own. I mean, take yourself; you don't hear me or Andy badgering you to find stuff out.'

'What stuff?' Mal asked defensively.

'Oh, I don't know, you being so interested in football all of a sudden, for one thing.'

'I always was,' Mal protested. 'I just hated the wick balls they used.'

Peter stepped on his cigarette butt.

'Aye, well, maybe that wasn't a good example,' he said.

Andy and Les were waiting by the goalposts of the first football pitch. Beyond them, at the front of the woods, Mal could make out the flame-blackened remains of the Eleventh Night bonfire. For a fleeting instant, his mind was seized by the recollection of himself clinging to the Gerry Fitt Pope, looking down the blank sheet of branches at the laughter-contorted faces, terrified he would crash through and go on falling, falling ...

Then, from somewhere inside the woods, he thought he heard the sound of men calling to each other as they worked. His father would be there now. When he focused again on Andy and Les, they no longer appeared to him as the same people he had stared at in his memory. Les, too, had had a change of hairstyle, although it was clear his mother would no more consider allowing him to have his hair cropped than she would let him grow it long. Instead, where before it had been thick all round, it had now been thinned out. It was the same length as always, there was just less of it. Short hair really did seem to be the whole go, right enough. Mal was wondering whether Mucker had had his done, and said so. Andy stroked his stubble proudly.

'Long hair's for poofs,' he said, 'They'd kick the shit out of you for it up the Shankill.'

He lit another cigarette in his new one-handed fashion and Les sidled over to Mal.

'Mucker's a sore point,' he whispered.

Nothing else followed and Mal decided he was best not asking anything more just then. Perhaps Peter was right, things did change, and if you couldn't accept the changes you simply got left behind. He was coming to see that, in this new order of things, the safest policy was not to pry too much. His return to Larkview was proving to be far less painful than he had feared. He'd be a mug to spoil it.

He ran a few yards infield with the ball at his feet.

'Andy,' he shouted. 'One-two.'

He stroked the ball with his instep, but it spun away to Andy's right and Peter only just saved it running off the pitches altogether. That flaming bump in Uncle Simon's ball; he was still making allowances for it. He cursed himself for not practising more last week.

'Great football,' Peter said, passing it accurately to Andy. 'All's you need now is a new pair of feet.'

That night, for the first time in many more months than Mal could remember, his father fell asleep in the armchair by the television immediately after dinner. He had been full of the chat at the table, giving Mal and his mother the lowdown on the boys he was working with. There was Phil the Flutter who always had a transistor in his hip pocket and an earphone in one ear, so he could keep up with the horse racing, and two big country lads from Fermanagh – nicknamed Bill and Ben – who lived in a hostel while they were in Belfast and only got home to their wives once a fortnight. There was a man called Monkey Green, who kept them all in stitches and was forever playing tricks on Harry Dawson. Powerful big fella, that Harry Dawson, Mr Martin said; they called him The Hammer. But he was a sad case all the same, there was something not quite right with him. Mal imagined Les, grown older and stronger, and indeed, the way his father told it, being on a building site was more like a bunch of mates having a good time together than actual work. They even called themselves a gang.

Mrs Martin unlaced her husband's boots while he dozed and slipped them off. She ran a licked fingertip along one toecap, dusty with powdered mud, streaking it with a wet shine. Using the arm of the chair, she helped herself up from her hunkers and made for the kitchen with the boots. But she changed her mind and glanced back at her husband's slouched figure. His shirt was open and pulled out from the waistband of his moleskin trousers and, under the thick chest hair, his skin was mottled pink by the sun. She set the boots on the hearth and looked out the living room window.

'What do you say we give the garden a quick going over before your daddy wakes?' she suggested.

Mal agreed readily and brought the tools from the garage to the front of the house. But when his mother asked him for the lawnmower he refused to let go of the handle.

'I'll mow,' he said.

His mother drew her head back a little and looked him up and down. Mal could tell what was going through her mind: he wasn't capable; he was spindly and potbellied like a child. But that was only because that was how she was used to thinking of him. She couldn't see the changes that were happening to him. Lately, at nights, his arms and legs had begun to throb with a dull but steady ache, deep down, inside his bones. Mal had no doubts what those pains signified and his brain raced with impatient excitement as he lay in bed, feeling himself growing up.

He inched his shoulders back and breathed in through his nose, so that his chest swelled and deflated the balloon of his stomach. But just then, Mr Crosier poked his flat, shiny head over the top of the hedge. One long branch of privet fluttered about his chins.

'Where's the worker?' he asked.

Mrs Martin gave a short laugh and fingered the clips at the back of her bun.

'Conked out by the TV,' she said.

'Ah, it's a hard life, and no mistake.' Mr Crosier sighed gloomily, then winked each eye in turn. 'Well, maybe you'll tell him when he comes round that if he waits on me in the morning I'll walk down the road with him again.'

Mal took advantage of the conversation to start mowing the grass, before his mother could raise any objections. As it was, she swung round at the very first click of the blades, her mouth opened to remonstrate.

But Mr Crosier was too quick for her. 'I see you've found another man for the jobs about the house.'

Mrs Martin joined in his good-natured laughter, but her smile was still uncertain. Mal drove the lawnmower forward powerfully, hauled it back, and drove forward again. His muscles grumbled to begin with, but, far from tiring, they seemed to gain more of an appetite the longer he worked. On and on he went, round the tiny square of hedge-bound garden, and, although he didn't once look to see, he knew that with every swathe he cut, his mother's smile became more convincing.

Mal was beginning to get fed up. He had been waiting by the chippy over half an hour for Peter and still there was no sign of him. He wouldn't have bothered standing so long if it weren't for the fact that – it being the day of the Junior Orange Walk – there were so few other people around that Saturday afternoon. Of all the days to get his hair cut, he had to pick the one when there was no one there to see it. He ran his hand up the back of his head, feeling the stiff crew-cut hairs bristle against his palm.

His mother and father had been dubious at first, couldn't understand why, after carping for months on end to have his hair long, he suddenly wanted it all chopped off. His mother was afraid, too, it'd make him look like a ruffian, until Mal listed the people who'd had it done already, finishing with Peter and Andy Hardy. His mother rubbed thoughtfully at the plate she was drying. Getting off the bus one day at the end of June, she had dropped a bag of potatoes on the footpath and Andy, who had been right behind her, was the only person who stopped to help. She had come home full of praise for his manners and was forever saying how smart he'd looked in his grammar school blazer. Mr Martin turned to her from the sink.

'Go on ahead. If that's what he wants, give him the money.' He touched her arm with a washing-up-wet hand. 'He's his mother's son all right. Dedicated follower of fashion.'

Mrs Martin aimed a flick at his behind with the tea towel and went for her purse.

The back of Mal's neck tingled now and felt red and raw, as

though the sun was singling out that one spot to shine on. He peered impatiently up Crawford Drive in search of Peter and rolled his caser backward and forward with the sole of his gutty. They had been playing with the caser so often that week, his initial insistence that he wasn't having it going on concrete or stones had progressively weakened and proved impossible to stick to. He was still careful and drew the line at having it kicked against a brick wall, but the odd bounce on the road now and again couldn't do it any harm. There were tiny scores on a couple of the leather panels, but you had to look very close to see them and to all outward appearances the caser remained superbly orange.

Mal was on the point of giving up on Peter altogether and going home when Sally Cleary came round the corner from the supermarket. They were both in the same class at school, though Sally sat at the back of the room, as far away as it was possible to get from Mal, who, being a new boy, had to spend the whole of his first term right up by the teacher's desk. He had spoken to her once or twice in the playground and thought she was very nice, thought Sally might even like him; but she was usually with a clutch of other girls and more often than not Mal was too shy to say anything to her.

They exchanged hellos, then each waited for the other to continue, and when neither of them did they both spoke at once.

'You enjoying your ...'

'Been away any ...'

They stopped at the same time.

'What were you going to say?' Mal asked.

'No,' Sally told him. 'You first.'

Now that there was such a thing being made of it, his question seemed pretty ridiculous.

'It was nothing,' he said. 'What about you?'

Sally smiled.

'Nothing.'

She began walking away and immediately Mal felt acutely the loss of a chance to get to know her better. By the first house on Crawford Drive, however, Sally turned again and called back.

'Like the haircut. Sexy.'

The prickly rawness spread from Mal's neck and covered his face. He was aware of his fingers, like they were somebody else's, creeping up over his chin and touching his lips. He was kissing them and, before he could stop himself, blowing along them in Sally's direction. He looked up quickly, as though the kiss had been a dart, accidentally discharged, and he was afraid it might have hurt her. But Sally was all right. She raised one hand to the side of her face.

'See you around,' she said.

When she was gone, Mal could not decide whether he had done the right thing blowing her a kiss. In fact, he didn't even know *why* he had; at the time it had just seemed the natural thing to do. Now, if he'd been Andy, or Peter, or anyone else, he could have lit a cigarette, hiding his face. The heat drained away from his cheeks, back down into his neck. He shook his money to one side of his pocket and counted the coins with his thumb. More than enough. He walked to the newsagent's and pushed open the door.

The pavilion toilets reeked of disinfectant and standing piss. The blue paint of the walls was interrupted at irregular intervals where the park-keeper had used thinners to remove graffiti. Some of the plaster-coloured blotches were already scribbled over again, however, and the inside of the cubicle door warned Fenians to beware and to Remember Burntollet.

Mal gave up trying to remember what Burntollet was himself and put a match to his fourth consecutive cigarette. Starting smoking was, as he had anticipated, turning out to be no big deal. He had accepted quite early in the week that he was bound to start sooner or later and that the right time would present itself without him hurrying it along. He had even concocted a story in readiness for buying them, rehearsing it over and over until he was word perfect: his aunt was visiting for the afternoon and had left a full box in her other handbag, so could she just have ten now to keep her going. He needn't have panicked though. The man behind the counter didn't bat an eyelid, not even when Mal added a book of matches and a packet of Polos to his order.

For a long while he did nothing in the cubicle except sniff the cigarettes through their silver foil, and when he did eventually take one out, he spent a full ten minutes more rolling it about his palm, squeezing it and weighing it. Firmer than he had expected, cleaner and more compact too. He sniffed again, placing the cigarette between his lips; a smell of drying firewood, which was lost a second later in a cloud of grey smoke as he brought a spluttering cardboard match to its tip.

He had always assumed the smoke would slip straight down his throat of its own accord and when it didn't he wondered how he was meant to go about swallowing it. He tried this way and that, but still the smoke remained in his mouth. It was acrid, but not unpleasant, and he told himself he could bear another few attempts. He let the smoke go and relaxed, urging his mind to wander. The sun was warm coming through the toilet's small, frosted window and he conjured a picture of his aunt and Cathy, lying side by side on their patio. But he was becoming bored always imagining them and he was already beginning to forget how exactly they looked while they sunbathed. He cast about for someone else and found Sally Cleary. In future, he decided, if anyone was to ask him who his girlfriend was, he would tell them it was Sally.

And then, somewhere around the third cigarette, he discovered he was inhaling. He had no idea how long he'd been doing it before he realised and he was never able afterwards to point to the precise moment at which it had begun. But then again, that was how everything seemed to happen nowadays. Like the Campbells, for instance. Mal couldn't say for sure when it was he first became aware that pressure had been put on them to leave and when, after that, he had come to understand why. Perhaps the full realisation was arrived at only gradually, too gradually in the end for the truth to come as any great surprise.

For that was another thing about that week he couldn't remember: when exactly he had simply ceased to be surprised by anything.

He pulled hard on his cigarette and threw it down the toilet with the other three. Outside, the sun was grown so intense it seemed to have melted into the sky itself, quivering the horizon with a warm fluidity, and Mal, dizzy from smoking, had to rest a hand on the pavilion wall to steady himself. He found Peter at the back of the pavilion, lying on the grass, cradling his head in his hands. Eddie Boyd was there too, twiddling a pole from hand to hand, like a stickman on the Twelfth. The pole was the very one he had used helping the binmen batter the rat those few weeks before, although Mal had all but stopped thinking of him in connection with that. He was just another of the boys he hung around with, indeed, if anything, the two of them had become more friendly lately. There were less people in the gang now, of course, which made things easier.

'Thought you were meeting me at the shops?' Peter said, looking at Mal through half-closed eyes.

Mal drew the cigarette box fractionally out of his jeans pocket.

'I was fed up waiting. Went for a quick fag.'

Peter's eyelids flickered apart long enough to take in Mal, cigarettes, haircut and all, then they drifted together again and he held out a drooping hand.

'Give's one,' he said.

'Away on,' Mal told him. 'Buy your own.'

Peter's hand continued its descent to the ground, like he hadn't really expected Mal to say anything else.

'What'll we do?' he asked.

'Fancy a kickabout?'

Mal flicked the caser towards Peter's stomach, but Peter sensed it coming and caught it in the nick of time. He bounced the ball from fist to fist, then batted it across the grass to Eddie.

'Not fucking football again,' he said. 'Andy's sure to want to play all day tomorrow as it is.'

'Tomorrow?' Mal asked. 'I thought there was a game on tonight?'

Peter shook his head.

'Not now there isn't.'

'Where have you been?' Eddie said, side-footing the ball against the wall. 'They're having a barney up the Shankill.'

'What?'

Mal retrieved the ball from him and sat on it, without a single thought for what he might be doing to the shape.

'What sort of barney?'

Peter raised himself on one elbow.

'It was on the lunchtime news – the parade was stoned again going past Unity Flats. The police are shit-scared there'll be murder there later, when the march comes back. They'll take the Flats apart.'

He sank back tiredly on to the grass.

'It was bound to happen,' he said.

Eddie came and sat with them.

'Wish I'd joined the Lodge in time,' he said wistfully.

Mal studied his companions' faces. Neither of them betrayed even the slightest trace of concern. But then, the afternoon was so quiet, it was hard to believe there was anything out of the ordinary happening in another part of the city. He looked to the left, in a vaguely westward direction, the direction, ultimately, of the Shankill and Unity Flats; but, just short of the dump, the view was blurred by a wall of air, made molten by the sun, bubbling about the estate.

The following morning, Mal and his parents went to the local Presbyterian church. They were aiming for the ten o'clock service, so that they'd be home in plenty of time for an early dinner. But when they arrived at ten to ten, the heavy wooden doors were locked and bolted from the inside. After a short time a caretaker, in slippers and an overall – under which he wore a shirt and tie – passed them, combing the white marbled stones of the drive with a rake.

'Early this morning,' he said.

'We were looking for the ten o'clock,' Mr Martin told him.

The man folded his hands on the nub of the rake, removing moss and leaves from the prongs with his slipper.

'No ten o'clock just now,' he said. 'Nor eleven thirty. Eleven only in the summer.'

He had a strong English accent and told the times like he was reading them from the Bible.

Mr and Mrs Martin stood uncomfortably on the broad stone steps, while Mal played at racing up and down the wheelchair ramp. Waiting for the eleven o'clock service upset all their orderly plans for the day: dinner was put back, tea delayed, and, in the end, Mal was much later getting to the park that evening than he had hoped.

A crowd of about twenty boys had made it there before him. The old system of a gang for each street seemed to have been done away with for good and this was what was left. It wasn't that there was never anybody else about; Mal still saw a lot of those who had used to be in the various gangs, but some people had obviously decided to keep themselves to themselves for the time being and it was just accepted that you didn't call for them.

They were gathered in a circle at the side of the pavilion, where Andy and Les were propped against the creosoted wall with Sonia Kerr in between them. Mal hadn't seen Sonia since the Eleventh Night, when she had hung drunkenly on Mucker's arm; but he had known long before this evening that she wasn't going out with him anymore. He clambered over the prostrate bodies and found a gap in the centre of the circle.

'Was it really as bad as it looked on the telly?' Eddie was asking Andy.

He meant the trouble at the parade. There'd been rioting ever since, and part of the reason why Mal and the other boys were at the park tonight was to hear what it was like from someone who had actually been there.

'Really that bad?' Andy mocked. 'Worse. That right, Les?'

'I'll say.'

'Fucking bottles, bricks, paving stones, the lot. Dirty bastards were even throwing shite out the windows.'

Eddie stuck two fingers in his mouth and pretended to puke.

'That's what you get moving Catholics in where they've no right to be,' Andy said, head nodding sagely. 'Keep them up the Falls, that's where they belong.'

There was a general murmur of agreement at that. Out of the corner of one eye, Mal noticed the person next to him tearing handfuls of grass from the ground, roots, soil and all. He glanced up to see Pickles Austin staring dead ahead at Andy, a look of intense concentration on his face. Mal remembered Pickles was a Catholic; it was sometimes easy to forget in the holidays when you didn't see people in their school uniforms. But Pickles had no need to worry. Andy probably just made a mistake, saying Catholics when he should have said Rebels. All Rebels were Catholics, but not all Catholics were Rebels, that's what Mucker said. The Campbells were Rebels because their father was interned in the fifties and that was why they had to leave. But Pickles's dad was a Protestant, so he was only half Catholic to begin with. No, Pickles had no need to worry.

'And were youse there when the Shankill went in to get them back after?'

'Damned right,' Andy said, without hesitation.

Les scratched his head, his skin colouring a light brown. A scowl puckered Andy's brow.

'We were there,' he explained. 'But then we'd so many kids

with us we decided we'd better get them off into the minibus before one of them got himself killed.'

There was a solemn pause while this was mulled over. He had a point, Andy, and there was a dead man in Tennent Street police station to prove it. The fact that the man had lived in the Flats was not considered important enough to contradict him. The discussion appeared to have reached a natural conclusion when there was one further, unexpected contribution from the floor.

'I'll bet youse had a hard job getting Mucker to leave.'

Only then when Pickles spoke did it strike Mal that he had not heard him utter so much as a single word the whole of that previous week. He couldn't help thinking he'd have been wiser keeping his mouth shut a while longer. Every face was now turned on him curiously; every face but one, that is. Andy peered about, as though having difficulty locating where the voice came from.

'Did somebody swear?'

Les grinned and chortled coarsely.

'Guess who it was?' he said, his face paling once more to its jaundiced shade.

Andy knew rightly who it was and ignored him.

'Austin,' he lectured, in his best headmaster's voice. 'Did your mummy never tell you shouldn't use bad words like that?'

Pickles was kneading the ground for all he was worth.

'Like what?' he said. 'Only asked about Mucker.'

'Mucker fucker,' Andy snapped. 'That's not a name we mention around here. I don't expect you would understand, but he wasn't even there. The Lodge wants nothing more to do with him. Get me? He's finished. Ask anybody. Ask Sonia here.'

Pickles was off the hook. Sonia shrank from the collective gaze, plucking self-consciously at a thread in her skirt.

'Tell him, Sonia.'

She snuffled and dabbed her red-raw nose with her wrist.

'Nothing to tell,' she mumbled.

Andy's eyes glinted, suddenly angrier. He twisted a hand in Sonia's hair and yanked her head towards his.

'Tell him what you told me,' he commanded. 'How after weeks of bragging about what he was going to do to you, when it came to the bit he wasn't up to anything and lay beside you in the woods, wanking himself off.'

Sonia tried to free her hair, but Andy only twisted his fist more tightly. His face was shrivelled purple with venom.

'Tell him,' he insisted.

'He did. All right. *He did!*' Sonia shouted.

Andy pushed her away. She covered her face and her head sagged to one side. Just above the collar of her blouse, where the oily smear of make-up ended and the darker tones of her suntan began, a patch of skin the size of a two-bob bit showed up, yellowed like a fading bruise.

Andy got to his feet, forcing a laugh. 'Fucking fruit. I tell you, he's finished.'

The others were slow taking his lead and he clapped his hands to rouse them.

'I thought there was meant to be a match here tonight? Let's get the teams picked and get on with it.'

It wasn't the best game they'd ever had, by any means. Perhaps, like Peter said, they had been playing too much football lately. Or maybe the problem was more the monotony of coming up against the same opponents day in, day out. That was Mal's only grumble with the new gang: though there was less danger now of being picked on (unless, of course, like Pickles, you did something *really* stupid), the fact that each day there seemed to be fewer and fewer people who were actually 'in' didn't make for much variation in the pool of players. And while there ought still to have been any number of permutations, the teams somehow always ended up the same, with Andy's invariably the winning one.

They had managed to get almost to the end of the first half when Gerardy and Barry McMahon came out of the woods by the bonfire site and headed for the middle of the playing fields where the game was in progress. Instead of the usual jeans, gutties and T-shirts, the two cousins wore cream shorts, with creases so stiff they looked starched, and short-sleeved button-up shirts. Eddie said you didn't have to be a genius to know where they had been and Peter said if Eddie knew then you mustn't have to be, right enough. For a time, though, the game continued regardless of them, until the ball ran out of play on the woods' side. Gerardy retrieved it and booted it back to Andy. Andy said nothing but turned his back on them, ball behind his head for the throw in.

'Pick us on?' Gerardy asked.

The teams are even,' Andy said and then shouted infield: 'Move would you. Somebody come to me.'

There was a flurry of movement as players from Andy's team ran towards him and then darted away again, pursued all the while by a marker from the other side. Mal ran too and, for a moment, forgot Gerardy and Barry, forgot almost why he was running, except that he had to keep Pickles in his sight.

'Sure, you could take one a side,' Barry McMahon said. 'That wouldn't make any difference.'

The players stopped running. Andy relaxed his catapult-sprung pose and balanced the ball in the crook of his arm.

'Well, if it'd make no difference, there's no point picking youse on in the first place, is there?'

Mal hadn't seen it like that before, but he was bound to say, the way Barry himself had set it up, Andy was right. Barry, though, was renowned for being a mouth and he wasn't giving in.

'But one more each would make it eleven a side. You'd have a proper game then.'

'Are you deaf, wee lad?' Andy shouted. 'This is a proper game and I said we've enough already.'

Barry was hefty for his age, but Andy was a good two years older and could have taken him no problem. If Barry had any sense, Mal thought, he'd give over and walk away while he was still able. Gerardy evidently thought so too, for he was trying urgently to drag his cousin after him. But Barry, it seemed, was stupid as well as deaf.

'How come you're doing all the talking?' he asked Andy. 'I bet that's not even your ball.'

Andy took a couple of steps towards him and Gerardy tugged more urgently than ever.

'For Jesus' sake, Barry, forget it, would you.'

'Makes no odds whose ball it is,' Andy began, then stopped. 'Suit yourself,' he said, and passed the caser to Mal. 'It's his. See what he says.'

Gerardy let go of Barry's arm and the two of them eyed Mal closely: the same look his mother had turned on him on Monday evening when he asked to mow the lawn. They were expecting him to be a soft touch, thinking he couldn't and wouldn't refuse them. Well he'd showed his mother and he would show the McMahons.

'Should have been here at the start if youse wanted to play.' He passed the ball back to Andy. 'Come on. Your throw.'

Andy had sat down in the meantime, idly inspecting his nails, as if Mal had been taking an important penalty and he was confident of the outcome. He stood up now, smirking. There was no need for him to thump Barry. Mal's word, as owner of the ball, was final. Gerardy had already started across the playing fields and Barry followed him, kicking his heels through the sandy soil.

'Hey,' Peter shouted behind them. 'We could do with a couple of linesmen, if youse are interested.'

The throw in was at long last taken. Nobody could control it and the ball broke to Pickles. Mal had lost him and he was on his own, but he was so busy looking after the McMahons that he didn't notice the man bearing down on him. Les barged into him from behind, winning the ball, but flattening him. Pickles jumped up, flaming.

'That's a flipping foul,' he blurted through the grit in his mouth.

Andy had beaten Les and ran on to blast the ball past the goalkeeper.

'Only seemed that way because you weren't fucking watching,' he told Pickles, so you'd hardly have guessed they were on the same side. 'Make up your mind: if you're going to play, play. If not, get off the pitch.'

Pickles stood by himself as the game went on around him. Then, wiping the sand from his mouth and shaking his head sadly, he turned away and trotted after Gerardy and Barry.

Andy's side added another quick goal to make the score 10–8. Half-time. Both teams went down for a breather. Pickles had drawn level with the McMahons on the very edge of the playing fields.

'Look at them run,' Les said. 'The dopy beggars.'

'You mean *Derry*beggars,' Mal quipped.

He did not usually risk making jokes, but the name seemed so apt when it flashed into his mind that he said it almost without thinking. The boys spoke the word over and over to themselves, laughing louder the more they grew accustomed to it.

Eddie cupped his hands round his mouth and yelled towards the road: 'Derrybeggars! Derrybeggars! Derrybeggars! Derrybeggars!'

And on like that until his voice cracked.

The second half dragged even more slowly than the first. Bit by bit darkness closed in, though for what seemed an age it hovered about the sidelines, as if allowing the boys time to finish. But somewhere around 16 all the game got bogged down. Legs were tiring, shots and passes going astray.

'Next goal the winner,' Mal called out.

Everyone speeded up, giving one last effort. But it was no use. Pickles's departure had cancelled out the slight edge Andy's team had had in the first half. They could have gone on forever the way they were playing, and still not have got a decider.

Andy said what they were all thinking. 'Aw, fuck this. It's a draw. Replay tomorrow.'

Bodies slumped with relief and darkness invaded the pitch. The boys drifted home in twos and threes, with only the Hardys, Les and Mal staying behind on the field. It was dark enough for Mal to smoke without worrying about anyone he might know spotting him from the houses opposite. He offered his fags all round, too glad of the rest to be bothered that none of the other three ever offered theirs. To the west, the setting sun had brushed the horizon with a thin strip of red, and towards the northern-most end of this strip the sky was flecked with spits of orange and yellow.

'What d'you suppose that is?' Mal asked.

'Unity Flats, with any luck,' Andy said.

Their faces glowed in random sequence as they smoked their cigarettes, watching the flashes leap on the edge of the red strip, like sparks from a dying fire.

When they had finished, they stamped their dog-ends into the grass and began the weary trek across the pitches to the hill. As they were passing along the bottom of the pavilion, they were stopped by a shrill finger-whistle from up the blind side.

'Who the fuck's that?' Andy said, squinting into the black-ness.

And that was all he said. Next moment, Mucker was on top of him, pummelling his head and shoulders with his fists.

'Finished, am I? Fruit, am I? We'll fucking see about that!'

After months of speculating and the occasional near thing, the long-awaited showdown was over in seconds. It was like watch-ing a re-enactment of the Eleventh Night fight: there was no jagged lighting this time, of course, but even in the darkness Mal could see the result was identical. Blood poured from Andy's nose and his left eye was already beginning to puff.

'Get him, Les,' Peter cried, and Mucker laid off Andy long enough to give his brother a smack too. Les came forward half-heartedly and Mucker dug him one in the belly. It didn't appear that hard to Mal, but Les keeled over anyway and looked thank-ful for it.

Andy was being hauled to his feet, hands stretched out in submission.

'Lay off, Mucker,' he spluttered. 'It was a joke, that's all.'

'You know what I think of your jokes,' Mucker said, lifting the back of his hand. Andy hid his face. 'And I suppose hitting a girl's a joke too?'

Andy looked out briefly from between his fingers.

'Did Sonia tell you that? She's a lying bitch.'

'Watch your fucking mouth.'

Mucker dead-legged him and Andy groaned, sinking to one knee.

'Sonia didn't say a word to me. And nor did wee Pickles, before you get any ideas. You've been watched the whole day – you're being watched all the time. Remember that. Touch either of them again and I'll be round for you. Hear?'

Andy had backed off to where Peter waited, with another bloody lip.

'Take your shite with you,' Mucker said, sticking his toe in Les's rump.

Les was up and away like a lilty and Mal was alone with Mucker. At the bottom of the hill, Andy stopped and yelled back to the pavilion.

'That's it, Press. You've had it now.'

'Any time,' Mucker shouted defiantly. He flicked the hair out of his eyes. 'Any time,' he said. Quieter.

He turned suddenly on Mal and grabbed him by the ear. 'And as for you, you're not even worth hitting. I could fart on you and knock you over.'

Mal slipped his clutches and retreated towards the pavilion. Then he stood stock-still, hearing a movement in the shadows behind him and a noise like a husky laugh. He recognised the smell before he heard the voice.

'Leave the child alone.'

Francy Hagan plodded out from the darkness.

'Hail Malkin,' he said. 'The Great Malacophilous!'

A thousand thoughts and questions careered across Mal's mind, seeming to ricochet off his very skull. But, over everything, one emotion held sway: amazement, complete in itself and compounded again and again by his lack of all such feeling in the past few days. In the same way that toothache was always worse in the returning than in the remembering, so this was astonishment and then some.

'Why the surprise?' Mucker asked. 'D'you think I could watch youse all on my own?'

Francy dredged up a gobful of phlegm and sent it thumping on to the grass.

'Like the haircut. Sexy.'

They were Sally's words exactly, but Francy's tone was beyond even the sarcastic. Where yesterday Mal's face had flushed, it burned now out of all control and he was unable to summon a single one of his new-found talents to his aid. Shock was being succeeded by an appalling sense of shame.

'See you're all tough these days,' Francy said. 'Smoking and everything.'

'Only the odd one,' Mal mumbled.

Francy clicked his thick, red-haired fingers, and Mal groped in his pocket for the cigarette box, pushing the cardboard tray out with his thumb. There were two left. Francy didn't even pause for thought: he took them both.

'Filthy habit,' he said. 'A wee lad your age.'

He snapped the filters, flicking them to the ground, and popped the cigarettes into his mouth. He grinned as he chewed, then gulped noisily, dangling his tongue out to show there was nothing left.

Mucker sniggered, chuckled, and in a minute was laughing hysterically. Francy simply grinned more broadly still, tongue hanging from the gaping blackness, preening the tufts of red hair about his mouth and chin.

3

Phil the Flutter put his entire pay packet on a horse in Saturday's 4.30 at Thirsk. Every last penny of it. He'd have bet his shirt too, if he hadn't had to walk through the city centre to get home. He'd had a tip from a friend in the know: the horse was a cert. Phil placed the bet on Thursday evening on his way from work and got early odds of 12/1. Between then and Saturday, the betting came in and in and every drop had Phil rubbing his hands together saying, boy-o-boy, did he have it made, and telling the others in the gang what mugs they were not taking advantage of his tip. By quarter past four on Saturday afternoon, when they clocked off at the site, Phil's horse was being paraded around the paddock over the water in Thirsk, 3/1 favourite.

That Monday morning, however, Phil arrived at work looking like a man on the way back from his own funeral. Just before the off in the big race, his horse had panicked in its stall, ducked out under the gate – knocking the jockey for six in the process – and galloped off down the track. There was a chase along the back straight, with the stable boy, the trainer and a gaggle of stewards tearing like mad in the horse's wake. They'd all but succeeded in directing it into the enclosure when, at the last minute, the horse seemed to get wind of what they were about and tried to escape by jumping the rails. Well, it may have been a good bet on the flat, but it was no steeplechaser; it landed full-square on the fence and toppled over in a heap on the other side. The vet was on the spot in a flash. Both back legs broken, he said; no option but to shoot the old thing. So they pulled the trigger and, at the same time, pulled the carpet clean from under Phil the Flutter's feet.

He'd managed to stave off his wife's demands for the house-keeping on Thursday and Friday, but when he turned up again on Saturday with nothing in his pocket, she gave him the rounds of the house. If he was to leave work empty-handed that night, then he might as well not bother going home at all. The upshot of the whole thing was that he'd to borrow his next week's pay in advance from Uncle Simon and he was now spending every free minute poring over the form guides, hoping to find a safe bet on which to recoup his losses.

'Could go on like that forever,' Mr Martin concluded. 'Who'd be a gambling man?'

'And who'd be married to one?' his wife replied, filling the teapot.

Mal found himself smiling at his father's story. It was a peculiar smile, in that it was formed, as far as Mal could tell, by the mutual consent of his lips, independent of his brain. That was not to say the smile was false; he had listened to every word of the tale and, if asked, would have said he'd enjoyed it. Yet, withal, he could not imagine from what quarter of his brain the order had come to make his mouth crease like that. It was as though the words were taken in, dealt with and stored somewhere on the very edges of his mind. For the centre felt hollow; as it had done since the previous evening, when he turned his back on the laughing figures by the pavilion and made his way home, alone, across the playing fields.

The teapot was placed on a cork mat where the brass bowl – rescued without comment, but duller these days – normally stood, and Mr Martin watched it, waiting on the tea drawing.

The smells of the food they had been eating hung heavily in the kitchen and dinette, so that they, too, seemed swollen and gorged. Mrs Martin opened the kitchen door like you would a notch on a belt. The television was on in the living room and, in exchange for the smell of fried cabbage, a newscaster's voice drifted through, telling them about the trouble. Rioting had gone on throughout Sunday and into the early hours of that day; it had been worst around the Unity Flats complex, at the junction of Peter's Hill and Upper Library Street, and in the Ardoyne area, north of the city. The newscaster had a pleasant, consoling sort of voice, even when talking about violence; polite too. He could have been a friend of Uncle Simon's.

Mr Martin lifted the teapot from the cork mat and swirled it twice before pouring a drop of coppery liquid into his wife's cup. It mingled with the milk, tanning it a strong brown.

'That's fine,' she said, and he filled all three cups almost to the rim.

Someone else was talking now in the front room. His voice was high-pitched, irascible and urgent. The newscaster attempted several times to calm him, but he was having a job getting a word in edgeways.

'This situation must not be allowed to obtain a minute longer. Not a minute longer. It's scandalous, is what it is. Women and children sleeping on the floor of a school dinner hall, whole families with nowhere to go. Scandalous is the only word for it. Since Saturday night they've been coming in their droves from Ardoyne and we can do nothing to help them.'

He paused for breath long enough for the newscaster to ask sympathetically just what it was he wanted done.

'Want done?' he replied, with never a hint of gratitude for the sympathy. 'We want the ministers sitting on their fat rich arses in Stormont to make Derrybeg a priority housing area.'

It was hard to say which of the two words – arses or Derrybeg – upset Mr and Mrs Martin most. The newscaster tried again to interrupt.

'They've ignored us too long as it is,' the angry man went on regardless. 'Starved the town of resources. Half the houses here aren't even fit to hold the people as is living in them, let alone give shelter to those that's been evicted and got nowhere else. The people of Derrybeg's fed up seeing houses built all around them, but never for them. Well, we'll not stand for any more. Either Stormont promises to allocate us the houses we need, or we'll go and take them anyway, for we'll not have our kin sleeping in the streets.'

The newscaster thanked him, which was a lot more than Mal's parents would have done, by the looks on their faces. They sat with their cups poised at their lips. Mal stashed it all away in his mind, but said nothing.

Later, at a time when the fading light outside would usually have led them to shut the blinds, the family were still sitting in shadow in the sombre living room, Mal on the settee, his mother and father in the armchairs either side of the fireplace. His parents had forgotten to let go of their teacups when they had finished with them; they hung from their fingers, empty now, save for the saturated leaves. A well of darkness was growing in the middle of the room between the three of them and the only movement on their faces was the black-and-white flickering of the television.

After a while, the process with the television was reversed and Mr Crosier's face appeared, reflected on the screen. Mr Martin jumped from his seat with evident relief and smiled towards the peering face at the front window.

'Cup of tea, Danny?'

Mr Crosier was being shown into the living room.

'Thanks, but I won't.'

'Well, take a chair there anyway,' Mr Martin urged him.

Mr Crosier ran a finger around the inside of his collar and in the darkness the folds of fat that did him for a neck wobbled whitely.

'Actually,' he said, 'I can't stop that long.'

He fell silent while Mr Martin scrabbled for the switch panel and turned on the main light. The room flashed suddenly yellow and Mr Crosier continued.

'I take it you saw the news this evening?'

Mr Martin had regained his chair and nodded seriously.

'Well, we ... That is, a few of the neighbours and myself were a bit disturbed – as I'm sure you were ...'

He stopped again, and Mal realised he was looking at him. He was smiling so good-naturedly that, for a second, Mal thought he must have told him a joke, and he smiled back, searching desperately through his mind to find it. Once more, though, he came up against the blank in the middle and could not get round it. Whatever was beyond that was, for the moment, out of reach. But his parents, too, were watching by this time, and he didn't need his whole brain to understand they would rather he wasn't there. He got up from the settee and left the room before he could be sent.

Kneeling on the edge of his bed by the windowsill, Mal counted the men gathered at the top of the hill: Mr Kennedy, the bus conductor, Tommy Duncan, who had the milk float, Billy Bell – either just going on or just coming off duty, for he had on his B Specials uniform – Tom Garrity, Elijah and Jonathan Smyllie, the twins, who were married on the same day, in the same church, and now lived next door to each other. Six from his own street and others besides from around the estate, some of whom he knew to see but couldn't put a name to. Perhaps fifteen in all, clustered about the street light. And leaning against the lamp post itself, holding forth to the rest, by all appearances, was the hulking figure of Bobby Parker.

A period of time elapsed – Mal could not have said whether it was long or short – and then the front door opened and closed below. The flat, shiny top of Mr Crosier's head came into view and the men at the lamp post turned to face him. When he was still some yards away he gave them the thumbs-up sign. On the extremity of the lamp's arc of light, his face obscured, someone was lighting a cigarette one-handed.

It was soon clear to Mal that no matter how pleased his father might have been at first to see Mr Crosier on Monday evening his visit was, ultimately, anything but welcome.

In the days that followed, he grew paler and ever more pre-occupied and, whereas the week before he had been cheerful in the mornings and ready for work bang on the dot, now he hung about the house to the last possible moment, as if hoping some-how he would simply forget to go. Whatever time he left, though, Mr Crosier would be waiting for him. Mal watched them each day as they walked out of Everest Street, Mr Crosier talking away, nineteen to the dozen, his father trudging along beside him, his head lowered, like Sammy Slipper in the old story.

By Thursday night, Mr Martin was visibly depressed. He stayed on in the dinette after the dinner dishes were washed up and the brass bowl was set back on the cleared table. Mrs Martin ushered her son into the living room and closed the door behind them. She put her feet up on the settee to read the paper and for a time looked very intense, turning the pages at regular intervals; but Mal could see that her eyes were roaming over the pictures and columns of newsprint, unable to settle anywhere. It was hardly surprising, though, for on the other side of the kitchen door, undermining all her attempts at concentration, the brass bowl was being rattled. Or, rather, whatever was in the bowl was being rattled, tipped on to the table, then scraped up and rattled again, in seemingly endless repetition. Finally, she slapped the crumpled paper against the cushions and swung her feet round on to the floor, cursing her husband with the word she had brought back from Pat and Simon's.

'Damn that man!'

She stalked off to the dinette and Mal settled into the cushion she had warmed, steeling himself, in an oddly detached way, for the inevitable argument. He quickly discovered, however, that even fights were apparently to be different from here on in. Only his mother's voice reached anything like a shout, and his father's dejected responses were mumbled and weak in comparison.

'Pull yourself together. What on earth's the matter?'

'You know.'

'That? All this is over that? A neighbour asks you a question, you give him an answer and days later you're still torturing yourself over it? Listen, this goes on all the time: they call it conversation.'

'It's what he asked me.'

'What did he ask you? It's a man with a torch guards that place, not the Secret Service. He could have phoned the company itself and found as much out from them.'

'But you know what they'll do.'

'No, I don't. And nor do you. Nobody told us anything. So long as we don't go poking our noses where we shouldn't we're none the wiser, and all the better off for it.'

Mr Martin sighed deeply. 'But, Simon …'

'Simon doesn't have to live here,' Mrs Martin beat him down. 'I do, God help me. And let me tell you, I've been an outcast in this street once already and I'm not about to go back to it.'

'I could end up with no job if anything was to happen.'

'Oh, give over. Simon's not going to lay you off now you're in.'

The bowl was rattled again, its contents scattered on the table, and Mrs Martin's temper peaked.

'And for heaven's sake, stop doing that!'

Coming back into the living room, she lifted the lid of the coal bucket that doubled, in the summer, as a bin, and shook the brass bowl over it. A few hairpins fell out and a pair of Monopoly dice.

Mal tried to call the argument up later that night in bed. But still he could get nothing to take hold in the centre of his brain.

The hollowness remained, indeed, seemed to spread as he lay there, pushing even the half-formed thoughts into steadily darker recesses, until his mind was entirely void and he tumbled into a deep, empty sleep.

At breakfast the next morning, his father was at the table once more, in his pyjamas now, with a pullover on over the jacket, staring dumbly at the solidifying yolk of a soft-boiled egg.

Mrs Martin leaned across in her seat and placed a hand on his temple.

'You're hot,' she said. 'Why don't you take a sick day?'

But Mr Martin pushed his chair back from the table and walked out of the kitchen.

'I'm going to get ready,' he told her.

A quarter of an hour later, however, when Mal went through to the front room, his father was standing by the window, still in his pyjamas and clearly never having gone upstairs at all.

Mr Crosier was waiting, as usual, at the top of the hill, but for a change he was not alone: Bobby Parker was there too this morning. Mal glanced at the clock on the mantelpiece: twenty-five past eight. His father had no chance of being dressed in time for work. Something of the same sort must have been going through Mr Crosier's mind at that very moment, for when Mal looked again he was checking his wristwatch. He pulled down his sleeve and smiled to Big Bobby. They tapped each other on the shoulders and went their different ways, Mr Crosier down the hill, Bobby up Larkview Avenue and out of sight towards the front of the estate.

Mrs Martin had been watching her husband from the kitchen. As he stepped back from the window she came to him and turned him about in her arms. For a few instants they stood together, motionless; then, slowly, Mr Martin's chin began to tremble and he buried his face in his wife's dressing gown.

One of the biggest gripes Mal's parents had with the Larkview house, after moving from the Belmont Road, was the ease with which noise travelled from room to room. Especially from the bathroom. The walls were only deal, they complained, and so badly soundproofed there was no getting even a minute's privacy. Still, flimsy walls had their advantages, and if it hadn't been for them, Mal never would have discovered just what was the matter with his father that morning. He had a bad dose of diarrhoea.

Though he had had no real inclination to go out over the doorstep since the weekend, the thought of spending the whole day at home with his mother and father in the mood they were in did not much appeal to Mal either. He footered about in the garage for a time, letting on he was driving the car, but he couldn't think where he was driving it to, and was soon bored. He gathered his caser from behind the lawnmower and kicked it down the driveway on to the street, still with no clear idea what he was going to do.

Just in front of the house, Les was toiling by, laden with bags of vegetables wrapped in newspaper and trying to keep up with his mother, who marched on ahead, trailing a bulging shopping trolley. Les was puffing with the effort and his only hello to Mal was a nod.

'Coming for a game after?' Mal called behind him.

'Uh-uh,' Les said, without breaking stride. Too busy.'

It seemed he wasn't alone there either. For not only was Everest Street itself hiving, but all the streets between it and the front of the estate, Mal noticed, were uncommonly full, considering the Twelfth Fortnight was over and the morning rush hour had been and gone. Friday was normally the day when most families did their groceries, but this was something else again. It could have been Bangor he was in.

At the roundabout, however, he stopped, staring across the road at the shopping precinct. There could be no doubting now where he was. There, on the side wall of the supermarket, a

Union Jack had been painted and, in tall letters below it – a warning and a challenge to anyone entering the estate – the words:

LARKVIEW IS PROD. DERRYBEGGARS GO HOME.

The kerbstones before the wall had also been painted: red, white and blue, red, white and blue, right the way round the corner to the shops.

Mal looked at the second part of the slogan curiously. His word. It was as if he'd entered a competition, dreaming up a motto for the estate, and was having his winning entry put on show. He wondered whether the correct reaction ought to be one of embarrassment or of pride, but as it turned out he felt neither.

The bin lorry cut suddenly between him and the wall and swung into the Hook. Andy Hardy was riding on the footplate at the back, his left eye blackened from Sunday night's thumping. It wasn't the binmen's day for Larkview – Fridays they were meant to do the crossroads below the estate. But then, Mal thought, with the holidays and what have you, they maybe hadn't got back into their proper routine yet. He crossed the road behind the lorry, into the jostle of shoppers. Eddie, his three younger brothers and little sister lounged in a loose line outside the supermarket. A handwritten sign in the window asked customers to bear with the management and kindly restrict themselves to one loaf of bread per person. As Mal was passing, Mrs Boyd came out one door with her shopping and handed a coin to Eddie, sending him straight in the other door and taking his place in the line.

Signs definitely seemed to be the order of the day. At the newsagent's there was one advertising special discounts on cartons of cigarettes and the chippy got in on the act with a request to people *not* to lean their bicycles against the window. Mal hung about the chippy wall with vague hopes of finding someone among the shoppers he could play with, but he was quickly resigned to the fact that there wasn't going to be a lot doing in that line. Everyone was in too much of a rush. Even Tommy Duncan appeared to have been smitten by the panic; his milk float was still on the road, hours after he should have finished his run. Mal's gaze followed the float's erratically jangling course past the newsagent's, along Crawford Drive. And then there was the bin lorry again, parked by the footpath now, at the point where the road began its slow curve round the back of the estate. Tommy pulled up behind it and got down from the cab for a chat with Andy and Bobby Parker. The three of them talked some time, resting their elbows on the milk float's crates of empties.

'No kisses today, Mal?'

Sally Cleary and her friend Jess were at the door of the newsagent's. Sally's mouth was open in exaggerated bewilderment, but the deep-red beam on her face was genuine enough.

Jess had started singing:

> Mal and Sally up a tree, k-i-s-s-i-n-g,
> Sal says Mal, oh let me go, Mal tells Sally no, no, no.

Mal didn't know where to put himself. People were walking by, elbowing one another, smiling at him and Sally. She could take no more and sought refuge in the newsagent's. Mal beat it round the corner, suddenly glad of the crowds and not altogether sure it was worth the trouble having Sally for a girlfriend if this was the sort of thing that happened. Jess chanted on:

> First comes love, then comes marriage,
> Then comes a baby in a carriage.

The line of Boyds outside the supermarket had altered again. Now, Eddie, his mother and the three brothers were waiting for the little sister. Each of the boys had a loaf of bread, and a shop assistant was busy on his knees beside them, scribbling the word 'person' off the sign and writing 'family' in capital letters above it. The exit door opened and the little girl emerged, clutching a barmbrack and a packet of wheaten scones. Mrs Martin was behind her.

'Hello,' Mal said. 'I didn't know you were going out.'

'Your daddy's sleeping,' she told him. 'I thought I'd get a couple of messages.'

She handed him one of the three carrier bags. 'Here, make yourself useful.'

Back in the house, the carrier bags were set on the sideboard for unpacking. Mal didn't mind this bit; he liked to see what they'd be having in the coming week. While his mother put away the toiletries and household goods in the cupboard under the sink, Mal opened the larder and got started on the foodstuffs: mandarin oranges, pineapple chunks, pear halves in syrup. Another tin of mandarin oranges; more pineapple chunks, and more pears. In fact, there were three tins of each, plus two of cling peaches and an extra-large can of fruit cocktail.

'Mum?' he asked. 'What's all the fruit for?'

His mother was unwrapping a toilet roll to take to the bathroom.

'The Spar was nearly out of peas and carrots,' she said. 'I didn't want to be running short.'

His father didn't feel like coming down for dinner that night and when the last dish had been dried and put away his mother yawned and said she was going upstairs for an hour or two for a lie down. Mal thought about playing outside, but one look into the street changed his mind. The daytime's air of frenetic activity had evaporated completely, leaving the road deserted and every house on it as quiet as his own. In one after the other, blinds were lowered and curtains drawn, long before the darkness finally occupied the estate. The evening gaped. An ache came on within Mal's mind, as though the weight of the thoughts stored on the periphery was becoming too great and was pressing in, threatening to dispel the vacuum. He shut his eyes tight and waited. Outside, where darkness reigned like a natural curfew, the houses stood silently, as if waiting too.

When he awoke, Mal found his mother and father in the front room with him. His father was dressed now and traces of his normal colouring were beginning to reappear low down on his cheeks about his unshaven jowls.

They were eating from a plate of sandwiches on a small, collapsible table between the two armchairs and talking in such loud voices that it was some time before Mal became fully conscious of the noise – like that of a sledgehammer on a sheet of tin – coming through the kitchen window from the back of the estate. At first, with no one else taking any notice of it, it seemed to Mal entirely possible that he was imagining the sound, that it was the lingering remains of a dream. But the ringing that resounded in his ears when the hammering eventually stopped convinced him that he had not been dreaming after all. His parents' conversation tailed off and they reached forward to the plate for a sandwich.

The second they began to eat, however, a short, hollow bang in the distance rattled the windows of the quiet house. There was another bang, then another, then three more in quick succession. Nobody could pretend they hadn't heard *them*, and nobody tried. Mrs Martin left her own armchair and sat on the arm of her husband's. She took his hand in hers, locking their fingers together.

It was already long past even Mal's new bedtime when the doorbell rang and disturbed their portrait pose. Mrs Martin un-crossed her legs stiffly and eased herself up from the arm of the chair. But Mr Martin checked her with a nervous, fluttering wave.

'I should go,' he said.

His walk was so slow and deliberate that if Mal hadn't known better he'd have said he had been drinking heavily. Halfway across the floor he paused before the mirror to moisten his lips with his tongue.

He had barely had time to open the front door when he was bundled back into the room by a breathless Uncle Simon. Aunt

222

Pat and the girls followed at his heels, rather more sedately, but it was obvious from their clothes that they hadn't come on anything so straightforward as a family social call. Aunt Pat was in a sleeveless, sequined dress, loosely draped with a shawl, Cathy in wet-look hot pants and knee-length boots. Alex was even wearing a new dress; it was a lot more flowery than the styles she normally went in for, a lot more feminine, in a grown-up sort of way. Uncle Simon had taken off his cravat and was winding it round his hand like a bandage.

His sister stood up, smiling a smile made up of equal parts welcome and puzzlement.

'This is a surprise,' she said.

'Surprise nothing,' Uncle Simon replied, scowling.

He headed straight for the television and switched it on.

'Sorry about today,' Mr Martin said, closing the living room door.

'Never mind that,' Uncle Simon snapped. 'It's tomorrow we should be worrying about now. I'm leaving Pat and the girls here. Get your coat and come on with me.'

'Simon? What do you think you're playing at?' Mrs Martin was horrified. 'He's in no shape to go anywhere.'

Aunt Pat was looking at her brother-in-law with great concern. Two rivulets of sweat traced the lines of his jaw and met in a drop at his fleshy underchin. She licked a finger and put it to his forehead.

'My God, but you're running a temperature,' she said.

'I've been telling him that all day,' Mrs Martin spoke for her husband. 'He'd a touch of gastric trouble and only just got up to see how he felt. It hasn't cleared any, though; I don't think he should go in to work tomorrow either.'

Uncle Simon had tried all three channels without finding whatever it was he was looking for and he thumped the off button angrily.

'We'll none of us be going in to work tomorrow at this rate.'

'I'll be okay if I wrap up,' Mr Martin said, removing Aunt

Pat's finger from his forehead. 'Where is it you want me to go, Simon?'

'You're not serious, are you?' Uncle Simon asked him. 'You mean to say you haven't heard the brouhaha outside?'

'What brouhaha?' his sister wanted to know. 'The estate's been like a morgue the whole night.'

She glanced furtively at Mal.

'A bit of banging earlier, nothing more.'

'A bit of banging! A *bit of banging*!' Uncle Simon repeated and his laugh only accentuated his anger. 'Is that all it was to you? A bit of banging?'

'Simon!' she stopped him. 'Is that all what was, for heaven's sake?'

But he pushed past her to the kitchen and it was left to Aunt Pat to explain.

'We were at a party in Malone Park – Dalton, the solicitor – when the police phoned. Somebody got into the building site this evening and went to town on it. Not a hut standing, by all accounts. Not a bit of machinery they didn't tamper with in some way.'

'That's dreadful,' Mrs Martin said, shocked but consoling. 'Poor Simon.'

'No need to feel sorry for me,' he snarled over the noise of a running tap. 'I'm damned if a penny for it's coming out of *my* pocket.'

Aunt Pat stroked the bridge of her nose, thinking. 'There was something else the police said. Now what was it?'

'The chapel,' Cathy helped her out and turned the TV back on.

'That's it,' Aunt Pat said, happy for the moment to have remembered. 'The chapel was petrol-bombed as well.'

Uncle Simon returned, clasping a glass of water. 'The one night in the week when there's no guard patrol. Senseless bloody yobbo vandalism.'

He drank down the water and left the glass on the mantel-piece.

'Come on, then, till we see what sort of mess this place is in,' he told Mr Martin.

Mal walked them to the front door and waited as they got into the car at the top of the street. All around, covered windows stared sightlessly from the houses' blank brick faces, but Mal could sense the people lurking behind them. He sensed, too, that somewhere on the very edge of his line of vision there was a telltale chink. His eyes darted from side to side in search of it, but always it seemed to stay one step ahead, and whenever his gaze fell squarely on a particular house where he was convinced it must be, the shaft of light had moved elsewhere. He closed the door and leaned against the wooden rays fanning out from the quarter sun lodged in the bottom left-hand corner of the frame. His head was pounding now, so insistent was the press of the thoughts forcing themselves in upon the diminishing space at his brain's core.

Back in the living room, Alex's dress was the focus of conversation.

'Well, dear knows, it took us long enough to talk her into one like this,' Aunt Pat mused. 'But, I must say, it was worth the wait.'

Alex fidgeted shyly.

'Wasn't it just,' Mrs Martin agreed. 'She looks every inch the woman.'

Mal seated himself on the cushion next to his cousin. Cathy, stretched out on the floor, already engrossed in the late film, shifted her weight from one hip to the other. Aunt Pat pointed to the sandwiches still sitting on the collapsible table.

'Could I have one of those?' she asked. 'Only we'd to leave the party before the buffet.'

Mrs Martin looked at the plate apologetically.

'I'm afraid they're a bit curled at the corners some of them,' she said. 'Wait and I'll make a fresh batch. The men'll likely want something when they get back anyway.'

Alex was spared further scrutiny and Mal was driven by a

sudden impulse to speak to her. He reached out a hand and touched her arm with tentative fingertips. Her skin was surprisingly rough and bristly, not at all, he thought, the skin of a woman. Alex did not say anything, did not look round, but gently lifted his hand and set it on the cushion between them. Whatever Mal had wanted to tell her would not come yet anyway.

Some time after midnight, a key turned in the front door lock and, to the accompanying stench of wood smoke and fire-fighting foam, Mr Martin entered the living room.

It was not he, however, but Uncle Simon, who introduced the immaculately uniformed stranger bringing up the rear. 'Inspector Maguire – my wife and sister.'

They all shook hands and the Inspector was offered a vacated armchair. Mr Martin, meantime, was bringing extra seating from the dinette. He arranged three hardback chairs in a semicircle before the living room door, then sank on to the settee beside his son. His face and clothes, like Uncle Simon's, were blackened and grubby, and when he rubbed his brow with the heel of his hand he streaked it an incongruous pink.

'The kettle's already hot,' his wife said and went through to the kitchen. 'It'll not be a minute boiling.'

'How was it?' Aunt Pat asked.

'Not as bad as we feared,' Uncle Simon replied. 'Not much on the site yet they could damage, thanks be. The huts are easy replaced and a few days in the garage should see to the hardware.'

'The chapel's gutted,' Inspector Maguire said.

'Oh, yes,' Uncle Simon added gravely. 'Made a right mess of the chapel.'

'Wooden building,' the Inspector went on. 'Too far gone by the time the fire brigade got there for them to save it. Tried to burn the priest's cottage too, but it got off with just smoke and water damage.'

'You'd wonder what sort of people could do a thing like that,' said Aunt Pat, and put her hand to her throat, as though, whoever they were, they might be lurking somewhere behind the furniture.

'Well, at least we know who one of them was,' Uncle Simon told her with a satisfied smirk. 'That right, Inspector?'

'Really?' Mrs Martin asked from the kitchen.

The policeman nodded his head, cautious, but confident. He was a thin-faced man with unusually full, slightly bluish lips that pursed before he spoke and gave the impression he was examining every word before releasing it.

'I think we can safely say that.'

'Caught right there and then in the woods,' Uncle Simon said. 'Admiring his own handiwork. Would you credit it? Nasty-looking being he was too. Young fella by the name of Press.'

The beleaguered space in Mal's mind gave out. Thoughts and memories tumbled in from every side; it was pandemonium in there, he couldn't think straight at all. Beside him, his father's thighs quivered with a faint but steady tremor, as if there was a tiny motor ticking over silently in the cushion beneath, causing them to vibrate. Mrs Martin appeared in the doorway, carrying a tray of steaming mugs.

'Press?' she said.

'That's correct,' the Inspector told her. 'Comes from this very street, I believe.'

'And did he confess to it?' asked Aunt Pat.

Uncle Simon looked at her, momentarily peeved; a look that said it was just like a woman to ask such a naive question. His brief, sideways smile to Inspector Maguire was all patronising allowances.

'Well, of course he didn't. But then you can hardly expect someone who's vandalised a building site – and set fire to a chapel – to be bothered telling the truth.'

'Bovril?' Mrs Martin proffered the tray. The Inspector smiled and took a mug.

'He was identified, though,' Uncle Simon continued. 'The priest, Father Riordan – decent sort – said he'd know him anywhere. Appears the wee lad had some kind of grudge against him and had been loitering out the back of the chapel lately.'

Aunt Pat tutted, distressed. 'You never know who you're living with,' she sympathised with her sister-in-law.

'But that's not the half of it.' Uncle Simon sat forward. 'Do you know what he did when he was stood there face to face with the priest, the man who positively identified him? Laughed. While the chapel blazed and the fire brigade was still fighting to save the poor man's cottage. Laughed. Imagine.'

'Capable of anything.'

It was Mrs Martin who said this. She had stopped before her husband and lowered the tray to him. For a time he appeared not to be interested, scratching his grimy fingernails on his trouser leg, then all at once he started and looked into her face. The tray was offered more insistently, until in the end he lifted a mug. Mrs Martin moved her foot discreetly off his toes and faced her brother, as though perplexed.

'You realise that's the same wee fella he had the run-in with on the Eleventh Night?'

'Aaaah!' Uncle Simon exclaimed. He made a fist against his forehead and walked to the fireplace. 'Of course, of course.'

'Only, I was thinking,' his sister's tone was almost reluctant: 'he hasn't been any too popular with the rest of the neighbours since it happened.'

'What's this?' asked Inspector Maguire.

Mr Martin raised a hand and shook his head. 'It's nothing.'

'I wouldn't call assault nothing,' Uncle Simon said.

'Let's hear no more about assault,' Mr Martin pleaded, getting to his feet and rummaging distractedly in his pockets. 'It's over and done with, and the boy's in enough trouble as it is.'

'Well, if he's in trouble,' Aunt Pat put in her tuppence-ha'penny's worth, 'it's because he got himself there.'

'Absolutely,' Uncle Simon supported her. 'And as far as the other thing goes, I would have thought, in light of what happened this evening, it was anything but over. Do you not agree, Inspector Maguire?'

The Inspector had balanced his mug on the arm of the chair and was unbuttoning the breast pocket of his tunic, lips puckered.

'I must say, if, as seems likely, it was revenge that drove him to petrol-bomb the chapel, there's a strong case for thinking a similar motive might have inspired the attack on the building site.'

He drew from his pocket a small notebook and an expensive-looking rolled-gold ball pen.

'I'd like to have all this clarified,' he said. 'Could we, perhaps ...?'

He glanced from Mr Martin to his wife, to the kitchen door.

'Yes, certainly,' Mrs Martin said.

She tucked the tray under one arm and held the kitchen door for her husband and the Inspector to pass through.

'There's going to be one sorry wee lad in that police station tonight,' Uncle Simon said as the door closed behind them. 'One sorry wee lad.'

In that instant, everything coalesced in Mal's mind: Mucker standing before the priest, laughing as he accused him. The pointing finger. Francy in the cul-de-sac, dying rat at his back, weighing the hatchet in his too-big hands. Bobby Parker's finger pointing from the bin lorry. Then you'll be sorry. Francy laughing.

Mal saw now how far he had kidded himself in the past weeks. Sitting in the rockery, in the shadow of the Cave Hill, overlooking the city, he had wondered why people didn't pull together a bit more to sort everything out; but what he hadn't seen was how easy it was to think such things up there at his aunt and uncle's house, with its patio and breakfast bar and long, long garden. Or maybe he could have seen it even then and, instead, simply chose to shut it out. Like the picture in Cathy's room and the eyes that reminded him too uncomfortably of the hard, beady

229

stare which challenged him from the dump toilet. And Alex. She had tried to warn him back then, but he didn't listen. He insisted on believing that everything he had imagined was possible. Indeed, it did appear possible when he returned to Larkview. The family belonged and, for a while, nothing mattered to him save that quarter square mile and the feeling of togetherness.

But it was no kind of togetherness really. Whatever didn't fit in, got excluded; that's what it boiled down to. Ardoyne, Unity Flats – Derrybeg, for that matter – all seemed as far away as Armagh, Rossville Flats and Londonderry itself had earlier that year. But just ignoring things didn't make them go away. So, Cathy's picture had been taken down; but it was hidden, not destroyed. Somewhere the eyes stared out, same as always.

Aunt Pat gave a short snore. Her cigarette had burnt itself out with a long ash in the ashtray on the mantelpiece. Cathy too was asleep, curled in a ball on the floor, arms pillowed beneath her head, and Uncle Simon was out of the room altogether. Alex's head rested on one hand, disappearing up inside the hair which drooped forward, hiding her face, and Mal couldn't tell if she was awake or not.

The need to talk to her had returned. Now, however, he knew exactly what he wanted to say. His touch this time was bolder, more urgent. But there was no response. Aunt Pat's snoring was growing erratic. He *had* to say something, there was no knowing when he would have another chance. He caught hold of Alex's dress by the hem of one short sleeve and tugged it lightly. Again she made no movement. A second, harder tug, though, jerked her head out of the cradle of her hand and jolted it to one side.

'What?' she demanded. Her eyes were clear and did not appear to have been closed.

'You were right,' Mal whispered.

He held a finger before his lips to tell her to talk more quietly, but Alex paid it no heed.

'I'm glad to hear it,' she said, louder than ever. 'About anything in particular?'

'The "next time",' Mal said, his words barely voiced. 'Remember?'

Aunt Pat stirred in her armchair and Cathy snuggled into a tighter ball.

Alex abandoned sarcasm and shook her head firmly. 'I have no idea what you're talking about.'

There were footsteps on the stairs; Mal trailed on Alex's sleeve until her shoulder was bared. 'You must remember.'

Her stare strayed to where his hand gripped her dress, and Mal could have been a tramp accosting her in the street.

'Would you mind not pawing me, small boy?' she said. 'This was new today.'

She snatched back her dress as the living room door opened, admitting Uncle Simon, scrubbed of dirt and wearing a shirt borrowed from Mal's father. Cathy roused herself and stretched and Aunt Pat came round groggily. Her lipstick had worn off and her meat-coloured lips were dry and cracked. Almost simultaneously the light was switched off in the dinette and Mal's parents and Inspector Maguire walked through from the kitchen to join them. The Inspector was rebuttoning the pocket of his tunic.

'Thank you very much for your help,' he said.

Uncle Simon passed an arm around his brother-in-law's shoulder and gave it a hefty squeeze.

'Buck up,' he said. 'Now you can forget about it.'

Mr Martin forced his eyebrows up briefly in response to his heartiness. Standing between the other two men, he looked dirtier and scruffier than ever, looked, in his dejection, for all the world like a man who had just been fleeced at cards. Uncle Simon had even got his shirt.

The patch of ground in front of the woods was still scabbed black; an almost perfect circle; a scab on top of a scab, reopened yearly so that the grass would never heal. Mal paced out its circumference: thirty-five giant steps in all. Here and there he came across charred lines, issuing from the rim of the ring where burning spars had fallen when the bonfire collapsed. He followed one such line to its extremity, then doubled back and let it guide him to the centre, stubbing his gutties through layers of debris and dust. It was easy to imagine a capsule had landed here and blasted off again, leaving only this scorched, desolate moonscape to show that it had ever been. Had blasted off and was circling now, somewhere out there in the no-atmosphere of space.

He remembered the view of the earth from the Apollo rocket. Tucked in the corner of the screen. Whole and apparently tranquil.

He had been taken in by it, just as surely as he had been taken in by the view of the city, spread out before him, from Uncle Simon's rockery. What he had seen was all the surface and surfaces could fool you. You only had to zoom in on Larkview to discover that.

He faced the estate. Streets descending in orderly steps to the park. This was the kindest prospect, the one the architects must have had in mind when they planned the estate. But Mal knew that, seen from Francy's mound, all this was chaos.

He looked beyond the playing fields to the dump and the solitary, drooping willow. A finger of smoke flexed itself weakly between the trees on his left. He struck out across the park knowing what he must do. He was going back to Francy Hagan.

4

Mal was in defiant mood as he strode along the bottom of the crazy-golf course and on to the frowzy sprawl of grass leading down to the dump. He tried to catch the eye of everyone he passed, but people on the streets fronting the park that morning seemed to be much more intent on the direction from which he was coming than the one in which he was headed. The events in the woods the night before were being discussed in doorways and pathways, gravely but excitedly, and Mal felt a stiffening of his conviction that what he was doing was right.

Reaching the fence, he assured himself that the toilet was squatting in its accustomed position before clambering over the wire and dropping down into the dump. His first thought was that there were more nettles than he had remembered; they had proliferated in his absence, spreading out on all sides in dense banks, greedily cluttering the rubbish, as though feeding off it. Twists of bramble cut in and out of them at intervals, making of the undergrowth a formidable second line of defence after the wire. He searched forlornly for the path Francy had shown him on his first visit and his eyes lit on the thorny patch where once he had made a footbridge of his father's boxes of grass clippings; but it too had grown wilder and he knew that if he was to attempt to stand on one of the few remaining exposed surfaces of cardboard it would not support him, but sink slowly beneath his feet.

The outlook was not an auspicious one. Mal was willing to admit that Francy's reception was more likely to be abusive than welcoming, yet neither that thought, nor the hostile jumble of weeds, was going to sway him. He was determined; and it was a determination bolstered by a sense of his own past failings. For it had been he who had betrayed Francy, he now realised, not Francy who had betrayed him.

He found a spot where the nettles were thin enough on the ground for him to make a first, tentative inroad, then inched forward, grimacing at every scratch and sting that penetrated the denim of his trouser legs, until his ankles, calves, knees and, eventually, thighs became one mass of burning itch and he ceased to feel any specific hurt. The dump's blue-green flies rose up in their scores with each step that he took, but whereas in the past they had flown a few feet ahead before landing, now they merely bounced lazily past his eyes and flopped straight down again to the waste mould.

At length, he halted in the clearance before the mound, peering to see through the fringe of hanging willow. Either the old tree had grown or – more probably – it had stooped even further in its decrepitude, for several of the spindly outer branches brushed the ground, bending double at the ends, as though growing back in upon themselves. Mal rolled his jeans to his knees and, tearing a handful of docken leaves from the ground, rubbed his legs to soothe the itching. All was silent.

'Francy?'

He called the name towards the sloping sheets of tin, but the reply, when it came, was from behind him.

'What?'

Mal wheeled round, disoriented, his resolve once again withered and all the old vulnerability laid bare by Francy's eternal capacity for the unexpected. And the surprise didn't end there;

for Francy was supported by a pair of wooden crutches, so long that they pushed his armpits almost level with his ears. But any idea that he might have been anything other than perfectly comfortable was immediately dispelled by a glance at his legs, which dangled, clear of the ground, crossed in an attitude of relaxation.

'Where did you come from?' asked Mal.

Francy breathed in – from force of habit through one side of his mouth only, though for once there was no cigarette there.

'You mean your mummy never told you?' he said.

He uncrossed his legs and dropped to the ground, pitching the crutches forward and propelling himself past Mal. At the top of the mound he gave a final push, let go of the crutches and landed plumb on the toilet's cushioned seat.

'What did you do to your legs?' Mal wanted to know.

Francy laid off screwing a cigarette into the corner of his mouth and pointed at the red welts, tinged green with rubbing, that scored Mal from the tops of his socks to the bottoms of his hitched-up jeans.

'What did you do to yours?'

Mal rolled his trousers to his ankles. He was getting nowhere. In turning his every question back upon him, Francy was keeping him firmly on the defensive. From now on, he thought, he would say nothing unless Francy spoke first. He waited while Francy sucked the scraggy butt into life and his breathing regulated itself with the rhythm of inhaling. He did not invite Mal to come any closer and Mal did not think it was his place to move just yet without being bidden.

'So you decided to come back?' Francy said at last. 'Don't tell me, your new friends deserted you – and after you getting the haircut.'

He chuckled quietly to himself and Mal wished what he had wished a hundred times since last Saturday: that he had never asked his mother to give him half a crown for the barber's.

'They didn't desert me,' he said. 'I just don't want anything more to do with them.'

Francy laughed good and proper at this, cigarette flicking in and out his mouth with his tongue.

'Fuck me, but you're a fickle little bastard,' he wheezed. 'How did that come about?'

Despite Francy's mocking, Mal was beginning to feel some of his earlier determination clawing its way back; the conversation was coming round to where he wanted it.

'Because of Mucker,' he said.

Francy sneered.

'Oh, aye? And since when was Mucker anything to you?'

'Since when,' Mal retorted, 'was he anything to you?'

Francy plucked the cigarette from his mouth and poked the filter with the hardened tip of his index finger.

'See fucking dog-ends these days,' he muttered.

He raised his head abruptly, his arched eyebrows banishing a frown. 'Don't suppose you've any fags on you?'

'Gave them up,' said Mal.

Francy nodded glumly.

'Of course,' he said. 'I should have guessed.'

He rummaged in his butt box until he found a smokable length. Mal was eager to continue, now that Francy's initial onslaught appeared to have been staved off. But Francy was in no hurry; he took his time lighting the cigarette, before hoisting himself on to the crutches and stalking around the mound. Mal endeavoured to hold his tongue, but impatience finally got the better of him.

'Are you not going to tell anyone it wasn't Mucker?'

'Are you not?' Francy shot back.

Mal's head drooped. He'd walked into it again and lost his fleeting foothold. But if Francy was trying to score off him he didn't pursue it.

'Sure, everyone knows already,' he said. 'Even the police, I wouldn't be surprised. They were dying to get him for something.

Anyway, say they didn't, who d'you reckon's going to believe me he was down here drinking when it happened?'

Mal didn't have to think too long to come up with the answer, but he remained silent beyond that, forcing himself to own up to something else that was lodged in his mind, unpalatable though it was.

'So youse were ... *real* mates?'

Francy splayed his crutches to steady himself.

'Why? You jealous?'

Mal didn't reply. It wasn't jealousy exactly, but when he had seen them together they were in Mucker's world, not Francy's. Now that he was on the dump, his thoughts ran on the den, the altar and the oath.

Francy grinned broadly, showing off his yellow-brown teeth, and folded his legs.

'Mucker,' he said, 'never intended being a mate of mine. You see, he finally worked out it was me that spoiled his bonfire and he wasn't a bit pleased. Seems he blamed everything that happened to him the last while on that.'

He probed Mal with that stare which made him feel his head was see-through and all the workings of his mind were exposed.

'So, he went and got a knife, the biggest knife he could find, and came looking for me. Might've had me and all, if it hadn't been for the booby traps. I was lying under the tree that day, dead to the world, when he charged through the branches. But he took the boxing glove smack in the bollocks and before he'd even the chance to count were they both still there I'd my wits about me and was making a grab for the hatchet.'

'You beat him, then?' Mal asked.

'Beat him?' Francy's tone was scathing. 'Wee lad, we're not talking John Wayne films here – all that circling and slashing shirts and quitting when you've the blade to the other fucker's throat. If one of us had won, he'd have been done the next day for murder.'

237

'So it was a draw?'

'A draw' – said Francy – 'and they'd have buried the two of us.'

'You mean youse never fought at all?'

Francy staggered backwards and gave a low whistle.

'There's no two ways about it, Malarkey, you have to be up right and fucking early to get one over on you.'

Mal knew how dim Francy must think him, but he had gone too far now to let it drop.

'Why didn't youse fight?'

'Why?'

Francy thought about it.

'We were crouched there, face to face, each waiting for the chance to do the other one in. For ages I was heartscared even to blink, in case he lunged at me. But in the end, I couldn't hold back. And when I did ... something happened. He looked, I don't know – smaller. His spurs were gaping and you could see right in his trousers. Dirt bird'd no knickers on him and there was me staring at this wee thing like a jelly baby dangling down: his dick. I swear to God, it was shrivelled away to next to nothing.' He crooked his little finger, pinching it at the topmost joint. 'That's when it hit me: all these years, they'd been filling our heads with that much shit, it was starting to get into our eyes. We were seeing things; seeing big men when we weren't any sort of men at all – just two wee lads squabbling over a dump and a frigging bonfire. They weren't worth the killing for ... So, I dropped the hatchet.'

Francy hauled in his cigarette and spat it – an intricate loop the loop – right down the neck of one of the bottles ranged at the foot of the mound.

Mal turned to him, impressed, but not astonished. 'You got that one in.'

But Francy was watching him, not the bottle. He spat again, less elaborately, and threw down the crutches.

'Ah, what's the fucking use.'

He trudged towards the tree, stopping as he parted the branches.

'Go away,' he said.

But when Francy came out again from the den in the early afternoon, Mal was still there.

'I thought I told you to leave?"

'So you did,' Mal said.

'Then why the fuck haven't you gone?'

All Mal's strategies had been exhausted and he had nothing left to commend him but the small, bald statement of truth.

'Because I don't want to.'

'Well, that's just your bad luck,' Francy snapped. 'Because I want you to.'

Mal willed himself not to flinch from Francy's glower.

'Are you going to make me?' he said.

Francy swiped a crutch from the ground, shaping as if to hurl it, and Mal sprang to his feet, running some yards, until he thought he was out of even Francy's range. There he halted and sat down, amid a cloud of bouncing flies, facing the mound. Francy lowered the crutch and took a seat himself. Opening his butt box, he began tipping the contents of various dog-ends into thin, white papers for rolling. It was a laborious process and one that Francy didn't seem to have quite got the hang of yet. From time to time, a paper pulled apart in the rolling and a stream of dried tobacco poured through the fissure to gather in a poke on his thigh. But Francy was persistent and each time it happened he would pinch the fine grains in his thick, spit-sticky fingers and start again, until he had a complete cigarette.

All the while, Mal waited, arms folded on his knees.

Francy's patience was the first to give this time, although late afternoon and early evening were already mingling and the streets outside the dump emptying of people when next he spoke.

'Is it not past your dinner time?'

Mal had stopped thinking about the time long ago.

'Probably,' he said.

'D'you not think you'd better be getting home, then?'

'No'.

Francy was wandering down off the mound.

'But you know what they'd do if they came searching for you and found you here with me.'

Mal nodded.

'They'd skin you alive.'

'I know.'

Francy stretched out on the grass beside him.

'And you're not bothered.'

Mal was indeed bothered, but there was nothing else for it.

'So why are you doing this?'

'Because,' said Mal, 'I gave you my solemn word on oath, and I broke it.'

Francy threw back his head, laughing.

'That?' he said and laughed some more. But when he saw Mal's grave eyes he stopped and raised himself on one elbow, unsmiling. 'And you're staying here till you've proved you're sorry, is that it?'

Mal looked down at his arms, folded on his knees.

'You're not serious, are you?'

'Yes,' Mal told him.

Francy winced and stood up, turning his back.

'No, no, no,' he said. 'You don't understand.'

'Understand what?'

'What's fucking going on here,' Francy said.

He flapped his arms in demented tick-tack, indicating the woods, the estate – the whole city, maybe – and started for the den. Mal watched him go, puzzling over that all-embracing gesture. Then, suddenly, the cloud lifted and his face broke into a smile: Francy was testing him. He closed his eyes to help him remember and slowly repeated aloud: 'Lesson number ... whatever: Their rules stop at the fence.'

He opened his eyes again. Francy was looking back, absent-mindedly scratching his crotch.

'All right,' he said at last, his voice flat and distant. 'I believe you. Come again tomorrow, if you like. Come any day. Why not.'

Mal scrambled off the ground.

'Thanks,' he said; and when he could think of nothing to add he said it again. 'Thanks.'

Francy humphed and jerked his scruffy chin towards the far end of the dump.

'Go, for fuck sake, before you get a leathering.'

After only a few steps, though, Mal pulled up.

'Francy?' he said. 'Where's that path you showed me?'

Francy was already back by his toilet. He narrowed his eyes, scanning the dump's disorder.

'Overgrown,' he said. 'I stopped using it.'

He picked up one of the crutches and threw it, javelin-like, to land at Mal's feet.

'Use that to beat the nettles down.'

Mal realised how badly he'd underestimated Francy's range earlier; he could've had his head off if he'd felt like it. He thrashed a track through the undergrowth and at the fence tucked the crutch away where he could find it again. As he straddled the wire, he caught sight of Francy, standing just where he had left him. Mal waved. Francy's head moved from side to side, a mass of red hair.

Work on the building site was suspended for a week while a report was made to the Housing Trust, and Mr Martin took advantage of the time off to get down to decorating the house. The living room and hall were stripped for papering and the furniture, television and telephone were all brought through to the dinette for the duration. Mal was not asked to help (though perhaps next week, his mother suggested, he could lend a hand painting the skirting boards) and, if anything, was in the way while he stayed in the house. So, as long as he made an appearance at dinner, his parents didn't seem to mind his frequent, prolonged absences, accepting his reply of 'with a friend' to their occasional enquiries as to where he was spending his time.

This unspoken arrangement with his parents only confirmed Mal in what he had already begun to feel: that his decision to return to the dump was to change forever his life on the estate. It was as if, in refusing to be cowed any longer by the dire warnings of his elders, he had broken through some invisible barrier, across which he now faced them. He was freer than he had ever been. The gang held no fears for him, and he moved through the groups of adults which seemed to form in those days wherever there was a wall to lean against (discussing IRA build-ups in the Falls, the Bogside and Derrybeg), hearing their gloomy talk and knowing he was beyond their reach. Francy made the rules, and everything was no more or less than he said it was.

The days were hot and still – too hot, Francy said, to be bothered going into the hut – but Mal was restless and eager to learn all that Francy could teach him. And so he learned to roll cigarettes from butts that you would have thought had nothing to offer, and even took up smoking again briefly to master French inhaling; he learned how to spit using his tongue for distance and how to light farts so that the flame shot straight out, instead of licking round the seat of his jeans. Francy, for his part, seemed content to sit in the willow's shade, propped against its peeling bark – heedless of the mites and spiders that crawled from it about his matted hair – watching Mal's efforts and smoking his attempted cigarettes, whatever their outcome. Even away from the sun he sweated freely, and each day the semi-circular stains under his arms spread out to include a newer, damper ring.

On Tuesday afternoon, after much coaxing, he showed Mal how he set the booby traps that protected the den.

'I can lay them,' he said casually, 'to allow for the wind, but at the same time so that the slightest other movement triggers them.'

He set them, took them down, and let Mal have a go. Then he said he'd show him one with the hatchet – a real killer, he called it. He sent Mal out on to the mound to prove to him how well disguised it was. Mal lay on the grass, following Francy's shadow as he worked. At length he stood still.

'Done,' he said. 'See anything?'

Mal scrutinised the limp branches.

'Not a thing,' he replied excitedly.

He hung back, waiting for the trap to be sprung, but Francy simply sat down against the tree trunk and lit a cigarette.

'Francy?' Mal shouted after a long pause. 'How do I get back in?'

Francy cackled coarsely, the phlegm rising in his throat.

'Same way I do,' he said, and spat. 'Work it out.'

Mal hadn't managed to work it out by the time he had to leave the dump for dinner. There were ways, he thought, sulking, and there were Francy Hagan ways; and he could light all the farts he wanted, he was still no closer to understanding *them*.

5

There were only two topics of conversation on the street corners the following morning: Mucker's court appearance and the Bogside. Mal already knew enough about both of them to make perfect sense of the snatches he picked up passing from group to group.

Mucker had been brought before the magistrate just after lunch on Tuesday; no mention now of the building site, the chapel, or even the fight on the Eleventh. Instead, he was charged simply with grievous bodily harm on a police officer. He'd bitten his ear off back at the barracks the night he was arrested. The judge remanded him in custody, due to the violent nature of the alleged offence and the fear that he might abscond if given bail.

Round about the time Mucker was being led down to the cells, stone-throwing on the fringes of the Apprentice Boys' march in Londonderry was exploding into an all-out riot between the Bogsiders and the RUC. The Bogside had been barricaded ever since and was calling itself Free Derry. The talk on the estate that Wednesday was of organising a busload of men to drive up there and help the police.

Francy waited on the toilet until Mal reached the end of the crutch-beaten path, then, getting to his feet, he nodded to the tree.

'Come into the hut,' he said.

Mal crouched low behind the corrugated-iron sheets, feeling about for the second passage. He could hear Francy up ahead, and when a hand was offered to him in the gloom he clasped it without a second thought. A sharp tug to the left, a few moments flat on his belly beneath snagging branches, and there he was, picking himself off the floor in the hut. It was all pretty much as he'd remembered it: the polythene ceiling and orange light; the altar draped with a bedspread, the bookcase, tables and chairs; the bundles of newspapers, books and files; the spitoon. Who'd have believed it was real?

'I came down here one night and couldn't find that passage,' he said.

Francy opened the window of the roadworks lamp and lit a cigarette from the ring of blue flame.

'Wouldn't be much of a secret hut if anyone who wanted could find their way in, would it?'

'No, I suppose not,' Mal agreed. 'But I'd been here just the day before and yet the more I searched for it the more I started thinking I'd imagined the whole thing.'

'Ah, well then, there you are,' Francy said cryptically. 'The real secret's believing. Most people find nothing, because nothing's what they expect to find.'

Mal had no idea what his expression was like at that moment, but if his mind was anything to go by it was completely clueless as to what Francy meant. Francy was watching him closely, with a look on his own face that Mal knew well: brows heavy and serious, eyes dancing darkly with the pleasure of seeing someone wrestling with and being floored by a devious conundrum.

'Listen,' he said tantalisingly. 'What if I was to tell you that the entrance to the passage was sealed from the inside?'

But Mal was beyond guessing.

'Give up,' he said. 'What if you were?'

Francy's eyes continued to quiz him a minute more, then he seemed to check himself and the mischievousness went out of them. He shambled to the corner by the altar and shoved the book wall with his shoulder. It rolled gently to the side.

'Wheels,' he said, matter-of-factly, and, pointing into the gap, added: 'How to lock yourself in and avoid your own booby traps.'

Behind the bookcase, a few feet from the impenetrable, tangled hedgerow of the end of the woods, the ground gave way and sloped steeply into a deep black hole.

'What's that?' Mal asked.

'A tunnel,' Francy said. 'I use it so's I'm never seen coming or going, only ever seen actually here. Anyone was to discover the front entrance, I'd be clear of here in seconds.'

Mal peered into the darkness, but Francy was already drawing the bookcase back into place.

'Ever seen rat holes? I'd've been found out ages back if people paid any fucking attention to rat holes.'

'Where does it lead to?' Mal asked.

'Use your head,' Francy told him. 'Where d'you think?'

Of course: the altar stones, the centre pole – where else but to the chapel ruins?

'Am I the only person knows about it?'

'And Mucker,' Francy said. He perched on a stool, upholstered with magazines. 'He took to mooning about the old chapel when he started getting the shove-off from his friends and admirers, hoping that there it would come to him who had done the dastardly deed that brought all this upon him. It came to him all right. One day, he was sitting in the half a window and saw someone crawl out into the bushes, only yards from where he'd hidden his tree. And that was me' – dangling his wrists as though handcuffed – 'caught by my own tunnel.'

He pulled his wrists apart and reached for the butt box.

'Unfortunately for Mucker, though, it was the tunnel got him caught too in the end. When the petrol bombs went off last Friday, Mucker was all for going to see what was up. I tried telling him to stay, but he'd had a skinful, we both had; he fired the head up and I let him go. So, while everyone else was scarpering across the playing fields to the estate, Mucker was headed along the tunnel into the depths of the woods. Pissed bastard must have wandered too far from the hole and when the police closed in had nowhere to run, for he never came back.'

From the softness in Francy's voice, you'd have thought Mucker was a favourite rat that had injured its leg. Mal steered the talk round again to the tunnel.

'Must've taken you a quer while to dig something that size,' he said.

'Did I say *I* made it?' Francy asked him.

He balanced his chair precariously on its hind legs and put his feet on the table.

'At one time' – he began – 'there was a stream ran all the way down from the hills, far side of Derrybeg, and joined up with other streams, somewhere below here, before flowing on into the Lagan. It was that stream dug the tunnel, diving underground and up again as it came through what's now the woods, but then was a forest. Little by little, though, the land round about was claimed for building and crop raising, the stream was dammed and channeled – turned every which way as it took people's fancy. Until, when Derrybeg got big enough to need a chapel of its own, they messed it about once too often, and the water just disappeared. And when it was gone, the bog that had once formed a barrier, right here, between the stream and dry land proper, vanished too. That was the dump.' He smirked. 'Always separate.'

Mal felt a tremor of excitement at the realisation of the history behind the book wall.

'And all these hundreds of years nobody found the tunnel?'

'Hundreds nothing,' Francy said.

'Sure, the first chapel ...'

'Don't tell me – King Billy came past on his way to the Boyne and destroyed it in a battle?' Francy chuckled coarsely. 'Nothing, but nothing any man ever made has survived here from King Billy's day; or the next Billy's, come to that. D'you know something? D'you know the oldest things for miles around here? The trees. See the one out there? That tree was rooted in the earth long before there was a chapel even dreamt of. And what do they do? These eejits that are never done spouting about the past? Tip their shite about it.'

He laughed so hard at the thought that he nearly cowped over on to the floor.

'No, the old chapel was much younger than that,' he said. 'The foundation stone's there yet, if you know where to look. 1875, it says.'

He had steadied himself again, feet on the table.

'Mind you, it was a great thing even in them days. People used to go out of their road for months after, just to stand and look at it. I'll tell you better than that – there was a party for all the local children the first Saturday it was finished and one of the Methodist ministers in the city brought a whole load of kids from his church to it. There was even a man came along with a camera. He sat the children down outside the chapel – Protestant, Catholic, Protestant, Catholic – and took their photo. My grandfather's father was in it.'

He had never before mentioned his family, but even this did nothing to ease Mal's disappointment. A century was a long time, of course, but a century ago there were photographs. There were no photographs of 1690, just drawings in books. Something had been taken away from him and only a very little given back in its place. The battle had been wiped out completely.

'Well, what did happen to it, then?' he asked testily.

'The usual,' said Francy. 'Torched.'

There was a silence between them while Francy searched for his matches.

'You've heard of Home Rule?' he said.

Not heard of, but seen. Graffiti pre-dating 'Remember Burntollet' and 'Larkview is Prod', as battered and faded as the walls it was painted on, a Belfast street poem: 'Home Rule, Rome Rule.' Like the two faces of a double-headed penny.

Mal hedged.

'Ach, don't be ashamed not knowing what it means,' Francy told him. 'Sure, who the fuck knows what anything means? They tell you one thing one day and something else altogether the next. Fucking beans means Heinz now.'

He was inspecting his hands, turning them around slowly before his face. They still looked mighty peculiar to Mal, though not for the reason they had formerly. They were peculiar now not because they were *big* hands, but because they were *hands*. Mal looked under the table at his own, seeing them as though for the first time. They were as funny in their own way as Francy's.

'All you can ever be sure,' Francy went on, 'is that whatever the other sort likes, you're supposed to hate. Anyway, in Derrybeg they thought Home Rule was the second banana. They had meetings and drum beatings and all sorts. But for every march they had, there was a bigger one the following day, saying they shouldn't be let get away with it, till eventually, the Friday it was all to be debated in the English Parliament, the pubs emptied this side of Belfast and a whole squad started down the main road out of the city to show those Rebels what *they* thought of their Home Rule.

'Chances are, though, they intended no more at first than to chuck a few rocks and prove they were bolder than the boldest Fenian man. But, by the time they got to Derrybeg, they'd forgotten all that and remembered only the chapel.

'Fuck, some of them there had been to that wee party only a lot of years before, to celebrate its building and had their picture took outside the door of it. But now? Now, it just looked like one great big Papish insult. So they went for it and all but razed it to the fucking ground.'

Here was Mal's glorious battle.

'Like the other night?' he asked, swallowing painfully.

'Like the other night,' Francy said. 'There wasn't enough could be done to the building site, so the chapel got it again.'

He put a match to the scrap of cigarette in the corner of his mouth, then held it over the table.

'We're a shocking lot for burning things,' he said.

A sharksfin of flame had reached the middle of the match. Mal shaped his mouth to blow it out, but Francy pinched his lips together, cutting off the breath.

'To waste is a sin,' he said. 'And the greatest waste of all is the waste of a fire.'

The flame glided lower and lower, blackening and twisting the matchstick as it neared the hardened skin of his fingertips. They touched with a sizzle. Mal flinched, the flame died and Francy wiggled his index finger, charred match soldered firmly to the end of it.

'Burning the chapel won't change anything,' he said, and banged the stool forward on to all four legs. 'Okay, they might never replace it this time, but them houses'll go ahead just the same. They'll build everywhere, and the woods will go, the park will go, then the dump'll go too.'

'No!' Mal objected vehemently. 'My dad's working on the site. I know. They're not coming this far down.'

Francy shrugged.

'Maybe not this year they won't. But some day, some day they will. It's no fucking big deal. I can't stay here forever, you know.'

'Why?' Mal asked. 'Why can't you?'

They had come full circle. Now it was Francy who looked at a loss. He struck his hand against the edge of the table, breaking off the matchstick, then walked into the gloom on the far side of the den and stood among the files. As Mal watched, the flower urn was transformed still further, becoming, momentarily, a spiturinal.

6

It had been a slow process to begin with, but, bit by bit, Mr Martin had succeeded in lifting himself out of the previous weekend's doldrums. The decorating helped, of course – he was always in his element when working around the house; but the real change came about after Mucker's court case. The fact that he'd finally been able to impress upon the police (and everyone else) that he didn't want to proceed with charges was pleasing enough, but when he realised that all allegations relating to the building site were also to be dropped, his day was complete. When Mal came down to breakfast on Thursday morning, however, his father was pacing the dinette floor, passing his hand repeatedly across his slicked hair in consternation.

'It doesn't seem right,' he said. 'Not right at all.'

On the settee, Mrs Martin was sipping a cup of coffee.

'I don't see there's any problem,' she said. 'Pat and Simon did it, and they couldn't be happier.'

Mr Martin stopped pacing and gnawed the side of his hand.

'Mal,' he said. 'What do you think for the pelmets – paper or paint?'

'Paint,' Mal told him.

'That's what I said.' He turned to his wife. 'See, he thinks we should paint them too.'

Mal sat on the armchair below the kitchen divide, watching the test card on TV. His parents' discussion ground on.

Francy did not make an appearance at the dump that morning, although Mal waited a good two hours, nor had he shown up when Mal returned in the afternoon. Rather than waste any more time hanging around, Mal decided to go back home to see if he could paint the skirting boards; it would save him having to stay in some day next week.

On the road before his driveway, two very young boys, carrying pot lids, were arguing with a small girl, who walked round and round in circles, jetting water from a Fairy Liquid bottle on to the dusty tarmac. It seemed they had been going to play riots, only nobody wanted to be the Bogsiders. One of the boys yanked Mal's belt as he passed.

'Will you tell her,' he said, pointing to the girl, 'she can't be the police?'

'Can,' she said.

'Can't, can't, can't,' the boy repeated. 'Can't 'cause you're a girl.'

The girl held up her Fairy Liquid bottle, wiggling it first at Mal, then at the two younger boys.

'Well, youse can't be the police either, if youse don't have a water cannon.'

She was no older than the gipsy girl Mal had seen in the amusement arcade in Bangor, inclined forty-five degrees to the side, nursing a baby.

'She's right there,' he said.

'Mmmneh!' The girl stuck her tongue out.

Just then, a car screeched into the street from the front of the estate, blaring its horn and scattering the terrified kids on to the footpath. It pulled up at the house beside the Clarks' and Billy Bell jumped out, tearing along his garden path, leaving the engine running and the door open behind him. Tommy Duncan, who was having a nap after his early morning milk run, lifted his blinds and leaned out of the bedroom window, and the two Mrs Smyllies ventured on to their adjoining doorsteps to investigate. Mal did not think he had ever seen the one without the other and, in fact, had as much difficulty telling them apart as he had their husbands. His mother said they were Free Presbyterians, though Mal couldn't quite see where the Free came from; their sombre clothes made him itch just looking at them, and they spoke so little that they might, for all he knew, have taken a vow of silence.

But Billy Bell was already on his way again, hurrying to the car, buttoning the high, black collar of his B Specials uniform.

Tommy Duncan whistled shrilly from his bedroom window. 'You been called up, Billy boy?'

Billy nodded and threw his cap on to the passenger seat. Buckled outside his tunic was a holster, so long you might almost have been forgiven for thinking it contained a fireman's hatchet, if it hadn't been for the curved butt protruding from the flap at the top.

'Well, by God, I hope you get to Londonderry,' said Tommy. 'Teach those twisters a lesson.'

The Mrs Smyllies gave Billy the thumbs-up and the kids he'd nearly knocked over coming into the street clapped and chased his car as he drove back out of it.

'It'll be all over now,' Tommy called to them. 'You'll see, the Bs won't stand for any of that Free Derry claptrap.'

Going into the house, Mal stopped by the kitchen door, watching his father slap paste on a narrow strip of wallpaper.

'Mal,' he said. 'Just the man. Stand there a minute while your mother and I get this up and tell us is it straight.'

His parents climbed on to stools and positioned the wallpaper over the pelmet.

'Did youse see all that outside?' Mal asked.

'*You*,' his mother corrected him. 'Ewes are female sheep.'

'How's it look?'

'Hanging to the right.'

The wallpaper slithered this way and that on the pasty pelmet as they tried to even it up.

'That'll do,' said Mal.

His father hopped down and helped his mother off her stool. 'See what?' he asked.

Mal told them about Billy Bell's call-up and the hatchet-sized gun.

'About time too,' his mother said, but his father sighed, stepping back to check the papered pelmet.

'I don't know,' he said. 'What'll it be next?'

He didn't have to wait long to find out. At five o'clock, the radio programme they were listening to broke off to bring them a report from Londonderry, and even before the announcer was finished reading it, Mr and Mrs Martin had dropped their brushes on to the papers spread to protect the carpet and were drifting into the street to join their bewildered neighbours. Men and women coming from work were being told the news by those who had been at home all along, and the little girl with the Fairy Liquid bottle was running from person to person.

'Who's side's the army on?' she asked. 'Who's side's the army on?'

None of the grown-ups could bring themselves to answer; it seemed to them that somebody had forgotten to tell the army itself. For, according to the radio, the British soldiers who had just marched on to the streets of Londonderry had not gone straight into the Bogside and finished the job off, but instead were ringing it with barbed wire and taking up position *facing* the police. Worse – the word was from people who'd seen it on TV – as the B Specials were being withdrawn, the rioters actually whooped and cheered.

Tommy Duncan, up and dressed now, wiggled a finger in each ear, as if they were playing tricks on him.

'Who said we needed them in the first place? Another couple of hours and there'd have been no Bogside for them to patrol.'

'Bloody IRA's getting off the hook,' Mr Crosier said, and scratched his flat bald patch.

Vera Garrity told them she'd heard from a girl at work that a Tricolour had been hoisted over the library in Derrybeg the night before.

'And if *they* start a revolt, how long will it be till we've the army here too, protecting them?' she asked.

The Garritys, like the Crosiers, were older than most other couples on Everest Street; their children were grown with families of their own, and that in itself was enough to ensure they were always given a respectful hearing. But the nodding heads now declared that, quite apart from anything else, this was a fair question.

'So, what I want to know,' she went on, and her neighbours were caught up in her logic, 'is who's going to protect us?'

Within an hour of the troops unrolling their barbed wire in Londonderry, the message had travelled from door to door around the estate that there was to be an open meeting at the park that night. They would decide then what steps should be taken to defend Larkview from an uprising in Derrybeg.

At dinner, though, Mr Martin suffered a recurrence of his gastric trouble, and when the time came, he was too busy stepping up and down to the toilet to be much use for any other sort of steps. His wife sent word across with Mal to Mr Crosier that she would be staying at home too, to keep an eye on him.

The dusk was already beginning to thicken when Mal came away from the Crosiers' door, but, what with the commotion of the day and the evening's meeting, he gambled on his parents not missing him for a while yet. He would have one last attempt at finding Francy before going back to the house. He scuttled down the hill, sticking close to the shadow of the houses in the hope of slipping unnoticed past the knot of youths assembling on the football pitches. As he turned into the cul-de-sac, however, a long figure broke away and bolted towards him. Peter Hardy.

'Hey, where are you off to?'

Mal stopped to let him catch up.

'You not coming to the meeting?'

He had had his crew cut trimmed still further and wore a white hanky, tied cowboy-fashion about his throat.

Mal realised it was just such a situation he had dreamt of when he first thought of becoming Francy's friend. He used the words he had longed to use then, though he didn't care now whether or not Peter was jealous, because he himself wasn't in the least bit jealous of Peter.

'Nah, thanks all the same, but I've something better to do.'

'Are you stupid or something?' Peter asked. 'Tonight's the big night. What d'you think it's all been for these past weeks? We could be heroes this time tomorrow.'

Mal gobbed on the ground. His spit was getting stronger.

'Like I said, I've something better to do.'

Peter hooked his arm with the hammerhead of a short, varnished stick and pulled him closer.

'Watch it, Martin. You might be able to fool the rest of them, but I've got my eleven-plus, don't forget. I know.'

He tapped his temple with the stick – a shillelagh, with 'Souvenir of Ireland' engraved on the handle. Mal thought now that the only puzzling thing about Peter was how he had managed to hide for so long the fact that he was a complete idiot.

'There's one person alone on this estate knows anything worth the knowing,' Mal told him. 'And eleven-plus or no eleven-plus, it certainly isn't you.'

For an instant, Peter was more perplexed than angry. He hesitated, then raised the shillelagh above his head. Too late though. Mal had already made his move and brought his knee up smartly into Peter's groin. He had never in his life hit anyone in a fight. Like smoking, it was much easier than he expected it would be.

'And if you're thinking of getting your brother and his mates to come after us, think again. Youse have none of youse seen the half of what Francy Hagan can do yet.'

Mal left Peter to limp back to the playing fields and ran on along the cul-de-sac, desperate to tell Francy what he had done for him and the dump. He grabbed the crutch from its hiding place and laid about him, cutting swathes through the nettles and brambles he'd already battered flat half a dozen times that week.

He could see Francy now, sitting on the toilet, staring at the ground, and where the weeds cleared he cast the crutch aside, calling: 'Francy, wait till you hear.'

The words died in his throat. Francy was tearing lumps off a loaf of bread, dunking them in a saucer of milk on his knees and throwing them on to the grass. There, each piece was being noisily fought over by a dozen or so grey-brown rats.

Seeing Mal, he stopped and rinsed his fingers in the milk. The rats continued to watch him expectantly, some of them clawing at the legs of his jeans.

'Want to try?' he asked Mal, and offered him the bread.

The rats' attention was torn now between the hovering loaf and Mal. He felt briefly the same churning in his stomach he had felt the first day he had come to the dump. All of a sudden, Francy's torso twisted and he flung the loaf far to the left, where it landed in the mangled remains of a pram, devoid of wheels and choked with dandelions. The rats tumbled over each other in their haste to reach the food and scampered up the pram's sides and hood.

'I've been back and forward all day calling on you,' Mal said, still a little shaken.

Francy looked like he couldn't care less. He set the saucer of milk on the ground and stood up, using the same hand to flick crumbs out of the waistband of his trousers. His other hand was holding a bundle of some sort tight against his zip. It was another rat, smaller than the others and, curled in upon itself, smaller still.

'Don't worry,' Francy said and laid it on the cushion. 'She's asleep.'

He rubbed his arms with red-rough hands.

'It's getting fucking cold,' he said.

It was too, but then, this was mid-August. Although the days were hot enough to make you think otherwise, there was a freshness in the cloudless night air that reminded you autumn wasn't far away. Mal had put on one of his school jumpers before leaving the house, but Francy wasn't dressed for the weather at all. He still wore the white T-shirt, run pink, that was the only thing Mal had ever seen him in, though tonight there was a new stain on it, broad and blue-purple, swelling from neck to belly, as if he had dribbled a drink down his front.

Francy turned and went into the hut without another word and, after an uncertain pause, Mal tagged along behind, telling himself he'd been coming to the dump long enough not to need an invitation every time. Francy was huddled over the roadworks lamp, warming his hands, and his thick sponge of hair sopped up its light, making the den so dim Mal could see little else but the central table. There was a peculiar smell in the hut, heavy and clinging – like emulsion paint, Mal thought. He sniffed himself and decided what he smelled were fumes coming off his clothes, made more noticeable by the low polythene ceiling.

'Where were you today?' he asked Francy.

'Even dump-dwellers have to have provisions,' Francy said.

'For the rats, you mean?'

Francy had taken out a cigarette and was lighting it.

'D'you feed them every day?' Mal asked, sitting down at the opposite side of the table.

'Got to,' Francy said. 'It's the only reason they let me stay on. Like rent. The rats were here first, don't forget. Had it all to themselves, until one day, when I was about the age you are now, I was being chased through the woods on my way home from school.'

'Chased?' Mal couldn't picture anybody chasing Francy Hagan.

'Half the class used to come after me, girls and all,' Francy said, making light of his surprise. 'But Mitch Campbell and Gerardy McMahon, they were the ringleaders. My own sort, not yours: their families had nothing either, but mine was bigger and I smelt like left sick ...'

Maybe it was Francy's acknowledgement of his own stink that did it, but at that moment the whole episode came to life for Mal, and he did not so much hear the rest of the narration as see it: Francy running scared, plunging through the bushes at the back of the chapel, hounded by the closing shouts and catcalls; then falling as the earth dipped and disappeared from beneath his feet and finding himself in the tunnel hole. A small Francy – a pot-bellied Francy, maybe – crawling up the tunnel's dirt and blackness, thinking that whatever was ahead could be no worse than what waited for him at the chapel ruins.

There was a feeling in Mal's chest like trapped wind. He thumped twice with his knuckles to make himself burp, but nothing came out and the feeling lingered on, as maddening as an unreachable itch between the shoulder blades. His concentration had been broken; the images became words, and then silence.

Francy was looking about the hut wistfully.

'There wasn't much light here in those days,' he said.

(There was next to none, Mal thought, these days.)

'Only what could penetrate the branches overhead – and that's a fair bit less than gets through now. But it was by that light, as I stepped from the tunnel, that I first made out the shapes of the rats. Fucking millions of them, it looked like, teeming over the floor and calling to each other. Ever been so scared you pissed yourself?'

If Mal had been he wasn't saying.

'Well, fuck, I pissed that day, I can tell you, and near shat to boot. And the sound of it and the smell of it set the rats screaming all the louder. But I knew – scared though I was – that if I wanted this place to retreat to I would have to get used to them and get them used to me. I held my breath till they settled, then crept away, and next time I came I had my school dinner with me, wrapped in a page torn out of my atlas. I left it at the lip of the tunnel and drew back to see would they eat.'

He snorted and swivelled the butt from one side of his mouth to the other.

'Would they eat?' he asked himself. 'They couldn't get enough of it. Each day after that I brought food and each day I stood a little closer, until, at the end of three weeks, I didn't move away at all, but held the food out to them in my hand. And in the half-darkness I saw one come forward and felt its snout rasp on my palm.'

He was rubbing a finger softly across his hand to show where the snout had touched him.

'The following afternoon' – he went on abruptly – 'I brought a stolen lamp with me – the nearest thing to real light, mind, ever to shine in here. And it could have been the sun itself I was carrying, the way the rats cowered in the shadows. But the food, you see, they were near dead for food, and when they'd blinked away their fright and skittered over to me, I knew I was going to be able to stay. And d'you know what I did? I got down on my knees and, with the rats weaving in and out them, I made myself a promise: never again would I be hunted by anyone; and I'd be looking after myself from now on.'

'Yes,' Mal said enthusiastically.

'What do you mean "yes"?' Francy snapped.

'That's what I want too. To be afraid of no one and answer to no one.'

Francy leaned across the table; the blue-purple staining was on the tufts of hair on his chin and bottom lip too.

'Come September,' he said, 'if they can't make me go back to school, my ma and da are being taken to court over the head of me.'

He slumped in his chair.

'Huh! The rats watched me move in and retired to the edges. But they knew all along that sooner or later the den would be theirs again. They weren't wrong either; rats seldom are. They're massing now to take back their own. Doesn't matter how many I bury nowadays, there's always more next time I look.'

Not even in his worst moments of temper was Francy's face as clouded as it was then, with the orange light colouring the spaces between the clusters of red freckles. But Mal's thoughts were on the many hundreds of rats – thousands, for all he knew – buried round about him. And yet always, Francy said, there were more. Dead and not dead. Like Bobo, Sadie's pekinese.

'Ever heard of Sammy Slipper?' he said suddenly.

'Who the fuck's he?' Francy asked.

'Sammy Slipper,' Mal told him, 'is a man from over the other side of town where I lived before – used to come in the shop my dad had there. And Sammy, you see, was married to Sadie and Sadie owned a girny wee dog called Bobo ...'

Although he knew what had suggested it, Mal did not know why he had begun to tell the story. Perhaps he thought it would make Francy smile, or, at least, coax him out of his moroseness. In a short time, however, he had ceased wondering altogether. Halting at first, unsure how each event followed the other, he soon found the tale taking shape of its own accord. Words that he wasn't even aware of knowing flowed into his mouth and arranged themselves in ways he would not normally have thought proper. And as he talked on, so he could see Sammy and Sadie – the dog too, for that matter – much better than ever he had when his father told the story to him. He was even fairly certain he remembered the street they lived in.

The tale tripped out of him, like a spring uncoiling: the dog collapsed, Sammy took it for dead, panicked, buried it and went off supposedly in search of it. And big, heartbroken Sadie was so ashamed at having done him down in the past she got her father to do a wee bit to the garden as a reward.

'Sammy,' he explained to Francy, 'was already on his way home, reckoning if he'd searched for that blasted dog a minute longer he'd be in no fit state to walk. Up the alley he came, shouting: "Darling, it's me; I'm sorry, but I haven't seen hide nor hair of poor Bobo." And then, just as he was in the gate, his father-in-law dug a spade into the garden, the bin bag ripped … And what do you think? Before their very eyes, out jumped Bobo. Sammy was no better versed in dog doctoring than the man in the moon – the thing was never dead at all; it had only passed out.'

He sucked his lip in anticipation of the inevitable question from Francy: 'How had the dog managed to stay alive?'

But Francy didn't ask it. In fact, he was scowling more irritably than before. He stubbed his cigarette on the table and knocked his chair over, standing up. Even without Francy eclipsing it, the lamp gave off precious little light. The flame burned low, as if starved of fuel, and the extremities of the hut remained in the murk.

'That's not how it goes,' Francy said.

Mal had come by now to believe implicitly everything Francy told him, no matter how unlikely or fanciful it sounded to begin with. But for once, he thought, he had blundered. He wasn't the one had lived up the Belmont Road and, sure, wasn't he only after saying he'd never heard of Sammy Slipper?

'Right then,' he said in a fit of pique. 'If you know so much, tell me how it does go.'

'It's much simpler than that,' said Francy, so quietly that Mal's anger seemed all the more unreasonable in comparison. 'A family's dog dies and, for want of anything better to do with the body, they tie it in a bin bag and bury it in the back garden. Years pass, the garden runs to seed and below, unseen in its polythene bag, the carcass rots. Eventually, the family sells up and another one moves in. First thing they want to do is build a greenhouse in the garden. When they're all set to begin, the father ceremon-ially stamps a spade into the ground – rips the dog bag and releases a stench so overpowering that one waft of it kills him on the spot. The End.'

The smell of fumes beneath the sagging ceiling was instantly more oppressive. Mal was nauseated.

'That's a disgusting ending.'

'It's a disgusting story altogether,' Francy said. 'Most stories people tell are.'

Mal was making for the front passage. It was impossible to draw breath in the den. He needed air.

'You must be mixing Sammy Slipper up with someone else.' he said. 'Sammy still lives in the same house.'

But, even as he spoke the words, he was losing sight of where exactly that house was.

'Don't be thick, there's no such person.'

Of course there wasn't. It occurred to Mal now that he had probably always known and had been waiting only to have it said. He had to get outside at once.

'Okay,' he shouted. 'I take it back.'

He ducked down the passage and stumbled through the willow branches on to the mound. The night was grown almost dark, but beyond the crazy-golf course the curling yellow flames of torches licked back the blackness and outlined a throng at the pavilion. Voices carried to the dump, an indistinct, communal murmur.

Francy overtook him and, placing a hand on both shoulders, dragged him down so that they knelt facing each other.

'I'm sorry for shouting,' Mal said. 'I was wrong.'

'No,' said Francy. 'It's my fault. What's it matter if the dog lived or rotted. Your version's as good as mine – a pack of fucking lies. It's all lies – the hut, the dump, everything. I wish I'd never got you into this.'

He shook Mal by the shoulders and his face moved in and then away, in and then away.

'I made the whole lot up. Do you hear me?'

But Mal was having difficulty keeping track of all there was to be heard. Somewhere in another part of the city a sound was beginning to rise: a dull, monotonous, drumming sound, chopped into uneven chunks by echoing cracks. A sound like nothing Mal had ever heard; yet he knew, without thinking, what it was.

It was the sound people had had in mind throughout that year when they prophesied that any day now the guns were coming out.

Francy's fingers were kneading his shoulders and his small, hard, black eyes had swollen fit to burst.

'But the rat charm,' Mal murmured. 'We're friends.'

'Oh, fuck the rat charm!' Francy screamed. 'One dies, another's born. You can always find a second dead rat here.'

Across the park, the meeting at the pavilion had been galvanised by the gunfire. Three loud whoops of assent rang out and then the cheering regulated itself into a simple chant: 'Out, Out, Out.'

Francy tried to get up, but Mal threw his arms about him and parting his lips kissed his open mouth. Rough-smooth face. A smell-taste of dirty nappies and emulsion paint.

A torch-led procession had set out from the pavilion and the chanting grew fainter: 'Out, Out, Out.'

Francy clawed Mal away and struggled to his feet. For one brief instant he stared at him. Then he was off, through the nettles and the brambles like they weren't even there, taking the wire in one leap and lolloping across the grass.

7

Mal rose slowly from his knees as Francy's ungainly figure grew more distant and ill-defined against the shadow of the park; like that of some huge, misproportioned moth, drawn to the receding torchlight. The imprint of his face still lingered on Mal's, its odd roughness reminiscent of the coarse feel of Alex's arm, the night of her last visit. Mal thought despondently how much alike were the expressions in his cousin's eyes then and that in Francy's just now, as he had turned from him and fled.

He could not imagine what had got into Francy that made him say what he did. He lowered himself on to the red cushions, feeling the toilet squat and sturdy beneath him, as though plumbed in. There was nothing remotely invented about *that*. And yet Francy had talked like the Larkview sceptics, who didn't believe there was a hut on the dump at all ... His thoughts ground to a halt and he found that he was walking towards the sloping sheets of tin. He was not checking, he told himself; he knew now why he had not discovered the entrance the time before. No, not checking, not trying to prove that he was right, but to prove, once and for all, that the others were wrong.

The passage had been left unobstructed and he was able to enter without difficulty. He stamped his feet on the hard, grass-worn earth and ran his hands over the table and chairs. It was as he had thought: there could be no doubting that they existed. His fingers traced the substance of the roadworks lamp and a new idea took root in his mind. If Francy *had* gone, *had* run away from his dump knowledge, then all of this, by rights, would pass to him, as the only true believer. He pictured himself alone here, master, and strove to contain a surge of excitement as he toured the inherited den, the walls of which, he now noticed, were curiously criss-crossed with lengths of hose and plastic tubing. He held the lamp above his head and approached the book wall. The piping there was run riot, impossibly snarled and all but blotting out the neat rows of books. Not far off, nestling among the newspapers and files, was an unfamiliar object, where the tubes seemed to begin and end; a barrel, with a hessian sack covering the top. Mal pulled back the sacking and a sharp smell stung his nostrils, watering his eyes. The fumes he had taken for paint were coming from here. Holding his breath, he peered into the barrel, tilting it slightly towards him. Oily liquid sloshed thickly against the side. Petrol.

There was a scratching at that moment in a darkened corner of the hut and a rapid screeching, like the cry of angry hunger. Mal forgot the barrel and began retreating carefully towards the front passage. For the second time that evening, some of the old fear clutched his innards: alone on the dump meant alone with the rats. Would he be able to feed them every day? And, if he wasn't, how long before they went for him and drove him out? Or worse?

No, he was not yet ready; in all probability he never would be. He knew it, the rats knew it. The dump was Francy's and Francy was the dump. They needed him. Mal had to get him back.

But there was no sign of him now as Mal looked out from the mound; no movement anywhere in the park, save the distance-dimmed flicker of torches, stationary by this time. Where?

The truth hit him like a thump in the guts. Brookeborough Close. Guilt and an awareness of his own stupidity swamped his brain: Francy did not flee *from* anything. He thought of the Campbells, gone overnight and already forgotten. But he had wasted enough time as it was, and every minute he shilly-shallied, pondering like a halfwit, was another one lost. He scrambled, as fast as he could in the gloom, over the disordered refuse, and once on the grass belted for all he was worth, his self-recriminations superseded by an apprehension so awful and real it appeared to depart from his body altogether and to chase him. It stayed on his tail right across the playing fields; and, in his agitation, Brookeborough Close seemed ever more like a refuge, less and less like the cause of his alarm. With every step he ran, the cementing darkness was diluted and the sinister, blurred mass thinned out to reveal the people who composed it.

Mal's chest ached from breathing through his open mouth and a stitch stabbed beneath his ribs. He pulled up, clutching his side, still some yards from the rear of the crowd. Nearest to him was a tall, lanky boy he didn't know, blowing off-key into a flute, while Eddie Boyd stomped beside him, twirling his broom pole and singing as he passed it round the back of his neck, from his left hand to his right:

> We'll fight for no surrender,
> We'll guard old Derry's walls,
> With heart and hand and sword and shield,
> We'll guard old Derry's walls.

Two girls laughed together, letting on they were jiving to the music. It was Sally Cleary and her friend Jess. Jess pulled Sally through her legs, attempting to twist and hop over her to pick her up again on the other side. But she couldn't keep hold and Sally skidded across the grass on her backside, skirt riding to her waist.

Jess shrieked. 'Look, Sally, look. There's your fella and he seen your knicks. Youse'll have to get married now.'

Flushed, but smiling, Sally dragged the hem of her skirt to her knees, while, behind her, Jess tried to hoist it again.

'D'you want to see more?' she asked Mal. 'Come on over to the woods and Sally'll let you see all you like.'

Sally's heart was thumping; there were lumps beneath her blouse where she was getting breasts. Mal had regained his breath and the stabbing pain was dulled. He made up his mind and squirmed under the linked arms of an elderly couple (the woman in her slippers, the man wearing reading glasses), wriggling and burrowing through the shifting bodies, until eventually he surfaced in the front row of a crescent, formed around a middle-terraced house, curving back in the centre, clear of the street and on to the grass. The street lamps had all been smashed, but, on either side of the garden, Bobby Parker and Andy Hardy each held two torches – sticks with oil-soaked rags twisted about the tops – lighting the most peculiar scene Mal had ever come across.

On the footpath, before the low garden wall, as though raised on a stage, a chesterfield suite was neatly arranged, and at one end of it a standard lamp had been placed, its plug dangling, redundant, on to a grating in the road below. From the middle cushion of the settee a boy of seven or eight, with red hair that was familiar for all that it was well groomed and kept in check, glared out ferociously – at Mal alone, or so it seemed. His arms were spread wide to take in five younger children, the smallest still in rubber pants, who huddled close to him. At the other end of the suite was a pile of mattresses, on top of which sat a carry-cot, chock-full of crockery and plastic fruit, and next to that a dining table, crowned with upturned chairs.

A woman was standing by the front door of the house. It was an unremarkable house, no better, no worse than any of its neighbours; but the woman on the doorstep, balancing a washing basket against her hip, was exceptional indeed. She had long, grey hair, coiled in a loose spring about one shoulder and reaching to her bosom. But she did not look old; her features were fine, unlined and very beautiful. So beautiful that Mal wanted to clap her. Was this the woman who – as Andy Hardy had told it – had yelled and squawked and cried like a wee doll the day the binmen kicked a hole in her bin? If it was, why had he not mentioned that she was a good many months pregnant? There was no missing it. But although the baby writhing inside her made her movements awkward and lumbering, her free hand was cupped beneath the heavy swell of her belly, supporting it with a graceful dignity, which Mal found all the more entrancing because he did not understand it.

Twins about Mal's age shuffled out behind her, sharing the weight of an old-fashioned cabinet television, and the woman set the washing basket on the gatepost and helped them by lifting the trailing lead clear of their feet.

No more than fifteen minutes could have elapsed since Francy leapt the fence surrounding the dump, yet everything was being conducted with such a minimum of fuss that the impression Mal had was of watching an age-old party game. A charade in which everyone knew their allotted role.

Muffled, self-conscious coughs sounded from the audience and were joined occasionally by the quick whip-whip-whip of the light breeze catching the torch flames. Behind it and below it all, the trill of the out-of-tune flute and Eddie's piping voice ran on like incidental music:

> When Derry's gates are open,
> And flags are flying high,
> God bless the ship that broke the boom
> On the Twelfth day of July.

A man backed out of the house, carrying one end of another prop, a black-lacquered wardrobe, turned turtle, doors flapping on the hinges. And then, bearing up the other end, Francy Hagan himself appeared. Some children in the crowd hissed at the sight of him, but the adults with them clipped their ears to shush them. Mal's pulse quickened and his fingernails pressed deep into his palms. The spectators might be fooled by Francy's dismal demeanour into thinking he was resigned to what was happening, but it was clear to Mal that his submission was the biggest act of all. Just when they least expected, he would shatter this orderly dumb-show and fall upon them, fists and feet flailing.

But Francy must have been biding his time, saving his strength for some grander finale than Mal could envisage, for he simply eased the wardrobe on to the footpath and headed back through the gate, without so much as a peep of protest.

They continued like that, in and out the front door in silent relay, for a full twenty minutes more, until it seemed the whole inside of the house must be on the outside. There were chests of drawers and storage jars, a black cast-iron kettle and an assortment of pots and pans; bathroom scales and bath towels, three mirrors, a large radiogram and a magazine rack, stuffed with copies of the *Reader's Digest*; headboards, bed frames, toys and games, a painting of a matador poised to kill a plunging bull; a box of plaster statues (that caused some of the grown-ups, and not the children this time, to hiss), an incomplete set of encyclopaedia, bound in imitation leather; a budgie cage without a budgie.

Then, bang on cue, an old diesel truck chugged into the close. It passed the inside-out house once, executed a stuttering three-point turn at the bottom of the street, and drew level with it again to park. Pickles was riding on the back, surrounded by the dark shapes of still more furniture; his father and Mr McMahon alighted from the driving compartment and lowered the tailboard. One by one, the possessions were loaded from the roadside on to the truck and when they were all aboard Mr Hagan handed the older children up among them to Mr Austin, who saw they were safely settled. The beautiful woman lifted the two youngest in either arm and climbed into the cab, ungainly but proud. Mal was sad to see her go and wished she could have stayed a little longer in the torchlight. But the truck pulled away noisily, leaving only Francy and his father on the stripped-bare kerb.

Mr Hagan had none of the look of his wife about him; where she was strikingly attractive, he was as unexceptional as the plain red brick of the house he was now so intent upon. He gazed at it, eyes widening, as though trying somehow to swallow it. From chimney to doorstep, they roved hungrily, from doorstep to chimney. At length, they glazed over; he stepped on to the road, Francy by his side, and started for the grass.

'Fifteen years,' he said. 'Since ever this estate was built.'

In their unexpected flatness, his words had the effect of breaking whatever spell it was that had maintained so long a silence. For a time, though, the silence reasserted itself, becoming, if anything, more unnatural and intense; even the flute fell quiet. But it was silence of a different order, like that of decency appalled by crimes committed in a hypnotic trance. Mr Crosier felt moved to place his steamroller bulk in the Hagans' path.

'It's not you,' he told Francy's father. 'Your own kind started this, don't forget. And that nutcase son of yours ...' He spread his hands. 'We've heard rumours. We'd be cutting our own throats having him any longer in our midst.'

Mr Hagan gripped Francy's shoulder and carried on towards the woods. To the rear of the assembly, Sally and Jess followed everyone else's lead and dropped their heads at the pair's approach. But Eddie Boyd was having none of it.

'Derrybeggars,' he sneered, and thumped the earth with his broom pole.

Embarrassment found an outlet in laughter; it began sporadically, but quickly became general. Kids were spitting by this time, marching alongside the man and his plodding son, pulling faces. Eddie poked Francy's ribs with the end of the pole.

'Want a fight? Want a fight?' he goaded, skipping like a fencer.

Francy'll clock him, Mal thought. Any second now he was going to wheel round, break Eddie's stick over his head and come back for the rest of them. Any second now. But every second Francy and his father moved further and further out of sight.

'So much for the big man,' Andy Hardy said. 'There was no bother from him.'

'He's more sense,' Bobby Parker said. 'He'll know not to show his Rebel face round here again.'

Mal shut his ears to their gloating talk, willing himself to disbelieve.

'No, no, no,' he repeated over and over in his head. 'No, no, no.'

But it was useless. This wasn't a game. Francy *was* going.

'*No!*' he yelled aloud.

Mr Crosier looked at him like he wasn't all there.

'What are you blethering about?' he asked.

Mal ignored him. He was dazed and, for the first time in weeks, he was feeling his age. He was suddenly acutely conscious of his body, weak, raw-boned and still immature, and the greater his awareness of it grew, the less control he seemed able to exercise over it. He tried to run, but his legs would do no more than splay and stagger ludicrously, like a newborn foal's.

'Francy,' he shouted. 'Francy, take me too!'

Confusion behind him speedily resolved itself into a stern command from Mr Crosier.

'Grab him, for dear sake, somebody that's more puff than me. His parents'll have a fit.'

Mal fell, got up, fell and got up again. 'Francy, take me too!'

There was a heroic response to Mr Crosier's call: Mal was rugby-tackled from behind and went down for the last time, pinned to the ground, Peter Hardy's crew-cut head close to his ear.

'Fenian lover.'

'Francy,' he cried. 'Francy.'

'One good turn ...' – Mr Crosier said. 'That's my motto.'

Mr and Mrs Martin thanked him and shut the front door. Mal sat in the living room on the paint-spattered newspapers. His nose ran, his tears flowed unrestrained and there was a sopping patch on his jeans where he'd wet himself. His parents glanced first at him, then at each other in silent mortification.

Breakfast was brought to his room next morning on a tray and placed on the floor by the door.

'Are you going to tell me?' his mother asked.

Mal stared blankly at his hands, down-turned on the sheets.

'There'll be no breakfast if you don't,' she said, her tone one of grim determination.

She left space for a response, but there was none.

'Fine by me,' she said and lifted the tray. 'We'll see if hunger will bring you to your senses.'

She paused on the threshold.

'I mean it now' – the last chance was dangled like a carrot on a stick – 'you'll go nowhere and see no one until we know.'

Still Mal said nothing. The door was locked from the outside, but a long time went by before Mal lifted his eyes. His breathing was even and unhurried. He didn't care. They could keep him locked there forever, he didn't want to go out, didn't want to see anyone again in his life. Except Francy.

The street was noisy that day; people who should have been at work hours before were still knocking about towards noon. No matter how hard he tried, Mal could not help but overhear what they were saying. It was like his window had become an outsized television screen: he could blot out the picture with his blinds, but there was no on–off switch and no volume control to get rid of the sound. Throughout the morning there were constant news reports and studio debates. Three dead at Divis and three more in Ardoyne ... Rebels cleaned out of Percy Street and Dover Street ... Protestants intimidated in Derrybeg ... Citizens' Defence Force formed, Bobby Parker elected Commander ... Question: Was it true the army was on its way? Were they going to disarm the RUC and disband the B Specials? Answer: Let them bloody well try.'

At lunchtime his mother returned with the tray and perched on the edge of the bed. Once more, Mal looked away.

'Well?' she asked.

He could smell bacon, eggs and dipped bread. He was hungry. 'Well what?'

'What was going on between you and that Hagan boy?' He wasn't that hungry, and he hoped he never would be. He gazed at the sheets.

'Your lunch is going cold.'

Mrs Martin was less composed than she had been earlier, and when Mal again refused to reply she clapped her hands in angry exasperation. 'At least look at me when I'm talking to you. Or has that filthy tramp made you forget all your manners?'

Mal finally obliged her, but his stare was fierce.

'He's not a filthy tramp,' he said. 'He's better than you any day of the week. And my daddy too.'

His mother's entire body seemed to tremble with rage, so that only her bun remained stationary, held in check by a visible shield of hairspray. She launched out an open hand and caught him a crack at the side of the head. Mal saw her bewilderment as she nursed her hand, and it was all he could do to keep himself from spitting.

'Fuck off,' he told her.

His mother's uncertainty vanished and her temper snapped completely. She hauled him from the bed and whaled into him about the bottom and legs until her arm was sore. But Mal had walked through nettles and brambles, scratched and torn his skin regularly crossing the dump. He could take this. His mother couldn't, though; she was in tears by now, attempting to force him back on to the mattress. But Mal made himself heavy and in the end she rushed sobbing from the room, slamming the door and twisting the key savagely in the lock. Mal pressed his ear to the carpet, following her crying into the living room.

There was a heated exchange and then his father flared up: 'I told you hitting him wouldn't get us anywhere.'

'But the things he said. He used "F" to me. *Me*, his own mother.'

He'd use it again too.

He did not hate his parents; indeed, in some small way, he thought maybe he understood more about them now than at any time before. He could not find the words for that understanding, but, instead, when he tried to explain it to himself, he saw Mr Hagan's gaze, trying to swallow his house, and the dignity of the beautiful woman as she climbed on to the truck. Saw himself, too, last night, body weak and useless ...

Recollection of that nightmarish loss of control scared him and made him yearn more than ever for Francy. Francy was not like the rest. Despite what he had seen with his own eyes, despite what Francy himself had said in the moments before he fled the dump, Mal would not accept he was gone for good. Francy would not allow them to put him out that easily. He *would* return. And so Mal got back into bed to wait. He could wait till hell froze over if necessary. There was a smell in the room of coagulating grease. His mother had forgotten the lunch tray.

Late in the afternoon, his father came to see him. He did not question him straight off, but walked for a time about the room, inspecting the pictures of footballers on the wall.

'I see Arsenal's due to play the Glens next month at the Oval,' he said. 'Fairs Cup. Your Uncle Simon was asking if we'd like tickets, but I wasn't sure you'd be interested.'

Mal buried his head under the blankets, sniffing his own sweat.

'Well, how does this sound,' his father suggested reasonably. 'I've to give him a ring and let him know this evening. So, if there's anything you want to talk to me about before then, just knock on the floor and we can sort it all out. Okay?'

Same thing, different approach.

'Okay,' his father answered himself.

Mal slept surprisingly well for a couple of hours and woke to find his room in darkness and the street television service working overtime:

Gunmen hiding out in Clonard Monastery ... Soldiers on the Falls ... Bombay Street blazing from end to end ...

Downstairs, the only noise was the scrape of wallpaper being removed from the pelmet mingled with faint strains of music filtering in from the radio in the dinette.

... Gang forming on Derrybeg side of the woods ... Bobby Parker's Defence Force gone to stop them coming through to Larkview ...

The pleasant confusion of his doze descended once more and was beginning to fuddle his thoughts when it was interrupted by an urgent newsflash, just in, the reporter so breathless he could only manage two words: a name; *that* name. Mal kicked away the covers and lifted a corner of the blind. There was bedlam outside. The hold had gone completely and shapes and outlines were dancing, out of control, across the picture. He didn't hear the name spoken again, but he didn't need to now, he had received the message loud and clear: Francy Hagan had been seen on the dump.

Hurriedly, he pulled a jumper and his best trousers over his pyjamas. He couldn't find any shoes, so put on three pairs of socks instead. Then he remembered the locked door. His spirits sank briefly as he wondered how he was going to get round it; but if Francy could make it back to the dump, surely to God he could think of some way to escape from his room? In the end he borrowed the solution from every jailbreak film he had ever seen. He stuffed his pillow and whatever clothes were to hand under the blankets, plumping them up until they vaguely resembled a curled body. A poor likeness really – they looked better on the screen – but it would do for the few seconds he needed. Raising his heel, he knocked on the floor as hard as his stockinged foot would allow. The scraping in the living room stopped, but beyond that, for several unbearable seconds, nothing else happened. He lifted his heel still higher and knocked again.

'There!' his father's voice said.

Before long his heavy tread was thumping on the stairs.

'Kindness,' he was saying. 'Not violence.'

Mal drew back against the wall in the shadow of the door as his father unlocked it and pushed it open.

'Son?' he said, switching on the light and moving towards the bed.

And in a wink, Mal was out of the room, his hands trembling, turning the key in the lock. He tried to pocket it, but fumbled in his haste and dropped it on the landing carpet. There was no time to stop; his father was already hammering on the door and, before he was two-thirds of the way downstairs, his mother was confronting him in the hall.

'Just where do you think you're going?' she asked, her sternness unable to mask her rising fear. 'Get back up those stairs this instant.'

Mal gripped the banister and gritted his teeth.

'Move!' he commanded her.

She took a step towards him and Mal picked the spot between her breasts, where, Francy's boxing glove had taught him, he could wind her best. He charged it with his head. His mother lurched backwards and fell, her eyes filled with terror.

He brushed past her and unsnibbed the front door. Out the drive and up the street he sprinted. Mr Martin was pounding on the bedroom door to be released, Mrs Martin was yelling to anyone who would listen to catch hold of her son. But no one was listening tonight. Mal lost himself in the steady stream pouring down the hill.

8

There was a little eddy at the foot of the hill, where people were jostling with one another about the street sign before going any further. A piece of card had been taped over the nameplate and a crude scrawl announced:

Act Two. Sale of a fucking lifetime.

The crowd spilled on to the unkempt grass – already much larger than the one which had congregated outside the Hagans' house to witness the eviction. Noisier too. Voices jabbered right and left, asking what the nutter was up to now and how the hell he'd slipped by the men at the woods. Mal could have answered their second question, but what it was Francy was at, he had no more of a notion than anyone else.

He was borne along on the tide which continued to swell as the Citizens' Defence Force – its intended business adjourned for the time being – joined from the left. It was swallowed up and broken up, until the men were so interspersed only their white armbands distinguished them from their neighbours. The whole jamboree came to a standstill some distance from the dump, apparently unsure what to do next. The chatter grew more excited, but Mal could see nothing and, when the shoving finally stopped, he peeled away from the main body, haring up the bank to the cul-de-sac.

The area around the willow tree was a mess of dump-found objects, garishly illuminated by three workmen's braziers, glowing and brimming with coals. And dominating it all was Francy. He doused the braziers with paraffin from a red can, causing them to flare even brighter, casting a three-way shadow, which grew out of a common pair of giant feet and loomed against the tree in one direction, down the dump in another, and across it, in a third, to the fence. He strode restlessly through the debris, chomping on a length of cigar and barking in a voice that, for all Mal had come to know it, sounded again as grating and unnerving as on that first day. Coarse, belly-dredged, boy-man's voice.

'Hurry, hurry, hurry! One night only. Everything must go. Hurry, hurry, hurry!'

There was still sufficient uncertainty on the other side of the fence for his patter to be greeted by smatterings of applause.

'The more the merrier. Roll up, roll up!'

Bobby Parker had an orange armband rather than a white one. He took it upon himself to give the lead and bustled decisively to the fore, face like thunder.

'Plenty of room up front,' Francy exhorted him. 'Move it now, or we'll be starting without you.'

Mal was so engrossed in the spectacle that his guard dropped and he forgot his exposed position. His parents were on top of him before he was even aware of their approach.

'You,' his father growled, twisting his wrists behind his back. 'Home.'

'Any more there?'

Mrs Martin rubbed her breastbone where Mal had struck her. But her eyes were on the dump, not her son.

'What in the world is happening here?'

Gradually Mr Martin released Mal's wrists. He drew his wife to him and Mal recalled how they had clustered together at the bonfire, a family briefly united.

'Good to see so many familiar faces,' Francy said. 'And even, I think – yes – even a few new ones tonight.'

Big Bobby was almost at the fence.

'You were warned, Hagan,' he said. 'Didn't you get the message yesterday?'

Francy scooped up a milk bottle filled with blue-purple liquid and lit the cloth taper stuffed in its neck. Bobby was already running. The petrol bomb broke on the very spot he had so hastily vacated, well short of the hesitant crowd – though the snake-tongues of flame persuaded them to fall back a little further anyway.

'That's enough now, pul-ease!' Francy shouted. 'Let's have a bit of fucking order in the stalls. Youse'll all get your share.'

He paced his littered pitch, weighing a second bottle in his hand, then stopped and flourished it above his head.

'Ladies and Gentlemen,' he said, and spat. 'Eyes down, peckers up and pray silence for lot number one.'

He rooted on the ground before the braziers and held up to view the thick, spineless and boardless book he had read from on the day he initiated Mal.

'Sick to death always having to take someone else's word for it? Then solve all your problems when you become the proud owner of this very attractive dictionary. Words upon words – every one you'll ever need and a few more besides – taken apart and listed individually for you to put together again, how you please, in the comfort of your own home. Who'll open the bidding?'

Now that the flames had died down, there were, even yet, those watching who were prepared to give Francy the benefit of the doubt and whose mood verged, once more, on the good-humoured. Others, however, had seen enough. Vera and Tom Garrity began walking away, Tom delivering his verdict on the proceedings with a two-fingered gesture. Immediately he did, though, a flapping noise behind his head caused him to contract his neck in fear. The dictionary whistled over his shoulder, halting him in his tracks.

'We have a buyer,' Francy said. 'Couple in the second row. Pay at the door and may you have many happy hours with it. Next ...'

He raised by its handle the pram into which the evening before he had thrown bread for the rats.

'... a novel variation on that old favourite, the infant perambulator. Ideal' – he pointed to the wheelless frame – 'for the baby that's going fucking nowhere. What do I hear?'

What he heard was precisely nothing. Faces stared at him; some sullen, some amused, all silently baffled. Dandelions fluttered from the inverted hood.

'Is it the dandelions bothering youse? "Wet the bed and have you any idea the price of nappies these days" – is that it? Ach, I'm cutting my own throat, but just to prove my heart's in the right place, youse can have it free, gratis.'

He spun twice on his heel, like an athlete with a hammer, and swung the pram out of the dump. It skimmed the smouldering grass on its belly, crash-landing.

'I know what youse're thinking: "he must be mad". Well, if that was mad, then fuck knows what youse'll say when youse see the next knock-down bargain.'

He paraded the mound, showing it off as gingerly as a priceless antique. The urn from the corner of the hut.

'An exclusive flowerpot, can also take spit, piss, snot and anything else you've got,' he rhymed, seeming to read from a legend on the base. He laid a hand on the red cushioned toilet seat. 'Say goodbye to those cold and lonely late-night treks.'

There was a sudden change in the audience's reaction. Grumbles of disgust welled from its ranks.

'Don't fret, there's plenty to go round,' Francy pacified them. 'No offers? Come on, you don't mean to tell me youse've all forgotten our battle cry. How does it go? – "Waste not, want not." Am I right, am I right? Or am I wrong? Right or wrong, wrong or right.'

He was almost singing the words, weaving in and out the

braziers, in and out, in a figure of eight. The three massive shadows wheeled about him, meeting and parting in a lewd, labyrinthine dance.

'Right or wrong, wrong or right. Which is it? WHICH!'

Watching Francy on his twisting course, Mal began to believe that he was following some ancient path, that he might tread it this night and beyond, on and on, time without end. But, behind the central brazier, Francy broke the measure and faced his public; arms spread wide apart, urn in the flat of one hand, a petrol bomb in the other. His voice rose and fell, as if in time to the loop of a skipping rope.

'Youse never knew – what to waste – and what the fuck – to keep.'

His arms see-sawed first to the left, then to the right, then gradually his head dipped back and steadied. His arms locked, rock rigid, and the urn and bottle were perfectly balanced. The lilt became a monotone.

'Oh, mother dear, my eyes are dim, I cannot see, I have not brought a spade with me, yet dead dogs lie where the English fear to tread and there's one born every minute ... Sold!' the last sound ripped from his throat, as though living; a wild, swooping, whoop of defiance. His head sprang forward and he pointed with the bottle. 'Sold, to the fat man with the sour-looking gob.'

The urn spiralled high in the air and smashed on the dried earth in front of Big Bobby. He stooped and collected the shattered fragments. From his vantage point on the bank, Mal saw him slowly piece the lettering together: 'PARKER. R.I.P.'

'This used to be on my father's grave,' Bobby said. 'We got a new one for him being ten years dead.'

His tone was muted at first, stunned by the effrontery, but steadily the anger rose and his temper became full-blooded. He shook the fragments at Francy.

'Where'd you get this? This was my bloody father's and there *is* spit in it too.'

282

'A fortunate purchase,' Francy told him. 'I'm sure the old soul will be delighted to have it back.'

He tossed the second petrol bomb to check any movement towards the fence. Fire spilt along the grass, then snapped back and billowed upwards in a plume, like a smokescreen conjured by a magician's wand.

'And talking of fathers ...'

Francy displayed a band of orange material, fringed with silver-gold thread. Small letters, numbers and signs glinted giltly in the braziers' light. A sash.

'I am, alas, unable to tell you who's owned this, but I have it on good authority it is very, very old. Still beautiful, though, and as you can see' – he shivered the fringe – 'the colours are fine indeed. Hardly worn, either. A lovely garment, I think you'll agree.' He tried it on, then wrapped it about his hands like a roll towel. 'And a handy thing for drying yourself.'

He passed the looped sash across his shoulders and set to rubbing lower and lower down his spine, till he was straddling it and pulling it in and out his legs.

'Or even' – he cackled – 'for wiping your arse.'

Simple disgust now was hardening into hate. Francy had gone too far, but he had also gone too far to stop.

'Better yet' – he coiled the sash around his neck, hoisting himself almost clear of the ground. Three shadows dangled, self-lynched – 'a good way to die.'

Men, women and children swarmed forward.

'Shut the fuck up,' Francy said.

He ran from brazier to brazier, lighting a taper on each and sending three more flaming bottles arching into the night. The advance was stopped and he produced a pair of scissors from the belt of his jeans, snipping frantically at the cloth. 'A bit for everyone.'

Signals were passing among the seething onlookers. They fanned out so that they faced the fence at every point along its length.

'A minute more, a minute more,' Francy implored, his words only just carrying above the increasing clamour.

He hurled another two petrol bombs, but his arm was clearly tiring, and they fell within the dump itself. The people outside took note and pressed closer to the fence.

'And the final item!'

A flag unfurled; first green, then white, then gold. Francy waved it, brandishing the scissors.

'A bit for everyone.'

His voice strained to command their attention. A boy's voice only now. It wavered, cracked, and sank without trace, lost in the roar the sight of the Tricolour had sparked. A corner of the flag flapped too close to a brazier, became entangled and caught light. Francy let go and scrabbled on the grass for a bottle, but his arsenal was exhausted. He stood, unarmed, starkly defined by the blazing flag. A single shadow lay down on the garbage behind him; stumpy trunk and outsized head.

The fence buckled beneath a renewed surge, then gave way, a confusion of wire, wood, arms and legs, tumbling into the dump. Francy kicked over the braziers and the coals rolled red-hot off the mound to collect in pools at its base. Hugging the red can to his chest, he tramped to the tree, his manner now leisurely and composed. At the curtain of branches he paused and looked to the cul-de-sac. The previous night, Mal had longed for him to make a stand of some kind, but he had not anticipated such a performance. Too late, he understood Francy's dangerous knowledge. He nodded his head, up and down, up and down, up and down. Francy bowed, spat a spit as affectionate as a blown kiss, and was gone.

Almost at once, the hedgerow began to radiate with a strange incandescence, like cramped neon lighting. Confounded by the outworks of nettles and brambles, all stopped now to watch and wonder. The light grew steadily more intense, until even Mal and his parents had to shield their eyes and the bushes themselves seemed to throb with pent-up energy. Then, suddenly, there was an explosion of ferocious heat. Everyone, save Mal, hit the deck as a fireball erupted from the mouth of the passage, blasting before it books, files and loose pages, engulfing the willow tree.

For some time afterwards little blobs of flame continued to rain down or skitter in crazy, dying squiggles across the mound. Those were the dump rats, on fire.

Slowly, people picked themselves up, unhurt. Tommy Duncan held a black baseball boot that had landed beside him. 'The mad Taig bastard,' he said. 'Trying to lure us into a trap.'

But Mal knew all about Francy and traps, and he didn't need a baseball boot to tell him the only person Francy had trapped was himself.

His father's hand clutched the nape of his neck. 'Oh, God.'

Mal became aware of stinging pains in his shoeless feet. His socks were wet and when he looked down he saw they were steeped in blood.

The estate was quiet, violence sated. Policemen sifted cautiously through the scorched gap at the tail end of the woods. They wore white or pink gloves and some had masks over their mouths and noses. They looked more like surgeons than policemen. Except that each carried a black bin bag.

A fence of orange tape cordoned off the area, and ropes, hitched to the willow's charred branches, were being tied to the towbar of a borrowed bulldozer. An armoured car, the first seen in Larkview, slowed and parked by the roadside beyond the grass. Two soldiers got out, nursing heavy rifles, and called a policeman to them. Then all three pored over a map spread on the armoured car's bonnet. One of the soldiers drew lines in pencil, the other took off his tin hat and scratched his head.

Mal's gaze drifted to the pavilion, to the wall that was already building itself into his brain. Even in the light of early morning the letters were burning white against the creosoted wood. Two feet high and still dripping.

'FRANCY HAGAN,' they read. 'REST IN PIECES.'

BOOK ENDS

opinions
interviews
and more

About
Glenn Patterson

Glenn Patterson began *Burning Your Own*, his first novel, while studying at the University of East Anglia, where he was taught by Malcolm Bradbury and Angela Carter. In 1989 he was appointed writer in the community for Lisburn and Craigavon by the Arts Council of Northern Ireland and started work on his second novel, *Fat Lad*, which was published in 1992. A year later he went to University College Cork as writer in residence, and the year after that became writer in residence at Queen's University Belfast.

Black Night at Big Thunder Mountain was published in 1995 and was followed in 1999 by *The International*. His fifth novel, *Number 5*, appeared in 2003, his sixth, *That Which Was*, in 2004. A collection of his journalism was published in 2006 under the title *Lapsed Protestant*. His most recent novel is *The Third Party* (2007), set in Hiroshima. A first full-length work of non-fiction, *Once Upon a Hill*, will be published in autumn 2008.

Glenn's television work includes documentaries for BBC, RTÉ, Channel 4 and Granada. He teaches creative writing at the Seamus Heaney Centre for Poetry in Queen's University Belfast and is a member of Aosdána.

Glenn Patterson on writing
Burning Your Own

The last words I typed of *Burning Your Own*, five
minutes before I left to deliver the manuscript to Michael
Shaw at the Curtis Brown Agency, were the first words
anyone else read: the title itself.* It was a spur of the moment
thing, an afterthought. Up until six minutes before I left I
had always referred to the novel as *Dogbag*, if only for the
amusement of my friend Tim Wilson, a writer of historical
novels and a compulsive watcher of snooker, often
simultaneously. Tim and I had met on the MA in Creative
Writing at the University of East Anglia. Actually we had
met there as undergraduates, but had both been attracted to
the university by the MA, one of only two then in the whole
of Britain and Ireland. By the time we enrolled on the
course in October 1985, Tim already had one novel (*Master
of Morholm*) accepted for publication and was writing a
second on commission. I had written, at most, four short
stories, none of which had been published anywhere, and
only one of which frankly could claim to have been hard
done by by the rejection. I wrote another two stories in my
first term on the MA, but I can't say I was much happier with
either of them.

I was living all the while in a house on Thorpe Road,
close to Norwich Railway Station, with four recent

* I didn't know much, at twenty-six, about publishing, but I knew that
the best way to avoid the slush pile was to reach across it and place
your novel into a named human being's hand.

graduates, including my girlfriend, Colette. Colette was
saving to do a masters of her own by waitressing in a nearby
Berni Inn. When she went out to work in the mornings I
went and sat at my desk; when she came back in the evening
I got up from it, for the twentieth and last time. Well, when
you're at home all day you will – literally – jump at any
diversion, although this particular house wasn't short on
distractions. Among our other housemates was a guitarist,
Spike (played in the Morags, shared a birthday – a destiny,
he would have said – with Jimi Hendrix), who must have
been one of the most conscientious people ever to strap on a
Stratocaster. From late morning on he would be practising
in the room at the opposite end of the landing from mine.
Once or twice a week he would be joined by his bass-player,
Vic, or 'Salad Pants' as Spike preferred, for reasons known
only to himself, to call him. Eventually Vic moved in too.

Took, who had the basement room, was a home-counties
soul-boy, a touch slow with rent and bills, but quick to bring
home the latest James Brown album or Cameo twelve-inch.
He was also given to fits of manic cleaning, whacking up the
volume on 'Word Up' so that he could hear it above the
vacuum, above his own vocal accompaniment.* Chufty, the
quietest, was also the least predictable. At any time of the
day, in any room of the house, he would throw back his
head and shout out the name of our favourite reggae singer
… *Eek-a-Mouse!*

And then, when all else fell silent, there was the TV.
Always, always there was the TV: *Masterteam, The Gong
Show, Racing from Kempton* (and from Haydock and from

---

* In a later novel, *The Third Party*, 'Word Up' is the song to which the
narrator, a Belfast businessman, dances around his Hiroshima hotel
room. Took's tastes, unlike the businessman's, ran to the Birthday
Party and Tom Waits and veteran punk band Chelsea, who wound up
on our living room floor one night. We *were* very close to the station.

Aintree). If there was nothing else to look at, we would even switch over to the news.

I walked into the living room one night in late November to find my housemates watching the early evening bulletin on the BBC. A hundred thousand people, a good half of them, it seemed, waving banners and flags, were packed into the streets in front of Belfast's City Hall. From a platform before the gates rang out a soon-to-be-famous (although now scarcely imaginable) 'Never, never, never!' Meanwhile some few hundred-thousandths of the protestors had smashed the windows of S.S. Moore's sports shop (maybe they thought the owner was related to SS RUC) and were pelting police with golf balls.

I think it was Took who turned to me and asked, 'What the fuck are they doing?'

It was his flag too they were protesting under, but he didn't recognise these people.

To tell you the truth, I had been letting on I didn't recognise them either since coming to study in England, but there was something pretty hard to ignore in a hundred thousand people. Apart from the Reverend Nevernevernever (or Pastor Notjustyet, as he turned out to be, bless his starched white collar) and the guys with the golf balls, the protestors did not look and sound to me like headcases. In fact the scenes were not a million miles away from those broadcast from all over Britain at the height of the recent miners' strike – a strike most of us in the living room that evening would have supported. (It's a mystery to me how the miners ever lost with the likes of Colette, Chufty, Took, Spike, Vic Salad Pants and me behind them.) It occurred to me that with the memory of that bitter, divisive dispute so

> It was his flag too they were protesting under, but he didn't recognise these people.

fresh in their minds, of communities split over whether to
stay on strike or go back to work, readers who would not
normally pick up a novel set in Northern Ireland might look
at events here as a little less alien and alienating. The politics
differed, but the strains felt by the individuals involved were
the same. It was not an excuse for violence from any quarter
to say that people in extreme circumstances will sometimes
do extreme things.

A month later, back in Belfast for the Christmas holiday, I
was talking to one of my brothers who reminded me of a
former neighbour who had joined the IRA in
the early seventies and had blown himself up,
aged sixteen, while taking part in a mortar
attack on police. Graffiti went up in our
estate the next day, gloating over the death:
'Rest in Pieces', it said. I wrote the phrase in
a notebook on my way back to Norwich in
the New Year. I think I knew already it was
the last line of a novel. I pinched the first from the Bible and
brought the opening chapter of *Untitled* (*Dogbag* came later)
to the first MA class of the new term.

It would be ten years and three novels before I wrote
another short story.

> People in
> extreme
> circumstances
> will sometimes
> do extreme
> things.

Carlo Gébler on reading
Burning Your Own

In the early nineties, before the paramilitary
ceasefires, I knew a London-born Belfast-based journalist
who reported on Northern Ireland for a quality broadsheet.
He compared the Troubles to an old warthog. When, he
said, this old curmudgeon was prodded he got angry and
had to kill people. Once he'd vented his rage, however, he'd
collapse exhausted, and all would be well until the next time
he was goaded into fury.

The warthog thesis ('It's just the bestial side of man's
nature, that's all the Troubles are'), and its many variants
were *the* popular explanation for Ulster's wretched late
twentieth-century history. And we, who lived here, though
we should have known better, we went along with it because
it freed us from having to critically examine our culpability,
while our neighbours in Ireland and Britain were also happy
with it because it meant they didn't have to examine their
contribution either.

But there were a few truth tellers who said the Troubles
weren't caused by man's animal nature: on the contrary,
sectarian animosity, they said, was a machine we had built
and that we primed and pumped and then set about its
infernal business. This select group included John Hewitt
and, after he published *Burning Your Own* (1988), Glenn
Patterson.

The novel is set on the largely Protestant Larkview estate
in south Belfast during the summer of 1969. The story is
told through the eyes of ten-year-old Mal and is primarily

concerned with his relationships – with his parents, with the teenagers on his estate, with his middle-class relatives, and most importantly of all with Francy Hagan, a fourteen-year-old Catholic savant who haunts the estate dump.

Burning Your Own is a book with numerous virtues. The writing is precise yet fluent. The topographical evocation of Larkview and its rural hinterland is flawless. Every character, whether major or minor, is a memorable creation, which given the large cast (very large for a novel so emphatically domestic) is critical to its success, for if they weren't all so memorable the reader would be lost.

> **The writing is precise yet fluent. The topographical evocation is flawless. Every character is a memorable creation.**

One aspect of the characterisation that I particularly relish is the author's alertness to what runs contrary to expectations. Francy's primary tormentors in childhood aren't Protestants from Larkview (where he's always lived) but Derrybeg Catholics, unnerved by his difference from them. And who at the end turns out to be Francy's unlikely, new, best drinking buddy? Answer: the deeply appalling and bigoted Mucker, who is converted to amity with Francy by the latter's amazing Christian generosity towards his old enemy.

Mal's parents are also full of surprises. The alcoholic Mr Martin seems, at first, to be much less sympathetic than his long-suffering wife. But, as Ulster polarizes, he emerges as the emollient peacemaker, while his wife emerges as the non-emollient anti-peacemaker, handy with her fists (at least if she's beating her son) and surprisingly ready to come to an accommodation with incipient Loyalism.

The novel explores Mal's relations with these imperfect parents, as it does all his relationships with all the other imperfect people in his world, with tenderness and wit, rather than scorn and judgment (which would have been so easy). Moreover, the book also gives a wonderfully precise sense of how Mal changes because of what these relationships teach him and, by carefully charting these, the author ensures, because he has change on every page, that this is a novel with the most fantastic forward momentum.

Meanwhile, as we watch Mal grow (and few books chart growth as convincingly as *Burning Your Own*), we are aware of huge events in the background – the first manned landing on the moon and Ulster's lurch into civil war. But until the end the powerful historical material is always kept in check and the focus is on Mal's maturation.

Then, in the appalling conclusion (so unexpected and yet, in retrospect, so inevitable), the personal and political collide. Mal has his epiphany: he realises what he really loves is Francy. He shows these feelings like a ten-year-old would, with a kiss, but Francy doesn't respond. He won't. He can't. He couldn't. Not given what is happening, which is nothing less than a repetition of what's gone on since the Plantation. The majority Protestant community has grown fearful of its minority neighbours and embarked on the course it always embarks on when it's frightened. This process started with small things, like not letting Catholics join in a game of football, and will end with the big thing – putting all the Catholics out.

> Mal has his epiphany: he realises what he really loves is Francy.

Against this background, of an old pattern reasserting itself, Mal yearns for Francy to accept him without having any idea how impossible, even insane, this is. For a start there'll be hell to pay if Mal's feelings are revealed (he'll be marked out as a Fenian lover), plus there just isn't the time or the space for Francy to reciprocate Mal's feelings, not given the cataclysm looming over the Hagan family, which is nothing less than their expulsion from Eden.

Once this happens Francy is faced with the terrible choice that thousands in Ulster faced at the time: he can either direct his rage against his persecutors (as his co-religionists who joined the IRA were to do), or he can direct his rage against himself. If he chooses the first path, Francy will have to hurt his neighbour's community. Does he want to do that? He's an ethical being and he'd rather not. On the other hand, if he chooses the second path, and turns his rage against himself, he'll be the only one hurt. So at the end, following his auction, he channels his fury inwards, literally burning himself out. By doing so, he saves the lives of others, perhaps even Mal, though of course Mal doesn't understand this, and it's this collision of Mal's ignorance and Francy's charity that makes the end so complex and bitter.

But it isn't only its end that makes *Burning Your Own* a great book (though it is extraordinary), it's the whole of it, and the sense that it communicates of a group of people in a particular place at a particular time in history and what it felt like to walk around in their shoes. And what a magical thing that is. I think so anyway, and I don't think one can ask for anything more. Finally, add in the fact that the characters in *Burning Your Own* are the ordinary people mostly missing from paramilitary- and security-personnel obsessed Troubles fiction, and the case that this is one of the great novels about Ulster at the start of its Troubles, is, I think, unassailable.

> This is one of the great novels about Ulster at the start of its Troubles.

BOOK
ENDS

The books behind
the book

Glenn Patterson

Midnight's Children won the Booker Prize in
1981, while I was working in Crane's Bookshop in Belfast.
I was too busy, however, collecting the complete works of
George Orwell in their black-jacketed Penguin editions to
pay Rushdie's novel much attention at the time. (As I recall
it anyway, *The White Hotel* by D.M. Thomas was the
punters' favourite in Crane's. I didn't read it either.) When I
left the bookshop for university I discovered that *Midnight's
Children* had got there ahead of me. I forget the name of the
course on which I first encountered it, something with a
'Post-' in the title at any rate. I will never forget, though, the
excitement of those opening pages, the realisation that this
was a book that spoke very directly to my own ideas and
experience. No, not 'spoke to', gave them fictional form.
When Rushdie wrote of 'a country which would never exist
except by the efforts of a phenomenal collective will . . . a
mass fantasy', he could have as easily been referring to
Northern Ireland as India. I did not aspire to write like
Rushdie, nor if I was being honest could I ever have hoped
to, but there is undoubtedly a grain of Saleem Sinai,
Midnight's Children's mythopoetic narrator, in the voice of
my own Francy Hagan: 'In the beginning . . . was the
dump.'*

---

* I go to my shelves and lift down my copy of *Midnight's Children* and
see I have written 'December 1985' on the title page. I was reading
it almost at the same time as I started *Burning Your Own*.

297

(At which point I suppose I should acknowledge the book from which the first three words are nicked. Unbelievable premise, but no end of great lines; and as for that final Revelation . . .)

By a strange coincidence there is another Francy-like character in *Billy Bathgate* by E.L. Doctorow, which was published the year after *Burning Your Own*. Billy's best friend – only friend when the novel starts – is a boy called Arnold Garbage, who 'never went to school ... lived [in the basement of the Max and Dora Diamond Home for Children] as if he were alone', and whose sole preoccupation is scouring the streets of New York pushing a baby carriage, looking to add 'new acquisitions to the great inventory of his life'. The inventory itself, in the book's closing pages, fills a half-page paragraph ending with 'tiny flags on toothpicks from all the nations of the world'.

Doctorow became another favourite writer.

what the critics say

'Glenn Patterson is a national treasure.'
IAN SANSOM

'Glenn Patterson has become the most serious and humane chronicler of Northern Ireland over the past thirty years, as well as one of the best contemporary Irish novelists.'
COLM TÓIBÍN

'No other novelist has proved as capable of capturing the heart of modern Belfast.'
EOIN McNAMEE, *Sunday Tribune*

'Compelling, confident, funny . . . and abundant in all kinds of clever touches. Patterson's vigour and flair keep us reading avidly as he exercises his capacity to make the everyday engrossing.'
Independent

'[Patterson] articulates the poetry of the ordinary with understated humour and pathos.'
Guardian

'an exceptional writer'
The Times

'intelligent and humane, endearing and insightful'
Sunday Business Post